THE PLAYBOY'S FUGITIVE BRIDE

BILLIONAIRE BRIDES OF GRANITE FALLS

ANA E ROSS

CEDAR TREES PUBLISHERS

THE PLAYBOY'S FUGITIVE BRIDE

Edited by Crazy Diamond Editing
Cover Design by Najla Qamber Designs

www.anaeross.com

ALSO BY ANA E ROSS

Billionaire Brides of Granite Falls Series

The Doctor's Secret Bride

The Mogul's Reluctant Bride

The Playboy's Fugitive Bride

The Tycoon's Temporary Bride

With These Four Rings: Wedding Bonus

Beyond Granite Falls Series

Loving Yasmine

Desire's Chase

Pleasing Mindy

Billionaire Island Brides Series

Seduced by Passion (2022)

To my patient, loyal fans who push and inspire me to keep going even when the journey seems unending, and to my Beta Readers, Shirlyn Renita, Sharon, and Shunta.

CHAPTER ONE

He was the epitome of masculinity as he strolled through the door of the ski cabin, bringing a draft of New England's frigid air with him. The rough-hewn floor groaned under his weight, and his hard muscles rippled beneath his skin-tight ski outfit as his sturdy legs transported his six-foot, three-inch frame across the room. He came to a stop in front of a wood stove, pulled off his mittens, and held large hands toward the roaring flames.

Nia's eyes glowed with a mixture of conflicting emotions as she gaped at the notorious Italian playboy—Massimo Luciano Andretti, sole heir to Andretti Industries, one of the largest textile manufacturers in the world.

With his smooth olive complexion, black, wavy, shoulder-length hair, a wide sensuous mouth, and eyes as blue as the Atlantic Ocean on a sunny day, Massimo was, by far, the sexiest exhibit in the billionaire bachelors' storefront window. No woman he set his sights on was safe. He captured them, pampered them, bedded them, then wiped his mouth and moved on to the next willing victim like an impartial judge at a pie-baking contest.

But Massimo's irresistible sex appeal wasn't the reason Nia had tracked him down to the resort mountain town of Granite Falls, New Hampshire. She had a six-year-old score to settle with the bastard who'd caused her father's death, and just recently placed the lives of her younger brother and herself in danger.

On his dying bed, her father had made her promise to forget about Massimo Andretti and to concentrate on taking care of herself and Aaron. He'd also made her promise that she would move as far away from Maine as possible. Nia had kept her promises and gone on with her life as best she could, even though she had never been able to put Massimo Andretti completely out of her mind since she'd first seen him six years ago.

Aaron had grown into a responsible young man and didn't need her protection from Maine's child welfare system anymore. He was a high school senior, and had recently received a full scholarship in engineering from MIT. Nia was so proud of him, and grateful that she'd had a chance to give him as normal a life as possible.

It wasn't easy, and many times she'd prayed for someone to come along and take the burden of parenthood away from her. But no one had come. She was all Aaron had, and he was all she had. Together, they'd survived a difficult past and had been looking forward to a better future.

But the past had a way of raiding a girl's present and stealing her future.

It showed up in the form of a letter from a loan shark named Eddie. Included in the letter was a copy of a six-year-old promissory note that bore her father's signature. Eddie wanted his money—interest, penalties, and late fees included. It was then Nia understood why her father had instructed her to get as far away from Maine as she could. Seemed she hadn't gone far enough. She'd definitely picked the wrong state in which to start fresh and hide from her past.

Nia had been puzzled as to how Eddie had tracked her down, especially when she'd been so careful to cover her tracks. She'd simply ignored it, hoping he would think she wasn't who he thought she was. But when a second letter arrived with a photo of Aaron's high school football team with his face circled, and another of him walking home from school that very week, Nia knew she was in real trouble. In the note, Eddie had promised that Aaron would be beaten to death in front of her, and then he would take his sweet time with her before slicing her throat. She had two months to produce the money.

She should have listened to her gut when it warned her not to let Aaron tryout for the football team, but how could she deny him that one little pleasure in his young pitiful life? He'd been denied so much, and she couldn't take that away from him, too. She never imagined that their high school would win the national championship and that their names and faces would be plastered all over the local news. The problem was that Aaron was the spitting image of their father. There was no denying who he was.

Nia quivered from the memories of reading that letter. There was no way she could come up with a million dollars—ever— much less in two months. Eddie was neither impressed nor pacified with the small installments she'd offered him, and had even suggested that she was a pretty little thing who could work it off in trade for him.

In her desperation, Nia's thoughts had gone to one man— Massimo Andretti. His actions, or lack of them, had created the problem. It was only fair that he fix it. She'd thought of writing to him, but recalling her father's numerous unsuccessful attempts to contact him six years ago, she'd decided it was a waste of time.

Luckily for her, the delivery of the second letter coincided with the breakup of Massimo's six-month engagement to a Boston heiress. Nia wasn't surprised when it fell apart. Massimo was an Andretti, and five months into the engagement, rumors of an affair began flying. Then, just two weeks ago, the bride-to-be canceled the wedding. Infidelity was synonymous with Andretti men. Massimo was merely proving he was hewn from the same adulterous piece of granite.

He hopped beds as frequently as he hopped the globe, which was pretty often, seeing he owned companies on every continent. His five-month engagement to the heiress was the longest relationship he'd ever had. He never denied the charges of infidelity, and he didn't even seem shaken up over the breakup. As far as the world knew, he hadn't yet zeroed in on his next catch. But with Massimo, one never knew.

The thought of associating herself with such an unscrupulous man made Nia sick to her stomach. But she had no choice. Her father owed Eddie. Massimo owed her. His broken promises had destroyed her family. This debt was not hers. It was Massimo's. And it was time he paid it.

Nia rubbed her palms along her arms and curled her fingers into the soft material of her cashmere sweater. Her new wardrobe and travel expenses had cost several thousand dollars, not to mention the high interest on her credit cards, but she couldn't approach Massimo looking like an underpaid schoolteacher. He was a man who appreciated classy women. She'd never seen a shabby-looking love interest on his arm.

A rush of uncertainly fluttered in her belly. What if Massimo didn't take her bait? What if he decided she wasn't worth the trouble? There was no doubt in her mind that Eddie would keep his promise to kill her and her brother if she failed to pay him in two months.

The day after she'd gotten the second letter, Nia had packed Aaron off to the Caribbean to stay with her friend who'd moved back there. She didn't want Eddie getting any ideas that he could kidnap and hold him as collateral until she paid the debt.

Besides, she couldn't leave him in New York by himself, and she couldn't bring him to Granite Falls on her clandestine mission, either.

She'd never lied to Aaron about anything, but she wasn't about to lay this kind of burden on him, so she'd simply told him that it was crucial he left the country. He wasn't happy about the disruption in his senior year, but he'd grown to trust her over the years and knew that she would only ask him to do something if it was vitally important. Since his high school was a superb prototype of twenty-first-century learning, he was able to carry on his studies via the Internet and satellite. Thank God for technology.

She'd been tempted to follow him across the ocean and forget about Massimo Andretti, but Eddie had found them once. He could find them again. This time, there would be no warning. He would just kill Aaron, use her up, and then kill her, too.

Nia's heart began to race as she watched Massimo slide his mittens back on. He was warm now and ready to go back out on the trail. Maybe she should let him go before her plan blew up in her face. Massimo Andretti could turn out to be far more dangerous than Eddie if he discovered she was about to swindle him.

No. She shook her head. There was no room for doubts and fears. Massimo was the only way to keep her and Aaron alive. She just had to convince this Andretti hound that she was his next willing victim.

Girding herself with resolve, Nia slid the metal strap of her knockoff Kate Spade purse over her shoulder and glided from the bench. Her legs felt like worn-out elastic as she covered the short distance to Massimo's side. "Beautiful day for skiing, isn't it?" she said, smiling up at him.

His head swung lazily to the other side. His thick long lashes lifted and his deep-blue gaze patrolled her face. "Then why aren't you out on the trails?"

Nia breathed through the sensual tremor that rocked her body. She never knew being this close to a man could be so unnerving, even one who presented a chilling aura. She forced her confused emotions into order and placidly said, "I enjoy watching other people."

His wide mouth pulled into a slight smile as his gaze moved slowly down the length of her then back up again. "Is that the way you get your kicks, watching other people?"

"It depends on what I'm watching them do." She held his hard gaze even as the provocative question and his deep voice made her insides quiver.

Interesting, Massimo thought as he surveyed the young woman with straight dark hair tumbling past her shoulders to the soft curve of her back. He'd felt an instant attraction towards her from the moment he walked into the cabin and spotted her sitting in the corner. If it weren't for the sticky matter of his marriage of convenience in less than a week, he would have joined her at the booth and been charming his way between her shapely thighs already.

He groaned inwardly as his eyes feasted on the slender brown-skinned kitten gazing up at him through brown, almond-shaped eyes. She was wearing black leather boots, a red cashmere sweater that accentuated her jutting breast, and body-hugging jeans that seductively emphasized her narrow waist, just-right hips, and a firm round derriere that would fit nicely in his palms. She clearly hadn't come to the mountain to ski.

He forced his gaze back to her pear-shaped face and full rosy lips, structuring a mouth so wide, visions of her kissing specific erogenous parts of his body sent a licentious need coursing through him. She was sinfully sexy in an unsettling innocent way.

He hadn't been with a woman in weeks, and just looking at her was pushing him close to the edge of his restraint.

As he continued to gaze into her eyes, a disturbing familiarity washed over Massimo. He'd seen those eyes before—sweet and radiant, with a bright rim around the pupils and a combination of gold and lighter brown shades within the irises. She was definitely not a one-night fling—even in his most inebriated state, he would have remembered enjoying such an enticing creature.

So, where had he seen those eyes before? "Do I know you? Have we met?" he asked, pulling his mittens from his hands and pushing them into his pockets.

She dropped her gaze and shook her head. "No, but I've wanted to meet you for a long time, Mr. Andretti. What woman doesn't?" She chuckled softly and tucked a handful of hair behind her ears with slender French-tipped fingers.

That mundane gesture and the way her lips unfolded like a rose glistering with morning dew caused a deep burning in the lowest regions of Massimo's belly. "I'm flattered, Miss—"

"Sylk. Nia Sylk."

As Massimo took the delicate hand she extended, he quivered at the thought of all that dark, fine, silk wrapped around him. "A very apropos name. Silk happens to be my favorite fabric. So soft and smooth and slick to the touch," he murmured, slowly caressing the back of her hand with his fingers.

"This *Sylk* is spelled with a *Y*," she said, pulling away from his grasp.

"Just as a rose by any other name is still a rose, silk is silk, whether it's spelled with an *I* or a *Y*."

Noting the flash of embarrassment that shrouded her face, Massimo knew he was right about her innocence. No sexually experienced woman would blush like that at such a mild overtone. *Enough with the games*, he thought with a hint of irritation. No need to toy with the prey since he couldn't gobble her up once he caught her. "To what do I owe the honor of your beautiful acquaintance, Miss Sylk?"

Nia's skin prickled with warm sensations that had nothing to do with the heat from the fire, but from his touch, his voice, and his overwhelming proximity. No wonder women willingly succumbed to him. The man was potent. *Lethal.* He knew his debilitating effect on the opposite sex and he took great satisfaction in exercising it.

She looked anxiously around the cabin. The two teenage boys who'd been trying on boots a few minutes ago had left, and the woman behind the rental counter was still engrossed in her sweater-knitting project. The place was deserted, not the kind of ski lodge that attracted many people. Luckily for her, it was the right time and place to cast her bait into the lake. Imposing an iron control on her nerves, Nia said in a low, steady voice, "I want to be your lover."

His eyes deepened to a cobalt blue. "You're definitely not shy, Miss Sylk. A properly raised woman would wait for a man to pursue her."

"Being properly raised doesn't mean you shouldn't go after what you want."

"Bold and beautiful. An intriguing combination." His eyes flinched like indigo lightning across a lake. "And what makes you think I would want you, Miss Sylk? Women who go around offering themselves to strange men don't interest me. I chase the women I want, not the other way around. You're taking all the fun out of the game," he added with a mocking downward turn of his mouth.

"I've never done anything like this before," Nia said, determined not to let his lack of interest deter her. Or was he just pretending? After all, he was a hound, and hounds never passed up opportunities.

"And I'm supposed to believe you because——"

"I'm a virgin."

Massimo bounced that unexpected bit of information around in his head. He'd had one virgin in his lifetime, and the experience had been so horrible, he'd sworn off them. But as he gazed into the seductive eyes of Miss Nia Sylk, the very thought of deflowering her, exploring the untouched landscape of her enticing little body made his cock throb. He was much more skillful now, and he was sure the experience would be pleasurable for both of them.

But he was getting married in five days.

Massimo stroked his lower lip with the pad of his thumb as he felt the familiar ache in his groin. If she glanced down, Miss Sylk would know exactly what he wished to do with her. He was never one to hide his desire for a woman. He wasn't into playing games. Games were for the inexperienced, the uncertain, and the cunning. And something told him that this inexperienced little kitten had a cunning game all plotted out with a trap at the end of her ball of yarn—just for him.

Keep your friends close and your enemies closer. Well, she wasn't an enemy, *yet*, but she just might become one when she found herself tangled up in her own ball of yarn. He'd be a fool to walk away without knowing why she'd approached him with such an indelicate offer.

For all he knew, Nia could be a Trojan horse his bastard half brother, Galen, had sent to keep him from fulfilling the requirements in his father's will. *Damn his father for putting him in this situation!*

It was just payback for his refusing to marry the innocent, young girl his father thought was a suitable match, ten years ago. Massimo had informed his father that he had no intentions of ever marrying any woman. He had no desire to break an innocent girl's heart like his father had broken his mother's—like all Andretti men were destined to do.

Luciano had gotten his revenge by stating in his will that if Massimo wanted to inherit Andretti Industries, he must marry on or before his thirty-fourth birthday and produce an heir within a year. Moreover, he had to remain faithfully married for three years or Andretti Industries would go to Galen. The old geezer couldn't control Massimo from his desk, so he figured he'd do it from his grave.

Massimo had had no idea of Galen's existence until the reading of his father's will, six years ago. The shocking information had sent Massimo into a psychological decline and begun a series of incidents that had almost cost him his life. But he'd recovered, and he was ready to fight anyone who got in the way of his goal.

And 'anyone' included Miss Nia Sylk, no matter how alluring she was.

"Hello?"

Massimo shook off the odious memories and surveyed the uninvited intrusion into his world. "So, you're a virgin. What's the big deal about virgins?"

What's the big deal? Nia balked at his cavalier response. He'd probably had more than his fair share of virgins. "I thought virgins were every man's fantasy, Mr. Andretti. I've heard that the pleasure of a virginal conquest for a man is equivalent to breaking in a wild horse. Merely a matter of triumph."

His thick eyebrows arched. "And where specifically did you hear that?"

I have no idea, Nia thought of the lame analogy. *Seriously?* Momentarily speechless, Nia could do nothing but stare at him. His apparent enjoyment of her inability to deliver a witty response grated on her already sensitive nerves. *You're doing this for Aaron. You have to play along. There's no room for failure.* She took a deliberate step backward, hoping her desperation wasn't too obvious. "Since you're not interested, I'll just—"

"How old are you, Miss Sylk?"

"Old enough to know what I want. I'm ready to be a woman in every sense of the word and I want you—a real man, to teach me, Mr. Andretti."

"Let me see some ID."

"You don't believe me?"

"Since I don't know you, I can't very well answer that question fairly. Your hesitation suggests you may have something to hide. Perhaps your name isn't even Nia Sylk." He turned and headed toward the door.

Crap. She couldn't let him leave now that she'd gotten his attention. She'd been waiting all week for this opportunity. Nia pulled her wallet from her purse, yanked out her driver's license, and rushed after him. "Here." She shoved it into his hands.

He studied the thin plastic. "So you're twenty-three, and from Brooklyn." He handed it back.

"Satisfied?"

"I'm not that easily satisfied, Miss Sylk."

The cynical twist of his lips and his suggestive gaze ignited fires inside her Nia had never experienced before. She didn't know exactly what she was supposed to feel when a man like Massimo Andretti looked at her that way. Since her father's death, she'd been too busy working to support herself and Aaron and stay under the radar of the law. She'd never had time for boyfriends.

She'd been looking forward to having a life, to finally engaging in all the things girls her age had been enjoying since they were teenagers—things she'd had to set aside while she was raising her little brother. She had a lot of catching up to do with partying with her girlfriends, with dating, with falling in love and losing her virginity to the man of her choice. She'd been looking forward to learning, growing, and discovering herself—who she really was.

Instead, here she was, playing a dangerous game with a scoundrel who could hurt her, destroy her innocence before she had time to embrace it. But if she didn't play along with Massimo, Aaron could die in front of her. So for that reason, with her heart beating wildly in her chest, Nia asked as casually as possible, "Well, are you going to take me up on my offer, Mr. Andretti?"

"What do you want in return for your... virginity?" He flipped his wrist indifferently.

Nia shrugged. "I'm not harboring any silly romantic notions, nor am I expecting any type of commitment, if that's what you think. I just want to fulfill a fantasy." That much was true. She'd been fantasizing about Massimo ever since she'd seen him, six years ago.

"You traveled all the way from Brooklyn to offer me your virginity with no ulterior motives. And when I've had my fill, you'll go back to Brooklyn with no hard feelings."

"Well, that and four million dollars."

A soft long whistle flowed through his pursed lips. "Is that what a virginity costs these days?"

"Since I haven't sold one before, I wouldn't know," she stated haughtily. She knew four million dollars meant nothing to him. He spent double that on some of his mistresses. He'd bought many of them villas to encourage them to go their ways quietly. It was the MO of Andretti men. They thought anything and anyone could be bought and discarded at will, and that they could change their minds on a deal without any explanation and without any regard to how it affected other people. Their callous behavior had cost her father his life. "Anyway, I'd like the money in cash, if you don't mind," Nia added with a dignified jut of her chin.

"Sure. Keep it clean and simple. No paper trails."

Under his withering gaze, Nia felt like a costly piece of marble being assessed for his private gallery. Perhaps this wasn't such a very good idea, she thought as the silence grew and thickened. The unreadable, changing expressions in his eyes worried her. What if he was contemplating turning her in for solicitation? The cards were stacked against her. She was a desperate schoolteacher drowning in debt. No one would believe her if she tried to deny the accusations.

On the other hand, Massimo was one of the wealthiest, most handsome, eligible bachelors on the planet. He didn't have to pay for sex. Everybody would believe his version of the…

"Deal."

Nia shook her head and blinked. Did he just say…

"*Andiamo*." He waved his hand in the air as if he'd just signed a contract on the purchase of a new car and continued on his way to the door.

"Wait!" Panic edged Nia's voice.

He stopped midstride and turned, his head tipped to one side. "Changing your mind, Miss Sylk? You're not quite ready to become a woman?"

"There are conditions to my proposal."

"Now you tell me. Well, let's hear them."

Nia's fist tightened around the cold metal of her purse strap. "I get half the money now and the other half after the— um—" She cleared her throat. "The deed is completed."

"Fair. Anything else?"

"I need time to get to know you better before I— before you — before we— consummate the agreement."

"Ahh!" He slapped his palm against his forehead in a clearly mocking manner. "You doubt my performance. Well, I assure you, Miss Sylk, no woman has ever left my bed unsatisfied. I can get my hands on some references if you'd like. I'm certain many of my former lovers would be happy to share their experiences with you. I've heard some of them even compare notes—positions, duration, locale. The kinds of things women brag about when they try to outperform each other. Perhaps one day you'll feel obliged to contribute to the blogs."

Nia gasped. If she didn't know it before, she knew now that she was making a pact with the most dangerous man on earth. Yes, they were just words, but they nevertheless sent heat rippling through her at the thought of rubbing skin and swapping bodily fluids with Massimo Andretti, and then blabbing about it. But that's not the reason she'd come looking for him.

"Well, I'm certain you're a master at the art of lovemaking, Mr. Andretti. It's one of the reasons I chose you. But all the same, I just can't jump into bed with you. A woman's first time should be special. She should feel comfortable and safe with her partner. I mean, we aren't even on a first name basis, yet."

"How much time, *Nia*?"

"One month." That should give her enough time to settle her debt with Eddie, make arrangements for a new life with Aaron somewhere out of the country, and escape from Granite Falls with her virginity still intact and two million of Massimo's dollars in tow—enough to make a decent life for her and Aaron. It wouldn't make up for five years of suffering, but it would bring her comfort to know she'd outwitted the notorious Massimo Andretti.

"One week," he said, pulling his mittens from his pockets and slipping them on.

"Three weeks," Nia countered.

"One."

"Two?"

"One. You'll have two million dollars on Friday. I'll have *you* next Tuesday, after which you'll receive the other two million. Fair?"

"Well—"

"That's my final offer."

"But—"

"Good day, Miss Sylk." He reached the door in two swift strides.

CHAPTER TWO

"Okay! I accept."

Massimo turned his head and stared blankly at her, obviously waiting for her to make the next move. Nia pulled a folded piece of paper from her purse and walked over to him. "Here's my contact information. Perhaps we can discuss the details of our arrangement over dinner tonight?"

"No."

"No?"

"You come with me now, Nia, or the deal is off." His eyes flashed imperiously and his tight lips indicated that the opportunities to negotiate were over.

Nia knew that if he walked out that door without her, she would never have this chance again. "Okay."

"Okay." He walked to a corner, dropped his weight down on a bench, and pulled a pair of humongous snow boots from under it.

While he changed out of his ski boots, Nia swallowing her defeat, and walked back to the table, picked up her parka, and pulled it on. She glanced over at the woman who'd abandoned her knitting needles and was now peering at her over the rim of her glasses. Nia wondered just how many women Massimo had picked up in this cabin. The woman would probably tell her if she had the guts to go over and ask. Thank goodness there were no other spectators around. Her father must be turning in his grave. His sweet little angel girl had turned into a...

Nia shut her mind against the nauseating term.

Feeling as if she'd just sold her soul to the devil, she followed Massimo out the door and into the cold March air. Tiny flurries landed on her face, immediately melting as they made contact with her flushed skin. She zippered her parka and arranged the hood over her head as Massimo draped his laced-together ski boots across his shoulders.

"Where are we going?" she asked as he retrieved his skis and poles from a hook on the side of the building and tucked them securely under one arm.

"Home." He started down the mountain toward the parking lot, leaving deep, giant footprints in the powdery snow.

Was home his villa on Crystal Lake, or was it the sprawling Andretti Estate on Mount Reservoir? Whichever, it was not a good idea to be cooped up behind four walls with Massimo. She hadn't planned on leaving with him today. She'd planned on returning to her hotel room to either gloat or groan—depending on whether or not he'd bitten her bait. Well, he'd bitten, and now she had to think of a way to slow down the process of her seduction which, judging from his long strides, he was in quite a hurry to begin.

"I can't go home with you, Massimo," Nia said, trying hard to keep the panic from her voice.

"Why?" The snow crunched under the weight of his boots.

"Well, it wouldn't look good for us to be living together."

The cold wind picked up his laugh and the pine trees echoed it around the mountain range. "You just offered to sell me your virginity for four million dollars and you're worried about what people will say if you move into my house?"

Nia knew it was a lame excuse, but he'd put her on the spot. "Well, I'm staying at a hotel and I'm committed for the week. I wouldn't get my money back if I left early. It's their policy."

"I guess you're staying at Hotel Andreas."

"Yes."

"I'm impressed."

He'd be, Nia thought. Hotel Andreas was the most expensive hotel in the area. It was costing her upwards of three hundred and fifty dollars a night and she'd been there for four nights already. But when you're planning to solicit the attention of one of the richest playboys in the universe, you want to look as impressive as possible. His cousin, Adam, with whom he shared a close relationship, owned the hotel, and when she'd set her plan in motion, Nia had taken that fact into consideration.

While familiarizing herself with the pattern of his daily life, she'd discovered that when Massimo was between affairs, he spent a great deal of time at his mountain estate and hardly ate out during that period. She'd also learned that he visited the bar at his cousin's hotel quite frequently—probably where he picked up most of his one-night stands. Since he was presently unattached, Nia had predicted that it'd be easy to meet him, and so had booked her stay at his cousin's hotel with the hopes of increasing her chances of running into him at the bar.

For the past four nights, Nia had dolled up and planted herself in a darkened corner of the bar that gave her a vantage point to observe without being observed. Unfortunately for her, last night was the first time Massimo had dropped in since she'd come to town. And doubly unfortunately, he was not alone.

"You travel in style," Massimo stated on a mild chuckle, not missing a step. "How do you like Hotel Andreas?"

"It's bleeding the life out of my bank account, but you're worth it, Massimo."

He laughed again. "I like a woman who speaks her mind. Don't worry about the bill. I'll pay it when we swing by the hotel to retrieve your belongings. Hopefully that'll stop the bleeding."

"I drove a rental here, so—um—" Nia fumbled for another excuse to stay her execution.

"I'll have the rental company pick up the car and I'll pay that bill, too. By Friday night, you'll have two million dollars in cash, a credit card, a new wardrobe, and a brand new car—any make or model of your choice." He stopped and turned suddenly causing her to bump full front into the brick wall he called a body.

Nia swore she'd broken a rib in the collision. He placed his free hand on her shoulder to keep her from falling at his feet.

Too close. He was too close. He smelled of man sweat and pristine snow. Earthy and inviting. Nia's breath caught in her throat.

"I have a reputation for taking care of all my women's needs. So tell me, Nia Sylk, did I forget anything?" he said, his gaze bold and stimulating as he peered down at her.

Nia shook her head, too winded to talk. It's a good thing she was breathless or she might have screwed herself by stating that she didn't need a car or a credit card since she wouldn't be around to use either of them. She'd definitely take the new wardrobe, though. She'd be stupid not to.

His eyes narrowed into blue slits. "How did you know I'd be here today? I don't usually ski on this deserted mountain and definitely not in the middle of the week or the day. I came here to escape and think. The last thing I expected was...well... your proposal to sell me your virginity."

Nia bit into her bottom lip as his words amplified the humiliation she was already experiencing from making the proposal in the first place. What must he be thinking of her? Like she should care. She swallowed her pride and stared right back at him. "I've been dressing up for the past four nights and waiting for you to make an appearance at the hotel bar, Massimo. You finally came by last night, but alas you weren't alone. I overheard you tell the man you were with that you would be skiing on this mountain today."

"So you've been stalking me, Nia Sylk?"

"Like I said, I've wanted to meet you for a long time."

"You could have stopped by Andretti Industries. That's how people usually gain an audience with me."

Nia tried hard to ignore the burning of her skin under his hand that was still firmly clasped on her shoulder. The cold March wind was no match for the heat Massimo's touch was causing inside her. She shuddered on a deep breath and pulled her parka tighter about her body. "I doubt I would have gotten past your security since I had no relevant business with you," she said. "I thought the bar was the best place to attract your attention." *It's where you pick up women.* She wished she had the courage to voice that thought.

"And now that you've attracted my attention, *cara mia*, I hope you understand what that means." A faint light seemed to flash in the depth of his eyes.

Nia's nerves tensed. As simple as his statement was, it felt like a threat. She dropped her gaze, fearing he would be able to detect her plan to con him out of his money.

"If you want to change your mind, do it now," he said softly, his hot breath misting the cold space between them, wrapping around her cold lips, warming them. "But be warned, Nia, it's the only chance you'll have to renege on this agreement. Once we get off this mountain, there's no turning back. I will hold you to your promise and claim everything you've offered me, right down to your last breathless moan of surrender."

Common sense told Nia to back down and run. But the thought of one of Eddie's goons jumping Aaron in an alley and beating him to death in front of her, filled her with the will to stay the course. She would do just about anything to keep Aaron safe, even play house with the devil if it came to that. She took a deep breath of the cold air and met Massimo's gaze again. "I'll stay."

A smirk played at the corner of his mouth. "You won't be disappointed." He released her, pulled his car fob from his pocket and pushed a button. He turned and began walking again, his head high, his body erect, his snow-dusted wavy hair dancing about his head in the breeze.

Nia stumbled to keep up with him, her mind spinning in a crazy mixture of hope, fear, and fury. *How had he done it, huh?* How had he taken her proposition and made it his? How had he turned her bargain into his own? If she weren't careful, he would carry out his threat to claim her body, then he'd walk away as if she had merely offered him a slice of chocolate cake with a cherry on top.

Even though she would have the money to pay off Eddie and enough to start new lives for her and Aaron, it would be a humiliating defeat if she fell victim to Massimo's sex appeal and surrendered the booty she'd offered him.

This was *her* game, damn it! She had made up all the rules and plotted the end results. She would not allow Massimo Andretti to bully her, sabotage her plan, and rewrite the outcome of her scheme.

When they reached the parking lot, Massimo called the rental company while she got her personal items from the car. That task completed, she followed him to his ride, a Mercedes-Benz G550. When he held the door for her, Nia glided on to the warm leather seat. She watched with anxiety as he walked around the front and climbed behind the steering wheel, immediately sucking up the air and space inside the vehicle. Every breath she took was saturated with the smell of leather and man. The sexual magnetism that made him so irresistible threatened to undo her.

Again, she pushed it aside, determined to stay focused on her mission, especially since she only had a week to see her plan through. When she'd ventured out on this mission, Nia wasn't certain Massimo would accept her offer. But whether or not he had, she'd known she couldn't return to her life in New York where—number one, he could track her down, and number two, where Eddie would be waiting for her. She needed time to finalize her plan of escape and wipe all traces of Nia Sylk off the face of the earth.

But Massimo had only given her one week.

"Why are you so quiet?" Massimo asked as they pulled onto the road. "I thought you'd be showering me with questions by now, trying to get to know me better as you so ardently put it."

"I'm just thinking."

"About?"

"Oh, my new wardrobe, new car, and my four million dollars."

He chuckled heartily. "You know, I've always preferred experienced women in my bed. I find innocence and inexperience boring. But," he added, nodding his head assuredly, "I think I may enjoy breaking you in. When I'm done with you, Miss Nia Sylk, you'll be so spoiled, you'll never want any other man to touch you."

Even though she knew he was taunting her, his words caused a tingling in the pit of Nia's stomach. "You're so sure of your sexual prowess, aren't you, Massimo? You may not have what it takes to satisfy me or keep up with me for that matter. I may just be the woman who brings you to your knees," she taunted right back.

His laugh grew harder as he tossed her a look that could melt a mile-thick Siberian iceberg. "Oh, *cara*, you *will* bring me to my knees. One way or the other, I *will* kneel before you. I can't wait to show you just how hot I can make your virgin engine hum. You might even blow a few gaskets."

"You still have to wait a week to find out, Massimo" Nia said, even as she squeezed her thighs together to combat the bolts of electricity that zinged between them.

"You're truly naïve when it comes to men, aren't you, Nia? We enjoy the chase, the anticipation of the kill almost as much as we enjoy the prey once we catch it. Believe me when I tell you that I'm already enjoying every second of this chase. I can wait, Nia. Question is, will you be able to?"

Turning her face toward the window, Nia smiled at the thought that by Saturday evening, she and two million of his dollars would be long gone. Her smile deepened as she envisioned him combing New York from one end to the other, looking for her when she wouldn't even be in the country.

Now that the threat to her and Aaron's lives might be gone, Nia settled into her seat and allowed powerful relief to fill her. For the first time in five years, she would be able to live without looking over her shoulder, and live well at that. There was so much she could do with a million dollars.

In a few days Massimo's promises, his threats and taunts would be a blur on the horizon of her mind. In the meantime, she had to play the role of a besotted lover to reduce his suspicions about her. "You're right," she said, turning her head to give him a seductive smile. "I can't wait to make love with you, Massimo, but like I said, I need it to be special."

"Oh, it will be special, Nia. Images of you quivering beneath me are already fueling my desire and determination to have you."

From the lustful gleam in his eyes, Nia imagined that he

probably intended to start ravishing her at a second past midnight next Monday, then at dawn Tuesday morning, he'd place her and her suitcase by the side of the road, lick his lips, and get back on his Casanovian journey as if she never even crossed his path.

Did she really think he was that gullible? Massimo thought as he navigated the SUV along a slippery country road. He knew she had no intentions of surrendering her virginity—willingly, that is. And he knew he'd have no trouble convincing her to spread her legs for him if he so desired. He wasn't yet sure if she was worth the trouble.

She claimed she'd never offered herself to a man before. It's possible she was telling the truth. Judging from her extravagant outfit, it was also possible that this virgin act was her MO to riches. And her little speech about Hotel Andreas bleeding her bank account, yeah right. How many wealthy idiots had she conned before? How many were out there scratching their heads wondering where she and their millions had disappeared to?

Again, his thoughts went to his half brother. After the shock of learning that he had a sibling had dissolved, Massimo had begun digging into the boy's background. Galen Carmichael was under the impression that his father died before he was born. He had no idea he was the progeny of one of the richest and most powerful men in the world. Having no interest in forming a relationship with him, Massimo had not contacted him.

Massimo assumed that a 'nondisclosure of paternity' was one of the deals his father had made with his whore, Judith Carmichael, when she disappeared from Granite Falls twenty-odd years ago with Galen already planted in her belly. Luciano had supported Galen financially and had provided him with as excellent an education as he'd provided Massimo, but the old man had left absolutely nothing for his bastard son.

Massimo gritted his teeth at the memory of walking into his father's office and finding him on the couch with Judith. He was only nine years old, and although he couldn't understand what he'd witnessed, he'd known that it was wrong. It was the beginning of his estranged relationship with his father. Massimo never told his mother about the affair between his father and his secretary, but he was certain she knew. Women had a way of sensing these things.

Massimo wondered if Judith had revealed the identity of his father to her son before her death, late last year. If that were the case, then he could understand Galen's interest in the vast empire their father had left behind. But then again, he thought as he stopped at a four-way stop, neither Galen nor Judith would have had knowledge of the contents of Luciano's last will and testament.

But if his assumptions were correct about the boy learning that Luciano was his father, and that he might have hired Nia—not to stop Massimo from gaining control of his inheritance, but so Galen could gain inside information about Andretti business—Massimo swore he'd bury both of them alive.

If they were indeed coconspirators, what was Nia's role in the plot? Was she just for hire or was she Galen's woman whom he'd pawned out? Had he seen her in a picture with Galen, maybe in the background of a photo his surveillance crew had sent him? Is that why her eyes seemed so familiar to him?

He had so many questions, and only two days to put this sexy Sylk puzzle together. By Friday... *Damn!*

Massimo applied the brakes as he came up on another intersection. Dafne, his fiancée, was arriving from Bellagio on Friday to sign the contracts on their marriage arrangement and settle in before they exchanged vows on Monday. His original plan was to fly to Italy tomorrow and finalize the deal there, but at his attorney's insistence that the contract be signed on U.S. soil, he'd arranged for her to come here. He would have to inform Dafne of the change in plans as soon as he got the chance. He couldn't very well have his potential lover and his potential wife sleeping under the same roof, could he?

Massimo took a deep breath as he released the gas pedal and gassed the SUV forward.

Desperation had pushed him into this marital agreement with Dafne Bellini, the daughter of a maid who worked at the Andretti home in Bellagio. He and Dafne had been friends since they were both five years old. She knew all his secrets. Even though their relationship had suffered some enormous strains over the years, she remained one of the four people in the world he trusted with his life.

So it was natural that he would turn to her after his breakup with Gabrielle had left him in a panic. Massimo had been astonished when Dafne offered to marry him as long as he did not make their engagement public. Except for that one encounter in their very distant past, neither of them had shown any sexual interest in each other. Their friendship was far more important than sex, and to keep it that way, Dafne had specified that she would produce his heir through nonsexual means only. Massimo could only hope that she would change her mind. He could not live without sex for the next three years of his life. No way in hell was that going to happen.

The fact that Dafne knew why he had to marry gave her a lot of power over him. Who knows what was going on in her mind now that she had him cornered up a tree like a leopard fleeing from a lion? Massimo knew firsthand how power could change a person. He hated being in this position, but he would be an idiot to surrender a company he'd spent most of his life building to a bastard half brother he despised. He wanted nothing to do with the offspring of Judith Carmichael, the woman he blamed for his own mother's untimely death.

Immediately following the reading of his father's will, Massimo had begun building his own empire. The product was *La Banca di Bianchi*, a chain of European banks he'd established in his mother's maiden name. In addition, he owned several companies, and was a major shareholder in numerous financial corporations throughout the globe. To guarantee that his interests were free and clear of Andretti Industries, he'd borrowed the investment funds from his friend, Bryce Fontaine, all of which he'd paid back with interest within two years. He really didn't need Andretti Industries, but he wasn't about to walk away from a conglomeration whose success he'd been contributing to since he was eleven years old, and there was no way in hell he was going to give up the house where he was born and raised, and where the fondest memories of his mother still lingered.

No Carmichael would ever set foot inside that house.

That fact was the deciding element in his agreement to marry Dafne. Nobody else but his lawyer, his two best friends, Bryce and Erik, and his cousin Adam knew he had to be married on or before next Saturday, but they were unaware of the deal between Dafne and him. Just last night, Bryce had commended him for sticking it to his father by letting his inheritance go. He was already a self-made billionaire, so why saddle himself with a wife—the one possession he'd sworn never ever to own?

But being controlled for three years was a more palatable toxin than ultimate defeat, Massimo decided as he pulled off Route 80 onto Andreas Way in downtown Granite Falls and headed toward the hotel.

Having Nia and Dafne under the same roof would leave room for questions, slipups, and revelations—revelations he preferred to keep from his half brother until he was unhappily married and holding the next generation of Andrettis in his arms. Until he knew exactly what Nia wanted with him, it was best he kept the women apart. It was a good thing Dafne wanted to keep their arrangement a secret. It would be difficult to explain the presence of one young woman in his house when he was engaged to marry another. To the world, he was still a bachelor, and he would remain thus for the next few days when he eventually announced the news of his marriage.

In the meantime, he would give Miss Sylk—if that really was her name—all the silk rope she needed to hang her own pretty little neck. Then he would spool her in for the bloody takedown.

Nia stepped off the elevator and into the lobby of the hotel in time to see the concierge hand Massimo a piece of paper she assumed was her bill.

I belong to him now, she thought as she watched him scrawl his signature on the receipt. He had bought her, just as he bought companies, yachts, jets, or whatever his avaricious heart desired. There was no turning back now, just as there had been no turning back six years ago when he reneged on the business agreement between their fathers.

Memories assailed Nia as she strolled ahead of the bellboy who carried her bags. She remembered how relieved her father had been the day he signed the contract with Luciano Andretti. She also remembered how worried he'd been in the months leading up to that day. By the time Luciano had agreed to help, her father had already mortgaged their family home and had cashed in his retirement and his children's college funds to keep the mill open.

According to Luciano, a paper mill—one of the remaining few in New England—was an asset to Andretti Industries. There had been plans to expand beyond paper production, plans that would be financially beneficial to both parties. But Massimo apparently thought differently, and after being told that the new CEO of Andretti Industries was no longer interested in honoring the contract with West Gate Paper Mills, her father had turned to a loan shark for help. When that money evaporated, the bank foreclosed on the mill, putting her father and a hundred and fifty other employees out of work. The final blow came when the bank foreclosed on their house, leaving her family homeless.

It hadn't eased Nia's pain when she'd learned that the new owner had renovated the mill, rehired most of the former employees, and turned it into the most prosperous in the area. Her father was already dead and she and Aaron had been forced to leave the only home they'd ever known.

And now to fulfill her father's request to take care of Aaron, she'd offered to become of all things—Massimo Andretti's whore. *His property*. His eagerness to shell out four million dollars —well, two, since she wouldn't be around to collect the other two million—just for the pleasure of bedding her gave her pause. Did he find her that irresistible? And should she trust him to adhere to the terms of their agreement?

As Nia joined Massimo at the concierge's desk, he turned and smiled down at her. "Have everything, *cara*?"

Nia nodded, the warmth in his voice and eyes making her tremble inside. Half an hour ago, he'd insisted on following her up to her room when a man with a French accent had approached him in the lobby.

When he stepped aside to converse with the man in French, Nia had taken the opportunity to bolt. She was thankful he'd been otherwise engaged, and that he hadn't bothered to come up after his conversation with the man was over. She didn't think it would have been wise to be alone with Massimo and a huge bed in a hotel room. She was honest enough to admit that it probably wouldn't take much for Massimo to persuade her to change her mind about waiting a week to make love.

She was after all a healthy young woman with hot blood running through her veins. And he was a hunk.

She forced a smile as Massimo folded his copy of the receipt and slipped it into the pocket of his parka. Stepping closer to her, he placed his hand on the small of her back and steered her toward the revolving doors, ahead of the bellboy who followed with her luggage.

They drove in silence through downtown Granite Falls—away from Crystal Lake that bordered one side of Hotel Andreas. Nia shifted uneasily on the seat when she realized he was taking her to the Andretti mansion on Mount Reservoir—a fortress that would be most difficult to escape from. She'd hoped that when he'd said he was taking her home, he'd meant the lakeside villa his succession of mistresses occupied during his affairs with them.

No such luck for her. To calm her anxiety, Nia took in her surroundings as they drove along. The streets, that a few days ago were crowded with weekend ski bunnies from the south, were now all but deserted. It was a lovely little town, a sort of unexpected mecca hidden at the foothills of the White Mountains, Nia thought as Massimo steered around a traffic circle surrounded by small businesses, local boutiques, cafés, restaurants, and other touristy shops, housed in beautifully renovated old mill buildings. The Aiken River that had powered the mills—many of which had been owned by the Andretti family for decades—now flowed unhindered behind the buildings.

Nia could only imagine how lovely the summers were here with the beaches teeming with the town's residents, noisy children playing on the shores, and small yachts cruising along the beautiful Crystal Lake. Too bad she couldn't stay long enough to enjoy some of it.

"Are you stopping at your office?" she asked as they traveled north on Industrial Drive and the glass tower that housed Andretti Industries headquarters loomed ahead of them. She could really use some time away from him. His nearness caused her mind to go into confusion and robbed her of her ability to think logically. And she needed to think and plot.

"No," was his only response as he passed Andretti Way that led to his office, made a left turn on to Route 80, crossed the Aiken River Bridge, and headed west into the mountains.

Nia took a glance at him and noted his set face, clamped mouth, and fixed eyes. His mood had definitely changed since she'd left him to go up to her hotel room to pack. Nia wondered if it had something to do with his conversation with the French man who'd approached him in the lobby. During the first few minutes of that conversation, even though she'd had no idea what they were talking about, Nia had detected tenseness in Massimo as if he'd received unpleasant news.

Sensing he was in no mood to talk, Nia left him alone to his brooding.

Finally Massimo pulled off the highway and started a climb up a steep paved road. A thick white forest with branches bowing laboriously from the weight of snow encased them. After a few minutes, he made another turn and drove along a somewhat level road that took them further into the mountain. A wrought-iron gate opened automatically as they approached it then closed behind them.

A cold shiver raced up Nia's spine. She felt like she'd just driven through the gates of hell with Satan at the helm. A flicker of real fear coursed through her veins as the gross enormity of what she had done took a heavy toll on her senses.

"Too late," Massimo said as they rounded a corner and

reached a small plateau that overlooked deep ravines and a labyrinth of lakes in the distance. He stopped the Mercedes, applied the parking brake, and unbuckled his seatbelt.

The sensual look in his eyes was unmistakable. As much as she resented him, Nia knew that if he touched her, she would instantly dissolve like a snowball on a hot tin roof.

"Come, Nia. I wish to taste you, now."

"Massimo, we haven't even had a date yet, and I don't kiss on the first date." Nia forced humor into her voice, but the quaking of her body belied the fear and desire she felt deep in her core.

With little effort, Massimo unfastened her seatbelt and pulled her halfway across the seat. "I'm a businessman, Nia. We made a deal. In business, it's always wise to sample the goods before the final purchase. I *will* sample the goods you offered. The last thing I need is a scared little kitten in my bed."

"I'm not scared of you," she lied out loud, hoping he couldn't hear the thumping of her heart against her chest.

"Prove it."

He slid closer and Nia almost fainted from the heady smell of male flesh and the hungry glare in his electric blue eyes. Her gaze dropped to his sexy mouth and she knew he could very well swallow her whole right here, right now. She licked her lips. "Massimo, I don't think—"

"Perfect. I don't want you to think. Just feel… me." He pulled her softly against him.

"Massimo, you promised—"

"Don't fight me, Nia. Let your body relax and enjoy the call of desire. It's good practice for next Monday when we seal our little agreement." He held her chin in his hand, and his mouth came down upon hers, soft and fluttering like a feather. He brushed his lips against hers then slowly traced his tongue along the outline, causing tiny explosions to erupt from ever pore of her body.

"*Aprire la sua boca,*" he whispered, clasping one hand at the back of her head and tangling his fingers in her hair. "*Avvolgere le braccia intorno al nio collo.*"

Nia didn't speak a word of Italian, but somehow she understood him. Her lips parted, and as his hot tongue swept inside her mouth, Nia wrapped her arms around his neck as he'd ordered. She clung to him as an invisible fire threatened to consume her, bone, blood, and flesh. Her heart drummed loudly as she surrendered to the enemy, as lust devoured revenge, and desire robbed her of all logic.

Massimo pulled up her sweater. His warm hand crawled along her ribcage and his long fingers expertly pulled down the lacy cups of her bra, baring her achy breasts to his touch.

Nia whimpered against his mouth as her nipples tingled and hardened against his smooth palm. He molded her breasts with skillful fingers, causing an intense yearning in her belly that quickly spread to the core of her throbbing sex. Moisture collected in her panties. She squeezed her thighs together to combat the pleasure, but quickly relaxed them when she realized it only intensified the ache.

Yielding to Massimo's seductions was against the rules. Her body and her mind had betrayed her. All she could count on now was her heart. It had to remain impassive to him. And she didn't think she could trust it.

"Do you still think I can't satisfy you, Nia?" he asked against her lips. He kept his hand on the heaving mound of one breast and continued caressing the hard nipple between his thumb and forefinger. "Do you find me inadequate?"

Nia squeezed her lids shut, refusing to answer. She couldn't talk. Shouldn't talk. Or she might foolishly ask him not to stop. As much as she loathed him, she had to admit that she'd been dreaming of kissing Massimo for six long years. She'd heard that sexual fantasies were a lot better than the real thing. Massimo

Andretti just blew that theory out the steamed-up windows of his SUV. Her fantasies about him were prayer vigils compared to his kiss and his touch.

"You're a very desirable woman, Nia Sylk. It will be extremely difficult keeping my hands off you for a week." He reluctantly released her breasts, pulled his hand from under her sweater and moved back to his side of the vehicle.

Nia's eyes slowly opened to encounter the passionate fire glowing in the sentient depths of his. She wanted to look away, break the spell, but it seemed some invisible cord held her transfixed. She was bewitched. She licked her burning, trembling lips.

"You have the most incredible brown eyes. They set my heart on fire each time I gaze into them," he said in a husky voice. "And when you lick your lips and stare at me like that..." He growled deep in his throat and shook his head, his black wavy hair brushing his shoulders. "You have to help me live up to our agreement, Nia. You have to stop being so damn sexy or I will not be held responsible for breaching our 'no sex for one week' agreement."

Help him? She couldn't even help herself, and she wasn't trying to be sexy.

With her heart pounding erratically, Nia scurried to her corner and pulled the lace back up over her breasts. It was just like Massimo not to clean up his own mess. She'd known that at some point they would kiss. It was what lovers do. What she didn't know was that a mere kiss would leave her this breathless, this weak.

She wasn't ready for this. *For him.* Thank God they would be sleeping in separate rooms. If she had to share a bed with this master-at-getting-what-he-wanted, she knew her resistance would be futile. She had to stay strong, get the money, then escape from Massimo's lair of seduction before it was too late.

As they continued up the mountain, another gate opened up, and two bulging, armed security guards in an expansive gatehouse waved them through. Yep, escaping from this prison would be much more difficult than it would have been from his lakeside villa. But she'd come with a will to escape Massimo Andretti, and where there was a will, there was always a way. She just had to be a little more creative in far less time than she'd originally anticipated.

They rounded a bend and the sprawling Andretti Estate popped into view—acres and acres of evergreen terrain with buildings of varying sizes and shapes scattered about. The main house, a white and blue limestone structure that comprised of three sections—a three-story center flanked by two-story wings on either side—dominated all the other buildings on the estate. A combination of evergreen and deciduous snow-dusted trees surrounded the intricate architecture, creating the picture of a stunning Italian citadel set in the middle of an arctic jungle.

Nia looked on breathlessly at the serendipitous surrounding as Massimo stopped in the courtyard—an extension of the middle section that expanded into a wide covered portico.

It was a fortress where the public was never allowed. One entered these grounds by invitation only. Electric fences, treacherous ravines, and armed guards kept the paparazzi at a distance. The few photographs Nia had seen in several issues of *Granite Falls People News* didn't do the estate the slightest bit of justice.

The earlier Andrettis were reportedly not social at all. After his father died, many thought that Massimo, the modern-day playboy, would open up his home and allow the public inside, but the world was still waiting with bated breath. It was as if they were guarding some dark family secret. Were there bodies buried on the grounds or trapped behind walls and stairwells?

Feeling a chill rush up her spine, Nia pulled her parka tightly about her shoulders as Massimo open the door of the Mercedes. He helped her down to the stone cut floor of the covered portico, then up a flight of steps toward the front door.

"My luggage," she said looking back.

"It'll be taken care of."

A teenage boy with curly blond hair emerged from a door on the side of the mansion. "*Buonasera, Signor Andretti,*" he called out to Massimo.

Massimo responded in a rush of Italian sentences. The boy nodded and gave Nia a shy smile before he climbed into the vehicle and drove off behind the house.

As the cold dry air swirled around her, Nia shivered. She wanted to go home, but when she remembered that she had no home to go to, and that she would never again have one if she backed out of this deal with Massimo, she swallowed the sob in her throat.

Massimo tried the knob on the front door and cursed under his breath when it didn't turn. He pushed a button on the wall.

A few minutes later, the heavy oak door opened and a robust woman greeted them. "*Jambo,* Massimo. You *forgit* you key *agin,*" she said in a thick accent Nia thought sounded African.

"I didn't forget my key, Azi. You insist on locking my door when I've repeatedly asked you to leave it unlocked."

She placed a hand over her heart and pretended to be affronted. "You're in a *gooood mooood* tonight, I see, Mr. Massimo. *Goood* t'ing I made one of your favorite *disheees* to soothe your grumpy *mooood,* eh? Her eyes widened as they settled on Nia. "And I see you have brought company. A lady friend, eh? Will she be stayin' fer dinna?" Her big white teeth glittered in the light from the ceiling.

Nia was suddenly overwhelmed with shame. She felt... soiled. This woman knew why she was here. With so many affairs to his credit, she was sure she was not the first woman Massimo had brought to his home. Why would this gentle-faced woman think she was any different from all the others who'd willingly given themselves to her boss? Good heavens, she was worse. She'd sold herself to him. If she walked through that door…

Just as she turned to bolt down the steps, Massimo's arm closed around her waist. He pushed her through the door into a spacious domed foyer that extended into a long hallway.

Nia glanced around the foyer with its vaulted brightly colored Italian Renaissance ceilings and walls. The interior architecture was just as magnificent as the exterior, but she thought the decoration and furniture could use a makeover to bring them into the modern sophistication of the twenty-first century.

"Yes, Azi, I have company." Massimo shrugged out of his parka, slid Nia's from her shoulders, and shoved them into Azi's hands. "Nia will be my guest for a few days." He turned to Nia. "My housekeeper, Azi. She will make your visit very comfortable."

Nia stared at Azi who seemed to enjoy teasing Massimo, and who was acting more like a grandmother than a housekeeper. She wondered at the true nature of their relationship.

"I'll prepare one of the guest rooms," Azi said.

"That won't be necessary. Nia will be sleeping in the master suit," Massimo said.

Nia's head snapped around. "We're not sharing a bedroom, Massimo. That was not the deal. Remember?"

Ignoring the hint of panic in her voice, Massimo sniffed the air. "Is that lobster I smell, Azi?"

"*Yeees*. One of your favorite dishes."

He noted the perturbed glance Azi cast in Nia's direction. He understood Azi's confusion and surprise. She was privy to his arrangement with Dafne, and was probably wondering what the hell he was doing bringing a strange young girl to the mansion just days before his nuptial. Hell, he was still puzzled as to why he'd brought Nia here instead of taking her to Crystal Lake where he housed his women.

Explaining the situation to Azi was inevitable, and he had no doubt that she would have a few spiteful laughs over it. In the meantime, he had to assert some kind of control over his household even if he had none over his life. He glanced at the Rolex on his wrist. "When will dinner be ready?"

"In about two hours. The stew has been standing for four, so far. Don't be late. It has to be eaten at *jeeest* the right moment."

"Excellent. We'll be on time. And we'll take dinner in the formal dining room."

"Okay. But did you *forgit* about—"

"That'll be all, Azi." He dismissed her with a flip of his wrist.

The minute Azi left, Nia attacked him. "Massimo Andretti, we had an agreement. We aren't supposed to—"

"And we won't," he said quietly, watching her eyes darken to a tempestuous brown, the amber specks flashing in the background like the remnants of a Fourth of July fireworks explosion. They were even sexier when she was mad.

"We agreed not to do... it.... until... for a week."

"Do what?"

"Have sex," she whispered as if the walls had ears. "You promised we wouldn't share a bed for a week."

"Have sex, yes. Share a bed, no. *You* laid down the law, Nia. *You* said you wanted to know me better. Well, my little virgin, you *will* know me better. You will know me so well, you'll be able to pick me out of a lineup blindfolded by simply running your hands along my naked body."

A shock ran through Nia. The one place she couldn't fight him was in the bedroom, and he knew it. He'd tricked her again.

Her arm came up.

Massimo caught her wrists, eased her backwards, and pinned her against the door with his body. "Don't you ever raise your hands to me again," he warned smoothly. "Or I will retaliate in the same way I did in the car. Only next time, it won't stop with just a kiss. I'll take you all the way for a slow, long, hard, and intensely enjoyable ride. Do you understand me, Nia Sylk?"

She continued to glare at him, fighting her way out of his grasp.

Massimo pressed his body deeper into hers, rotating his hips slightly, giving her the full brunt of his arousal. He felt her weaken. He relaxed his hold. At about five feet, six inches, the top of her head barely made it to his chest, yet she dared defy him. No other woman had ever challenged him this way. They were too afraid he would cut them loose. He didn't know about breaking in horses, but Nia Sylk was one temerarious kitten he looked forward to taming.

"You will share my bed and lie between my silk sheets, Nia Sylk," he whispered against her cheek. "Every night, until I claim what you offered. Next time you make a bargain, be specific in your negotiations. As a businessman, I had to learn the hard way to never assume anything. It could make a *punda* out of you. That's 'donkey' in Swahili, in case you're wondering."

Massimo's jaws clenched. If he'd know the cost of assuming, Maurice Spencer, the former executor of his father's estate would not have had the opportunity to almost destroy Andretti Industries. His father had trusted Maurice and thought the company would be safe in his hands until Massimo reached the required age of thirty, but Luciano was obviously wrong again. In his attempt to control Massimo, the company he'd slaved at all his life had almost followed him into the grave.

Several years later, Massimo was still trying to clean up the mess Spencer had made. On that disturbing memory, Massimo extracted his body from Nia's. "Follow me," he said to her.

Still trembling—more from his touch than from anger, Nia followed him down the mirrored corridor. She need not fear his wrath, she realized with a despondent cry in her heart. He had other means of controlling her. Suddenly, tricking him out of his money didn't seem like the best route to take anymore. She was seriously concerned about what the lasting effects her association with him would have on her heart.

"Massimo?" she asked, as the corridor ended into a mostly white sitting room. "How do I know I can trust you not to break our agreement?"

He bypassed two flights of stairs and stopped at a glass-encased elevator. "You can trust me, Nia. I give you my word. We will not consummate our agreement for a week, unless you change your mind. A man's word is his honor. I am a man of honor. You trust me, don't you?"

As they entered the elevator, Nia's mind skittered back to the day, six years ago, when he'd uttered the same words to a room full of factory workers. She'd snuck into the building against her father's wishes and lurked in the back of the cafeteria behind the employees as Massimo promised that he would honor the contract his then recently-deceased father had made with hers.

Nia remembered thinking in her fluttering seventeen-year-old heart that he was the hottest guy she'd ever seen—even hotter than Ian Somerhalder—her idol up until the moment she saw Massimo Andretti. Like the first thing that pops into every infatuated teenage girl's head, she'd fantasized about marrying the Italian hunk and having his babies one day.

Such foolish, childish dreams!

She would so love to tell this forked-tongue jerk just what he could do with his honor, but instead she smiled easily at him. "Yes, I trust you, Massimo."

CHAPTER THREE

Massimo opened a door on the third floor and stood back for Nia to precede him into the room. Adrenaline coursed through his veins as Jabari leaped off the floor and charged toward them.

Nia screamed and jumped back against his chest.

He hastily pulled her behind him, grabbed a canister from a table near the door and raised it as he shouted to the animal. Jabari stopped his charge halfway across the room, dropped to the floor, and eyed Massimo through bright amber eyes.

Without turning his back on Jabari, Massimo motioned Nia back into the hallway. "Stay here and don't move a muscle." He closed the door with his heel.

He walked toward the animal, canister in one hand, ready to spray. He gestured toward a large cage with the other. He let out his breath when Jabari rose and walked into the cage that shut automatically behind him. "Sit, Jabari."

Jabari dropped to the floor, his front legs extended and his head upright.

Knowing the animal posed no further threat to Nia, Massimo

dropped the canister and rushed across the room, half expecting her to be gone. He opened the door and sighed in relief when he found her standing right where he'd left her, perhaps too frightened to move.

He pulled her inside and wrapped his arms about her. Her heart was racing a mile a minute. He pressed her face against his chest and ran his hands down her arms and back with sure steady strokes.

He had been so caught up with Nia's proposal, then preoccupied with the information he'd received in the hotel lobby that he'd completely forgotten about Jabari. *Damn it*. Azi had been trying to remind him that Jabari was here when he dismissed her so impatiently. His ego could have caused Nia harm. "I'm sorry he scared you," he whispered.

"What is it?" She curled her trembling body further into his, and tightened her arms about his waist.

Massimo's heart rocked against his chest. "A leopard. My pet leopard." He loved the way she leaned fully into his strength. She smelled lovely, like sun and snow and strawberries dipped in smooth chocolate whip. He wanted to lick her all over then gulp her down with a glass of champagne.

"Does he usually come after your women like that?"

Massimo placed his hand under her chin, lifting her face to his. Fear spiked in her earthy eyes. "Jabari has never met any of my... women."

"So why'd you bring me to him? So he could scare me into submission?"

"Oh no, pussycat. I would never deliberately put you into harm's way. I totally forgot about Jabari." He chuckled, but then his heart stumbled on a beat as he experienced that strange familiarity about her again. He'd seen her in his dreams, many times before, but she claimed they'd never met. He shook off the

eeriness. "My head has been spinning ever since I met you."
Literally.

"Most men who want a big animal as a best friend get a German shepherd or a Doberman. You got a leopard."

"I love pussy...cats."

She rolled her eyes and eased out of his embrace. "Wild exotic ones, obviously." She gestured to several pictures of big cats in a variety of vast landscapes on a wall.

You are wild and exotic, he thought, watching the play of emotions on her face as her eyes settled on a pair of leopards captured in the act of mating. He smiled when she swallowed and turned quickly away. The thought that she was probably burning up inside amused him. "Jabari isn't wild," he said. "I've raised him from a cub. He was a present from my *nono*, my grandfather."

She rolled her eyes at that too. Pretty eccentric, he agreed.

He remembered feeling lost and hopeless when the family had traveled to Kenya to scatter his mother's ashes. It was then that *Nono* had brought him the cute little orphan cub. *Nono* had told him he hoped they brought each other comfort. Massimo hadn't known it then, but years later when he'd returned to Kenya to scatter his father's ashes in the jungle, Jabari had turned out to be the most valuable gift he'd ever received.

Massimo pressed his palm against the right side of his torso. Even through his ski clothes and flannel shirt, he could feel the raised rounded scar of his wound from where the rhino's horn had gouged him. It had stopped aching over the years, and had simply become a numb reminder of the precariousness of life. If it weren't for Jabari's exceptional strength and ingenuity, he would have perished in that Kenyan jungle. Man and cat had bonded on a superior level that near-fatal day.

He usually made up stories at his lovers' enquiries about the cause of the scar. Would he tell Nia the truth when her curiosity got the better of her? He shook his head. What was he thinking? Nia would never see his scar since they would never be intimate, not in the light of day, anyway.

"Does he live here with you?" she asked, pulling his thoughts back to the present. "I know some states prohibit keeping exotic animals as pets. Is New Hampshire one of them?"

"No, and yes," he said answering her questions in chronological order.

"So I guess you're breaking the law in having him in your home."

He chuckled at her supercilious crack about his character. "I'm not breaking any laws, Nia. Only USDA licensed exhibitors are allowed to own wildcats in this state. But I have what is called a Category B license."

"What's that?"

"In order to qualify for that special permit, I had to procure two thousand hours of paid experience with a licensed exhibitor. I can house Jabari on the estate, but I cannot allow him to have any direct contact with the public."

"Is that why no one knows about him?"

"Basically. Only those I trust."

"I've heard about those two Australians who formed a lifetime bond with their lion, Christian," she said. "They bought him when he was just a cub, raised him, and then released him back into the wild in Kenya. Even after that, when they went back to Kenya to visit him, he remembered them. Until I watched that documentation, I never thought it possible for humans and wildcats to bond on such a mutually deep and trusting level."

"It is possible, Nia," he said softly, touched at her knowledge and understanding.

"Where does Jabari live?"

"Jabari spends most of his time on a reservation in Kenya. I travel there often to visit him. He's here for his biannual check-up."

"Is he okay?" she asked with surprising concern.

"Well, he's almost twenty-five years old."

"That's old for a cat."

He nodded on a deep sigh. Jabari had been in his life since he was ten years old, and the thought of him dying brought Massimo much anguish. "Yes, but he's in perfect health, although not as strong as he used to be. His roar is much more dangerous than his bite these days."

"Glad to hear that."

He chuckled. "I usually fly Howard, his vet, to Kenya, but Howard's suffering from an ear infection and can't fly, so I brought Jabari to him." He'd also wanted to spend some time with his old friend before Dafne arrived, and before they settled down into marital nightmare, but he couldn't share that information with Nia. "He's heading back to Kenya tomorrow," Massimo said, just then deciding to cut Jabari's stay by one day. He did not have the luxury to assimilate Nia into Jabari's life at the moment. Time was of the essence since he knew she would try to run away in two days. On the other hand, Jabari was a jealous cat that needed constant affection that Mass could not offer with Nia around. A brief introduction would have to work for now. "Come meet him." He led her over to the cage. He knelt on the floor and slapped his palms against his thighs. "Jabari, come here."

Jabari stared at him through vigilant bright-yellow eyes before shifting his gaze to Nia.

Nia's hand gripped his shoulder when Jabari let out a high-pitched snarl followed by a low purring hiss. Massimo recognized the sound as one of abidance and friendship. "It's okay." He patted Nia's death-grip on his shoulder. He smiled when Jabari rose from the floor of the cage and walked towards them in as graceful a stride as his short legs would allow. His strong muscles rippled under his tawny coat, covered with dark circular rosettes.

Nia held her breath as the cat came closer. Even though he was now cased behind a sturdy enclosure, and Massimo had said he was potentially harmless, she was still afraid of him. But she took comfort in the knowledge that Massimo was here to protect her. But then again, if his pet leopard had gobbled her up, he would've been denied the pleasure of devouring her himself at the end of the week, wouldn't he?

She tried not to dwell on how safe she'd felt in his arms moments ago. If he could shield her from a big cat, he sure had the means to shield her from a loan shark like Eddie. The way he'd held her moments ago was different from the way he'd held her in the car. That was passion. This was protection.

She couldn't tell which she liked more, but it was amazing to have a pair of strong male arms about her. She hadn't had that since her father's death. Lately when she was having a gloomy day, Aaron tried to cheer her up, but he was just a boy. She needed the kind of security a full-grown man could offer.

Nia glanced down at the cat purring contentedly as Massimo reached a finger between the wires and stroked behind his black-tipped ears. He was almost six feet long from his orange colored nose with a black streak running the length of it, to his exceptionally long spotted tail. She'd guess he weighed close to two hundred pounds. He could have mauled her quite terribly, she thought, taking a brooding glance at Jabari's broad head, powerful jaws, and strong teeth. Again, she was thankful for Massimo's quick move to get between her and his cat.

"Squat down beside me and give me your hand," Massimo said. "Don't worry. He can't harm you from inside the cage."

Nia's first instinct was to refuse, but remembering why she'd followed Massimo home, she reckoned it would play in her favor to make friends with his cat. It might even cause him to doubt his own suspicions about her. She squatted down beside him and placed her hand in his.

She held her breath as Massimo placed their entwined fingers against the wire and lined them up to Jabari's nose. His breath was warm and moist on her fingertips and it caused a tingle along her spine. As she stared into his amber eyes, Nia felt as if she was staring at an old friend. "You're a beautiful cat, Jabari Andretti. And it's my pleasure to meet you."

Jabari dropped his head on his paws and made a deep low growl in his throat. The sound was thrilling, almost erotic, and it generated a feeling of danger and uncertainty in Nia—the same danger and uncertainty she'd felt when Massimo had kissed her. It was as if he and his cat's sexuality were morphed into one.

"He likes you," Massimo said, smiling at her.

"He's quite the charmer. Much like his owner," she replied, withdrawing her hand from his. In an effort to avoid his intensely disturbing eyes, Nia glanced around the room. Skylights ran the length of the cathedral ceiling, allowing in patches of the fading afternoon light. The furnishings were comprised of posh dark brown leather sofas and chairs, marble tables, and Italian and Persian floor rugs. A fully equipped kitchenette and a small dining table on the far side of the room, overlooking the mountains completed the suite—a real bachelor's pad that represented Massimo's male dominance and power.

Involuntarily, her eyes were drawn to the mating leopards on the wall. The female was on her stomach with the powerful front paws of the male holding her captive against a bed of long grass. His sharp teeth were sunk into the back of her neck. Nia's eyes grew wide when she noticed the dark streak that ran the length of the male's nose.

She took a quick glance back at Jabari. The resemblance was

undeniable. She glanced at Massimo and she felt the heat rising under her skin at the apparent amusement on his face.

"Yes, it is Jabari," he said without hesitation. "I've been capturing all aspects of his life since he was a cub. Mating just happens to be one of them. It's a basic animalistic act that we humans enjoy immensely. You'll agree soon enough, *cara*."

Perhaps, but not with you, she thought, even as she wondered if Massimo was in the habit of capturing himself in the act as well. Did he take pictures and make videos for his private collection? What would it be like to watch the two of them making love—the erotic sight of their bodies thrusting against each other, the sounds of their passionate moans echoing around the room? The thought caused a powerful ache between Nia's legs, and she swallowed the low moan that threatened to erupt from her throat.

Massimo chuckled as he took in the look of embarrassment and desire on Nia's face. She was the most sensual woman he'd ever met. Everything she did turned him on. He doubted she knew the effect she had on men. It was hard to believe she was still a virgin.

Massimo knew without a doubt that if he hadn't promised Dafne not to take another lover before their wedding, at this very moment, Nia Sylk would be lying naked in his bed with her silken brown legs wrapped securely around his waist, their bodies moving in exquisite harmony as he rode her to the pinnacles of pleasure again and again. He knew too, that she was the kind of woman a man would find hard to leave, to purge from his system. He'd better not let her get too deeply embedded under his skin since he had other pressing obligations to fulfill.

He swore his heart laughed at his folly in thinking he would still go through with his plan to marry Dafne after the explosive desire that had seized him when he'd kissed Nia.

She was addictive. He reached out and trailed a finger along her cheek. Her skin was so soft and smooth. *"Como sei graziosa bella e molto dolce." Very beautiful and sweet.* Indeed.

Nia had no idea what Massimo had said, but the magic in his touch and the husky tremor in his voice told her it was something passionate. Feeling the power in his fingertips tugging on her insides, she pulled away and stood up.

Massimo Andretti took great pride in his ability to seduce women. His kind would say and do anything to encourage a woman to take off her clothes. He'd told her that he enjoyed the chase. And from his multiple short-lived relationships, it seemed as if that's all he enjoyed.

She stepped back as Massimo stood up and spoke to Jabari. The cat leaped up, stretched like a lazy feline, and strolled to the back of the cage where he disappeared into a gargantuan kitty door.

"Is that Italian you were speaking to him?" Nia asked.

"Yes. He also understands English and Swahili."

"Where did you learn to speak Swahili?"

"In a Masai village in Kenya."

"Oh yeah, you did say you visit Kenya often to see Jabari, but what's an Italian-American boy doing at a Masai village?"

Laughing, he raked his fingers through his hair. "You're a curious little kitten, aren't you? I promise to tell you all about Kenya one day. And I'll teach you Italian and Swahili, or any of the other three languages I speak, if you so desire."

Teach her foreign languages? Was he hoping she'd stick around that long? "That might prove to be a most difficult feat. I have enough trouble with English as it is."

"There is a language that requires no words although the mouth and tongue are fully engaged. I'm most anxious to teach you that language, Nia."

Massimo's husky voice hummed with titillating promises causing Nia's heart to race so fast, her temples throbbed from the pulsation. Her mouth filled up with saliva as she glanced at an unopened door that led to the inner quarters of the master suit—the place where she would sleep next to Massimo for two long torturous nights until she made her escape.

She hoped she made it out unscathed.

Massimo savored his last spoonful of lobster bisque as he watched Nia finish off her second helping. He understood the enthusiasm with which she'd approached her dinner—rich, creamy, and loaded with calories as it was. Azi's culinary skills were some of the best in the world. Ever since he was a little boy, he was always happy to come home to Azi's kitchen. There really was no cooking like home cooking.

Yet Massimo felt Nia would have displayed the same amount of zeal if she'd been served a less appetizing dish. It was a welcome change to watch a woman enjoy her food without giving a thought to the width of her waistline or her thighs.

He, on the other hand, was giving them a lot of thought. So much thought that while Nia was dressing for dinner, he'd put a call through to his friend, Paul Dawson, an FBI special agent in New York, and asked him to run a check on her.

He'd called Dafne to let her know that her move to the States was on hold. He'd simply told her that something had come up. *Boy, had something come up,* he thought as his growing erection pulsed against his thigh. Dafne's nonchalant response had reminded him that it might be three long years before he would enjoy the silky feel of a woman's skin beneath his palm again.

That possibility didn't sit well with Massimo. Not at all, he thought as Nia finally put her spoon down and gave him a smile that deepened his ache for her. She was so damned beautiful. He wondered if her appetite for sex would match the one she had for food. "You have a very healthy appetite," he remarked over the rim of his wine glass.

Nia eyed Massimo through lowered lashes. The light of desire that illuminated his mellow blue eyes told her that he wasn't just talking about her appetite for food. She'd felt him watching her as she finished off her second bowl of lobster bisque. She'd been tempted to stop halfway through it for etiquette's sake, but God the bisque was the most delicious dish she'd ever tasted. And seeing that she wouldn't be around to enjoy this kind of cooking for long, she'd taken her time enjoying it. She couldn't care less if Massimo thought she was a pig.

"Do you always attack your food that way?" he asked, smiling as he twirled the long stem of his wine glass between his equally long fingers.

"They don't serve food like this where I come from." *Nor where I'm going* Nia thought of the island of Dulcina where Aaron was hiding out. It wouldn't be a bad place to settle down once her business with Eddie and Massimo was behind her.

Her friend, Josie, a native of the island, had always tried to get her to visit, but the funds were never available for her to take a vacation. Josie had recently married her childhood sweetheart and moved back to Dulcina. Another friend, Amber, had found love on the island and moved there also.

Even Aaron seemed to have settled in and was enjoying himself in Paradise. During their Skype session last night, he'd talked about Josie's father as if the man was some kind of super hero. It seemed that what Aaron needed all along was some bonding and masculine guidance—the one thing Nia could never give him.

Aaron had a bright future ahead of him, but he had to be alive and well in order to enjoy it. Massimo's million would secure both his safety and his future. Massimo owed them. If he'd held up his end of the bargain between Andretti Industries and West Gate Mills, her father wouldn't have had to borrow money from Eddie. If he hadn't lost the mill, her father would be alive today, and neither Aaron's nor her safety would be an issue.

"Brooklyn?"

"What?" Nia said as Massimo's voice broke into her thoughts.

"They don't serve food like this in Brooklyn you were saying?"

"Right." She held out her glass for another refill of the wine Massimo had fished out of his underground wine cellar.

He picked up the bottle and filled up her glass. "You should go easy. This wine is very effective. It's been maturing for years."

"I can hold my liquor." Ignoring his warning, Nia took a long swallow from her glass, welcoming the cool feel of the white fruity liquid splashing against her throat. Nia had no idea how many glasses she'd consumed. She'd stopped counting at three.

"So what do you do there?"

"What do you mean?" she asked licking her lips slowly.

His eyes narrowed and he grunted softly. "I assume you have a job, a career of some sort?"

"I teach math at a private school. I'm on winter break, just in case you're wondering why I wasn't in the classroom today," she added.

"I suppose you've thought about resigning."

"Why would I resign?" She planted her elbows on the table and, resting her chin in her hands, smiled sweetly at him.

"Well, you can't very well be teaching in Brooklyn while you're acting the role of my lover here in Granite Falls. Do the math."

"I don't plan on resigning, just taking a leave of absence." An involuntary giggle spilled from her lips. "With your track record, I'll probably be back at work in a week, anyway."

His hearty laughter bounced off the walls of the dining

room. "Well, I just assumed you'd resign seeing you'll be a brand new multimillionaire once we consummate our agreement. I guess I'm a *punda* in that regard."

Nia blinked several times and shifted uneasily on the chair. The wine was working its evil on her senses, affecting her ability to harness her tongue. If she weren't careful, Massimo's cleverly crafted questions would cause her to say something that would give her away.

She glanced at her half-empty glass on the table, then pushed it away, out of reach. "I love teaching," she said, placing her hands on her lap. "I don't see why I should give it up just because I'll have money. I plan to save my millions for retirement."

"Hmm. That's a very good plan. Be sure to invest it wisely."

"I will." She picked up her water glass and took a big long gulp from it.

He sat back and folded his arms across his chest, his face breaking into a sinister grin. Or perhaps she should say a profusion of sinister grins, since he seemed to be leering at her in multiple layers. Nia felt the sides of her mouth tremble as an unwarranted smile parted her lips.

Oh yeah, she was drunk. She raised a hand to her mouth to stifle a laugh.

"The thought of you as a schoolteacher turns me on," he remarked, watching her closely.

"Just about anything in a dress turns you on, Massimo. Even a slippery snake slithering along in a grass skirt would get a rise out of you." She giggled at the image of Massimo stealing stealthily behind a snake through a field of tall grass. What would he do with it once he caught it?

He joined her humor, chuckling heartily. "*You* turn me on, Nia Sylk. Everything you do, everything you say. The sound of your sexy voice, the sparkle in your beautiful brown eyes, the way you flip your wrists to tuck your hair behind your delicate ears.

The way your slender fingers caress the stem of your wine glass, the way you walk, twisting your hips and sweet little backside just so." He made a smooth undulating motion with his hands.

"And your breasts..." He shaped his palms to the size of two medium-size melons. "*Mama, che belle tettone.* Voluptuous, firm, and full, the way I like them on a woman. They fit perfectly in my hands, and I can't wait to suck them into my mouth. *Bellisima!*" he exclaimed, placing his fingers to his lips and making a loud smacking sound with his mouth. He finished with that deft snap of his wrist Italians were famous for.

Nia crossed her arms in an effort to stop the throbbing of her swelling breasts and the hardening of her nipples against her lacy bra. "You have a two-track mind, Massimo Andretti. All you think about is sex and money."

"Most women appreciate my mind, and soon you will too since our relationship is built on sex and money. Sex for money to be exact. Lots of sex for lots of money," he added with a low throaty laugh.

Massimo's dirty talk was causing all kinds of havoc to Nia's system. She felt flushed and lightheaded and, unwittingly, she thought of the photo of Jabari in the act of mating. She felt like a female jungle cat that had been cornered by a persistent male. Like the cat, she had two options—run or mate. Since she couldn't do either, Nia reached for her wine glass and finished the contents in one swallow.

She hated Massimo's ability to arouse these unwanted and frustrating desires in her. And judging from the smile on his lips, she knew that he knew the effect the wine was having on her. Massimo wasn't the kind of man to pass up an opportunity, but she hoped he had enough scruples to resist the temptation to force himself on an intoxicated woman.

She hoped.

From his vast experience with the opposite sex, Massimo knew Nia was at the moment struggling to control the need to mate. How he was going to hold up his end of the bargain and not make love to her was a puzzle to him. Just the thought of having her in his bed and knowing he couldn't take her was already driving him insane.

If he had any sense, he'd have Azi prepare one of the guest rooms and warn Nia to lock herself inside it. But he'd already laid down the law—they were sharing a bed—and so it would be. Andrettis didn't renege on their promises or their threats for that matter—not even when their lives depended on it.

As he watched Nia struggle with her feelings, Massimo knew it was time to bring the night to an end. The sooner they were both asleep, the safer she'd be from him. He'd already asked Azi to leave a pot of her magical tea in his suite. He didn't trust himself with Nia, and he had no intentions of diving head first into something he knew nothing about.

Until he heard back from Paul, he would have to find other ways to resist her. He knew Azi's tea would work its magic in a matter of minutes. It was the same tea the Masai tribe had kept pouring down his throat when he'd had his unfortunate run-in with the rhino all those years ago. That tea, in a much more powerful dose than Azi's, had kept him from going insane from the unbearable pain. It was the most effective natural sedative he knew. That tea may have also been responsible for the hallucinations he'd experienced about a pair of sparkling brown eyes that had kept his mind focused and off the excruciating pain.

He had to stop dwelling on the past when his present and his future were so unstable. "Would you like anything else, Nia?" he asked finishing the one glass of wine he'd been nursing all evening.

"Like what?"

"Tea. Dessert. Azi makes a mean devil's food cake. It's my favorite indulgence."

"I'm full," she said patting her stomach. "But you are free to have some."

From the look she tossed him, Massimo was sure that in her mind, she'd tacked on *Devil* to the end of the sentence. "*Andiamo a letto, poi.* Let's go to bed," he translated for her benefit.

The trepidation in her eyes told Massimo that this was the moment Nia had been dreading since he told her they would be sharing a bed—sex or no sex. She'd been gulping down the eighty-thousand-dollar bottle of *Romanee Conti* all night in an effort to self-intoxicate and deter his advances.

He was never one to miss an opportunity where a slightly drunk but experienced woman was concerned, but he would never seduce an innocent inebriated girl—no matter how alluring she was. He could have told Nia that her drinking binge was unnecessary, but he'd gotten great pleasure from watching her simmer in her own sauce. He saw no harm in having a little fun with her before his impending nuptials next week. It might be the last time in three years he would have fun with a woman.

He rose and walked around the table to stand behind her chair. When his fingers brushed against the warm silkiness of her arm, she shuddered and gazed up at him. Her eyes were bewitching as they glimmered in the light from the fireplace and the wrought iron chandelier above the table. They haunted him. *Where had he seen them?*

"Vieni, *cara*," he said, helping her to her feet. He would worry about her eyes tomorrow.

She wobbled a little as she stood up and Massimo immediately circled her waist to lend her support. Once she was steady, he followed her out into the corridor, staying close should she stumble, but far enough to admire the gentle curves of her hips and buttocks moving beneath her black knee-length dress.

He was now the proud owner of two gorgeous cats, he thought as he watched the glossy mane of straight black hair bounce against her back as she walked. Just as Jabari possessed the grace and charm of ultimate feline beauty, Nia displayed all the charisma of the quintessential female.

As he imagined Nia purring in pleasure beneath him, Massimo thought of calling Dafne again, this time to tell her that their arrangement was off. Ever since he met Nia, he'd been having trouble making a decision and sticking to it.

He would possess her. He would possess her not.

He'd never been this indecisive about anything in his entire life. He was known for making articulate and prudent decisions then following through until they passed or failed muster just like his ancestors before him. It was the stick-to-itiveness upon which Andretti Industries prospered. Nia Sylk was slowly stripping him of that power.

"Massimo?" Nia turned and gazed up at him.

"Yes, pussycat?" His heart pounded against his chest when she licked her lips with her little pink tongue.

She stood on her tiptoes and draped her arms around his neck. "Would... would it be... wrong if I... I asked you to... to kiss me?"

"No, pussycat. It wouldn't be wrong at all." He tucked strands of hair behind her ears.

She was so damned desirable.

He was so damned hard.

"I... I know I... asked you to wait... before we... you know——"

"*Piccola, mia.*" Massimo growled as his arms circled her. He'd promised to break his promise, only if she asked. Was she asking?

He should be flogged for the lewd images flowing through his head. The fact that she was drunk didn't seem like much of a deterrent now against such pungent temptation. He was going to hell. God help him, he was already there. He eased her onto the elevator and drew her close, pressing her sweet, soft body into his. She felt absolutely divine, and smelled just as...

He bent his head and covered her tender waiting mouth with his, kissing her deeply and rapaciously. When they stepped off the elevator, Massimo led Nia down the hall toward his bedroom like a butcher leading an unsuspecting lamb to the slaughter.

CHAPTER FOUR

*T*he kiss was deep. Deep and thrilling. His hot tongue wrapped around hers, probing, thrusting, sucking a response out of her. His hands were everywhere on her body. On her breasts, molding and kneading until her nipples became so hard they were painful to the touch. She shuddered as his fingers trailed slowly down her belly to the junction of her thighs, nestling against the entrance to her moistened sex. He whispered something in a foreign tongue, and she opened for him. His voice was hypnotic. She felt warm and full and achy...

"Nia..."

He leaned over her, fully clothed while she lay naked and vulnerable on the bed. He smiled then lowered his head to suck a nipple into his mouth. She whimpered...

'Nia. Wake up, sleepyhead."

"No. Go away."

Her body was alive, pumping with urgency. She reached for him, wanting him...

"If you don't wake up, pussycat, I will get back into bed with you. And we will spend the entire day making passionate love."

Nia's eyes flew open. She gasped when she saw Massimo sitting on the side of the bed, a wicked grin on his face. She jumped up as reality struck her. Then she hurriedly dived back into the mattress when she realized she was naked. She grabbed for the silk sheet, pulling it all the way up to her chin. When and how did she get naked?

"Sweet dreams?" Massimo's eyes drank in the erotic picture she presented. A full pouting mouth and long dark lashes fanning enormous aphrodisiac eyes. He had been watching her seductive little movements on the mattress, fighting the temptation to crawl back into bed and finish where they left off last night.

"My dreams are off limits to you."

"Were you dreaming about me, about us, pussycat?"

"Don't you wish." She cut her eyes at him. "And stop calling me pussycat."

He leaned closer and planted his palms on either side of her body. "But you do purr like one. And after last night—"

"Last night?"

Massimo cast his mouth downward in a feigned wave of disappointment. "Don't you remember?"

She shook her head and clutched the sheet tighter to her throat.

"Let me see." Noticing her death grip on the sheet, Massimo altruistically reached out and brushed away the strands of hair that had fallen across her face. "Immediately following dinner, you asked me to kiss you."

Her forehead creased in confusion. "I did?"

"*Si*. You begged me, actually."

She gulped. "And... and... wha... what happened... next?"

"What happened next? Well, you threw your arms around me and refused to let me go. You were all over me and I couldn't get you off, even after I repeatedly reminded you about the 'no sex for a week' clause in our agreement. You said it was a stupid clause. You couldn't imagine my delight at hearing those words. So I picked you up and brought you to bed. I even had to undress you. It was a struggle, but well worth the effort after we—"

"We didn't! Did we?" Nia's mind reeled as she fought through the foggy images. She remembered dinner, the tasty lobster bisque, and all that fine wine. She remembered getting on the elevator, but everything else was a blur. Everything except the vivid images of Massimo's hard naked body lying next to hers, holding her, kissing her, molding her to him. But that was a dream. *It had to be a dream!*

"Oh, Nia, you really know how to emasculate a man. Here I was, thinking I'd been so thorough in my lovemaking, that I'd satisfied you beyond your wildest imaginations, only to hear that you don't even remember making love with me at all."

Nia's fists curled around the silky fabric of the sheet. *They had done it.* And she couldn't even remember. She closed her eyes as sobs of defeat and contempt threatened to spill from deep inside her. *Damn him!* She should have known she couldn't trust him.

She opened her eyes and glared at him. "You bastard! You took advantage of an innocent, drunk girl. I should have known you couldn't keep your word. You lied, just like you—" She stopped and turned away at the near slip.

What did it matter, anyway? He'd ruined everything. Her entire plan had blown up in her face. When he gave her that money on Saturday, she would really become a generously paid whore. She would have sold her virginity for two million dollars once she accepted that money. It wasn't like she had the privilege of walking away without it to save her dignity. She had to accept it to save Aaron's life.

She turned and glared at him. "You miserable, filthy son-of—"

"Tsh, tsh. Such fury, pussycat. And such vulgarity from the mouth of a schoolteacher. I hope you never use such language in the presence of your young impressionable students. Although," he continued, raising a hand to stop her from speaking, "if I had a teacher who looked like you, I wouldn't give a damn what kind of words came out of her mouth. You'd be my favorite and I'd be so delighted to be your pet. I'd bring you apples everyday, and strawberries and oranges, too, if you wanted them."

Nia saw the devilish twinkle in the depths of Massimo's eyes and his mouth quivering with humor. *Jerk.* He was toying with her. "I've never spoken this way before. You seem to bring out the worst in me." *Six years worth of bottled-up frustrations to be exact.* "Maybe I talk to you that way because it's the only type of language you seem to understand." She reached for a pillow to knock the ridiculous smirk off his face.

Massimo was on her in a heartbeat. He captured her hands and pinned them to the mattress above her head. The silk sheet slid off her shoulders, exposing one brown-ripe breast and one darker-shaded smooth wide nipple. The sight of that voluptuous lonely breast tempted him beyond reason and caused a hot ache to grow in his throat. He remembered the smooth taste in his mouth.

He held his breath as his eyes raked down her petite frame. The only thing standing in his way was the silky barrier of that sheet. He knew what her skin felt like under his palms. *Boy, did he know.* It was silk of the Sylk. He had shaped and molded her body to his last night. He had kissed her and caressed her until Azi's tea had rendered him unconscious.

What Massimo didn't know until now was what Nia looked like. For obvious reasons, he'd undressed her in the dark then left the bed before the light of dawn, just so he wouldn't have to fight with his conscience and his desire for her. The added pleasure of seeing her naked would have pushed him right over the edge, as it was doing now. He focused his gaze on her face.

Fury rioted through her

Lust surged through him.

"Don't you fret your pretty little head, Nia. When we do *it*, there will be no doubts in your mind. I will leave my mark on you, with you, and most assuredly inside you. You wouldn't have to wonder whether or not we mated, pussycat. You *will* know. I promised not to make love to you for a week and I'm sticking to it. Hard as it is. Pun intended." With reluctance, he released her and pulled the cover up over her chest.

Nia let out an audible sigh of relief, grateful that her game was still on.

"Are you hungry?" he asked, shooting to his feet.

What a stupid question. Despite the fact that she wanted to punch him when she thought he'd taken advantage of her, she still had a burning hunger for him. To her dismay, a tiny part of her dared to develop a speck of respect for him. All things considered, he could have taken her last night and there was not a damn thing she could have done about it, drunk as she was.

She didn't know whether to resent or commend him for keeping his word.

"Azi has already started breakfast." Massimo's voice pulled her back to the subject of food. "I don't know what you like, so I instructed her to prepare an assortment of dishes." "You didn't have to do that. I'm not a fussy eater."

"I noticed that last night. I like it. Too many women starve themselves thinking that men like skin and bones." There was a spark of some indefinable emotion in his eyes. "I appreciate a toned, healthy-looking woman. Like you, *cara*."

Nia could only imagine how enticing she looked lying naked in his bed while he was fully clothed in a crisp white button-down shirt and a pair of dark suit slacks. A swath of wavy black hair rested casually on his forehead. Even fully dressed, he exhibited an aura of sexuality unmatched by any other man she'd ever met. She could so easily fall...

Thoughts of Aaron reminded Nia of the reason she was in

Massimo's bed and she pushed the silly fantasies away. Some of her anger evaporated, leaving embarrassment at her tirade, and confusion at the fact that she wanted to hurt Massimo and make him want her at the same time. "I'm sorry for my outburst when I thought you—"

"No apologies necessary. I know how it feels to be betrayed. When someone you trust breaks a promise, it brings out the worst in you. I despise liars."

Nia frowned. Was this the same man who had lied to her father, broken a promise that had caused his death? The world was full of people who condemned others for the very same flaws they themselves possessed. She supposed Massimo was one of those self-righteous hypocrites.

"We have a lot to accomplish today." Massimo strolled around to the other side of the bed and picked up a remote control from his nightstand. He pressed a button and the red and ivory satin drapes slithered soundlessly apart.

Nia blinked as the bright sunlight hit her face. Still clutching the sheet to her body, she sat up and leaned her back against the cushioned headboard. She glanced at the clock on the nightstand. It was only eight-thirty. "It's still early."

A ray of sunlight caught his eyes as he stared at her. "I'm surprised you think so. Aren't you usually in school around this time?"

"Yeah, but I'm on vacation, remember?"

Massimo set the remote back on the nightstand and picked up his Rolex. "Unlike you, *cara*, I'm not on vacation. I don't have the luxury of lying around in bed all day. I have a billion-dollar company to run. People all over the world depend on me for their livelihood."

Did he grow a conscience with age? Her father had depended on him, and had been deadly disappointed. Too bad Massimo hadn't developed his sense of obligation six years ago.

If he had, she wouldn't be lying naked in his bed right now. "You have a company to run, but I don't see why I have to get up so early." She had her own errands today, none of which she could do with him breathing down her neck.

"Well, there's the matter of your new wardrobe, transportation, and two million dollars that needs to be turned into cash within two days. Oh yes, and a credit card. I can't have you interrupting a board meeting to ask if you can have a few dollars to buy some tampons and a soda."

"I don't drink soda."

"Well, you'll need tampons at some point."

But I'll be gone by then, Nia thought as she watched him slip the watch onto his wrist. The only thing she wanted from Massimo was her two million dollars. But until she saw that cash—better still until she held those crisp hundred-dollar bills in the palms of her hands, she had to continue playing the game she'd made up and whose rules he was trying to change.

"You have a two-thirty appointment at the country club today," he said imperiously as if he were giving orders to one of his employees whom he expected to obey without question.

"For what?"

"Your nails, hair, a facial, and a full body massage."

Nia glanced at her nails then rushed the fingers of one hand through her tousled hair. "I'm good."

"Not good enough for the event tonight."

Her eyes widened. "Event? What event?"

His smile was guarded. "I'm sure you've heard about the charity event that's taking place at the Fontaine Conference Center tonight."

Nia nodded. "I'd have to be deaf and blind not to know about it." The event—a dinner that cost two thousand dollars a plate, and a silent auction of high-ticketed prizes like weekend getaways, seven-day cruises, expensive cars, and a collection of watercolor landscapes from a newly discovered local artist—was being sponsored by the Children of the Future Foundation. It was reported that a number of Hollywood celebrities who had vacation homes in the region were expected to attend.

"What about it?" Nia asked.

He smiled easily. "You'll be going as my date. I want you glowing."

"But... I..."

His head tilted to one side. "Are you ashamed of being seen with me in public, Nia?"

Nia averted her gaze and stared out the wall of glass at the white hills in the distance. As much as she would love this once-in-a-lifetime opportunity to attend such a splendid affair, it'd be a mistake, especially since she knew that swarms of reporters and their cameras buzzed about Massimo like bees on a petal. An event like this would attract even more paparazzi.

She could just imagine tomorrow's headlines in the local newspapers and the article in the next issue of *Granite Falls People News*: *The Italian Playboy Wins Again. Who's The Mystery Woman On Andretti's Arm? Massimo Andretti's Latest Conquest: How Long Will She Last?*

If her face were made public, it would be virtually impossible for her to hide from him, even on a remote little island like Dulcina. He had the resources to track her down to the ends of the earth, and knowing him, she knew he would put a BOLO out on her.

But even more frightening was the possibility of Eddie seeing a picture of them together. Eddie was a shark, and if he discovered she was associated with Massimo Andretti—one of the richest men in the world, one million dollars would suddenly become insufficient for him. He would try to blackmail her for the rest of her life.

Nia was feeling the heat of her deceit already. She might not be able to make her way out of this one, she realized with a shudder. Why hadn't she thought of this possibility when she set out to con Massimo? She really hadn't thought this plan through very well, had she?

"Are you ashamed the world will know you're my latest conquest, Nia?"

Think of Aaron, she told herself. *You can do it for him.* "No, Massimo, I'm not ashamed. It just took me by surprise that you'd want to make our relationship public so soon." Panic choked her, but she managed to hold herself together. "I mean, what are you going to tell people when they ask how we met? That I offered you my virginity for two mi…" She cleared her throat at another near miss. "For four million dollars?"

He chuckled, his blue eyes taking on a glossy hue. "You should know by now that I never tell people anything, Nia. I let them draw their own conclusions."

Thinking back on all she'd heard about him over the years, Nia had to agree. He was the most private public figure she knew. Nobody knew about Jabari. Nobody knew where he'd disappeared to six years ago when he ordered the then CEO of Andretti Industries to sell her father's mill.

He hadn't even defended himself against Gabrielle's accusations of infidelity. He never discussed his personal relationships. It was the women who did all the talking. *They* fueled the gossip frenzy. "Well, I appreciate your discretion," she said, "because I wouldn't want people thinking that I'm a…"

"Whore?" he finished when she trailed off. "Ah, pussycat, you made yourself a whore when you offered to sell me your virginity. If you want to change your mind, we can forget about the money and just become lovers. We can start right now," he said gazing down at her with sexy cobalt eyes. "You can live here for the duration of the relationship and once it's over we'll part ways— mutually satisfied, I hope. Since I'm in the habit of taking care of my ex-lovers, you know you'll have a substantial parting gift. Theoretically, you wouldn't be a whore, just another woman I've had the pleasure of enjoying."

Lust filled his eyes as he dropped down on the bed. "What'd you say, pussycat, shall we mate?" he asked, leaning so close to her, she felt his hot breath on her face.

Nia tried to deny the pulsing ache between her thighs and the moisture seeping from her body onto the mattress. She took deep gulping breaths and willed herself not to throw off the silk cover, lay back, spread her legs, and let Massimo have her. She knew his words were cleverly crafted to make her want to do just that. Would he follow through if she fell victim to his wicked charm? Her gaze skidded from his eyes to his sexy lips. "I'll think about it," she said on an equally cleverly crafted smile.

"Ah, pussycat, it's so nice when we agree, isn't it?" He placed a quick kiss on her forehead and pushed to his feet. "Don't loiter in bed. There's much to be done today."

He descended the steps and walked across the floor. "Oh, I almost forgot," he said, turning at the door. "You'll also be accompanying me to a very important business meeting tomorrow night."

Nia pursed her lips. "Why do I need to attend a business meeting with you? I don't know anything about your business."

"You don't need to know anything about my business. You just need to be by my side."

"Well, suppose I don't want to go."

His mouth parted on a wide smile. "It's not a request, *cara*. You will be there by my side. We're involved now, which means when I attend a function that requires a date, you will dangle from my arm, dressed to kill with a big smile on your beautiful face. So make sure you select outfits that are appropriate for each occasions. I'll say hot and sultry for tonight and elegant for tomorrow. Joanne's Boutique on Main Street is the place to shop.

I'll let them know you'll be coming." He closed the door behind him.

Nia picked up a pillow and tossed it at the closed door. She punched another pillow and screamed in frustration. Damn him! He was playing her, just as assuredly as she was playing him. There was no pretending anymore. The game was officially on. Perhaps it was on since last night, she thought with dismay as the events of the night became clear as day. He'd warned her at dinner not to drink too much of that fine wine he kept pouring into her glass each time she held it out for a refill. And her pert response was, "I can hold my liquor."

Feeling like a complete idiot, Nia covered her face with her hands as memories of Massimo caressing and kissing her body made her blush. She even remembered begging him to make love to her. What had stopped him from fulfilling her request? It couldn't be honor since she already knew he had none.

Nia flung back the covers and hopped out of bed. Descending the three steps, she walked across the fluffy white carpet, then down a marble corridor that led to a huge shower stall.

Massimo was mapping out her day, making plans for her as if he owned her. She was not used to people telling her how to run her life. She'd been taking care of herself since she was seventeen. She made her own decisions. She decided when she went to bed and when she got up in the morning. She booked her own hair and nail appointments—every once in a long while.

Massimo Andretti did not own her. And he would be very aware of that quite soon.

As she stood under the warm shower sprays, Nia thought about Massimo's important business meeting tomorrow night. If he honored their agreement, she would have her two million dollars by then. Escaping from this fortress would have been easy while he was preoccupied elsewhere with Andretti business. But no, he had to order her presence at the meeting. She was sure it was a calculated move to keep an eye on her.

Nia smiled as she lathered the shampoo into her hair. Massimo thought he had her cornered, that he'd captured her knight and her bishop in this human game of chess they were playing. But she still had a few pawns left, and they were working overtime to protect their queen.

At some point during the meeting, he'd have to leave her side to mingle with his colleagues, and if that didn't work, she would excuse herself to go to the bathroom and just never return. She didn't think he would follow her to the ladies' room, but just in case he was blatant enough to do it, she would feign illness and leave for home early. If the meeting was as important as he said it was, he would have to stay behind, giving her the perfect opportunity to vanish quietly into the night with his money.

She'd have to keep a low profile until the dust settled. She might have to cut and dye her hair since her face would be made public tonight. She'd done it six years ago when she ran away from Maine. Being on the run was nothing new to Nia. She'd perfected the art of staying hidden with new names and new identities for her and Aaron.

The time had come to change again. Both she and her brother were past eighteen so she wasn't concerned about Maine Child Welfare Services coming after them. What could they do, now? Put them back into foster care? The thought pulled a snicker out of her.

Although she'd set her plan in motion in New York by obtaining a passport, credit cards, and opening a bank account in the name her parents had given her, there was still a lot to be done. Foremost was resigning from Ellswood Charter School. She couldn't just leave them high and dry since she'd need a strong reference for a new teaching position—a position she'd thought she had a month to find.

Then there was the matter of booking a Saturday morning flight from Manchester to New York then one from New York to Miami. Then finally a cruise from Miami to the Bahamas if she could find one at this short notice. Zigzagging her way to Dulcina using a new name was a sure way to keep Massimo from tracking her down.

He would be looking for Nia Sylk, but she would have disappeared without a crumb trail.

Nia chuckled as she imagined Saturday's headlines: "*Two Gone in Three Weeks: Is Massimo Andretti Losing His Touch With The Ladies?*"

That should bring him down a peg or two. The joke was surely on Massimo. He was about to become the biggest *punda* on the planet.

&

Massimo walked into his home office on the second floor of the west wing and locked the door behind him. Dropping into a huge leather chair behind an elaborate desk, he picked up his secure phone and dialed a number.

In a matter of seconds, a man's voice boomed, "Dawson," from the other end.

"Paul. It's Massimo."

"Hey, Mass, can you hold a minute?"

"Sure." Massimo leaned back in his chair and thought of the night he met Paul in a restaurant in Paris. Paul had been unsuccessfully trying to order a meal through a waitress who spoke no English, when Massimo walked by. He'd been happy to help out a fellow American in a foreign country and had invited Paul to join him, Adam, Bryce, and Erik at their table.

At the time, Erik was married to Cassie and Bryce and Pilar were newlyweds. Their lives had changed so much since then.

Paul was inducted into the circle that night, and he and Adam had struck up a close-knit relationship—closer than the rest of them, perhaps because both their hearts had been broken by women they loved. Misery loved company, Massimo supposed.

Having an FBI agent as a friend was a good thing when you needed to have someone investigated. There was no agency more thorough than the Federal Bureau of Investigation. They had a plethora of resources and legitimate access to information that a P.I. didn't.

Why hadn't he thought of putting Paul on the missing persons case he'd been trying to solve for years? The private investigator he'd hired had tracked the family to Philadelphia, but after that the trail had gone cold. They had simply disappeared off the face of the earth.

Not a day passed by that Massimo didn't feel a pang of guilt for what had happened to that family. He was obsessed with righting the horrible wrong that had been done to them. It was the last mess left by Maurice Spencer that Massimo had to clean up.

"Sorry about that," Paul's voice jarred Massimo back to the present issue. "I'm working on a top-priority case. It's personal, too."

"Serious?"

The agent hesitated before responding. "Yes, and no. I'll fill you in later."

"And my trivial affair is diverting your attention."

"Hey, what's the use of a friend if you can't count on him when you're in need? I don't mind a trivial diversion once in a while. As a matter of fact, I was planning on buzzing you this morning."

Massimo pulled a ballpoint pen from its holder on his desk and grabbed a notepad. "I suppose you wouldn't have been thinking of getting in touch if you didn't have something to report." He got straight to the point. Nia would be coming downstairs soon and he needed everything wrapped up by then.

"The lady is who she says she is. She's been teaching math at Ellswood Charter School in Brooklyn for the past two years and she also works part-time as a tutor at a community college."

Massimo's fingers slithered lightly across the pad as he jotted down the information. "Where did she go to college?"

"Rutgers in Newark. She studied Applied Mathematics and gained her Bachelor's in three years."

Bold, beautiful, and intelligent. "Has she ever been in trouble with the law?"

"Not even a parking violation. I took the liberty of calling her school this morning under the guise of a potential part-time employer. Everybody knows teachers are grossly underpaid so no alarm on their part."

"What's the verdict?"

"Well, it's closed for winter vacation, but the principal was in and she thinks very highly of her. To quote the principal, 'Miss Sylk is competent and patient. Very much loved and favored by her students, and respected by her peers'."

"Wow, that's a stellar recommendation."

"I'll say." After a pause, Paul said, "There's a downside, though."

"What?" Massimo held his breath, his fingers tightening around the pen.

"She's up to her neck in debt. All her credit cards are maxed out. She has trouble paying her bills and she's delinquent on her student loan payments."

"Well," Massimo said, letting out his breath, "times are tough. Do you have the contact information for her creditors? All of them, even her student loans," he added, realizing he had no idea where to begin looking up information on federal loans. He'd never had to worry about money his whole life.

"As a matter of fact, I do."

Massimo wrote quickly. "Her medical records?" he said, moving on.

"Clean. No history of mental or any other medical diseases." Paul paused. "And yes, according to her records, she is still a virgin."

"Hmm." Powerful relief filled Massimo. She wasn't lying about that. "And has she ever traveled outside of the U.S. to the U.K. specifically?"

"No, man. She doesn't even own a passport."

Massimo breathed another sigh of relief. At least he could rule out her association with Galen. It was just a coincidence that Galen had booked a flight to New York at around the same time Nia would be in Granite Falls. He was due to arrive next week. His suspicions of Nia's relationship with his half brother had increased exponentially after the P.I. he had on Galen's track relayed the information in the lobby of Hotel Andreas yesterday.

Massimo had immediately put a stop to his bastard brother's travels to make sure he stayed in England, at least for the time being. He could not deal with another distraction right now. He would pick up his investigation on Galen once he was married and his inheritance secured.

It was a relief to know that Nia wasn't in cahoots with anyone, but herself. *But why?*

"Who's this girl, Mass? And why are you having her investigated?" Paul asked.

"It's business."

"Other than sexual, what kind of business can you possibly have with a virgin schoolteacher from Brooklyn?"

Wouldn't he love to know? "What about her family? Does she have any relatives?" he prompted to impede Paul's interrogation. The man was an FBI agent. Probing was his specialty.

"Well, actually, she——"

"Massimo?"

Massimo swiveled around as he heard Nia call his name. "We'll have to finish this conversation later, Paul. The lady is at my door."

"She's at Andretti Estate? But you never——"

"Yes."

Paul chuckled. "You dirty dog. You just broke up with Gabrielle and you're already back in the game. I guess Miss Sylk won't be a virgin much longer."

"You know me too well, my friend."

"I should call the boys so we can make bets on how long this one will last."

A smile played at the corners of Massimo's mouth. He hadn't missed Nia's slip this morning when she'd asked if he was going to tell people she offered him her virginity for two million dollars. The girl needed some serious lessons in the Art of Deception. "Heads up, buddy," he said to Paul. "Three full days, if it was all up to her."

"Three days? Man, your exploits are getting shorter and shorter. Are you trying to break some kind of record?"

"I'm trying to break something. Not quite sure what it is yet."

"Massimo?" Nia called again.

"I do have to go, Paul. Thanks for the info," he said as the doorknob rattled. "I'll be in touch again, soon. I have another matter I'd like you to check into when you have the time. I'll have my secretary email you the file later today."

"Okay. Anything for you, my friend."

Massimo hung up the phone, tossed the pad into his desk drawer and locked it.

"Why is your office locked?" Nia asked when he opened the door.

He shrugged. "Force of habit. I prefer not to be disturbed by the help when I'm conducting business."

"But Azi seems to be the only help around here."

"Help, nonetheless. Were you looking for me for any particular reason?"

"Azi says breakfast is ready."

Massimo took in her attire—a pair of designer jeans and a turquoise sweater. *Simple, yet sexy.* Her hair was pulled back into a ponytail, dramatizing her high cheekbones and almond-shaped eyes, and her smooth brown skin glowed with an innate vitality. He would love to take her back to his bed and have her for breakfast. The thought of her hot juices flowing into his mouth as he brought her to an earthshattering climax cause a lump to lodge itself in Massimo's throat.

She had no idea how close he'd come to living out his fantasy earlier in his bedroom—ripping the sheet from her body and riding her into the sunset. The only thing that had stopped him was the fact that he had no clue who she was, or what she really wanted with him. But now that he had credible and pleasing information about her...

Massimo drew her to him and pressed her face into his chest. She was really a teacher, and she was adored by her students and admired by her peers. According to her principal, she was kind and patient. Those were the very qualities he desired in the mother of his child. The fact that Nia was the sexiest, feistiest woman he'd ever met were added bonuses.

What on earth had propelled her to step outside of her character and offer to sell herself for four million dollars? It had to be more than the fact that she was buried in debt—a debt she'd incurred recently by making several large cash advances on her credit cards.

What kind of trouble was she in? Who had she borrowed from and had to repay? Was it a loan shark or some other questionable individual? New York City was rife with shady characters ready to pounce on inexperienced, innocent young women like Nia. Had she had the misfortune of falling prey to one of them? She was only twenty-three, and although she put on a brave act, her youth and innocence rendered her defenseless against the harsh realities of life.

A consuming need to protect Nia surged through Massimo's veins. The reason she had sought him out to solve her financial problems didn't seem important anymore. He didn't care, just thankful she'd come to him. Another wealthy man might not have been as honorable and considerate as he, even though she might not think him honorable at all.

His arms tightened possessively about her. He buried his face in her hair where traces of ginger and grapefruit from her shampoo and conditioner still lingered. *Simple and refreshing*—a nice change from the strong nauseating fragrances a lot of women used. He liked the fact that she was different.

"You're suffocating me," she said, struggling to break free.

"Sorry, pussycat." He relaxed his hold and stepped back to gaze into her hauntingly familiar eyes. Since she wasn't conspiring against him with Galen, he could not have seen her in the background of any surveillance photos. She wasn't a model or a movie star, so he would not have seen her in a magazine or on TV. So where had he seen her, and why was it only her eyes that were familiar? He would have remembered her entire body if he'd seen it once. It was just her eyes. "Are you sure we haven't met before, Nia?" he asked as frustration gnawed at his insides.

She dropped her gaze to the floor, just as she'd done yesterday when he asked her the same question.

"I'm positive, Massimo. We have never met," she said raising her head to smile at him wide-eyed.

Little liar, he thought on a smile. They had met before. It was up to him to find out where and when. As he gazed at her, he realized there was only one possibility. He had to have met her just before he set out for Kenya to scatter his father's remains in the Mara Lands. He wondered if she knew she talked in her sleep. She'd been tossing and mumbling during the early hours of dawn, but he'd been too tired to make sense out of her nonsense. He smiled inside, deciding to keep that bit of knowledge to himself. He might be able to coax the truth out of her tonight.

"Our breakfast is getting cold," she said, her eyes twinkling with eagerness. "We should go eat. It smells delicious."

You smell delicious. Massimo had a long day ahead of him, starting with an international satellite conference in a couple of hours. He placed his hand on the small of Nia's back and steered her into the direction of the dining room. Bliss crept through him. He faltered at the unexpected emotion.

In less than twenty-four hours, Nia Sylk had managed to spin her silken threads around his head. Now that he knew she was not involved with Luciano's bastard son and that she was who she said she was, and even though he was certain there was a lot more Nia wasn't telling him, his thoughts about her were nevertheless heading in a different direction.

He just had to be careful that her silken threads didn't extend to his heart.

CHAPTER FIVE

Nia pulled the wool dress from the hanger and slid it over her head. She wrapped the belt around her waist, tied it in the front, and stared at her reflection in the trifold mirror.

It was almost one o'clock, and she hadn't completed one single task on her list.

Since Massimo's international satellite conference was postponed until midafternoon he'd insisted on accompanying her to Joanne's Boutique after they picked up her new Mercedes. To make matters worse, she had that stupid spa appointment at two-thirty.

During breakfast, Massimo had told her that the charity event was to begin at seven, but that he'd arranged for her to meet his cousin, Adam, and friends, Bryce and Erik at the country club for drinks at six. Afterwards, they would drive across town to the Fontaine Conference Center where she would meet Bryce's wife, Kaya, and Erik's wife, Michelle.

That didn't give her much time to take care of her business, keep her spa appointments, go back to the mansion, and get dressed in time to drive to the country club.

Her planning time was getting shorter and shorter, Nia

thought with a frustrated twist of her lips. First, from one month to one week, then from two days to one, since she wasn't sure what time Massimo would give her the money tomorrow. From the way things looked, once she left Granite Falls, she'd have to stay in Miami until Tuesday, at least. Since she would be boarding the cruise ship under a different name, she had to get all of Nia Sylk's personal business taken care of before she left the country.

"I have to get to work, Nia."

"You didn't have to come with me, Massimo. I'm quite capable of picking out my own clothes. I've been doing it since I was twelve." The memory of losing her mother at that early age caused her heart to skip a beat.

"I'm sure you are capable, but I know what I want to see on you, pussycat."

Nia opened the door. "Stop calling me pussycat, especially in public." She fought her body's reaction to his mesmeric lure.

"Then stop hissing like one. Besides, we're all alone."

That was true. The man had so much clout he'd requested absolute privacy and ordered the store closed to the public while Nia tried on her new wardrobe.

"Come on, let's see it."

Nia stepped from the seclusion of the dressing stall and into the waiting lounge. "What?" she asked at the scowl on Massimo's face.

"I don't care for it. It makes you look… drab—like a nineteenth-century schoolteacher.

"I *am* a schoolteacher," Nia quipped, hands on hips. "*I* like it." *Just because you don't.* The color was all wrong for her. The puffed shoulders, long sleeves, and turtleneck did make her look drab. One thing she could say about him was that he had a good eye for fashion. She wondered if his women always looked as if they stepped off a Milan runway because he dressed them himself.

She watched, transfixed, as Massimo began stroking his lower lip with the pad of his thumb. It was a seductive habit that made her blood heat up under her skin each time he did it. She felt every stroke, every caress deep in the recess of her being.

"I'll tell you what," he said, walking over to her. "If you agree to take the red silk one you refused earlier, I'll let you keep this ghastly-looking thing."

The red silk one could hardly be called a dress. It was strapless, backless, revealed just a tad too much cleavage for her comfort, and it clung to her like a second skin. She would not be caught dead in that iniquitous garb. "Well, I don't like it that much," she told him.

"What a pity. Think of the lover's squabble we'll have when I request that you wear the red one to dinner and you decide on this instead. It would be interesting to see what happens when I order you to take it off at the dinner table."

"Fine. I'll keep them both." Not wishing to waste anymore time arguing with him, she ripped off the belt and threw it at him. She wouldn't be here long enough to wear either one of them, anyway. Let him eat that for dinner.

Massimo chuckled as she disappeared back into the dressing stall. He picked up the belt from the floor and tucked it into the pocket of his slacks. Images of Nia spread-eagle on his bed with her arms tethered to the bedpost by the strip of wool sent a delicious shudder ripping through his gut.

He'd never had to fantasize about a woman before. He was usually inside them just hours after meeting them. He'd never had to wonder for long how their hot flesh would feel clamped around his hard cock. This waiting game Nia had cooked up was a new challenge for him, and he had to say he was enjoying it. It just made the victory of her impending defeat much sweeter.

Massimo recalled his massive arousal this morning when he awoke to find Nia's soft, bare bottom nestled against his groin. It had taken every ounce of willpower for him to drag his aching body off that bed and take Jabari for a cold brisk walk. On his return to the house, he'd made arrangements for Jabari and his handler, Servio, to be taken to the jet for their return to Kenya. Once he'd said his good-byes, he'd gone to his home gym for a vigorous workout and an equally vigorous swim in the indoor pool. He had to release all that pent-up energy somehow.

But his need for Nia had swiftly reinstated itself when he walked back into his bedroom to find her writhing under the sheets, no doubt dreaming about him. He'd wanted to strip off his clothes, join her in bed, and fulfill her dreams in the worst way. The only thing that stopped him was his promise not to make love to her for a week. He would not breach their contract. He wanted her to trust him. But there was only so much temptation a man could take.

During breakfast, his mind had worked overtime on engineering and presenting a sink-or-swim counter contract offer to Nia. One she could not refuse. By the time they were headed into town, Massimo had decided that once he got to his office, he was calling Dafne to release her from their arrangement. It was crazy to give anybody—especially a woman—that much power over him. He was taking back control of his life and his future.

Since he had to marry to keep his inheritance, why not marry a woman he knew could offer him the kind of pleasure he demanded in bed? Nia had already agreed to sleep with him for his money. He saw no harm in marrying her in exchange for that same money. She'd claimed that she wasn't harboring any silly romantic notions about them. Well, neither was he. It would be a temporary business liaison with benefits, not a romantic love affair with complications.

He would offer her the same settlement he'd offered Dafne.

Probably a little more since he would be depriving her of her virginity. Ten million should compensate for her loss, and once her duty was fulfilled, she was free to go back to New York or any other place in the world she desired—seeing she would be his wealthy ex-wife and mother of his child.

Pulling the red dress from the 'no' rack and selecting a couple other items from a table, Massimo strode to the door that led to the sales floor. He called to a clerk who was busy straightening out a table laden with silk scarves.

She glided over to him. "Yes, Mr. Andretti?"

"We've set aside the outfits we're keeping." He held out the dress and items. "Have these delivered to the country club ASAP. Miss Sylk is not to know about it."

"Yes, sir."

Massimo detected the curiosity in her eyes. He could only imagine the avalanche of rumor about Massimo Andretti's new love interest that would soon be speeding through Granite Falls. And just as Paul had reminded him this morning, there would be bets on how long he'd keep this one. For the first time in his life, Massimo was not amused by the gossip surrounding his personal life.

Nia was not just another love interest. She was to become his unwilling bride. Andretti men might not be in love with their wives, but they protected them at all cost. He wished he could drag Nia down to city hall and put the Andretti mark on her today—stop the speculations before they began, but he knew she wouldn't go along with it. She'd have no reason to. He had to corner her between a snow bank and a running plow where she would have no alternative but to marry him.

"Would you like me to deliver the rest of the wardrobe to your lake house, sir?"

At the clerk's question, Massimo made a mental note to get rid of that house. It was his belated eighteenth birthday gift from his father after Massimo was caught trying to sneak his real birthday present—a cute little brunette—into the Andretti mansion. He'd never forget the look of desperation on Luciano Andretti's face when he handed his young hormone-driven son the key to the villa, along with a case of condoms, and commanded him never to bring his flings to the Andretti Estate. That honor, he'd adamantly emphasized, was reserved for Andretti wives only.

Until yesterday, Massimo had never disobeyed his father's command. Was never even tempted, not even with Gabrielle, who'd been deeply hurt at his reluctance to take her to his family home. It just didn't feel right to him. As it turned out, it wasn't, or more specifically, *she* wasn't right for him. His actions in taking Nia to the Andretti Estate, yesterday, were as spontaneous as they were inexplicable. It was as if his heart knew its inevitable fate from the moment he laid eyes on Nia Sylk.

"Mr. Andretti?"

Massimo stared at the clerk. "Yes."

"The wardrobe, sir. Should I deliver it to the villa?"

"No. I'll have someone pick it up later today. Just have it ready to go." He pulled out his wallet and dropped a credit card on the counter before walking back into the dressing lounge.

Nia emerged from the dressing stall. She wore the same jeans and sweater she'd worn into town. Any other woman would have been sporting one of the new outfits he'd just bought.

"You didn't have to buy me so many clothes, Massimo," she said, going over to the mirror to pull her hair back into its ponytail. "I feel like it's such a waste. That money could have been given to charity. There are many needy children in this world."

For a woman who'd offered him sex for four million dollars, she sure was unimpressed with material things—so very different from the women he was used to. She was more concerned about the basic needs of the unfortunate, and after his conversation with Paul this morning, he understood why. She was one of the unfortunate. She had hit rock bottom herself.

"I fund several charities, *cara*," he said in his own defense. "I support orphanages around the globe and award college scholarships to worthy students every year." Bianchi Incorporated was one such organization he supported in his mother's memory. It was a dream she'd brought to fruition just before she died. "And tonight, I'm writing an enormous check for the CFF. Who could fault me for splurging on someone I care about?"

"You care about me?"

"Yes," he said, just then deciding she'd become a most valuable asset to him, if not the most valuable since she would be bearing his heir, the future of Andretti Industries and Bianchi Incorporated. A prudent man would protect and cherish such an asset. He liked to think of himself as a prudent man. "Is that so hard to believe?"

"You don't know me."

"Then help me get to know you."

"I'm rather boring."

"I doubt that, pussycat." As he watched her brush her long black hair, Massimo realized that giving up his freedom in exchange for his inheritance didn't seem like a daunting ordeal anymore. With a spitfire like Nia for a wife, he would never be bored in the bedroom. If their son inherited Nia's fiery temperament and the Andretti astute business sense, the boy would be a force to be reckoned with in the corporate world.

Pleased with this particular decision, Massimo strolled across the floor and stood behind Nia. His hands closed over hers as she finished resetting her hair. He felt her quiver at the contact. He laced their fingers together and clasped his arms around her, bringing their joined hands to rest against her stomach. His son would be well nourished as he grew in her belly, he thought, recalling Nia's healthy appetite at dinner last night and at breakfast this morning.

He glanced down at their entwined limbs, loving the contrast in colors—his, tanned from the sun, and hers, a darker natural shade of brown—erotic and earthy. Their son's skin tone would be somewhere in between—olive. He would be a most adorable child whom Massimo hoped would inherit his mother's smile and beautiful brown eyes—eyes that would remind him of Nia once the term of their contract expired and she made her departure from his life.

Their eyes locked in the mirror. Hers, warm and sensuous— his, intense and desirous.

Massimo's breath caught in his throat as an ineffable trepidation overwhelmed him. When it came to women, he was always in control. He could turn his affections on and off like a faucet. He decided when a relationship began and when it ended. There were no lingering drips once he'd made that decision—he made sure of that with the generous settlements he provided his ex-lovers to leave him alone.

And there would be no lingering drips with Nia. She was a means to an end. A very delicious means. No need to get his heart involved. Andretti men only loved two things—sex and money—a fact Nia had contemptuously pointed out last night. Andretti wives were in the habit of withdrawing emotionally and physically once their duties were accomplished. Some, like his mother, foolishly fell in love with men like his father who were incapable of reciprocating that love.

Which was Nia's fate? Massimo wondered, mildly. Would she love him and try to make their marriage work, or would she become cold and bitter and wither away when he couldn't love her?

"I do have to get to the office," he said, staring at her

reflection in the mirror. "And you have your spa appointments at two-thirty. Don't be late."

She gave him a radiant smile that made his heart skip a beat. "Thanks for the clothes and the car, Massimo. I really appreciate them."

You can thank me properly tomorrow night once you're my wife and lying naked under me while I fill you up to the hilt. Your moans and the writhing of your sexy little body will let me know how appreciative you are.

"You can show your full appreciation next Monday when we seal our deal," he said out loud. He spun her around, planted a wet kiss on her lips, and left before he lost control.

Alone in the dressing room, Nia took several deep breaths to regain her wits. Since she wasn't going to be around to thank him, she wasn't flustered by Massimo's threats about showing her appreciation on Monday. She actually smiled through the rush of warmth his words had generated in her. It was all physical, she told herself—just the natural reaction of a girl to a boy. Nothing more.

She stared derisively at the new clothes he'd just shelled out thousands of dollars on. Yesterday, when he told her she would have a new wardrobe, she'd thought of keeping it, but as she glanced at the colorful array of dresses, sweaters, skirts, and pantsuits hanging on the rolling racks, she realized that most of them would be useless on a tropical island.

They were indeed a lovely waste of money, she thought, running her hands along the assortment of fabric—silk, satin, wool, linen, and dozens more she'd never heard of. She didn't know there were so many kinds of fabric until Massimo began describing them as she modeled for him. But fabrics and textiles were his specialty. Some of these fabrics were probably manufactured in an Andretti factory somewhere in the world.

Nia turned at the knock on the door. "Come in," she called.

One of the clerks came in and handed her a cordless phone.

"Mr. Andretti is on the line," she said and walked back out, closing the door.

Wondering why Massimo would be calling her when he'd just left her less than ten minutes ago, Nia raised the receiver to her ear. "Hello?"

"*Cara,* I just realized I don't have your cellphone number. What is it?"

Nia went into panic mode. "I... I don't have a cellphone." She hated lying, yet again, but she'd been calling Aaron in Dulcina on that phone. If Massimo knew her carrier and her number, he could track her there once she disappeared.

"No cellphone?"

"I lost it... yesterday," she added as a precaution. Longer than a day, and he'd want to know why she hadn't replaced it. Not being in possession of a cellphone these days seemed to be an invitation for interrogation from those who thought the mobile device was as vital to life as the air they breathed. "I think I might have dropped it on my way up the mountain in pursuit of you."

"Is that so? Have you informed your carrier? You don't want someone racking up unauthorized charges in your name."

"Yes, I did."

"When?"

"When?"

"Yes, Nia, when did you call your carrier?"

"You think I'm lying to you?"

"I don't know, Nia. Are you?"

Nia sensed that he was not just asking if she were lying about the cellphone but about everything else she'd told him since they met. He'd been practically glued to her side since she approached him in the cabin, and she hadn't made any phone calls since then. His suspicion and curiosity were reasonable.

Nia took a deep breath. "I'm not lying to you, Massimo," she lied. "When I got back to Hotel Andreas, I realized that my phone was missing. I called my carrier from my room while you were otherwise occupied in the lobby."

"I suppose you haven't gotten a new one yet."

"I haven't had time. I'll probably do it later today."

There was a long pause before he spoke again. "No need. Why don't you swing by Andretti Industries on your way to the country club and I'll have a corporate one ready for you."

Sure. It probably had a GPS just like her brand new Mercedes so he could keep tabs on her. She wouldn't be surprised if he had listening devices installed in that car. "Massimo, you don't have to—"

"I won't have you driving around without a phone, Nia. Suppose you get into an accident and need to call for help. These country roads can be extremely dangerous in the winter."

"In that case, OnStar will kick in, I'm sure." She was getting good. Her lips spread into a smile.

"I'm not about to argue with you, pussycat. I expect you—"

"Massimo, go tend to Andretti affairs and leave me alone to mine." Nia pushed the end button and tossed the phone on the chaise lounge. She picked up her coat, shrugged into it, and stormed out of the room.

To hell with him!

He'd already taken up most of her day. She was not wasting another minute bending to his imperial commands. She had more important things to do.

He could use her slot to get his own nails and hair done, get himself a facial and a full body massage. Then right after she got her two million dollars tomorrow, Massimo Andretti could go take a flying leap off Mount Washington straight into Crystal Lake for all she cared.

CHAPTER SIX

At five minutes to six, Nia entered an impressively decorated room at Granite Falls Country Club. She dropped her shawl on the back of a chair, set her purse on a table, and stared into a crackling fireplace as she recalled the last few hours of her life.

When she arrived at the club—two hours late for her appointment, a young man was waiting for her in the foyer. He'd hesitantly stated that Mr. Andretti had instructed him to take possession of her car. When she asked how she would get home to prepare for the night's event, he informed her that everything she needed was already delivered to the club and that Mr. Andretti would meet her here at six.

Fuming, Nia had asked to use the club's phone to call Massimo. He was conveniently in a meeting.

'Everything' turned out to be the red dress she'd sworn not to be caught dead in, a pair of six-inch silver stilettos—her size, surprisingly—a pair of black lacy panties, no bra, since she couldn't wear one with the dress, a silver, diamond-studded clutch, a white cashmere shawl, and a diamond and ruby necklace with a matching bracelet and earrings.

Since her jeans and sweater mysteriously disappeared when she donned a robe in preparation to be pampered like an Andretti woman, she had no other choice but to wear the clothes Massimo had picked out for her. He'd even told the hair specialist that he wanted her hair up off her neck in a French chignon, with a few curly tendrils falling down her cheeks and shoulders.

The man had a lot of balls. What did he hope to accomplish by bossing her around? Was this the reason his relationships were short-lived? No woman could take his domineering attitude, no matter how much money he threw at her. Somebody needed to tell him that no woman liked the constant feel of a boot heel on her neck.

When she walked out of Joanne's Boutique, Nia had been tempted to forget her plan and get the hell out of Granite Falls and away from Massimo. But thoughts of Aaron lying in an alley beaten to death kept her on course. Just one more day and she'd be free of Massimo forever.

"Cara."

Nia turned to see Massimo in the doorway. It was impossible to stay mad at him, she realized in despair as her annoyance dissipated at the sight of him. He looked irresistible in a dashing black and white tuxedo, his wavy black hair flowing from his face like a crest. He was every woman's wish, and every man's envy. He'd been her dream since she was seventeen. Just a dream, she reminded herself as butterflies started fluttering around in her belly.

He strolled toward her, and when he was close, she licked her lips as the faint yet heady smell of sandalwood and spice wafted up her nostrils.

"You look absolutely stunning," he said.

The tremor in his voice and the sensuous light in his eyes made her knees weak. At least he wasn't staring at her chest, like most men did when they talked to a woman. As a matter of fact, Massimo always looked her in the eyes when he talked to her, Nia realized. She clasped her hands together in front of her and cleared her throat. "I'd better look stunning since you picked out every stitch of clothing I'm wearing."

His lips parted into a seductive smile. "Don't remind me, pussycat. I'm already aching from visions of those black lacy panties nestled against your—"

Nia gasped as electricity shot through her. "Is sex all you think about, Massimo?" she asked pertly.

"What else am I to think about? Sex is all you offered me."

"Exactly. I didn't ask to be presented to the public and paraded in front of your friends."

"Being pampered is one of the roles of being my lover. And it serves to heighten the anticipation of my claiming what you offered. Although the rest of the world would think that I've already had you, only you and I know the truth."

"Right, I forgot your motto: Capture. Devour. Pamper. Release." She was pleased at how nonchalant she sounded while discussing their agreement.

He chuckled softly. "You know me well, pussycat." His face softened, his eyes twinkling in the light from the overhead chandelier and the fire. "Only a virgin, or a very inexperienced woman would blush at such playful banter. But I'm confident that this time next week, you'll be welcoming my sexual taunts, perhaps trying out some of your own? It makes for wonderful foreplay," he added with a hopeful lilt in his voice.

Feeling the familiar tingle of her skin only Massimo could generate, Nia shifted her gaze to the wintery scene on the other side of a window. This time next week she'd be in the sunny Caribbean. Massimo would just have to find someone else to stroke his big ego.

"I'm surprised they were able to pull this off when you were two hours late for your appointment," Massimo said.

Delighted with the change of subject, Nia said, "Three attendants worked on me simultaneously. One did my pedicure, another my manicure, while the third did my hair. I had a quick facial, but had to forgo the full-body massage." She dared not tell him what else she'd had done at his expense. It was her little secret. "They are quite talented," she continued on a tantalizing smile. "I've never looked this polished, even after an entire day of preparation."

"Why were you so late?"

"I had some business to take care of." She dropped her gaze to his wide chest.

"What kind of business?"

"Personal."

"Tell me." His voice was irascibly patient.

Nia crossed her arms and meeting his gaze again, she began relaying her prepared tale. "When I came to Granite Falls, I didn't know if you'd take me up on my offer, so I left my life as it was. But now… well… I have to rearrange my personal affairs in New York."

"I thought you said you weren't planning to change your life much. You mentioned returning to your teaching post after I've had my fill of you."

"It's not a huge change, but since I'll be a multimillionaire, I thought I'd move into a nicer apartment—maybe even purchase one in a better neighborhood."

He nodded agreeably. "Makes sense. If you need help with the move and need to be present to make other arrangement, I can fly you to New York in my private jet."

"There's no need. I've taken care of everything."

"So what specifically did you need to do that took so much time?" He folded his arms and probed her with his piercing eyes.

After she left Joanne's Boutique, she'd stopped at the library to type up her resignation, then she'd headed to the post office to mail it. After that, she'd stopped at Mountainview Café and made some calls over a bowl of homemade chicken gumbo soup and a cappuccino.

She'd managed to book a Saturday morning flight out of Manchester to JFK. From there she would take a taxi to the location where Eddie had instructed her to drop off his money within the two-month period. Nia had checked out the place before she left New York. Apparently it was a branch of Eddie's corporation that was operating under the guise of a check-cashing business. The cloak of anonymity suited Nia just fine. She never wanted to meet that man.

She'd called her landlord to let him know she was breaking her lease, which would be up in a month—one of the reasons she'd asked Massimo for a month. Her security deposit and four rooms of fairly decent furniture that she offered the landlord were enough to cover her remaining rent and pay the penalty for breaking her lease.

Next, she'd called Aaron and asked him to start looking into rental properties on Dulcina. She told him she wouldn't be contacting him again until late next week. He had lots of questions. She provided no answers.

It was a good thing she'd packed up her personal belongings before she left New York. If she'd known she only had a week to terminate her old life and plan her new one, Nia would have mailed the boxes to Dulcina herself. Her landlord had agreed to store them then put them on a freighter to Dulcina once she was settled. If she didn't have so many memories of her parents in those boxes, Nia would just forget about them.

Before she left New York, Nia had withdrawn the last of her meager rainy-day savings, but had decided not to close her account. She didn't want to give the impression that she was terminating her present life and leaving town forever. Since she didn't know exactly where Eddie's eyes were stationed, it was best she kept things as normal as possible.

No stranger to the art of deception, Nia had disguised herself and changed her rental cars several times on her way to Granite Falls. She'd checked into one hotel as herself in Connecticut, checked out disguised as young boy later that night, and driven off in a different rental car. As far as she knew, no one had followed her.

The day she arrived, she put the cash along with her new passport in a safety deposit box at Granite Falls Savings Bank. So after lunch, she drove to the bank and wired some money to her landlord's account to pay for storing her stuff, for his troubles, and also for his silence should anyone come asking about her.

She couldn't tell Massimo all that, so she offered him a small version of the truth. "I had to call my landlord to break my lease and arrange to have my stuff put into storage. I also called my school to tell them I was taking a leave of absence, and my friends to let them know I was okay. I mean, I just kind of disappeared."

He measured her with a cool appraising look. "And that took three hours?"

She held his suspicious gaze without flinching. "I have lots of friends."

"Hmm. So, I suppose you got your cellphone problem fixed."

"What?"

His bushy eyebrows arched. "Your cellphone. You never came by Andretti Industries, so I assume you replaced the one you'd lost."

Nia stared into the granite fireplace. If she said she'd gotten a new phone, he'd ask to see it, and he would want the number. Since she'd tossed the phone into the Aiken River after making all her calls, she didn't have one to show him. She couldn't tell

Massimo that she'd lost a second phone that quickly. If she said she hadn't replaced it yet, he'd want to know how she'd made all her calls to New York.

"I'm waiting, Nia. How did you make those calls? Did you borrow someone's phone to conduct your business?"

Nia bit into her lower lip. *Think. Think, girl. You managed to get Maine Child Welfare Services off your tail when you were seventeen, you can surely cook up a plausible excuse about a cellphone to throw Massimo off your scent.*

She met his gaze. "I made my calls from the computer café on the circle. I know how busy you were, Massimo, and didn't want to bother you, so I just used a pay phone at the café."

He planted his feet apart and scowled down at her. "Really? So if I—"

Whatever he was about to say was lost in the flood of male voices in the hall. As Massimo swore under his breath, Nia peeked around him to see three dashing handsome men crowding the doorway.

"In here," one said, stepping into the room.

Nia felt like running over and kissing the dark giant she recognized as Bryce Fontaine. He was followed by Erik LaCrosse and Adam Andreas—all members of the Granite Falls Billionaires Club. Like Massimo, they were regularly featured in *Granite Falls People News*. The only difference was that these men's sexual escapades weren't as infamous as Massimo's.

Bryce had been close, but no cigar. He'd left that lifestyle behind for marriage, and was now the proud father of two-month old twins. He and Kaya were also raising her deceased sister's three children. Erik and Michelle had three children— Precious, Little Erik, and Tiffany. Like his cousin Massimo, Adam was still single.

Nia wondered which one of the two would be the first to follow their friends into marital bliss. She would bank her money on Adam, she thought gazing at the handsome hunk with a head of thick black hair that was even longer than hers. Massimo was still too egocentric for marriage and family. She couldn't imagine him putting anyone else's needs ahead of his own. Having a family would force him to make sacrifices. He was not the kind to do so.

"Mass." Bryce approached them.

Nia looked on as the men exchanged greetings and hugs. She felt very small in their towering presence. Bryce was at least two inches taller than Massimo. He was known as a global giant in the business world. Erik was the most sought-after OB/GYN on the east coast, but he also practiced pediatrics for the children of his closest friends, and Adam owned Andreas International, an exclusive chain of hotels and restaurants around the world. Tables at his restaurants were booked months in advance and required a hefty nonrefundable deposit.

Nia had been tempted to have lunch at the hotel while she'd been lying in wait for Massimo, but when she saw the prices of the salads, she'd sought out the less expensive restaurants in town. She hoped Andreas was catering the gala tonight. It'd be wonderful to finally know what the culinary buzz was all about.

"And, who's this lovely little jewel of the Nile?" Adam asked, smiling down at her.

"You didn't tell us you'd be bringing a date," Erik said.

"If we'd known, we would have had Kaya and Michelle meet us here instead of at the center," Bryce chimed in.

Massimo pressed his palm into the small of Nia's back and propelled her gently forward. "This is Nia Sylk. Nia, meet my two closest friends, Bryce Fontaine and Erik LaCrosse, and my cousin, Adam Andreas." He placed his hands possessively on her shoulder.

"It's a pleasure." Nia smiled shyly up at the men.

"The pleasure is all ours, Nia." Bryce gave her an affectionate smile.

They took turns shaking and kissing the back of her hand, and each time their lips connected with her skin, she felt Massimo's grip tighten on her shoulders.

"Shall we sit?" Massimo led her across the room to a red sofa and sat down so closely beside her, their thighs touched. Nia tried very hard not to pull away. A woman who'd asked to become a man's lover was supposed to try to get closer to him, not try to avoid him.

The three men occupied the chairs on the opposite side of the low table between them. They all watched her intently, reminding Nia that she was in the presence of some of the most powerful men in the country, perhaps the world. She was beginning to feel the heat of the tense silence when an attendant entered the room.

"What would you care to drink, *cara?*" Massimo asked her.

"Red wine, please."

Massimo rattled off an Italian wine to the attendant then added, "And we'll have our usual."

The attendant left as quickly and quietly as he'd arrived.

Nia listened quietly as the men discussed the details of the gala. The proceeds of the evening would go toward the construction of the headquarters for the Children of the Future Foundation. It was to be built in Evergreen, a neighboring town, but would serve children from all over the country—children who were disadvantaged, abused, and addicted to drugs and alcohol.

Erik's wife, Michelle, was the founder of the organization, so Nia understood his uninhibited excitement about the evening. The pride he had for his wife was evident.

Many of New England's elite were expected to visit this little mecca nestled in the foothills of the White Mountain National

Forest. As she listened to the conversation, Nia learned that some were even travelling from as far as Connecticut. But Nia was certain most of them were just coming to see if they could get a glimpse of the Hollywood celebrities, even have their pictures taken with them.

Nia's brain was in turmoil as she anticipated being caught up in the dizzying spotlight. She hadn't signed up for this kind of attention. Her plan was to get in, get her money, and get out without anyone knowing she was even here. She should have included a 'no-publicity' clause in her verbal contract with Massimo. Since yesterday, he'd been indicating that she was not a very good negotiator. She had to agree that she had a lot to learn.

Finally, Adam turned to her and began the interrogation she knew was inevitable. "We must be boring you with all this chatter, Nia. So it's your turn. Tell us, where are you from?"

Nia straightened her shoulders and forced a smile. "New York. Brooklyn."

"Is that where you and Massimo met?"

"No. We... we met here in Granite Falls."

"She was actually staying at your hotel, cousin," Massimo stated, staring at Adam.

"And I missed her?" Adam's mouth drooped in disappointment. "If I'd only seen her first."

"I don't think it would have mattered," Massimo said with an unpleasant twist to his mouth.

"Have you forgotten our motto: First see, first—"

"Are we forgetting that the lady is sitting among us? You two need to stop squabbling over her as if she were the only bone in the yard," Bryce said, looking from Massimo to Adam like a displeased father at his quarreling boys.

"I agree," Erik piped in. He smiled at Nia. "You must forgive them, Nia. They've been competing with each other since they were children. Their fathers encouraged this family rivalry, so it has become a natural parade for both of them. I can understand Massimo's possessive behavior toward you."

Adam held his cousin's gaze. "Since you and Gabrielle broke up, we just thought you—"

"*Abbastanza*, Adam," Massimo growled at his cousin.

"So when did you and Massimo meet?" Bryce asked, moving the conversation back to her. "I would think it must be some time ago and he's been keeping you a secret for the grand announcement," he stated, his black eyes fixed on Massimo.

What the heck is going on? Nia looked from one man to the other. They were speaking in code and sending each other peculiar glances as if they were keeping some big secret from her.

"Yesterday, actually," Massimo provided in a very calm voice that held no traces of the annoyance he'd exhibited just moments ago.

"Weren't you skiing yesterday?" Erik asked.

Massimo's gaze caught hers. "That's where we met." He reached over and curled his fingers around her clenched hands that were lying on her lap. She was surprised at the comfort his touch offered to her jittery nerves.

"So you're a skier." Bryce said. "You must be very skilled to have caught Massimo's attention. He's very competitive on the slopes."

The attendant returned with their drinks. Pulling her hands from under Massimo's, Nia grabbed her glass and took a few quick sips even before the men received theirs. She wished she'd ordered something much stronger than wine. If she ever needed to get drunk, now was the time.

"So, how did you two meet?" Bryce repeated after the attendant left.

"It was the most interesting introduction I've ever had," Massimo told him.

"All your introductions with women are interesting, Massimo," Erik teased.

Massimo gazed placidly at her over the rim of his glass. "Oh, this one was.... unprecedented. I was totally unprepared for it. Wouldn't have expected it in a million years, not even four million," he added, his deep voice rich with derision.

The men laughed.

Nia cringed.

"What was so different about this one?" Adam asked with obvious traces of jealousy in his voice.

Nia's pulse began to beat erratically as four pairs of curious eyes turned on her. When she'd first met them, she'd wondered why Massimo hadn't already told them about her. Was it so he could embarrass her in front of them? Even Massimo couldn't be this cruel.

Massimo chuckled. "I'll let Nia tell you about it. You'll like her version better."

Even worse than embarrassing her, he was putting her on the spot. Nia's thoughts scampered vaguely around as the three men leaned forward in their seats—ears, eyes, and mouths agape. She felt like her breath was being sucked right out of her. She took a giant gulp of her wine.

"Go on, Nia. You have our undivided attention," Erik coaxed.

Massimo reached out and fingered a loose tendril of hair that was resting on her cheek. The back of his fingers brushed her skin ever so softly as he toyed with the strand.

Nia swallowed a whimper and wrapped her hands around her wine goblet to stop the tremors his touch was evoking. He knew she wouldn't dare pull away in front of his friends. She had to play the role of an enamored lover. How she would love to toss her wine into his devilish face.

She inhaled deeply and hoped her voice would hold. "I... I

don't really ski... *well*," she added, realizing she'd have to disclose the real reason she was on the mountain if she admitted she wasn't a skier. "I'm a city girl. I can hardly keep my balance on roller skates. So it was no surprise to me that I fell flat on my face while going around a bend. But—" She turned and gave Massimo a genuinely sweet smile, "my knight in a shining ski suit saw me fall and glided to my rescue. He picked me up, dusted me off, and the rest as they say is history."

Anxiety spurted through her as the men, who were obviously prepared for an exceptional story, sat back in their seats and looked at each other with mild disappointment at her dull tale.

"Wow, that's routine compared to my first meeting with Michelle." Erik was the first to speak. "She refused to take no for an answer and barged her way into my home, then my life, and eventually my heart."

"I hear you, brother. Kaya wanted to slap me just minutes after we met. If she could have reached my face, I know she would have. It took me a month to bring her around." Bryce chuckled, as he sipped from his glass.

"Not to rain on your parade guys, but Nia's and my meeting wasn't as routine as you think. Was it, *cara*?"

"Are we missing something?" A frown ruffled Erik's brow.

"Just that I fell deliberately to attract his attention." At the outburst from the men, Nia was pleased with her quick wit. She glowered at Massimo.

"Leave it to my cousin to stumble upon a beautiful damsel in accidental or deliberate distress. When it comes to lovely women, he's one of the luckiest men alive. And just let me say, Nia, you are by far the loveliest woman he's ever had the opportunity to meet."

Adam's expression stilled and grew serious as he stared at his cousin. "What are your intentions with Nia, Massimo?" he asked blatantly, an indescribably challenge in his eyes and voice. "I only just met her, but I feel that there's something special about her. She seems different from all the other women you've dated. So tell me, is she simply a drive-by, or are you smart enough to hold on to her, get to know her, see where it leads. You only have—"

"Adam," Bryce and Erik shouted simultaneously, their glances shifting cautiously from Massimo to Adam.

Nia took a sideway glance at Massimo. There was a lethal calmness in his eyes as he stared at his cousin. "Nia and my relationship is none of your business, Adam, but if you must know, she's not a drive-by. I plan to keep her around for a very long time."

His last statement caused Nia's bones to quiver. She took a sip of wine to hide her anxiety.

"Good," Adam said with a contented grin on his face. His eyes were soft as he stared at Nia. "We would all love to know more about you, Nia. Welcome to Granite Falls and our family." He raised his glass. "To Nia and Massimo."

"Here, here," the others acquiesced, raising their glasses.

In spite of her uneasiness, warmth flowed through Nia at the welcome. She liked Massimo's friends, and his cousin. She felt a little sad that she wouldn't be sticking around to join their family. It would be nice to have such powerful force in her corner. A worm like Eddie wouldn't dare look at her, much less threaten her if he knew the kind of company she was now keeping.

In the midst of the cheers, Massimo wrapped his arm around her and pulled her so closely against him, the heat from his body fused with hers. "I've been dying to tell you that you're a horrible little liar, pussycat," he whispered for her ears alone.

Nia felt like she'd been doused with a bucket of ice water. What did he mean he'd been dying to...

"I didn't see lights at the lake house last night." Bryce cut into her distressed thoughts. "I live on Crystal Lake, for the time being," he added for her benefit. "Now that I have a wife and a rapidly growing family, I just began the construction on a bigger house."

"Oh don't be so modest, Bryce. He's building an estate on Mount Reservoir," Erik said, smiling at Nia.

"And once you and Michelle move into the LaCrosse Estate, we'll all be happy neighbors," Massimo added with a grin. He ran his warm palm slowly up and down Nia's bare arm and shoulders and along the baseline of her hair, sending explosive currents racing through her.

Nia gasped as she felt her breath literally being cut off.

"And to respond to your statement, Bryce," he continued. "Nia and I spent the night at the mansion." He sent Nia a seductive smile, deliberately misleading his friends into thinking they'd slept together. Well they had, but not in the way he was suggesting.

A tense silence enveloped the room as the four men exchanged those peculiar glances again.

Nia's body fought to blanket the hysteria of delight rising inside her at Massimo's caresses while her mind worked to decipher his comment about her being a bad liar and the strange expressions on his friends' faces when he told them he'd taken her to his mansion. Well, Massimo did tell her that she was the first woman he'd ever taken to the mansion. But why was it such a big deal?

Then there was Adam's blatant question about Massimo's intentions for her, and Erik's and Bryce's attempt to cut Adam off in midsentence. What was he about to say, and why did Massimo's intentions toward her matter to him, to any of them?

Voices suddenly gushed in from the hallway. A mob stormed into the room. The bright lights of a camera momentarily blinded Nia. She was so startled by the invasion, she tipped her glass, spilling wine all over the front of her dress.

She heard Massimo swear as he pushed to his feet to stand

between her and the mob, blocking their view of her. His three large friends joined him at the line for reinforcement.

"Is it true Mr. Andretti? Have you taken a new lover? Who is she?"

As the infamous chaos of Massimo Andretti's world enveloped her, Nia closed her eyes. Her life as she knew it was over. She wished she and her red wine-stained dress would just meld into the red sofa and disappear.

"Gentlemen, ladies, please, have a little respect." Massimo and his line of generals forced the crowd back into the hallway. How the hell did they know he was here? He'd arranged to meet his friends at the club in order to avoid this very fiasco. Why weren't they at the conference center groveling over pre-event tidbits?

For small-town paparazzi, they were the most ferocious vultures he'd ever encountered.

He should have kept Nia hidden until after their marriage. Perhaps he should have taken her to Africa with Jabari this morning—hidden her in the Masai village, the only place on this earth where he found a little bit of peace. Massimo wished he could snap his fingers and whisk Nia into the middle of the Mara Lands right now.

"You were seen leaving Bristol Mountain with a young woman, yesterday, Mr. Andretti. The buzz around town is that you bought her a new car and wardrobe today. Is that her?" Lester Cobbs, a reporter from the local television station tried to peek around Massimo for a better look at Nia.

He and his camera were pushed back by Bryce.

"Lester, you should know by now that I make announcements only when I'm ready." Massimo blinked as cameras flashed in his face. At least Nia was safe for now. The last thing he wanted was for her to be photographed with that awful wine stain on her dress. Not the way he wanted to introduce his future wife to the public.

"What kind of important announcement are you about to make, Mr. Andretti?" A reporter from the daily newspaper asked.

"Yes, curious minds want to know."

"Is it that you'll be bored with her by tomorrow?"

"Or maybe tonight," another chirped in.

In the midst of their laughter, Massimo heard Nia gasp behind him.

He clenched his jaws. He should have known better than to subject Nia to this circus. He swallowed his rage. His well-laid plans were being waylaid. He didn't want Nia to know about his intentions until he had her where he wanted her. But he couldn't have the media publishing ugly gossip about her, either. She was special and pure, and that's the way he wanted to keep her— well, at least in the eyes of the public. No one but Nia and himself would ever know the truth about the way they'd met.

Since tongues were already wagging, it was best they wagged the truth. "Well, if you must know, Miss Sylk—"

"Silk? Is that her real name? Sounds provocative."

Another round of laughter erupted from the crowd.

"Is she as soft and smooth as her name implies?"

Blood hammered against Massimo's temples. He'd wondered the same thing when Nia first approached him with her audacious proposal. Hearing the thought verbalized from another's lips made him sick to the stomach. He hadn't realized until this very moment what a big pointless joke his life was. He wanted to punch some faces, break a few cameras, but that would demonstrate weakness. Andretti men weren't weak.

"Miss Sylk and I will be married within a week," he gritted out between clenched teeth.

A hush fell in the hallway as all jaws dropped, including those of his friends. Massimo used the moment to snatch Lester Cobb's camera before jumping back into the room and slamming the door. His lips thinned in rage at the footsteps clambering down the hall like a stampede of wild beasts on the African plain.

He turned around to find an openmouthed Nia glaring at him, fury and contempt shooting from her eyes.

CHAPTER SEVEN

Pulling herself out of a daze, Nia shot to her feet, her chest rising and falling with the force of her breathing. Her stomach churned. Her legs were shaking so hard, she was afraid she would collapse on the floor.

How dare he make such a bombshell announcement about *her* future? How dare he broadcast her name to the world? At no time did they ever discuss marriage. It never even crossed her mind. Only a spoiled, insecure, gold-digging narcissist would marry a man like him.

As he walked steadily toward her, his squared shoulders, the firm line around his mouth, and the intense look of resolve in his eyes told her he had no regrets about what he'd just done.

"Massimo—"

"Nia—"

"Um... Mass..."

At the sound of Erik's voice, Nia looked at the three men hovering close to the door. She'd completely forgotten they were still in the room. When Massimo dropped his bombshell, they'd seemed just as stunned as she was.

"We... we should leave you two alone." Erik sent her an apologetic smile.

"I think that's a great idea," Bryce added.

"We'll catch up later, cousin. It was really nice meeting you, Nia."

The three men raced from the room like a swarm of bees was after them.

"Are you out of your mind, Massimo Andretti?" Nia shouted.

Ignoring her question, he calmly opened the camera he'd snatched from the reporter, yanked out the small chip and tossed it into the fire. "Am I out of my mind? Perhaps a little," he said in a barely composed voice as he set the camera on the mantel.

Even in her anger, Nia was grateful for his quick reaction in shielding her from the media, and his thoughtfulness to confiscate the only picture they had of her. That still did not give him the right to...

"You have no right to tell anyone that I'm marrying you much less broadcast it to the world." Anxiety spiked her voice at the realization that the news might very well reach Brooklyn and Eddie. He, along with her friends and acquaintances in New York, would know where she was, which would complicate her plans and her life even more—something she didn't realize was possible.

Since she'd tossed her phone and didn't dare try to Skype with Aaron from the mansion, he and everyone else she knew might try to contact her through Andretti Industries. Massimo would question them. And they would spill the truth not realizing that she was trying to conceal her identity from him.

God, this plan of hers had turned into such a mess!

Nia pressed her hands against the sides of her head and squeezed. She wanted to cry.

"I had to tell them something to stop the insulting questions about you. It worked. They're gone."

She folded her arms and jutted her chin at him. "Why does it matter what they say about your reputation? It's not like you aren't used to it."

"I am used to it, but you aren't." He watched her through keenly observant eyes. "I'm sure you're aware of the unfavorable manner in which my former lovers have been portrayed."

"I would have gotten over it, Massimo." *By Saturday evening Nia Sylk will be old news, and by next Tuesday, she'll be dead news.* "Are you forgetting that once our... *little contract* is fulfilled, I'll be leaving?"

His smile had a spark of eroticism. "You don't think I'll let you go immediately following the fulfillment of our... um… *little contract*, do you? You didn't put a time limit on this arrangement. That makes it indefinite."

Nia's mind momentarily froze as he pointed out yet another flaw in her negotiation skills. No wonder the man was so successful in the business world. He covered every tiny detail of his deals.

"I plan to keep you around for a very long time, Nia Sylk," he continued, seemingly satisfied that he'd rendered her speechless. "I look forward to taking my time pleasuring you and teaching you how to pleasure me. You'll be slaking my passion and warming my bed for many a cold winter nights, my little pussycat. You can count on that."

Nia willed her mind to throttle the dizzying excitement his passion-filled promises evoked in her. "Well, at some point, the affair *will* be over and you *will* let me go. You're going to look like a fool when a wedding doesn't take place. The second one in a few weeks."

"I'm no fool, Nia Sylk. Don't you ever forget that."

The silken thread of warning in his voice sent a chill down her spine. Feeling the probing heat from his eyes, Nia walked to the window and stared at the snow-covered golf course and the lake beyond it. Just before the mob had descended upon them, Massimo had called her a horrible little liar. Somehow she knew he wasn't just talking about the silly story she'd told his friends about their first encounter, but about every lie she'd spoken since they met.

It didn't surprise her. Any intelligent man would have figured her out by now. Massimo just stated he was no fool. What he didn't know was that Nia Sylk wasn't simply running away from him. In a few days, she would cease to exist. He could spend all his money on every private investigator on the planet, and he still wouldn't be able to find her.

Pleased with her adeptness at handling herself so far, Nia turned to face him. "I'm just saying, your reputation as the irresistible playboy of the century will be ruined, Massimo."

He closed the distance she'd put between them. "So you care about my reputation, now? And here I was, thinking you only wanted sex and money from me."

"Sex and money was all I asked for."

"I'm offering you more sex and more money."

"You don't need to marry for sex, Massimo. You're a rich playboy."

"Even playboys get tired of the games at some point, Nia," he said with a resigned twist to his lips. "You just witnessed the circus I'm constantly pulled into. Perhaps I want a little balance in my life."

"And a wife will give you balance?"

"A wife and a child." His voice was calm, his gaze steady. "I spend a great deal of time with both Erik and Bryce's families. I see how happy and balanced they are. I'm man enough to admit that I envy them that kind of stability. It would be nice to have a woman waiting at home for me at the end of the day."

Maybe he was telling the truth, Nia thought. He and

Gabrielle Berkeley were supposed to be married by now, but he'd messed that up. "You couldn't even be faithful to Gabrielle for six months," she stated on a shrug.

"Gabrielle wasn't right for me."

Right or not, it didn't give him the right to cheat on her. "Well, neither am I. I told you I wasn't harboring any romantic notions about you. That hasn't changed," Nia said, almost choking on the big fat lie as it fell from her lips.

He placed his hand under her chin and raised her face. "I'm not talking romance, either. A marriage between us will be purely business. If you agree to become my wife and give me an heir, I promise to take care of you, Nia. I will respect you, protect you, and treat you well. You'll live like a queen."

He dropped his hand from her chin and pulled his ringing cell from his jacket pocket. "Excuse me for one moment." He walked to the other side of the room.

A dull ache settled in the pit of Nia's stomach as she gazed at the powerful man who'd just told the world they were getting married. She'd imagined this moment when the man of her dreams would ask her to be his bride, bear his children, and spend the rest of her life with him.

Although this was not the way she'd expected a proposal to take place, it was the most tempting offer she would ever have. Becoming Mrs. Massimo Andretti was no trifling accomplishment. Millions of women would be kissing his feet just for offering them the chance to bear his name. She was not one of them.

Besides, there were too many obstacles standing between her and Massimo walking off into marital bliss and happily ever after. They lived in separate worlds, traveled in different circles. There was no love between them and, foremost of all, she could not betray her father's memory by marrying the man who was responsible for his death.

And even if she could love Massimo past that monumental fact, his track record with women was enough to give her pause. At some point, men like Massimo got tired of their women, be it mistress or wife, and went in search of new adventures. Marriage to him was purely a business contract that could be rendered null and void at any time. To her, it was a love commitment between a man and a woman. When she committed herself to her husband, it would be for love, and it would be forever.

Love and forever were two things Massimo Andretti could not offer her.

But he could offer Aaron security and a promising future.

Nia raised her hand and gazed at the diamond bracelet on her wrist. She ran her fingers along the necklace around her throat and the dangling earrings in her lobes. The set probably cost more than Aaron's tuition at MIT. She thought of her new car and new wardrobe and of the Andretti mansion she would call home if she married Massimo.

Aaron would have access to opportunities and luxuries she could never provide in a million years, and definitely not with a million dollars that would be eaten up by the time she paid off her debts, her college loans, and helped Aaron get through college.

For many years following their father's death, they'd gone hungry, had been cold in the winter and hot in the summer. They had slept on bare floors, and lived without electricity and running water while she tried to support them on various menial minimum wage jobs.

Marrying Massimo would be like winning the lottery.

He said she would live like a queen. He'd promised to respect her, protect her, and even now as her body tingled from the memory of his passionate kisses and the possessive way his skillful hands brought her body to life, the fact that he never promised to love her or be faithful to her caused a raw and primitive longing in her soul.

"The vultures are gone. It's safe to leave."

Nia turned at his voice. She watched him slip his cell into his pocket, pull her shawl from the back of the chair and her purse from the table where she'd tossed them less than an hour ago. He walked over to her, pressed her purse into her hand, and methodically slipped her shawl over her shoulders as if he'd performed the actions a thousand times before. Without uttering a word, he opened a door at the back of the room, led her along a corridor, down a short flight of stairs, and into the waiting limo parked under an enclosed porch.

"Where are we going?" Nia asked in a panic. Surely he wouldn't force her to attend that function now, not after that public fiasco and surely not in a wine-stained dress.

"Home. Your dress is ruined, and quite frankly I've had enough chaos for one night. I'd like a warm quiet place to relax and enjoy the rest of the evening, and you."

As they drove away, Nia's mind fluttered away in anxiety. The night was young and the more time she spent with Massimo, the weaker her defenses became. And she was sure he had plans to seduce her tonight. Being cooped up alone in the mansion with him was not a good thing. "You can attend your event, you know," she said. "I can take care of myself for the evening."

He chuckled softly. "Not a chance, pussycat. We have unfinished business. If I can't convince you to marry me for my money, I'll have to convince you to marry me for sex. Since you're not drunk tonight, you will be acutely aware of what my hands and mouth will be doing to you.

Nia pulled her shawl tighter around her and huddled against the door of the limo. If he thought they were sleeping in the same bed tonight, he could think again. She would sleep with Azi if that's what she had to do to keep Massimo away from her. She did not trust herself to be near him. She wasn't strong enough to fight this wanton need he'd spawned inside her.

He'd promised he wouldn't take her before the week was up, except if she asked him to. Nia knew if he touched her tonight, she would beg him to go the distance.

"You must be famished."

Why was it whenever she was thinking about making love with him, he brought up the subject of food? She was aware of the old saying that the two things that kept a man truly satisfied were good food and good sex. Massimo had had access to both all his life. And it seemed he was determined to continue nurturing his cravings for food and sex with Azi in his kitchen and Nia in his bed.

"I'm just tired," she said, realizing that it was true. She'd had a full day.

"I'll have Azi prepare us something."

Nia's stomach growled with hunger as he discussed dinner with Azi in what she suspected was Swahili. She was starving. She hadn't eaten since noon, and she'd been looking forward to gorging herself on Andreas' cuisine at the gala. But there was no way she was going to sit down at any table and have dinner with Massimo.

Massimo would be eating alone, tonight. He would be sleeping alone, too.

As soon as they entered the mansion, Nia made a dash down the hall, but Massimo caught up with her before she could make her escape.

"Something smells wonderful," he said as he removed her shawl and dropped in on a lounge in the hallway.

"Everything Azi cooks smells wonderful," she responded, distraught that she would probably go to bed hungry. The smell from the kitchen deepened her hunger pangs.

Massimo shrugged out of his jacket, ripped off his bow tie

and dropped them next to the shawl. His eyes scanned her face. "How do you like the diamonds?"

Nia fingered the jewels at her throat. "They're lovely. I've never worn anything this... extravagant."

"Get used to it, *cara*. I plan to shower you with diamonds, sapphires, emeralds, rubies, and whatever else your little heart desires."

The things he thought made a woman happy. The only things she desired from him were her two million dollars and her freedom.

"All you have to do is say yes to marrying me." His mercurial eyes twinkled in the lights from the alabaster lamps on the walls.

He placed his hands on her shoulders and caressed her neck with the pads of his thumbs, sending a series of electrical shocks through her. "We make a beautiful couple, *cara*. We'll make a beautiful son. Don't you think?" His voice was barely a whisper.

He gazed into her eyes as he slowly loosened her hair from its bun. The black tresses fell like a heavy curtain down her back. He drew her closer, and held her fast with one hand at the small of her back, the other under her chin, his long fingers spanning the scope of her face. He bent his knees and crouched down. His warm breath fanned her cheeks. Her heart jack-knifed in her throat when she felt his heavy arousal pressing against her belly. He slowly lowered his head and brushed his lips over hers.

"Marry me, Nia," he rasped in a husky voice. "Make love with me tonight. Let me show you how incredible it can be between us. Let me put out the fire I know is burning inside you, *cara*. It's the same fire that's eating me alive. Let's ride the flame together."

Nia's breath came out in hard harsh gasps. She felt her breasts swelling and her nipples tingling. She wondered how her throat could be so dry when her panties were so wet. She fought the desire to stand on tiptoe and bring her hot sex in alignment with Massimo's erection burning a hole in her belly.

In an attempt to moisturize her dry lips, her tongue grazed Massimo's mouth that hovered just inches from hers. She felt him tremble on a groan at the unexpected caress. Their gazes tangled and lust sizzled between them as his other arm circled her, drawing her into his body. A moan escaped her lips as her mind and her body began a heated squabble.

"Let's mate, pussycat." He licked one corner of her mouth with long wet strokes—much like the way a jungle cat would lick its mate. His tongue was hot and strong and smooth.

Nia felt like she would burst out of her skin if she didn't…

Snap out of it, girl. You know what he's doing. You can't give in.

Nia closed her eyes and called on the few rational nerves in her body that hadn't yet fallen victim to Massimo's seduction.

No. "No!" She pulled completely free and took a step back from him. "Not… not here," she said, pressing her hand to her racing heart and glancing up and down the hallway. *Not anywhere.*

The sensuous flame lingered in his eyes. His lips parted on a smile. "Right. Let's take it to the bedroom." He glanced down at the red stain on her dress. "Pity, such a lovely dress. Why don't you go on upstairs and put on something more comfortable. I'll go see what Azi has prepared and bring it up. I know from experience that it's not good to make love on an empty stomach."

Nia didn't need to be told twice. It was the chance she'd been praying for in the car. She'd be a fool not to take it. As Massimo went in the direction of the kitchen, she raced the other way like a rocket, and into the elevator. In the master suite, she flew through the living room, grateful that Jabari was gone. She didn't need to deal with an unpredictable cat as well as his tenacious master.

Once she got to the bedroom, Nia closed and locked the door then leaned against it, taking deep gulps of air into her desperate lungs. It wasn't long before the gold lever rattled. She stepped away and stared at it. Angst spurted through her when it rattled again.

"Nia," Massimo called from the opposite side. "Why is the door locked?"

A few silent moments expired. Then the heavy oak door shook as he threw his weight against it. She heard him swear, probably more from anger than pain.

"Nia, open this door, right now, or I'll be forced to break it down."

"I doubt that. It's about six inches thick. Not even you are that strong, Massimo." Nia backed further into the bedroom, just in case she was mistaken about his strength.

He lunged at the door again. This time, he swore in a foreign tongue.

"You should stop before you hurt yourself."

"If I do, would you come out and kiss my bruises?"

"I'm not falling for that, Massimo."

"Azi prepared some delicious roasted chicken. I know how much you enjoy her cooking."

Nia pressed her hands against her stomach as another series of hunger pangs ripped through her. Just like him to use her weakness against her. She wished she'd remembered to grab a snack from the kitchenette. "That's not going to work, either," she said. "We're not sharing a bed tonight. Get that through your thick skull."

"Damn it, Nia!" His fist resounded against the wood. "You're locking me out of my own bedroom. Where am I supposed to sleep?"

Nia huffed. "It's a big house, Massimo. Pick another room."

"You will pay for this, pussycat. I promise you."

Whatever punishment he was planning for her, it couldn't be worse than having to spend the night in his bed with his hands and mouth doing lewd things to her buck-naked body. Nia held her breath, waiting for more protests from him. When she heard his footsteps moving away from the door, she let it out, raced up the steps, and threw herself on the mattress.

She'd won the battle tonight, but the war was far from over.

Tomorrow would bring another round of challenges.

CHAPTER EIGHT

"The package you've been waiting for just arrived, Mr. Andretti."

Massimo glanced up from his computer screen as his executive assistant, an attractive brunette, walked over to his desk and handed him a large white envelope.

"Thank you, April." He winced as he took it from her. "What time is Mr. Lynd expected to be out of court?" he enquired of his attorney who was supposed to have delivered the papers in person.

"At around three o'clock."

"What about Mr. Dawson, have you been able to locate him yet?"

"Not yet. All I've been told is that he's away on an assignment and they're not sure when he will be available."

"Thanks, April. That will be all for now."

Massimo's brows furrowed as he leaned back in his chair and folded his arms.

Yesterday, while Nia was busy picking out her new wardrobe at the boutique, he'd called April and had her fax the Norwood file to Paul. Massimo was in the middle of his satellite conference when Paul left a message on his voicemail that he'd already discovered some pertinent information about Shaina Norwood, one of the members of the family Massimo had been looking for. Dawson thought he might have found her and promised to call Massimo with the details later that day.

By the time Massimo had a chance to return the call, the FBI agent had fallen off the face of the earth. He wondered if it had anything to do with the huge case Paul had mentioned working on. Had he gone undercover? If he had, who knows how long he'd be gone.

Massimo's lips twisted wryly. After years of searching, the one person who it seemed could help solve the case of the disappearing Norwoods was suddenly unavailable. He had no other choice but to wait until Paul reemerged to relay the information he'd discovered about Shaina Norwood. He'd waited five years. He could wait a few more days, or weeks, or even months.

In the meantime, he had more important issues to tend to, like making damn sure one particular young woman never got the chance to disappear on him. And if by some stroke of luck she did manage to escape, he was prepared to move heaven and earth to find her and bring her back to his bed where she belonged.

Massimo picked up the envelope his assistant had brought in. He winced again at the slight ache in his shoulder. Opening the flap of the envelope, he pulled out the papers and quickly scanned through the contract.

The prenup was comparable to the one he had drawn up for Dafne—with three slight changes: the size of the settlement Nia would receive when they inevitably parted ways, the number of heirs he wanted from her, and the number of years they would remain married.

He'd been lonely as an only child growing up in that huge

house. His loneliness was one of the reasons he'd formed such a tight bond with Adam and Erik, and later Bryce when he moved to Granite Falls as a teenager. His best friends were also only children. It was no fun not having siblings to fight with and connive with. Both Bryce and Erik had told him that their experiences as only children was the main reason they wanted to have as many babies as their wives would allow.

Massimo sighed. If it weren't for his father's infidelity, he would have had a little sister. She'd be around Nia's age and just as beautiful. He was certain the two of them would have become quick friends and coconspirators against him. A wishful smile curved Massimo's lips as he envisioned them doing girly things together, but he quickly pushed it away and ordered his heart not to get involved in his business with Nia Sylk.

In his will, his father had mandated that he remained married for three years and produce one heir, but Massimo was asking for no fewer than three children during seven years of marriage with Nia. He was going to test the seven-year itch myth. He had no doubts he would still be satisfying Nia sexually, and if she was still pleasing him, he saw no need for either of them to end the marriage, or stop replenishing the earth with little humans if she was willing to keep going.

Massimo was mildly grateful that Luciano had not specified that his wife be of Italian heritage as his forefathers had requested of their sons. His choice of the sacrificial lamb was completely left up to him.

As he thought about the way they'd met, Massimo realized that it was not he, but either destiny or circumstance that had chosen Nia to be that lamb. If she hadn't come looking for him, he might never have known she existed. Their paths had crossed at the right time, and whether by destiny or circumstance, they would be married—happily or not—by the end of the day.

If their marriage remained amicable and civil after seven

years, they would grow old together, watch their children become adults, marry, and have children of their own. And they would spoil their grandchildren, just like his *nono* had spoiled him.

Massimo's eyes misted at thoughts of his grandfather. He glanced around his office from which his great-grandfather, Bruno, his grandfather, Piero, and his father, Luciano, had run Andretti Industries. It had been remodeled several times over the years, and when he took over as CEO five years ago, Massimo had given the top floor of the building a complete overhaul by combining the two offices into one. The walls and floors had been gutted, and all the antique furniture had been replaced—all except the leather chair he now occupied and which had been upholstered several times over the past twenty-two years. It held too many pleasant memories, he thought allowing his mind to take a wary stroll down Memory Lane.

A year after his mother died, Luciano began grooming him to take over the company. At eleven years old, he was given an office at Andretti Industries, situated across the hall from his father and grandfather's. His assistant now occupied that space. Back then, it had been equipped with a sprawling desk and all the luxuries fit for an aspiring CEO, including a telephone, the only one in the building with a direct line to his father and grandfather's offices. His chair was extra large for a boy his size.

"Cresci in esso, quello piccolo," Nonno Piero had stated with a twinkle in his eyes as he'd brought Massimo over to the chair. Massimo smiled as he recalled the comfort and reassurance in his grandfather's touch whenever the old man ruffled his hair. He loved his grandfather and he did grow into the chair, he thought, leaning back and testing its strength.

While other children his age were engaged in sports, he was traveling the world, making business deals and orchestrating the takeover of corporations—foreign and domestic. Luciano had enrolled him in several language schools even before he could talk, so conducting business in foreign languages was a piece of cake for him.

He'd enjoyed the wheeling and dealing of the business world until around age sixteen when his grandfather died. Shortly after, his hormones kicked in and he started noticing girls. He began spending less and less time at the office and more in the back seat of his fire-red Ferrari with the girl of the night, or week, or month, depending on her level of experience. He liked them experienced. Even at that age, he knew he wouldn't be with any girl long enough to teach her the art of lovemaking.

After he'd found his father with his secretary and witnessed the pain the affair had caused his mother, perhaps even her death, Massimo had sworn that the curse of the Andrettis would end with his father.

That oath was the reason he hopped beds so frequently and ended his relationships before they began. He was never giving any woman the chance to get under his skin, nor would he allow himself to be emotionally trapped by one. But his father was determined to see him live the hell of a married man, incapable of being loyal. And now here he was, forced to marry a woman he knew had the power to turn his world upside down.

Massimo set the folder aside and left his chair. He walked over to the glass wall that afforded an unobstructed view of the Aiken River and the Presidential Range of the White Mountain National Forest.

Convincing Nia to accept his proposal would be tantamount to climbing one of those mountains barefoot in the snow with a two-hundred-pound pack on his back. But if there was one thing Massimo had proven in the business world, it was that where there was a will, there was always a way to break it.

Nia had her will. And he knew just how to break it.

Massimo smiled as he recalled Nia's brilliant move in locking him out of his bedroom last night. She had *checked* him. He could have *checkmated* her and gained access through a secret passage, but that wasn't the way he planned to capture his queen. Forgoing the comfort of a guest room, he'd camped out on the sofa in the room next door. He didn't know if Nia was mad enough to try to sneak away in the middle of the night without her two million dollars. He hadn't been willing to take that chance, but since she didn't attempt to escape he was now certain that she would stay until tomorrow night when he handed her the cash.

After eliminating all possibilities of Nia being harassed by the paparazzi, he'd left before she woke. He had a lot to accomplish and he was certain his little fugitive bride-to-be did, too. He assumed Nia thought he was having her followed, but the truth was he couldn't care less what she did within the borders of Granite Falls and the surrounding towns. He had no doubt she was quite resolute and resourceful in her endeavors to deceive him, but she would soon learn that he was not a man to be double-crossed.

He'd been chasing women since he was a teenager and he'd never met a woman who tested him, maddened him, or agitated him as much as Nia Sylk. He'd never been this excited about pursuing a woman before. He felt like a male leopard on the scent of a female, just waiting for the object of his desire to lie down in submission so he could make his move.

Their encounter would be intense and they would mate for hours on end.

The anticipation of finally trapping Nia's sexy, chocolate body under him and thrusting triumphantly into her virgin heat caused Massimo's sex to swell and pulse with vigor. The ache was so potent, he pressed his palm against his erection to ease the pain.

Massimo never knew that the need for a woman could cause such physical agony to a man. Then again, he'd never had to wait to make love to a woman before. This was a new experience for him.

Something told him that he was in for a lot of new experiences in his life. He didn't know how he felt about that.

❧

"I'm sorry, Miss, but you need a credit card to rent one of our cars."

Nia peered through her sunglasses at the young man behind the counter of the auto rental company. This was the third and last agency in the neighboring town of Evergreen she'd tried to rent from today, and had been turned down.

"I understand that..." She checked the name on his badge. "Trent, but my wallet was stolen." She was so tired of making up stories, but she couldn't use her card, or her license after Massimo made that ridiculous announcement about their impending marriage last night.

Since the names *Sylk* and *Andretti* were linked together and plastered across the headlines this morning, all she had to do was produce her name and the entire region would bow down to her. But she hadn't come to Granite Falls to be pampered and revered like an Andretti whore.

She battered her eyelashes then sighed when she realized Trent couldn't see her attempt to charm him through the dark shades. "Come on, Trent, just this once? It's just for one night." She dug through her bag and pulled out a wad of cash. "I'm willing to leave all this as collateral," she said, waving it under his nose.

Trent gave her a sympathetic, albeit, stiff smile. "You don't have a license, Miss—" He paused, obviously waiting for her to supply a name. When she didn't, he shrugged his shoulders in a dismissive manner. "We can't rent you a car without a license. Nobody will rent you a car without a license."

Nia stared at Trent as she tried to subdue the anger boiling inside her. There really was no need to get upset with him. He was just following the policies of his company and pointing out the truth. The fact was that she did look a bit shady with her dark sunglasses and the hood of her parka pulled over her head. If she were in Trent's shoes, she wouldn't lease a tricycle to someone who was dressed like her, either. In fact, she'd probably call the authorities.

Although Massimo had destroyed the only picture the reporters had managed to snap of her, she still had to take precautions. She was not the only Sylk in the world, but she was certain she was the only one in Granite Falls. Massimo hadn't given up her first name to the public, but everyone would put two and two together if they knew her last name was Sylk.

Nia stuffed the wad of cash back into her bag, walked to the door, and glanced up and down the snow-banked streets. Massimo had gone to great lengths to protect her from the public, but that didn't mean he was above having her followed. Satisfied that she was not being watched, Nia stepped out into the brisk air and hurried to the taxicab waiting on the other side of the street. She knew her cab fare would be enormous, but she couldn't drive the Mercedes around with that GPS installed in it.

"Back to Granite Falls," she said as she climbed into the back seat of the cab. As the taxi took off, she stared out the window and suppressed the need to scream as they headed north on Interstate 93.

Her day had started out promisingly when she'd awaken to find that Massimo had already left for the office. She was sure he was still furious that she'd locked him out of his bedroom last night. Probably a first for him, she thought as her mouth spread into an involuntary smile.

She'd found a sealed envelope taped to the bedroom door with a note inside from Massimo:

Nia,

I'll be home for lunch around 12:30. I cordially request your presence at the table. I will have your two million dollars with me, the first installment of our little agreement. You'll have the other two million next Tuesday as promised after we close the deal. I can't wait!

Ciao, cara.

Massimo.

Was he taking back his proposal? She'd crumbled the note in her fist. Perhaps one of his friends had talked some sense into him. What kind of man proposed to a woman just a day after meeting her? And what kind of woman said, yes? *Really.*

Not wishing to have that kind of information lying around for Azi to read, Nia had tossed the note into the fireplace. She didn't need Azi or anyone else wondering what kind of deal she'd made with Massimo for four million dollars.

Things, however, began to fall apart when she'd turned on the TV. Talk of her and Massimo dominated the local channel: *Who was the new mystery woman in Massimo Andretti's life? Was she a one-night stand from his past? Was she the affair he had while engaged to Gabrielle Berkeley? Why the rush to marry? Is she pregnant with Andretti's heir?*

Numbed with disgust, Nia had crawled back into bed with the intentions of staying there all day until she remembered that she had unfinished business in town. Retrieving her passport and money from the bank, renting a getaway car and parking it in an accessible location were at the top of her list.

The thought of running into a bevy of reporters on her way into town had made her even sicker to her stomach, but Massimo was way ahead of the game—probably from force of habit. There had been no mob on the other side of the wrought iron gate that protected the house, nor at the end of Andretti Drive, the private road that led to the estate. Instead, armed guards were stationed along Andretti Drive and Mount Reservoir Way—the road that connected the mountain to Route 80.

It was only when Nia had encountered the human barricade of more armed guards and a couple local police officers stationed at the intersection of Mount Reservoir Way and Route 80 that she fully realized the length to which Massimo would go to protect his property. He'd obviously gained the compliance of the other residents of the mountain to keep the public out. Only residents were allowed in, and since nobody knew what kind of car she drove, Nia had cruised past the crowd of reporters—some, she recognized from last night's fiasco—and headed toward downtown Granite Falls without any problems.

It both excited and scared her that any one man had that much power. It had scared her even more that she was about to deceive that very man. But it was either deceive Massimo or risk her and her brother's lives.

After leaving the Mercedes in the parking lot of a supermarket, Nia's first stop had been to the bank. She'd been a bit hesitant to go in. What if someone recognized her and sounded the alarm? Massimo wasn't there to protect her. She would have been all alone with no idea how to deal with that kind of nuisance.

She'd scanned the employees until she found an elderly man she hoped didn't keep up with the local gossip and who was oblivious to the hype surrounding her name.

She'd chosen well. The old man didn't blink an eye when she'd shown him her I.D.

Securing a reliable car that would get her to Manchester safely had proven to be a much more difficult task. If she'd foreseen this particular problem, she'd have kept the car she'd rented when she first came to town. But hindsight wasn't foresight.

"Where to, Miss?"

Nia took stock of her surroundings and realized they were approaching the exit from the highway to Granite Falls. "You can drop me off at Jakes-Rent-A-Wreck on Oak Street," she told the driver. "It's my last stop."

She'd exhausted all the decent options in Granite Falls and the surrounding towns. Not to mention the hefty cab fare she was racking up. The only option she had left was to head back to Jake's Rent-A-Wreck and hand over a sizable amount of cash for a piece of junk. She hoped the beat-up sedan—the most promising car on the lot she'd turned down this morning—was still available. Since she couldn't rent a car without identification, she would just have to talk Jake into selling her his cheapest wreck for cash—no questions asked.

When the driver pulled to a stop, Nia glanced at the meter and almost fainted. *You're doing it for Aaron,* she consoled herself. She pulled some cash from her bag, counted off the fare, plus a tip, slid open the glass partition, and thanked the driver for her patience.

As she stepped inside the barbed-wired fence of Jake's Rent-A-Wreck, the church bell began to chime out the hour. She would miss this antiquated custom when she left Granite Falls. She had just enough time to negotiate the purchase of a wreck and park it in a secluded area before heading back to the mansion to claim her two million dollars.

There was just one more detail she had to figure out: how to get two million dollars in cash out of a heavily guarded mansion and into her getaway car.

CHAPTER NINE

"I suppose it's safe to say that you enjoyed your lunch?"

"I suppose." Nia set her folded napkin on the table next to her plate and raised her gaze to meet Massimo's. "It was a good lunch," she added patting her stuffed stomach and resisting the urge to unsnap the button of her jeans and pull down the zipper, just a fraction.

"Your uninhibited appetite for food is inspiring. I love to watch you eat," he added in a lazily seductive tone, his blue eyes dazzling in the afternoon sunlight that streamed through the glass of the four-season balcony off the master suite.

Nia studied him guardedly, certain there was a lot more he would love to watch her do. "Well, if you must know, I didn't have breakfast this morning."

"Pity." His mouth pulled down into a frown. "I asked Azi to make your favorites. You especially liked her spinach quiche and sausage egg casserole, if I recall correctly from yesterday."

"You recall correctly." Nia took a sip of the tea Azi had served with their meal of pork braised in milk with carrots, mashed potato, and a side of spinach sautéed in garlic. "I was too upset to eat after I saw the news this morning. Can you believe they're wondering if I'm the woman who broke up you and Gabrielle? And the nerve of them to suggest that I'm pregnant."

"It's not that farfetched if you do the math. Many unplanned pregnancies have sent countless couples racing to the altar."

"Well, both you and I know that I'm not pregnant, and since we're not planning to start a family, it's a moot point," Nia said, swiping her wrists dismissively. The thought of Massimo Andretti's heir growing in her belly sent mixed feelings dashing through her.

"You seem rather disgusted by the thought," he said. "I do apologize for subjecting you to this madness," he continued when she didn't respond. "You came to Granite Falls for one purpose only—to sleep with me for four million dollars. I remember you specifically said that there were no strings attached. I apologize for complicating your life by announcing to the world that we would be married next week."

You have no idea how complicated you made it. Nia watched him over the rim of her mug as more bouts of confusion flowed through her. Was he playing her? "You really mean that?"

"I do, wholeheartedly," he said, placing his hand against his heart and offering her a forgiving smile. "Perhaps I got carried away with the warm welcome my friends were showering on you. Then there was my cousin grilling me about my intentions for you. I got the feeling that he was making a play for you. He has done that in the past, you know."

Nia watched him closely, trying to figure him out. If he was playing her, he was doing a damned good job of covering it up. Something told her not to trust him. It was the same something that had told her not to let Aaron tryout for his high school football team. If she'd listened to that something, she wouldn't be in this mess. "Well Erik did say you and Adam have been fighting over everything since you were kids," she said to move the conversation along.

He leaned forward and folded his arms across the tabletop. "So you can understand my reaction when the mob descended upon us. My first instinct was to protect you by informing the world, including my cousin, that you were mine."

"It's nice," Nia said, her face breaking into an unexpected grin.

"What's nice?"

"Having someone leap to my defense."

"I protect what's mine." His eyes were warm as he gazed into hers.

"You made that very clear this morning with the armed guards patrolling the roads and the police barricades at the main entrance into the mountain. Because of your protective instincts, not to mention your infinite power, I was able to spend a stress-free day." *Well, kind of.*

He studied her for a long moment before asking, "Why did you need to leave the mansion, anyway? You have everything you need here."

"Yeah right, like you didn't have me followed." Nia crossed her fingers under the table. Even though she hadn't actually seen anyone following her this morning, it didn't mean Massimo hadn't put a tail on her. She was sure his spies were trained to stay out of sight, much like Eddie's.

"I didn't," he said softly.

The gentle tone in his eyes and voice told Nia that he was telling the truth. "I had some business to take care of," she offered grudgingly.

"What kind of business?"

"Personal."

He stared at her, waiting for more.

"I needed tampons," she said derisively. "You didn't have any lying around, or did you, and I just missed them?"

He chuckled. "No, *cara*. I don't keep tampons around, and since Azi is past the age of reproduction, I suppose you had no other choice but to leave the safety of the mansion. But if you'd called, I would have been happy to stop at the drugstore on my way home and pick some up for you."

Nia giggled.

"What's so funny?" he asked with a frown.

"You, standing in the feminine aisle of the drugstore trying to figure out what kind of tampons to buy for me."

His frown deepened. "You mean there are different kinds?"

Nia was certain he was toying with her. A playboy like Massimo would surely know women had a selection of tampons to choose from, just as men had a variety of condoms to meet their individual needs.

"I guess I would have just bought one of every kind and let you choose."

"Well your thoughtfulness this morning spared you the embarrassment, and I had a pleasant tampon-purchase experience. Thank you."

"No need to thank me, Nia. I created the mess by publicizing an impending marriage between us, so it's only right I clean it up."

I wish you'd cleaned up the one you made six years ago. Better still, I wish you hadn't created one. "It takes a real man to admit that he's made a mistake, especially to the world."

"I can't make you want to marry me, Nia." He shrugged dismissively and leaned back in his chair.

"No, you can't." Nia pulled a leg up under her. "And hypothetically speaking, even if I did marry you, what would we tell our children when they asked how we met? Can you imagine sitting them down and telling them that their mother offered to sell you her virginity for four million dollars, and that you actually took her up on the offer? What scandal!"

He threw his head back and laughed out loud. The richness of his humor wrapped around Nia like warm velvet and made her heart tremble in response. His laugh was marvelously catching and soon she was chuckling along with him, reveling in the few rapturous moments of enjoyment. It felt wonderful to share laughter with him, something she never thought was possible when she set out to con him.

There was a genuinely fun side to him that made her giddy, like she was seventeen again. This is the man Nia had fantasized about for six years—one who was charming and funny. This is who she'd hoped he would be—a man who would make her laugh like her father used to make her mother laugh.

"Actually," he said, remnants of laughter still in his voice, "I think I would enjoy telling our children and grandchildren about our initial encounter. If you marry me—hypothetically speaking of course—our story would no doubt be the favorite topic of discussion at many a Thanksgiving and Christmas dinners. You would be the Pretty Woman of Granite Falls."

Nia blinked. "You've seen *Pretty Woman*?"

"Several times."

There he went, surprising her again. When she'd told him that she wanted to get to know him before they made love, Nia hadn't expected this kind of 'knowing'. In fact, she hadn't expected any kind of 'knowing' since asking for time was part of her plan to keep him at bay.

She felt herself relaxing in this simple, ordinary side of Massimo Andretti. It was a side that could easily break out of that rigid shell of a man he portrayed in his business suits. A side that could change from eating gourmet meals in his isolated castle to wolfing down hamburgers and fries at a noisy pizza joint. It was a side that could skip the business drama of the boardroom to sit beside her at the movies, holding her hand while they shared a large popcorn and a box of chocolate-covered raisins. This side of him was so appealing, it seemed more intimate than sex. It was his soul in all its meekness.

"But Vivian only asked Edward for four thousand dollars in exchange for her services for one week," he said, breaking into her thoughts.

Nia's lips pursed on a smile. "Well, she asked for four, but he bargained her down to three."

"Perhaps I should have bargained you down to three million, then?" His eyes were enigmatic, filled with mystery and enchantment.

"Vivian was no virgin," Nia stated with a frisky lift in her voice. "I deserve extra for that. Believe me, I'm worth the three million, nine hundred and ninety-seven thousand dollars extra."

"No argument there," he said with a smile.

"But Vivian managed to capture Edward's heart in the end," the romantic little girl in her added. "It goes to show that a wealthy sophisticated man can fall in love with a woman with a shameful past."

"It's a fairytale, Nia." A doleful tone crept into his voice.

"It can still happen. You don't have to be perfect for the perfect someone to love you. Edward was locked away in an emotional prison, and it took an imperfect, unexpected woman to free him from that prison. He'd had so many failed relationships, including the one with his father, that it had warped his perspective about trust, love, and happily ever after."

"If you believe so much in happily ever after, why aren't you chasing your dreams instead of playing hooker with me?"

His words and the vehemence in his voice took Nia by surprise. She particularly didn't like the word 'playing'. She shrugged off the ominous feeling. "I didn't say I believe in it. I just said it's out there for those who do believe."

A frown settled into his features and he pulled his gaze from hers. He wrapped his long fingers around his mug and stared off into the cold white vastness on the other side of the glass-encased balcony.

Nia shuddered as if Massimo had summoned the cold onto the balcony. Even the fire that had been crackling merrily nearby seemed to ebb in the chill. As she sipped the last of her tea, Nia wondered where he'd gone as much as she wondered about his change in temper.

She'd returned from her trip into town to find Massimo waiting for her in the foyer in what she considered a very cheery mood. She'd expected him to berate her for locking him out of his bedroom last night, but he'd said not a word about it, nor had he brought up the subject of marriage or their little arrangement until now.

Well, she was the one who had broached the subject, which made her even more suspicious of him. The man was a chameleon—changing from one mood or language to the other in the bat of an eyelash.

While they ate, he'd kept the conversation light by asking her about her teaching career and her life in New York City. His questions had made her sad. She loved her job and her students, and she was going to miss them so much. Massimo had also shared a little about his life growing up in Granite Falls.

He'd spoken affectionately about his grandfather, Piero, with whom he'd had a close relationship, closer than the one he'd had with his father she suspected since he hadn't even mentioned his father. Nia wondered if he hated his father for the openly multiple affairs he had while married to his mother. If her father had publicly humiliated her mother like that, she would hate him too.

Nia remembered the boyish grin on Massimo's face when he spoke of his *nono* who had taught him ice fishing, rock-climbing, gliding, deep-sea snorkeling, and a host of other skills he thought a young boy should know. A licensed pilot himself, his grandfather had taught him how to fly a helicopter, and Massimo had offered to take Nia up for a ride one day soon.

The man was complex, among other things, she thought, studying the smoothness of his olive skin stretched taut over the elegant ridges of his cheekbones, his straight, fine nose, and strong, square jawline. He was indeed a very handsome and irresistible man.

If their circumstances were different, she could see herself falling for him, loving him, marrying him and having his babies. He could so easily have been her imperfect someone. If she were honest with herself, Nia would have to admit that she was a little disappointed he'd offered to recant his announcement about their marriage.

The world would see her as another inadequate, insufficient woman who couldn't keep Massimo's attention even for a week. She would look like the fool, his latest discarded victim. Nia couldn't tell if she'd prefer being known as his unhappy wife or his jilted fiancée. Both positions were equally distasteful, but since she wouldn't be around when he made his announcement, it really didn't matter.

Nia turned her head to take in one last, lingering view of her breathtaking surroundings. When she left, she would take along this pleasant memory of sitting here with Massimo engaging in light chatter and enjoying scrumptious meals with him. She would...

Wait a minute! Nia's mind floundered as ripples of suspicion settled in her stomach. Massimo hadn't said they weren't getting married, nor had he offered to recant the announcement regarding their nuptials. He'd said that he couldn't make her want to marry him. What kind of ambiguous talk was that? His words had been carefully wrapped in neutral shades, and as she began to strip away the layers of meaning, his subtle deceit became clear to Nia. He had plans for her.

She turned to encounter a warm smile playing at the corners of his mouth. "Massimo, did you—" She held her breath and tongue as he turned his head and looked at her. It was the same unwelcome look he'd given her the first time she'd approached him in the cabin, like she'd walked uninvited onto his private, sacred stage. What affectionate memory of his had she interrupted?

"Yes, I brought the money, Nia. I did promise. I keep my promises."

"Well I wasn't suggesting—"

"Would you like to see your two million dollars?" His eyes were aglow with an ineffable emotion.

"Well, yes. I would love to see it." *Chameleon.*

Her suspicions instantly altered to relief that her charade was coming to an end, a successful one at that. She didn't have the energy to continue down this deceptive path for another day. Massimo's constant proximity was making it impossible for her to stay focused. She was suddenly grateful that he'd given her one week, instead of the four she'd initially asked for.

Nia took deep breaths to calm her jittering nerves as Massimo walked around the table toward her. Two million dollars was all she'd come to Granite Falls for. The thought of laying her eyes on all that money was enough to make her leap with joy, but she managed to hide her delight. She was so close, so close to saving Aaron's life, of giving him the life he deserved, the life their father would have provided if he were still alive.

This was her real life.

Those little stolen moments of enjoyment she and Massimo just shared were silly snippets from the infatuated heart of a seventeen-year-old girl.

That was a fairy tale.

She stood up when Massimo held her chair and moved it out of her way. He stood back and, with his hand, indicated for her to precede him into the living room of the master suite.

"This way," he said taking up the lead. "Down the hall to the vault."

Nia followed him into the hallway. It was impossible for her not to admire the tight outline of his buttocks under his trousers —he had a beautiful ass. And the way his powerful well-muscled body moved with easy grace and virility under his white silk shirt made her heart race. There was no hesitation in his step, no slouching in his mile-wide shoulders.

He was a man who knew where he was headed, one who would not be sidetracked with trivial nuisances. Nia wondered if he considered her a nuisance. Had she forced him to take a detour from his carefully planned-out life? If he did think of her that way, she wasn't making any apologies.

Hell, coming to Granite Falls was a detour for her. Her life was perfectly fine until the broken promises from his New Hampshire chicken coop came to roost on her New York doorstep.

She halted when he stopped at a door almost at the end of the hall. He'd skipped this room during the tour he'd given her two nights ago. The house was gigantic—one wing of the first floor complete with an Olympic-size swimming pool, sauna, steam room, hot tub, the works, and even a massage room. He'd also shown her his modern, fully equipped 'man cave' as he called it, where he entertained Erik, Bryce, and Adam, once in a while. They could shot pool, play mini golf, tennis, and racquetball in that cave. A spacious movie theatre and state-of-the-art surround sound stereo system had been installed for relaxing pleasure.

Massimo had told her that the first floor used to be the servants' quarters in the old days, but since he had no servants, he'd turned it into his cave. Azi occupied one of the guest rooms on the second floor where the kitchen, dining and living rooms, library, study, ballroom, and a few more unused rooms were situated. Nia had wondered why he hadn't renovated the rest of the house—probably because he spent most of his time at his lakeside villa with his lover of the week.

Nia guessed he hadn't trusted her enough then to bring her into his family vault. Did he trust her now? she wondered as he began to punch some numbers into a silver-plated electronic keypad on the wall next to the door.

"I guess this is where you keep the family jewels," she said to lighten the brooding atmosphere that had followed them from the balcony.

"Nope, I keep those in my pants." His response was as rapid as it was intimately effective, casting visions of his 'family jewels' across her mind.

"And you're welcome to see them anytime you want. I would even let you play with a couple of stones, but you'll have to be extremely careful since they're rather delicate and responsive to the touch. You don't have to wait until Wednesday, Nia. I can show them to you tonight."

Nia felt herself swimming through a haze of wanton desires as her heart hammered against her ribs. "Wednesday is good," she said, whipping those feelings into shape. "I'm getting to know multiple sides of you, and I like that. I need more time like we had at lunch. There was no pressure or expectations, just two adults enjoying a delicious meal and each other's company."

"I like that, too, *cara*. I'll have to see that we spend more quality, platonic time together." He gazed down at her with intensely warm eyes. "I never thought I'd admit this to you, or even to myself, but I'm glad you made us wait before we make love. It's a new experience for me. Perhaps good things do come to those who wait. It'll make our coming together much more phenomenal, I think."

Butterflies fluttered around in Nia's belly as an ache grew in her throat. For six years she'd fantasized about making love with Massimo Andretti, and now that she had the opportunity the unfortunate circumstances surrounding their relationship had rendered it impossible.

Why did he have to lie to her father? Why hadn't he just kept his promise?

If he hadn't lied, her inner voice argued, *you wouldn't be standing here with him right now. You are not the type of woman Massimo Andretti totes about on his arm. The real you, the insignificant daughter of a washed-up mill owner would never have attracted Massimo Andretti's attention. Who is the real 'you' anyway?*

"After you."

Nia silenced the voice of rational reasoning in her head and stepped through the door when Massimo pushed it open. It was pitch-dark for a second until he flipped a switch and flooded the room with soft light.

Nia walked further into the room. The only furniture was a marble table with four black leather chairs around it. Two walls were made up of rows of safety deposit boxes of varying sizes like those she'd find in a bank vault.

Another wall was lined with a set of black velvet drapes that extended from the black marble floor to the silver steel-finished ceiling. There were no windows in the room and the only exit was the door through which she'd entered.

Hearing a metallic click behind her, Nia turned around.

"It locks automatically when you enter and leave," Massimo said. "You have to punch in a different combination of numbers to get out," he continued, pointing at another silver-plated electronic device on the wall next to the door. "A thief might get in, but if he or she doesn't have both combinations, there's no getting out."

Nia swallowed. How the hell was she supposed to retrieve her money tonight if it was locked away in Fort Knox?

"Don't worry," Massimo stated, as if reading her mind. "You'll have the combinations. I only come in here when I absolutely have to, and Azi comes in once a week to dust and vacuum the drapes. You can come in and roll around in your dough as often as you want. Just make sure you remember the code to get out or you may find yourself locked in here for a while."

"I think I'll take it to another room and roll around in it there." She ran her hands up and down the sleeves of her aqua wool sweater. "It's kind of chilly in here."

He moved away from the door and walked in her direction. "The vault is climate and light-controlled to protect the paintings and other family heirlooms."

"I don't see any paintings, but I figure the heirlooms are stored inside there." She flared her hand at the walls of safety deposit boxes. Which one held her two million? And when was he going to end her suspense? He had to know she was dying to have that money in her possession.

He walked to the table, picked up a remote control and pressed a button. The black drapes parted.

"Wow," Nia exclaimed at the numerous paintings on the wall.

"My ancestors," he said, strolling toward the family wall. "You said you wanted to know me better. Here's your chance."

Nia drew closer for a better look. She immediately recognized some of the faces from the research she'd started on the Andretti family when she first met and fell into infatuation with Massimo. Her research had come to a halt after Massimo had broken his promise to her father. She'd stopped giving a damn about him or any other Andretti, so there was a lot she didn't know about his family history. She still didn't give a damn, but she had to pretend she cared for a few more hours.

"This is my great-great-grandfather, Luca." Massimo folded his arms and stared up at a brown-eyed, frail-looking, heavily bearded man. "He was barely a man when he left Bellagio to seek his fortune in America. He used his expertise in candle and silk production from a factory in Italy where he used to work, and started his own company in New York City."

Nia detected pride in Massimo's voice as he talked about his ancestor. She wished she could share her family history about her ancestor, Thomas, a young runaway slave who'd made his way to Maine and started his own paper mill. As far as she knew, it was the only paper mill in America that was started and owned by a black family.

Thomas had named his mill West Gate after the west gate of the plantation he'd made his escape from all those generations ago. One west gate had given him freedom; the other had brought him success. Then an Andretti had slammed it shut, destroying the dream Thomas had brought to life.

Nia knew her father had been plagued with shame at losing their family legacy. She wished she had the means to buy it back, restore her family heritage, and make her father proud. Maybe one day when Eddie wasn't a threat anymore and Aaron was settled in his life, she might find a way to buy back her family mill. In the meantime, like the saying goes, there was no point crying over spilled milk, or in this case shredded paper.

"Is that Luca's wife?" Nia asked referring to the portrait of the plump, rosy-cheeked woman next to Luca.

"Yes. That's Rigarda. She wasn't too happy about leaving her home, menial as it was, for the shores of an unknown land."

Nia thought she looked like a ghost compared to her dark-complexioned husband. There wasn't even a hint of a smile on her face, and her hazel eyes looked vacant. Women back then didn't have a lot to smile about she supposed, especially one who was forced to leave her home behind. She could so identify with Rigarda.

"She died when my great-grandfather, Bruno, was an infant," Massimo said. "It's rumored that their marriage was arranged and that she died of a broken heart, pining away for the true love she'd left behind in Bellagio."

"Thank God for the suffrage movement," Nia murmured, "or we'd still have a lot of unhappy women pining away for their true loves."

His blue eyes darkened like a cloud, heavy with rain. "Did it ever occur to you that these men were also forced into these marriages, that they too were unhappy? They didn't have the luxury of pining away when they had to make a living to support their families. Arranged marriages are archaic, but not defunct. Many cultures still practice it today."

"You're right," she said, holding his gaze, even as she wondered at the acerbity in his voice. "It's not just the women who suffer through these arranged marriages. The men do, too. I guess we should just be grateful that we live in a culture where it isn't practiced."

He pressed his lips tightly together and took a side step to the next painting. "This is Bruno."

Nia's gaze shifted to the stoic portrait of Bruno, from whom Massimo had inherited his fathomless blue eyes, she noted. He was large and bearded with a round head, thin lips, and a bulbous nose. Massimo was lucky he hadn't inherited his nose as well. As she stared at him, Nia thought he was smirking at her.

"Bruno moved Andretti Industries from New York to New Hampshire and turned it into one of the most prosperous textile factories in the world," Massimo said. "The first thing he did was purchase land on this mountain. Then he went back to Bellagio and purchased as much land as he could get his hands on. As a boy, I spent a lot of time there with my mother."

"Is that where she was from?"

"She was born and raised in Como, but she worked in Bellagio. She took the *traghetto* up and down Lake Como everyday." He paused. "I wish I'd known Bruno and my great-grandmother, Nora," he said, smiling up at the portrait of the brown-eyed, delicate-looking woman next to Bruno. "He was a shrewd businessman."

"I guess you take after him."

His eyes narrowed to glacial slits. "You think I'm shrewd, Nia?"

"I mean in a good way. You have to be shrewd to succeed and survive in this world." The fact that she was standing in front of his family wall of fame attested to her own shrewdness for survival.

He seemed to be satisfied with her response and returned to his roots. "And this is my *nono.*" An affectionate smile curved his lips.

Nia felt a warm glow flow through her when she gazed into Piero's soft blue eyes. He was tall, clean-shaven, and slightly built. Massimo had inherited his straight high nose. He was definitely smiling at her she thought. She had a feeling that if she'd met him, she would have liked him.

Last, was the tall and imposing Luciano—Massimo's father—and his brown-eyed wife. Nia stared at Luciano, the man whose death was the beginning of her family's demise. Although he'd been willing to save her father's mill, the man's personal character disgusted her. He was a cheat, like all Andretti males before him. They were incapable of fidelity, even the much-loved Piero—one fact Massimo had omitted from his walk through the pages of his family's history. Massimo's fate of being an unfaithful husband had been decided even before he was born—

simply because he was an Andretti. He couldn't even remain faithful for six months. How could anyone expect him to remain faithful for years? *Maybe that's why he has a hard time believing in love and fairytales. What's your excuse?*

Nia dismissed the annoying voice in her head with a sigh, and focused her attention on the portrait of the woman next to Luciano. Massimo's resemblance to his mother was extremely striking, especially their wide mouths and full lips. He had her smile, but while hers was soft and inviting in a reserved way, his was openly sexy and tantalizing in a predatory masculine way. Nia's eyes wandered to a painting of him—perhaps around twelve or thirteen years old. Even at that young age, she could sense the animal magnetism in him. He was undeniably a…

"I guess you've figured out that these are my parents, Luciano and Giuliana," he said, smiling down at her.

"Your mother was very beautiful," she said.

A shadow passed across his face. "She was."

Nia swore she saw his eyes mist as he gazed at the portrait of his mother. "Do you—"

"I think I've bored you long enough, *cara*." He turned his back on the wall and closed the drapes, bringing an end to talk of his family history. "I do have to conduct some business in my home office before our dinner meeting tonight."

"Thanks for sharing, Massimo. I feel much closer to you." Nia had no idea if that admission had come from her heart or if it was part of her charade. She felt as if her worlds of reality and fiction were blending into one and she couldn't tell the difference between them anymore.

"Sit here," he said, pulling out one of the chairs from under the table. "I will bring you what you came here for."

Barely able to contain her excitement, Nia dropped into the seat and watched him walk to the far right corner of the room. He placed his right hand against the side of the wall and a door swung open. He reached inside the small compartment and pulled out a key.

Nia could hear her heart drumming wildly in her ears as Massimo opened one of the safety boxes and pulled out a black briefcase. He brought it over, placed it on the table in front of her, and opened it.

Nia's eyes almost popped out of her head when she saw the rows of neatly stacked hundred dollar bills in the briefcase. She'd never seen that much cash in her life, and she knew that after she paid Eddie his million and deposited the balance into her account, she would never see that much ever again. It was a once-in-a-lifetime experience.

Just to make sure she wasn't stuck between the gray areas of reality and fiction, she ran her fingers along the top row of bills, squelching the urge to burst into happy giggles or jump up and do the happy dance at the feel of the smooth paper beneath her fingers.

She'd done it.

Her next step would be to count it out into two equal portions. Once Massimo locked himself in his home office, she'd take it back to the bedroom and roll around in it.

"It's all there," Massimo said, standing so closely to her, she could feel the heat from his body seeping into her skin. "But if you want to count it, go ahead."

Nia drew back her hand. "No. It's okay. I trust you."

"I'm glad to hear you say that you trust me, because I trust you, too. These are for you," he added, pressing the key he'd taken from the panel, and a piece of paper into her hands.

"The combinations." Nia stared at the hand-written numbers on the paper.

"You can take your time and let the fact that we're really going through with this deal sink in. Stay in here as long as you like, and when you're ready to leave, you can put the briefcase back into the safety box, and the key into the compartment with all the other keys. It's just an extra precaution in case someone manages to break into the vault."

And who the heck could break into this vault when access to this estate is damn near impossible? Plus, do you really expect me to put my key back into a compartment that opens only to your fingerprints?

"Thanks, Massimo." As Nia gazed up at him, she realized that it would be wise to at least give him a kiss, offer him a taste of what he thought he'd be getting on Wednesday. After all, she was supposed to be excited about their impending sexual encounter, but then again, he hadn't made any passes at her today, either, which caused her suspicions about him to mount again. What was he up to?

He bent down and dropped a quick kiss on her forehead before leaving.

"I don't trust you, and you shouldn't trust me, Massimo Andretti," Nia said, when the door clicked behind him.

CHAPTER TEN

"Are you sure no reporters will be there tonight?" Nia asked Massimo as the limo began its journey from the mansion to Fontaine Conference Center. She didn't need that kind of attention or distraction while she made her escape.

"I'm one hundred percent sure, *cara*. It's just a business meeting. Bryce will be there, so at least you'll know one other person besides me."

"He's a really nice man. Large, but nice," Nia stated on a smile, remembering how Bryce had planted his Goliath frame beside Massimo, Adam, and Erik to shield her from the local press. The bond of brotherhood between the four men was obvious. They didn't even know her, yet the simple fact that she was with Massimo propelled them into action at the slightest sign of trouble. She wondered if they would have been so eager to jump to her defense if they knew she was about to swindle their friend out of two million dollars. "I must remember to thank him and Erik and Adam for helping you out yesterday."

"That's what friends do. Help each other in times of need."

"Have you ever been in need, Massimo?" Nia studied his profile in the dimly lit limo. He'd shared a lot of himself at

150

lunch, but there was still so much she didn't know about him. *Why do you care? You're leaving in a little bit.* "You were born with the proverbial silver—" She paused. "No, in your case, platinum spoon in your mouth. What could you possibly have ever been in need of?"

"Plenty." There was a faraway, almost regretful tilt to his tone. "And I have been lucky enough to have friends who have come to my rescue time and time again. What about you? You spoke a lot about your students today, but nothing about friends or family. Do you have friends you can count on, Nia?"

She'd deliberately not talked about her friends and family. The less Massimo knew about her, the less likely it would be for him to find her once she left this town behind. "I get on with my coworkers," she said on a shrug.

"Just get on? Do you ever go out together—to the movies, dinner, drinks?"

"Sometimes." Not nearly enough as she would have loved. With a teenage boy to support and keep out of trouble, there just wasn't time for anyone or anything else in her life. If she'd had time for boyfriends, the chances she'd still be a virgin were slim— a fact she was grateful for since it was the only reason Massimo had accepted her proposal.

She sucked in her breath when Massimo reached out and picked up her hand that was lying on the seat. He laced his fingers through hers as if it were a natural thing for him to do.

"I could be your friend, you know. You can tell me anything, anything at all, *cara.* Everything that's wrong in your life, I'll make right again, or at least try to."

Can you bring my father back from the dead?

Nia blinked back the tears that stung the back of her eyes. She could not let Massimo's all-of-a-sudden gentle attitude get to her. Yes, they'd spend a pleasant afternoon together, but she knew better than to trust the devil. She had no idea what it was, but she was certain he had his own plans to sabotage her escape tonight, a plan she was certain he'd put into place the day they met.

In spite of his suspicions about her, he'd adhered to their agreement. She had the money in her possession; now all she had to figure out was how she was going to get from Fontaine Conference Center back to the house to retrieve the briefcase, and then back into town and her getaway car. She couldn't just walk out of the Center since she knew Massimo would have his guards posted at the exits. But she was sure the answer to carrying out the final details would come to her by the end of dinner.

"What about family?" Massimo interrupted her escape mapping. "Do you have any?"

Nia cleared her throat. "No... No... I'm an only child."

"We have something in common, then. We're both alone in the world. I've been alone since my father died. We weren't close," he added, a steely edge drifting into his voice. "I didn't agree with many of his principles or choices. We fought frequently, but he was the only family I had after my mother and my grandfather died." His fingers tightened around hers.

"I know your mother died while giving birth to your baby sister," she said. The story about the death of the wife of the textile tycoon, Luciano Andretti, was public knowledge. Nia had read about that period of Massimo's life on the Internet. He was only ten. No details of her death had been leaked to the public. "What happened? Was something wrong with the baby?"

Nia watched his Adam's apple vibrate above the knot of his black tie as he fought to control some emotion. "If you don't want to talk about it, I understand."

"Mom went into premature labor." His voice faded, losing some of its steely edge. "She started hemorrhaging and died half an hour after giving birth. Aria's lungs weren't developed enough and she followed within seconds. It was the longest thirty minutes of my life." He paused and swallowed. "Even after twenty-four years, I still miss her. I feel as if I was robbed of the most important person in my life."

Nia knew exactly how he felt. She was twelve and Aaron was seven when their mother died from a brain aneurysm. It was the saddest day of her life. She'd stood at her mother's bedside, along with her father and brother, praying for a miracle as the life ebbed slowly out of her.

The ensuing six years were difficult. She'd felt her father's love for her and Aaron. He took exceptional care of them, making sure they never wanted for anything, but he was never the same after her mother died. Gone was the comical, teasing father she'd known—the one who used to chase her and Aaron around the house, climb the willow tree in their backyard with them when they were hiding from their mother, color with them, and who, when she was really little, would let her put makeup on his face, barrettes in his hair, and paint his nails glittery pink when they played dress-up. And when she'd gotten her period for the first time, he'd sat her down and told her about sex. He was a remarkable father.

A strong, remarkable man who'd been broken by Massimo Andretti. Nia remembered the many nights she'd lain awake and listen to her father cry after he lost the mill. She'd cried along with him, and when morning came they tucked their pain away and went about their day, keeping up appearances for Aaron's sake. He was too young to be burdened with the dismal uncertainty of their future.

Then there were times Nia had watched her dad staring off into space with a smile on his face. His brown eyes would light up as if he could see her mother. It was the same smile she'd seen on his face when she stood at his side and watched him take his last breath. He was finally at peace with the love of his life—forever. Now that was a fairy tale that had come true.

Her father's death was the beginning of a life of difficulty and turmoil for her and Aaron. Her father didn't have medical insurance and the hospital had come after her, his next of kin. To add to her woes, child welfare services had placed Aaron in a foster home because they'd been staying in a homeless shelter when their father died. The first chance she got, Nia had taken Aaron and fled Maine, leaving child welfare services and that medical bill behind. She hadn't known about Eddie until a short while ago.

Taking a deep breath, Nia forced her emotions under control. If she continued evoking memories of her past, she just might break down and cry and she couldn't do that in front of Massimo, the man who'd made her an orphan and caused her a lifetime of heartache.

"How old were you when you lost your parents?" Massimo asked, caressing the inside of her wrist with his fingers.

She sucked in her breath at the currents whipping through her body. "My mother died from a brain aneurysm when I was twelve and my father passed away a few years ago." Nia clenched her teeth tightly as she felt her body begin to shake. She tried, but she could no longer hold back the tears that rolled down her cheeks.

Massimo's arms immediately circled her and she found herself cradled against his huge frame, her cheek resting on his chest. She felt as safe and cherished as she used to in her father's embrace. She was very much aware of the steady beating of Massimo's heart beneath her ears as she fought back her grief. It was soothing. It made her want to lay down her arms at his feet, end the war, and surrender completely to him. But she couldn't. *He was the enemy.*

Nia gathered the strength to pull herself together and

struggled out of Massimo's arms. She pulled a napkin from a holder close to her and dabbed at her eyes. She'd ruined her makeup, but that was the least of her problems tonight. She took a deep steadying breath and straightened her shoulders. "I'm fine now."

"Our experiences are very similar, *cara*," he said taking her hand again. "We both lost our mothers at very tender ages and were raised by our fathers."

Nia never thought of them in that way. She never thought of them in any way, except when she was a doting teenager and thought he was God's gift to women.

"Was he a loving father to you? Did you have a good relationship?"

"He was the best," she said, her mind flooding with happy memories.

His mouth curved with tenderness. "It's a frightening feeling being alone in the world. Perhaps we could find a way to help each other heal. Alleviate each other's loneliness?"

Nia's guard snapped back into place as the grand seducer was unmasked. She pulled her hand from his. "You of all people should know that sex doesn't fill the void in anyone's life, Massimo. If it could, you wouldn't be lonely still."

Was that why he had so many affairs? Was he searching for someone or something to fill the void in his life? Did he move so quickly and frequently between women because he couldn't find fulfillment from any of them? The man's life seems to be an eternal quest. She was just another prescription in his search for a cure for whatever ailment he was suffering from.

"You're wrong, *cara*. My interest in you is more than sexual." His eyes were filled with warmth and passion as he leaned closer to her. "I will prove it to you one day."

"How?"

"I don't know, yet."

"There's actually something the omniscient Massimo Andretti doesn't know?"

He sighed and leaned back into the seat. "Yes, Nia, there are quite a few things in this life that baffle me. But," he added with a note of determination in his voice, "I know that one day, you will grow to like me."

"What makes you think I don't already like you?"

His bushy brows arched upward. "Do you?"

Nia turned her head and gazed out at the dark moving shadows as the limo sped along the highway. Truth is, she was beginning to like Massimo Andretti—the one she'd spent the afternoon with. And just now when he shared his pain with her, Nia felt herself warming to him in a very unexpected way. Instinct told her that she was the first woman with whom he'd talked about his mother.

Knowing that he'd shared an intimate part of himself should give her a sense of empowerment, but instead it had become an awakening experience that left her reeling in an ever-vaster sea of confusion. When she left Brooklyn to find him, there was only one thing she'd wanted from him: two million dollars. She had the money and she was just hours away from ridding herself of her nemesis, but the harder she tried to ignore the truth, the more it persisted.

She needed Massimo's money to save her and Aaron's life, but deep down in her heart, Nia knew she wanted more from him, had always wanted more from him. The feelings she thought she had for him for the past six years weren't anger and hate at all. She'd been infatuated with him, and now that infatuation was rapidly turning into something else. Something she dared not put a name to.

"You look very beautiful, Nia."

At the sound of his husky voice, Nia turned and gazed up into his coral blue eyes—tranquil now. Blushing under the intensity of his gaze, she glanced down at the black evening dress he'd picked out for her to wear tonight.

It was simply elegant with an off-the-shoulder neckline that was accented with tiny pearls and sparkling sequins. It had an empire waist that extended into a soft flowing skirt that swept the floor. Each time she moved, Nia was aware of the soft fabric caressing her legs and ankles. She ran her hand down the sheer long sleeves and across the bodice that were perfectly detailed with the silkiest black appliqués.

The dress was beautiful, and it made her feel feminine and desirable. Massimo had asked her to wear her hair down and so her long wavy mane cascaded off her bare shoulders and lay against her back like a lustrous satin drape—at least that's how he'd described it when he saw her.

"The credit is all yours, Massimo," she said, turning to face him again.

His face lighted into an appreciative smile. "Ah, I can't take all the credit. It probably wouldn't look half as good on another woman. It's perfect for you and on you. I'll be the envy of every man tonight."

Heat warmed the surface under Nia's skin as she remembered the look of enthrallment on his face when he'd stood at the bottom of the stairs gazing up to where she stood at the top. She'd felt like a princess and her breath had caught in her throat as Massimo, looking irresistible and devilishly handsome in his black silk suit, snow-white silk shirt and black tie, had ascended the stairs toward her. She'd almost fainted from sheer bliss when he took her hand and escorted her downstairs.

She was Cinderella on her way to the ball with her handsome prince, but at the stroke of midnight, she'd be gone.

Things could have been different, she thought, recalling the day Massimo had visited the mill shortly after his father died. He'd seemed sincere in his promises, especially the one to stop by the mill regularly to keep abreast of its renovations. His words had given her hope that they would later meet during one of his visits.

Her stilettos weren't made of glass, Nia thought, bringing her thoughts back to the present, but she would leave one on Massimo's nightstand to remind him of the woman who'd duped him. "You have exceptional taste, Massimo," she said, giving him a smile, and deciding then to enjoy the rest of the evening until she could vanish quietly into the night.

"In clothes, or women?"

"Both. I have to give you that," she answered with a hint of modesty. "At lunch you briefly mentioned that the meeting tonight had to do with energy production, and a company you and Bryce started together," she said, to change the subject to something less personal.

The lacy panties Massimo had placed on the bed for her to wear were already wet. She'd been trying to ignore the spasmodic little tremors and electric bolts of desire that had been crashing through her body since Massimo told her she looked beautiful. Or perhaps they'd begun an hour ago when she slipped the lacy panties over her hips, knowing full well that Massimo's hands had been all over them. Her sex pulsed as if he were stroking his long fingers across her soft flesh. "You didn't elaborate, though."

"I didn't want to bore you with the details."

He was probably tired of women falling asleep when he tried to tell them about his business, what he did on a day-by-day basis. "I wouldn't be bored, and since you demanded that I accompany you, I think I should know a little bit about what's going on. I don't want to seem like a total idiot during light conversation."

He uttered a short chuckle. "Ah, Nia, one thing I would never mistake you for is an idiot."

Nia frowned at his compliment. *Was it a compliment?*

"But since you asked, Fonandt Energy is the largest and most productive wind farm in the Northeast. Bryce and I are thinking of expanding nationally and eventually globally, of course."

"Of course," Nia concurred with a shrug.

He absorbed her sarcasm with a smile and continued to hold her gaze steady. "In a nutshell, something needs to be done about global warming. Bryce and I, along with several other wind farm owners from the US and around the world are convening to address alternatives to energy. Dignitaries from several third-world countries will also be attending, mainly to choose a company like Fonandt Energy to service their countries' needs, whether to build, aid, or takeover the operations of current inefficient and unproductive farms."

You'd probably want to takeover.

"In the past year Bryce and I, like our competitors, visited several of these countries to gauge the possibilities for wind energy. It would be life-changing for people in undeveloped countries to receive the gift of light, indoor plumbing, and clean water—basics of life that are too expensive now." His voice rang with enthusiasm and conviction. "Bottom line: at the end of the evening only one company will have the contracts to service these countries. Of course, Bryce and I want that company to be none other than Fonandt Energy."

"That's a good cause," Nia said, noting the pale blue rays around his iris brighten. "Global warming is a huge problem, and if nothing is done to reverse, or at least control its effects on our atmosphere, there won't be a world to leave to future generations."

"Precisely. As you know, Andretti Industries owns numerous factories throughout the world. I proposed investing in wind farms and geothermal energy to both my father and grandfather, years ago. I pointed out the benefits for our mill employees working in safer, cleaner environments. They thought it was too costly to initiate such a project. I was furious at their lack of concern for the planet, especially when our factories contribute so much to the depleting ozone layer every single day."

"Not to mention the chemical waste that needs to be disposed of properly on a daily basis. At the rate we're going, planet earth will eventually become a giant chemical waste dump if we do nothing to stop the destruction," Nia supplied.

"I'm surprised you're so passionate about the subject, *cara*. The women with whom I associate—" He stopped and took a deep breath. "The women with whom I *used* to associate cared only about the latest clothes, hairstyle, and diet and exercise fads. Although I sense that you far exceed any other woman I've known in beauty, brains, and personality—a fact that touches me deeply, I would never have thought of you as an environmentalist. I'm impressed," he added on a soft and gentle note. "Something else we have in common."

Nia dropped her gaze at both his curiosity about her eco-friendliness and his compliment that placed her above all the other women in his life. If he only knew he was about to eat those sweet words, he'd have a stroke.

"Well, I'm not a tree-hugger or anything like that," she said, deliberately avoiding a response to his praises. "But I've always been conscious about waste disposal." Wind farm energy had always been of significant interest to her father. Nia remembered his disappointment when Luciano had crushed the idea during the negotiations between Andretti Industries and West Gate Mills. "For as far back as I can remember, my family has always recycled. We drank tap water and my mother never used plastic wrap or aluminum foil. She sewed her own reusable shopping bags—some of which I still use today. What you're doing is admirable. It's nice of you to care."

"And why wouldn't I care?"

Because you didn't six years ago. If you'd only taken the time to speak with my father, you would have found that his concerns about our planet mirror yours. I could even see you two becoming great business partners, even friends. "Most tycoons couldn't care less about our planet. I suppose greed and ignorance are what drive their indifference for the welfare of the universe."

"I think I should give you the floor tonight instead of letting you leave with the other spouses after dinner. With your—"

Nia put her hands up to silence him. "Thanks for the vote of confidence, but I'll stick with the spouses. You said Bryce's wife, Kaya, would be there. I missed the opportunity to meet her and Michelle last night."

"Unfortunately Kaya will not be present. One of the twins isn't feeling well. When I spoke with her this afternoon, she asked me to pass along her regrets."

Nia tried to suppress her elation. She was certain she would have liked meeting Kaya Fontaine, but the fewer people she bonded with, the easier it would be for her to melt into obscurity once she left Granite Falls.

"You'll meet her on Sunday," Massimo said.

Only if she'll be a passenger on the Royal Caribbean cruise ship. "I'm looking forward to it," she lied without batting a lash.

"I'm glad it's you who's accompanying me tonight. I couldn't ask for a lovelier date. The woman I'd planned on taking can't hold a candle to you, pussycat."

It was the first time he'd called her pussycat all day. Unexpectedly, it didn't bother her like it had before. In fact, she almost liked it, except... She gave him a level look. "Massimo, were you already in another relationship when I approached you?"

"No. *She's* one of those friends-in-need I mentioned earlier."

"Good, because I wouldn't want to get my eyes scratched out or my hair pulled from the roots by some jealous, jilted lover."

"Something tells me you're quite capable of taking care of yourself, Nia Sylk."

She giggled. "Yeah, I can take care of myself. Been doing it since my father died. But since I never had a boyfriend, I never had to deal with that kind of jealously."

"And you wouldn't with me. I may have been a playboy, Nia, but I was always monogamous."

"So the rumors about you cheating on your fiancée aren't true?"

"There was no infidelity on my part. Gabby and I broke up for a completely different reason—reasons I do not care to discuss since it concerns no one but her and me."

That, Nia surmised was probably true. No one could ever accuse Massimo Andretti of infidelity. He was faithful to his lovers. But then again, all his affairs were short-lived. It was very unlikely that he could be faithful to a wife who would be around for a much longer period of time. "So why don't you tell the truth about the breakup and restore your reputation?"

"What reputation?" His lips curved into a smile.

"You like people thinking you're a jerk, don't you?" She absentmindedly toyed with a diamond-studded onyx earing in one earlobe.

"I don't care what people think of me, *cara*. It's what I do that matters. My actions and what I know in my heart to be true are what count. I always try to do right by people."

Really?

"What good would it do anyway?" He threw his hands in the air dismissively. "It's all in the past. Gabrielle has gone on with her life, and so have I. Speaking of which—" He shoved his hand into the right pocket of his jacket and pulled out a small black velvet box. "I would like you to wear this tonight." He flipped the box open.

Nia's eyes bulged and her mouth dropped open at the sight

of the huge sparkling diamond ring. She pressed her hand against her palpitating chest. "Massimo, we spoke about this marriage thing this afternoon."

"I understand. But last night I announced to the world that we were getting married. Since I haven't yet recanted, it would seem very odd to my associates if my intended wife weren't flashing a large diamond on her finger. I'm an Andretti. It's what's expected of me."

"I'm not that kind of woman. Material things don't matter to me."

"That's a quality I find fascinating." He pried the diamond from the box and reached out a hand for hers. "Wear it tonight. Indulge me."

Nia pursed her lips as she gazed at the diamond. "If I do this for you, I want something in return."

"Ah, pussycat, you're finally learning the art of negotiating. You should come work for me. You'd be a valuable asset to Andretti Industries."

His white teeth dazzling against his olive skin reminded Nia of the photo of Jabari in pursuit of the female he'd later conquered and pinned beneath him.

"What do you want?" he asked, his voice and eyes full of expectation.

"You stay out of my bed until it's time to consummate our arrangement."

A puzzled frown replaced the grin on his face, and for a moment Nia thought he would decline, but his features eventually relaxed. "Okay. I promise to stay out of your bed until it's time to consummate our arrangement."

Satisfied, Nia allowed him to slip the ring on her finger.

Triumph twinkled in his eyes and he bowed his head and kissed the sparkling jewel. "Perfect fit," he whispered, taking her coat from the seat next to him and draping it over her shoulder.

As they came to a stop, Nia couldn't deny the evidence any longer, and so admitted the truth graciously to herself: Massimo Andretti wasn't the lying, deceitful, uncaring asshole she'd thought him all these years. He had his issues with relationships with the opposite sex, but other than that, he'd matured into an admirable man who could change the world for the better. He wasn't set apart, but like her and everyone else, he suffered from pain and loss and loneliness—but never a lack of confidence and authority, she noted as her heart fluttered away. He cared about people, the universe of which she was a part.

He didn't care about your father, and he's dead.

But people change. They deserved second chances, don't they?

Your father will never have a second chance, but you and Aaron will after tonight. Stick to the plan.

"Vieni, cara, mia."

Nia silenced the voices in her head and glanced up at Massimo standing at the door of the limo with his hand outstretched to her. She picked up her clutch with one hand and placed the other in Massimo's. Like Massimo had promised her, there were no reporters with flashing cameras lurking in the courtyard.

As she stepped into the luxurious warmth of Fontaine Conference Center, Nia felt a multitude of eyes on her, but she stood tall and proud as Massimo slid her coat from her shoulders and handed it to the attendant waiting at the door. As she gazed back at the curious faces of the women seated on the plush sofas and the open admiration of the men standing nearby, Nia unexpectedly found herself reveling in the fact that she was the woman on Massimo Andretti's arm tonight.

Nia smiled up at him when he took her arm and laced it through his. Her heart began pounding at his nearness, of the warmth seeping through their clothes, and the effect of his soft touch on her wrist.

"I hope you and Bryce win tonight, Massimo," she said for lack of something better to say, or perhaps it was to prevent her from saying something stupid.

"*Grazie,* Nia." He pulled her close, pressed his warm lips to her forehead and whispered, "Now let's go save the universe."

Massimo paced the hallway outside the ladies room. He'd been in the middle of negotiations when April texted him that Nia had left the lounge where the guests who weren't involved in the negotiations had convened after dinner. A local band provided entertainment as they socialized and hopefully formed new friendships.

Although his guards were patrolling all exits from the building, Massimo was taking no chances. A drop-dead beauty like Nia could convince even the most resolute, intellectual man to exchange his soul for one nibble of her exquisite delights. When it came to women like Nia, men were weak and often stupid, himself included—and Nia was no dummy. She was intelligent and calculating.

Massimo liked to tell himself that it was his suspicions about Galen that had compelled him to take Nia up on her proposal, but he knew better. He'd been hooked from, "*Beautiful day for skiing, isn't it?*" Or was it, "*I enjoy watching other people*"? Or could it be, "*I want to be your lover*"? Whichever. Point was: he'd been hooked.

His guards, most of whom had more muscle than brains, could easily fall under her spell. One bat of her sweeping lashes and a flash of her alluring smile would have them considering the possibilities. The fact that they could easily fall victim to Nia's

Machiavellian plan was one of the reasons Massimo had requested April's 'tailing' services tonight.

Considering that he had his own plan in motion, he could have just let Nia leave. But he knew she would probably have called a taxi, and the last thing he wished was for her to fall prey to the paparazzi again. The thought of a pack of crazy reporters chasing her along the dark country roads was too troubling. If she wanted to skip out, it was best she did so in the limo with a driver he trusted.

So the moment he received April's text, Massimo had left the conference room and practically ran across the center toward the vicinity of the lounge. He'd gotten there in time to see Nia disappear into the ladies' room on the other side of the hall. He'd called out to her, but she'd either not heard him or simply decided to ignore him.

Massimo dropped his weight into one of the two sofas nearby and allowed his mind to travel back to their afternoon together. Sharing lunch with her on the balcony had brought back so many memories of his childhood—most poignant was sitting on his mother's lap as she read to him from his favorite children's books.

He'd envisioned Nia reading to their children while he watched from the doorway like his father used to do. He could easily get used to such tender moments—sharing quiet meals and enlightening conversation with his wife.

Massimo sighed at the ease with which he'd opened up to Nia and told her about the day his mother died. Dafne was the only other woman with whom he'd ever shared those moments. He closed his eyes as memories of that rainy day came unbidden to the surface of his mind.

His parents had just eaten lunch together in a private little room of their own. Massimo remembered his mother receiving a phone call shortly after his father returned to the office. He remembered the ghostly look on his mother's face as she dropped the receiver then collapsed on the floor. Up to this day, Massimo had no idea who that call was from or what the caller had told his mother. All he knew was that whatever news his mother had received, it had sent her into early labor and ultimately to her grave.

When they returned from Kenya after scattering his mother's ashes, his father had locked the door to that special room and never crossed the threshold again. For the past twenty-four years, Azi was the only person who went in there to dust and ventilate once in a while. Massimo had often wondered if the memories of that room were too painful for his father. Could it be that he had indeed loved his wife, but was too stubborn or too proud to admit it?

Remorse was the only emotion Luciano had needed to show in order to redeem himself in Massimo's eyes. He just wanted him to say he was sorry for his affair with Judith Carmichael, and for betraying his wife. But Luciano refused to grant him that tiny favor.

Even though he'd been unfaithful, his father had been loving and gentle with his mother, but according to a conversation Massimo had overheard between his father and his grandfather, Luciano had admitted that he'd told his wife he loved her three times, only: the day he'd asked her to marry him, the day of their wedding, and the day Massimo was born. Luciano had loved Giuliana for considering him as a potential mate, for finally accepting him, and for giving him an heir—the three most significant events of his life.

Massimo sighed. He had to admit that his father had his faults, but cruelty was not one of them. Luciano was a philanthropist, but most people never knew that about him. He gave away grocery gift cards to families in need. He paid off student loans and medical bills for the uninsured and poorly insured. He gave money to young entrepreneurs to jumpstart their businesses—Joanne Lambert, owner of Joanne's Boutique was one of them, and he took others under his tutelage. Bryce had been his favorite.

Massimo remembered asking his father why he wished to remain anonymous when he performed those acts of kindness for the ordinary citizens of Granite Falls. *"If you let people know you have a heart, they'll try to break it,"* Luciano had responded.

Did his father's belief extend to his mother?

Massimo looked up as he heard the door to the ladies' room open. The woman who came through it wasn't Nia, but one he recognized from dinner. She smiled at him and hurried on her way, her dress making a swishing sound behind her.

He pushed to his feet and began pacing again. He'd followed his father's advice when he'd bought West Gate Paper Mill, one of the factories Spencer's actions had caused to collapse. He'd implemented the renovations his father had promised and then some, rehired all the employees, raised their salaries, and increased their benefits. It was a thriving mill now, better than it had ever been. And he'd kept the name Andretti out of the contracts. Remorse was a sign of guilt and he was neither guilty nor remorseful. He had nothing to be ashamed of when it came to that Maine mill. Nobody knew who owned it, and he meant to keep it that way until…

Massimo stopped his pacing when he saw Nia emerge from the bathroom. His heart began to pound so hard, he was afraid it would rip right through his ribcage. Dear God, no woman had ever come close to having this kind of effect on him—making him weak and speechless. He stood transfixed as she began walking toward him in what felt like very slow motion.

Her wide-eyed expression told him she was surprised if not a bit annoyed to see him. She looked ravishing in her dress, her breasts pulled nice and high under the sheer fabric of the bodice.

His eyes wandered to the pair of diamond studs in her ears. Except for the glittering rock on her finger, the earrings were the only jewelry she wore.

The pair was a Tiffany original and has been part of the Andretti wives collection for generations. The collection consisted of pieces by Harry Winston, Buccellati, and Van Cleef & Arpels, to name a few of the finest jewelers in the world. Massimo's mother was the last Andretti wife to wear the earrings, and Massimo decided that they looked perfect on Nia—the next Mrs. Andretti.

From the way the eyes of the other men had kept wandering back to her during dinner, Massimo knew he was the envy of every man here tonight. He'd heard under-breath comments about Nia's smooth and impeccable chocolate skin, her mesmerizing almond-shaped eyes and her sexy body. He'd even heard a Texan remark that she was too good for Massimo. Massimo had smiled at the truism.

Nia might be too good for him, but she was unmistakably good *for* him. He'd only known her for three days if he counted the day he met her, yet he was already feeling the effects of the changes her presence in his life was having on him. There were a lot of beautiful single women at dinner tonight, yet he hadn't lusted after any of them—not even a little. But each time his eyes connected with Nia's his heart stopped beating.

Being complimented for having a gorgeous woman on his arm was nothing new to Massimo, but he could never remember feeling the sense of pride and completeness he felt at knowing that the world knew Nia belonged to him.

"*Cara,*" he said, when she stopped in front of him.

"What are you doing here?" She frowned up at him then pressed her palm against her stomach and closed her eyes on a sharp intake of air.

Ignoring her question, he placed his hand over hers then

drew back quickly as a swift fire rushed through his gut. "Are you not feeling well?"

"Not really. Must be something I ate."

"I'd agree with you if you'd actually eaten something." She'd hardly touched any of the four courses they'd been served at dinner. Very unlike Nia, who so loved to eat. "What's wrong?"

She took a deep breath. "I'll be fine. Just go on back to your meeting." She winced and pressed her stomach again.

"Oh, pussycat." Massimo placed his hands on her shoulders. "Is it that time of the month for you?"

"That's personal." Her eyelids crash-landed.

He placed a finger under her chin and forced her to meet his gaze. "We'll be lovers in a few days, Nia. Nothing can be more personal than that."

She tugged her chin free and took a step back from him.

"So, is it?"

"Yes. I usually have a bit of discomfort in the beginning. I'd like to leave early, if it wouldn't cause problems for you."

He searched her eyes. She'd told him that she'd gone into town this morning to purchase tampons. *Was she telling the truth or was it a cover for the real reason she needed to leave the safety of the mansion?* She had her two million dollars, so she had no reason to remain in Granite Falls. And tonight presented the perfect opportunity for her to make her escape while he was otherwise occupied.

"If you're not feeling well, you should go home," he said, deciding to indulge her since he knew a little tummy ache won't get in the way of her plans. She was a cunning little pussycat.

Her gaze shifted toward the door of the lounge as music, chatter, and laughter seeped from inside. "I don't want to jeopardize your chances for securing the contracts for Fonandt Energy."

"You're more important than anything else that's going on in my life right now, *cara*." He drew her close and pressed her face into his chest. She had no idea how true that was. He hugged her tighter, bathing himself in her warmth and the exhilarating ginger scent of her hair. He was so looking forward to making sweet slow love to her tonight, but if she had her period, he might have to wait to plant his heir inside her. A couple weeks won't matter that much.

Massimo glanced up when the door opened.

April stuck her head out. "Mr. Andretti. I was just about to go—"

"April." He quickly interrupted her, knowing what she was about to say.

"Is everything okay?" she asked, her gaze dropping to Nia in his arms.

"Nia isn't feeling well. She'll be heading home early."

"I can drive her, and stay with her until you get home," she offered, stepping into the hallway and closing the door.

Nia struggled out of his embrace. "That won't be necessary, April. Azi is home. She'll take care of me."

"Yes," Massimo said, liking that she'd referred to the mansion as home. What she didn't know was that it was Azi's night off. She was out at the movies with Erik's housekeeper. "Nia doesn't need a babysitter."

"But thanks for your offer," Nia added, giving April a sweet smile.

April stared at him, waiting for his instructions.

"I'll see Nia to the car. Please give them her apologies," he added, jutting his head toward the door.

"Will do, boss. I hope you feel better soon, Nia."

"Thanks, April, and it was really nice meeting you," Nia said.

As he led Nia toward the front entrance of the building, Massimo pulled out his cell and speed-dialed his driver. He collected her coat from the coatroom attendant, and by the time he guided her through the automatic glass doors, John was waiting in the courtyard. He opened the door when he saw them approaching.

"I'll be home as soon as the meeting is over," Massimo said as he helped her into the back seat.

"Take your time. I'm not going anywhere."

Massimo smiled at her blatant lie. He leaned into the limo and brushed his lips against hers, solely for the benefit of his driver and a couple men near the entrance who'd come outside for a smoke. He'd announced their engagement last night, and she was wearing his ring tonight, so they'd better act as if they were in love, or at least in lust. "I'll see you at home, *cara*."

He attempted to pull back when Nia threw her arms around his neck. She pulled him close and his heart catapulted to his throat when she glued her warm, moist lips to his.

CHAPTER ELEVEN

Nia's passionate kiss was the last thing Massimo expected, but he wasn't going to stop her. He was a man on the edge who'd been without a woman for weeks. So when her soft lips parted beneath his, he slid his tongue inside her mouth and gently probed the roof with the tip of his tongue. When she sighed and opened wider, he twirled his tongue around hers, slowly and fervently.

As the surprise wore off and the heat built inside him, Massimo fought against his desire to increase the pace and show Nia just how intense his passion for her had grown over the past three days. Most women welcomed his avaricious appetite in bed, but he held himself in check because he didn't want to scare his inexperienced wife-to-be, especially since he had to convince her to marry him before the night was over. But then again, it probably wasn't a bad idea to give her a little initiative.

"Take a walk, John," he commanded his driver before slamming the limo door, blocking out the world and the courtyard lights. The windows were heavily tinted and the car was soundproof, so he didn't have to worry about nosy passersby as he showed Nia just how fantastic making love with him could be.

He pushed her coat off and, wrapping his arms about her, Massimo slumped back against the seat and spread-eagled her atop him with her dress bunched up around her waist and her legs straddling his thighs. Recalling an embarrassing situation where he'd had to walk back into a meeting with a wet crotch after a bathroom quickie, Massimo set Nia on the seat again.

"One second," he said at the confusion in her eyes. He hurriedly shrugged out of his jacket, unbuckled his belt, unzipped his fly, and shucked his trousers halfway down his thighs. He circled Nia's waist, and lifting her up, he settled her on the hard ridge of his shaft. He gathered the material of her dress and tucked it into the bottom of her bra, leaving her middle section bare for his viewing pleasure.

She pressed her hands against his chest, threw her head back, and began to slide back and forth on top of him. "Make love to me, Massimo. I want you. I want you," she whispered as a series of sharp gasps burst from her throat.

The husky request was enough to drive Massimo crazy, but he held himself in control.

The soft ceiling lights allowed Massimo a wistful view of Nia's taut flat belly, and the erotic place where their sexes were connected. One deft swipe of the waistband of his briefs and one swift flip of her panty crotch and he'd be sheathed inside her tight hot flesh.

With a groan, his gaze came to feast on her hard nipples pushing against the thin material of her dress. It was with great effort that he thwarted his desire to unzip her dress, release her luscious mounds from the constriction of her bra and suck them into his mouth.

When his name spilled from her lips, he shifted his gaze to her enchanting face. Her eyes were closed and her long thick lashes were spread like black fins on her cheekbones. Her rosy lips were parted and her little pink tongue darted nervously back and forth across them. She was sex itself.

He caressed her silky legs, trailing his fingers higher and higher to the softer flesh of her thighs. She whimpered as his eager hands climbed higher still, seeking out the rounded softness of her derrière. He'd love to slip an exploratory finger inside her, but that was pushing it—pushing him. Cupping her buttocks, he pulled her into him as he thrust upward.

She bucked again and again as more ragged sighs erupted from deep inside her.

Powerless to resist the urge any longer, Massimo unzipped her dress and slid it off her shoulders and down her arms. He reached inside her bra and cupped her naked breasts, kneading the swollen flesh in his palm and squeezing her smooth nipples until they turned to little pebbles between his fingers.

Massimo could not remember ever being this hard, ever experiencing the kind of heat that was now sizzling in his belly, the fire burning in his loins and swirling along his veins. He was a volcano on the verge of eruption. It took every ounce of control in his body not to grant Nia's wish, spread her out on the seat and bury himself deep inside her virgin body.

But he didn't want her first time to be in a limousine in front of the Fontaine Conference Center with his driver and strangers lurking outside. Granted that this would be a very daring and erotic experience, but he wanted her first time to be special, in a place where he'd never made love to any other woman—in his bed at the Andretti mansion.

It dawned on Massimo that he too would be experiencing a first. It would be the first time he would make love to a woman without wearing a condom. The thought of the fusion of Nia's and his naked flesh was enough to blow his mind, and his load.

He reminded himself that this appetizing foreplay was not for him. It was for Nia. She had ordered it, and it was up to him to make certain she devoured every little morsel laid out before her—down to the explosive sexual release she'd soon have.

Massimo buried his mouth in the hollow of Nia's neck and alternately began to lick her with his tongue, nip at her with his teeth, and graze her with his lips. He pushed his hips upwards making sure that each thrust brought the solid ridge of his shaft into direct contact with the little knob of flesh that housed the core of her sexuality.

"Purr, Nia. Purr for me. Purr like the sultry little pussycat you are." He toyed with her breasts and nipples and mercilessly teased the sensitive skin of her neck until she locked her hands at the back of his neck and began to writhe deliriously against him, her heart pounding like a violent jungle drum against his palms.

"Mass…imoooo… Oh my God, I'm cooooming…" Her knees clamped on to his hips in a painful grip as her body began to convulse like a ten-point Pacific earthquake.

"Yes, Nia, you most certainly are!" He pulled his face from her neck and placed his mouth over hers, not a moment too soon. Her body tensed tight as a bowstring and then a high-pitched scream like a mating she-leopard's spilled from deep within her.

Massimo swallowed the primitive cry of pleasure as her body collapsed against him, weak and spent. He wrapped his arms about her, holding her tightly against his heart until her breathing slowed and she relaxed into his body like a contented kitten.

"Oh, pussycat, you are the most passionate woman I've ever met," he said, as pleasurable anticipation mounted inside him. *Men have started wars and murdered their brothers for this little piece of heaven, right here.*

She raised her head and stared at him. Her eyes were dilated with passion and appeared a much deeper brown...like dark, rich molasses, her lips swollen from his kisses, and damp tresses of hair clung to the sides of her face. She was a beautiful sight and Massimo wanted to gaze upon that wanton look of desire and satisfaction for the rest of his life.

She glanced at her dress with the hem still tucked inside her bra. "That wasn't very ladylike of me, was it? Especially making the first move."

Massimo chuckled. "Oh, quite the contrary, my love." He tucked the errant strands of hair behind her ears. "I like a lady who makes the first move. A bold young woman once told me that being properly bred doesn't mean you shouldn't go after what you want."

"That was just to raise your interest." A shy smile ruffled her lips.

"And my interest is undoubtedly raised, *cara mia.*" As if to verify his words, his cock pulsed with excitement. They both trembled involuntarily. It was his cue to put physical distance between them. There was only so much temptation a man could take. He'd reached his limit for the week. He lifted her off his lap and set her on the seat.

She turned away and began fixing her clothes.

Massimo smiled as he reveled in the hot sticky feel of her bodily fluids seeping through his briefs and into his skin. With a deep sigh, he pulled up his trousers and tucked his shirt back in. The smell of sex saturated the air and probably his clothes too.

As he watched her bring order back to her appearance, Massimo thought of the first time he'd kissed her in the SUV, and how she'd straightened her clothes then, too. The next time they were intimate, there would be no clothes to straighten.

He applauded her for making the first move tonight in an attempt to explore her own sexual prowess, and God, was she a wild sexy thing. Thrills rushed up and down his spine as he imagined what she'd be like in a week, a month, years, once they discovered each other's erogenous zones and began testing the depths and limits of each other's passion.

With her clothes back in place, she turned to him. "It's important you know that I've never done this with anyone before. I've kissed boys, but I've never allowed any of them to get this far —not even cop a feel."

He brushed his knuckles along her cheeks. "Well, Miss Sylk, I feel very honored that you allowed me to cop a feel. A few of them," he added on a smile.

She may not have done it with anyone before, but Massimo was certain Nia was used to pleasuring herself. She was perfectly aware of the pot of climatic gold waiting at the end of her ride down his rainbow. It was not her first orgasm, but it was her first brought on by a man. He couldn't wait to teach her how to achieve deeper depths and higher heights of passion.

Massimo was suddenly into virgins. And he'd be *in* one soon.

"Well," she said, as if reading his mind, "you… you should go back to your meeting."

Sure, just use me then kick me out. He wanted to say to hell with the meeting and go home with her, finish this thing she'd started. But he knew making love to her wouldn't be enough to convince her to marry him. He still had to back her into a corner. "You'll probably be asleep by the time I get home. Do you still want me to stay out of your bed, *cara?* Or should I wake you so we can pick up from here?"

Her lips parted, but she said nothing.

Massimo knew she would not answer, could not, since she wasn't planning on being there when he did get home. All doubts about her not feeling well were gone. And if she were on her period, his shirttail would have been stained.

In a few hours, they would be sharing a bed. He would be buried deep inside her while she was having her second orgasm, or her third or fourth—depending on the limit of his control.

She glanced out the window as the church bell began to chime out the hour. "I so like that," she said, grinning. "I don't hear that in New York City."

"Yes, it is a quaint custom, but it gives you a homey feeling… which reminds me, how do you feel about church?"

She narrowed her eyes in confusion. "Why?"

"Bryce and Kaya's twins are being christened on Sunday and they asked me to be godfather. I'd like you to accompany me to church. Then we're going to their home for lunch."

"Do you attend church regularly?"

He shrugged. "Not as often as I should, but if you have something against God and all things religious, I understand."

"I don't have anything against God. I like Him, actually." She gave him a half smile. "I used to attend church with my parents when I was little."

"So, is that a 'Yes'?"

"Yes, I'll go with you."

"I'll let them know you'll be accompanying me." *As my wife.* That much he was certain of. "Good night, Nia." Placing a quick kiss on her forehead, Massimo stepped out of the limo and sucked the cold night air into his lungs in an effort to bring his senses back to normal.

He signaled for John, who'd sought refuge from the cold inside the center. "Take her home and return pronto," he said, very much aware of the uncomfortable look on his driver's face. John had been a trusted chauffeur for the Andretti family for several years. Between him and his father, the poor man had been subjected to more embarrassing situations than he could count. But thanks to one very sexy, exceptionally beautiful young woman, all that was about to change. His playboy days were really over. If he wasn't certain of it before, Massimo was absolutely certain now.

As the limo disappeared from view, Massimo walked back

into the center and made his way back to the conference room. He knew that for Nia, that passionate encounter was 'Goodbye'. She'd wanted to make love so she would have something to remember him by.

He'd offered her the world, not as his lover, but as his wife, and she had turned him down. He didn't think there was a woman alive who wouldn't jump at the chance to be an Andretti wife.

And now the one woman in the world whom he needed to marry within the week and bear his heir within a year was running away from him, claiming that it was because of his infamous reputation with women. Massimo knew it was much more than that, especially after what had just transpired between them. There was a war going on inside her—her head saying one thing and her body saying another.

She was acting as if they had a history. If they did, it was lost with the others prior to the time the rhino attacked him. He couldn't even remember the actual attack, just the moments before it, and then the sensation of being dragged along the ground. It wasn't until weeks later when he'd awakened from a coma that he learned Jabari had dragged his bleeding body back to the Masai village. Neither therapy nor a series of neurological treatment had helped in restoring all his memories. His doctors had told him some might return if his mind was jogged by something or someone associated with them.

Could it be that he'd met Nia just before he left for Africa? Had he done something to hurt her? If that was the case, she would have been a teenager, still in high school, and far too young for the kind of female relationships he sought back then. There was only one answer: he must have hurt someone close to her, perhaps a relative. Perhaps money was involved and she'd tracked him down to seek revenge, steal back what he'd stolen.

How? How had he hurt Nia? Where had he seen her before?

Massimo halted in his tracks as an image began to form in his mind. He closed his eyes, and tried to will the memories back to life. *A silver-plated picture frame, a navy blue khimar, soft brown eyes gazing out at him through the tiny slits… Darkness surrounded him and those eyes, those eyes were his light, his guide…*

"Hey, Andretti."

Massimo swore as the image dissolved into mist. He opened his eyes and hastily pulled his scattered thoughts into order.

"Where the hell have you been, man?" Bryce asked, walking towards him. "You got a text and disappeared. They're eating me alive in there."

"Nia isn't feeling well."

"Sorry to hear that. Is she gonna be okay?"

"Yeah, yeah." He flared his hand in the air. "Just a little stomachache. She'll be fine. I just needed to see her to the car."

Bryce looked him over suspiciously. "And it took you half an hour to do that?"

"Have you seen my fiancée? You don't just place a woman like that into a limo and close the door. You go in with her and say goodnight properly."

Bryce chuckled. "I hear you, man. I've been married for a year now and every night I still give my wife a proper goodnight."

"I hope I can say that in a year," Massimo stated, as they began walking.

Bryce's forehead crinkled. "Look, Mass. I probably shouldn't butt into your business since I married Kaya within a couple weeks of meeting her, and none of you were here to at least try to talk me out of it."

"You probably wouldn't have listened to us, anyway."

Bryce shrugged. "Probably not. However, as your friends, we have the right to be heard."

Massimo spread his hands in compliance.

"The boys and I are a bit concerned about your rash decision to marry a woman you don't know. At least I knew of Kaya's existence before I met her. She was practically family."

"Your concerns are valid, Bryce, but unnecessary, nonetheless. I have it under control." Massimo hoped his friend would drop it, but knew he won't. Like he said, they were friends, and that's what friends did—butted into each other's business whether you wanted them to or not.

"I'm sure you do, but I'm just saying, you met this girl, took her to the Andretti mansion—the one place you've never taken any other woman, then the next day you announce your engagement. Don't get me wrong, I mean, she seems nice and she's gorgeous, and you'd have to be a fool, blind, and, or dead from the waist down to not want to have a relationship with her. But marrying a stranger? How do you know your brother didn't send her to spy on you? And you know we don't believe that story she told us about the way you met," he added with a skeptical edge to this voice. "So what's the real story?"

Massimo smiled as he recalled the ridiculous story Nia had told when he'd introduced her to his friends. She thought fast on her feet. That was good. "I had the same suspicions when Nia approached me, Bryce. She has no ties to Galen. However, I couldn't pass up her proposition—"

"She approached you with a proposition? What does she want from you?"

"I can't tell you that, but I can say that I'm happy we met, and just in the nick of time."

"So it's really all about your inheritance? You swore a long time ago that you'd never get married because of—you know, the Andretti curse. You built your own empire, free of Andretti money so you wouldn't have to bend to your father's demands."

Massimo grimaced.

"You obviously changed your mind when you asked Gabrielle

to marry you, but when that fell through, we thought you'd finally given up on trying to keep Andretti Industries. But now I can't help wondering, like everyone else, if you called off your wedding to Gabby because you'd met Nia. She isn't really pregnant, is she?"

Massimo shook his head. "No. One has nothing to do with the other, and no, Nia isn't pregnant." *Yet.* "But yes, marrying her has everything to do with my inheritance. I never told you, but Dafne offered to marry me after Gabby and I broke up."

"You've known Dafne all your life, and she's an attractive woman. A good friend with-benefits kind of thing. Why didn't you accept *her* proposition?"

Massimo chuckled cynically. "Oh, I did, but she wanted my Italian balls on a platinum platter, literally. She had stipulations of her own," he added, as they turned a corner. "My heir was to be conceived by artificial insemination. And three years with no sex wasn't appealing to me."

"Ouch!"

"My sentiments exactly. I would have gone along with it just to hold on to the mansion. But then Nia showed up and provided me with an alternative. And I know you pointed out that she's a stranger, but I had her thoroughly investigated, just as I'm certain you had Kaya investigated before you married her."

Bryce gave him a sheepish grin. "All right. We're not stupid men. We don't jump into situations with our eyes closed. Point taken."

Massimo nodded. "Nia came highly recommended. Her colleagues only have good things to say about her. She's never even had a traffic violation, but," he added rushing his fingers through his hair, "there are things about her that concern me."

Bryce quirked an eyebrow. "Like what?"

"I feel that we've met before, and that the memory is lost with the others I have trouble recalling. But she swore we hadn't met."

"And you're still going through with the marriage?"

Massimo shrugged. "I'm a desperate man, Bryce. What can I say? I need her. I don't think she's dangerous. I feel that she's in danger, though. I feel I need to protect her."

As they came to a stop outside the conference room, Bryce placed his hand on Massimo's shoulder. "You know you don't have to marry her to protect her, right? But the heart wants what the heart wants, I suppose."

"I'm not in love with her. I just thought that if I have to marry for money, why not marry for sex? She's a means to an end. That's all." His heart kicked him in the ribs.

Bryce laughed out loud. "That's the same bull crap I told myself when I married Kaya. Take my advice—just go with your heart. It'll save you a whole lot of pain down the road."

I'm already in pain, Massimo thought to himself as he opened the door to the conference room and stepped inside.

As the limo took off, Nia drew her legs up under her and let the tears she'd been holding back fall. She would never forget the feel of his firm lips on hers, his strong arms wrapped about her, the taste of his warm breath in her mouth, or the restless tingling of her skin from the magical touch of his fingertips. She'd felt excitement and anxiety all in the same breath as she abandoned herself to the spurts of awakening desire.

Her craving for him had superseded everything else: her senses, her dignity, her morals. She didn't know that passion could drive her so insane that she cared about nothing else, not even that they were in a limousine in a public place with the driver and strangers standing around outside. She'd wanted one thing, and one thing only: for Massimo to put out the fire burning her up from the inside. Just once, she wanted to know what it would be like to be taken by the man she loved.

Nia wrapped her arms about her body. She felt like a traitor for succumbing to Massimo's sex appeal. Her father must be turning over in his grave. She pressed her hands into her stomach as a sharp familiar pain ripped through her midsection, signaling the onset of her ovulation. Another reminder that she should be grateful Massimo hadn't granted her request to make love to her. She was sure he didn't have any condoms on him and the last thing she needed was an Andretti in her belly.

Her father would not appreciate her mixing her bloodline with the Andrettis since it was an Andretti who had brought him to financial ruin and who was responsible, albeit indirectly, for his death. If it was one thing the Norwoods were it was loyal to each other.

"Family must always come first," her father used to tell her. *"Family takes care of family, no matter what."*

It was loyalty that had given her the courage to snatch Aaron from his foster home and run. It was loyalty that had given her the strength to look after him, raise him from a boy to a man. It was loyalty that had driven her to Granite Falls to save his life.

She'd saved him five years ago, and she would save him again tonight as soon as she got out of Granite Falls.

Massimo had made it so easy, she thought as the limo climbed up Andretti Drive. She'd been at her wits end in the bathroom, trying to figure out how to convince John to take her back to the estate without alerting Massimo. She'd hoped that when she told him she wasn't feeling well, he'd just comply with her wishes. And just in case Massimo was summoned, she knew he would not have argued with her in front of his driver or anyone else who might have been present. She'd been prepared to make a scene if she had to.

She'd almost peed herself when she'd emerged from the

ladies' room to find Massimo waiting for her, but it turned out to be a stroke of luck and played out well in her favor.

Soon Massimo would be a distant memory, Nia thought as the limo came to a stop in the lighted courtyard and John got out to open the door for her.

CHAPTER TWELVE

Nia pressed down on the gas pedal as she drove along Route 80. She was the only motorist on the road, which suited her fine. All she had to do now was get to the beat-up car she'd purchased today, transfer her luggage and take off down the highway to Manchester.

She hoped to be miles away from Granite Falls by the time Massimo got home from his meeting and discovered his fiancée and his two million dollars had flown the coop.

It was such a relief when she'd gotten to the mansion to find that Azi was out for the evening. With no one to deter her, Nia had packed as quickly as possible, stuffing all the clothes she'd brought to Granite Falls along with some that Massimo had bought her into two large suitcases she'd found in one of the empty bedrooms. Among those she left was the red dress he'd forced her to wear last night, but at the last minute she'd grabbed the ugly gray one he'd tricked her into buying and tossed it into the suitcase just before closing it. She'd keep it as a memento of their feud and the fact that she'd won.

A smile of victory parted Nia's lips as she imagined the look of utter bewilderment on Massimo's face when he walked into the master suite to find his bed and her closet empty. She wished…

Nia glanced in her rearview mirror and frowned. A cruiser with flashing lights was barreling toward her. She glanced at her speedometer and hastily eased up off the gas. She was going ten miles over the posted speed limit, and was still the only car on the road. Surely, he wasn't stopping her for such a trivial traffic violation. People sped along this road all the time. Even Massimo and his driver were in the habit of going well over the speed limit, and the law didn't seem to care until tonight.

With the cruiser practically riding her tail, Nia slowed way down and pulled to the side of the road. This was her first traffic violation. She hoped the officer would take that into consideration and let her off with a warning. She rolled down her window as the burly frame of the officer approached her car. "Good evenignt, Officer—" She squinted up at his badge. "Jordan."

"Registration and license, please," he demanded in a dry tone.

A thick fog hovered at the cave of his mouth where his warm breath and the cold night air collided. He was a veteran cop, probably in his early fifties, and displayed the no-nonsense air of authority that came with time and experience on the police force. "What's the problem, Officer?" Nia asked in a calm voice as she tried to hide her intimidation.

"You were speeding, Ma'am."

She blinked as the bright beam of his flashlight hit her face. "I didn't realize I was speeding." Nia had heard somewhere that when a cop stopped you, you should never admit to anything. Innocent until proven guilty was the good old American way, and until this cop showed her the reading on his radar, she'd swear she was driving under the speed limit.

Officer Jordan shifted the stream of light from her face to the backseat, bobbing it around as if he was looking for something. "Registration and license, please," he reiterated, and brought the beam back to her face.

So he was going to be a hard-ass. With a sigh of frustration, Nia reached into the glove compartment and pulled out the registration, then she rummaged through her purse and fished out her license. She handed them over. Maybe when he saw the names Andretti and Sylk, he'd realize she was Massimo's fiancée, apologize profusely for his blunder, and send her on her way. For once, Nia was happy Massimo had publicly linked her name with his.

This was clearly not her night, Nia thought as the officer frowned at the documents, placed his hand on the handle of his pistol and stepped back. "Miss Sylk, I'm going to have to ask you to step out of the car."

Icy fear twisted around Nia's heart. Had her past finally caught up to her? Had her many years on the run come to an end? Her mind flashed back almost five years ago to the day in Philadelphia when her neighbors had told her that a strange man had been asking questions about her. Certain it was Maine's social services on her tail, she'd packed up Aaron, run to New York, and changed their names.

"Ma'am, please get out of the car."

Nia swallowed the lump in her throat. "Why? What did I do?"

"You've committed a crime."

A crime? Kidnapping? Was there a statue of limitation on kidnaping in Maine? That's something she hadn't checked into. *False identification?* Had they finally connected Nia Sylk with Shaina Norwood? Had she opened Pandora's box when she applied for a passport in her real name? "Wha… what kind of crime did I allegedly commit, Officer?" she asked in a shaky voice.

"Grand theft auto."

Nia's eyes popped wide. "What?"

"This vehicle was reported stolen a short while ago."

"By whom?" *As if she didn't know.* "Who reported it stolen?" she asked, needing confirmation.

"Massimo Andretti, the owner, Ma'am."

"I'm the owner! He bought it for me!" She knew what her declarations implied about her relationship with Massimo, but that was the least of her worries at the moment.

"That may well be the case, Ma'am, but until you produce a document that shows you own this vehicle, I'm going to have to place you under arrest. So, I will ask again, nicely. Would you please step out of the car, Miss Sylk?" His eyes were an icy gray, his thin lips clamped tight.

Nia's fear exploded into fury. She yanked the door open and jumped out. She hadn't taken the time to change and shivered as the frigid night air crawled beneath her coat, penetrated the thin material of her dinner dress, and wrapped about her like a frosty blanket.

Officer Jordan unsnapped his cuffs from his duty belt. "Turn around and place your hands behind your back."

Resisting arrest, whether or not it was warranted was not a smart thing to do. It was a misdemeanor and although it carried a less severe penalty than a felony, Nia could not afford the mountain of problems that would ensue after such an offense. As much as she hated it, it was better she played this Massimo's way. He was ruthless, and probably very pissed off that she'd tried to deceive him, steal from him. He was going to teach her a lesson.

Not knowing if this arrest was bogus or real, Nia turned around, placed her hands behind her back, and cringed when the cold metal of the handcuffs snapped around her wrists.

Officer Jordan read her her Miranda Rights then led her to his cruiser.

From the back seat, Nia watched him stroll back to the Mercedes and pop the trunk. He was bent over it for several moments before he straightened up and began talking on his radio.

He'd found her briefcase with her two million dollars. She could not explain that away without incriminating herself, admitting that she'd offered Massimo Andretti sex for four million dollars, when all she was really doing was conning him out of two. None of it sounded good.

Nia wished she'd asked for a bank check instead of cash.

Was that why he hadn't made love to her tonight—so he could come off as the victim who hadn't fully participated in her indecent plot? Damn him!

Nia had no idea if it was fear, anger, disgust, or just plain spite that forced the bile up her esophagus and into her mouth. But she nonetheless felt a rush of powerful relief as she bent forward and emptied her stomach on the floor of the cruiser.

Let Massimo Andretti clean that up.

"You have a visitor, Miss Sylk."

"I bet I do." Nia rose from the narrow cot in the eight-by-four cell in which she'd been locked for the past two hours or so. She swore Jabari's cage was a lot roomier than her cell. Being locked up, having your privileges taken away and placed in someone else's control was no way to live. As Nia had sat on the cot, she'd come to realize that life on the run was just as much a prison as the bars that limited her physical movements.

They'd given her the customary one phone call, and she'd wasted it on the only person who could get her out of this mess —the very man who'd gotten her into it.

Again.

He'd promised to come right over and bail her out.

The last time an Andretti had made a promise to a Norwood, she'd lost her father.

What was it going to cost her this time? She prayed to God that it wasn't her brother.

She stared at the ruddy-faced officer as he unlocked her cell —the only one of the eight that was occupied. She followed him along a corridor and around a corner, grateful that at least they hadn't handcuffed her again. They passed the room where he had fingerprinted her and lined her up for her mug shots. Afterwards, he'd taken her to a multi-stall bathroom so she could wash the stench of vomit from her body.

Once alone, Nia had taken a quick cramped shower in a stall as big as a locker, then pulled out the gray dress from the top of her suitcase and put it on. She was wearing the second of the two dresses she'd sworn she'd not be in Granite Falls long enough to wear.

Her master scheme was falling apart right in front of her and she was powerless to do anything about it.

Nia sighed as a feeling of hopelessness descended on her. They'd taken her luggage, her money, the Andretti family jewelry she'd been wearing and that damned engagement ring she'd forgotten to take off before she fled. As far as she was concerned, the four cops who made up the entire Granite Falls Police Department were in cahoots with Massimo Andretti.

She was the outsider, who'd fallen victim to a twisted plot.

She wasn't even a person anymore. She was now number 315678.

The boy-officer led her down a short flight of stairs, into a shorter, but wider hallway, and stopped at the first door on the right. "Your visitor is waiting inside," he said, and hastily sped back the way they had come.

Nia glanced around the brightly lit hallway with two holding benches and a water cooler lining one wall, while an oversized bulletin board with an array of three-by-five cards, colorful Post-it notes, and additional bulletins lined the other wall. The other three doors were closed and seemed unoccupied, casting a feeling of pessimism in the air. If this was New York, she was certain the interrogation rooms would be crowded with criminals and cops trying to squeeze the truth of them. The front lobby and the holding cells would be crawling with newly arrested perpetrators, waiting their turn to be questioned. Tonight, she was the only perpetrator on the block in this quiet, mountain town.

For the first time since she left New York, Nia missed the din of the big city.

Taking a deep breath, she tried to shake off the gloom in the air. She still had some fight left. She placed her hand on the doorknob, and debated whether she should confront Massimo or just turn around and go back to her cell, call a public defender and let him try to get the bogus charges dropped so she could make it to New York to pay Eddie. She didn't care what happened after that. At least the threats to her and Aaron's lives would be gone.

But if Massimo had gone to such lengths to keep her in town, she knew she wasn't going anywhere until he got what he wanted. Whatever that was.

She peered through the narrow pane of glass in the door. Massimo was seated behind a table with his smartphone glued to his ear and his head bent over some papers sprawled across the top of the table. A large white envelope and a brown folder sat on the end of the table closest to the door.

He was conducting business as usual as if he hadn't a care in the world, and he'd obviously taken the time to go home and change, she thought, her gaze washing over his magnificent body, dressed in a dark green sweater and a dark pair of slacks. She studied the side of his face and swallowed at the faint shadow of a beard dusting his jawline and chin. Her knees grew weak at the memory of pressing up against his hard frame in the limousine, of his hands roaming along her body, cupping her breast.

A weak sigh escaped Nia, and furious at the arousal in her treacherous body, she opened the door, stepped inside, and closed it with a resounding slam. His head jerked up and he immediately stood to his feet when he saw her. He ended his call and dropped his phone on the stack of papers, then had the audacity to throw her a handsomely devilish smile—the smile of sweet victory, made more provocative by his five o'clock shadow.

"Why?" Nia glared at him, unable to believe he was the same man in whose arms she'd experienced such a mind-blowing orgasm only hours ago. The memories sickened her.

"You think I was just going to let you waltz off into the sunset with two million of my dollars, Nia? I was suspicious of you the moment you offered to sell me your virginity. I was convinced of your devious plot when you asked that we wait before making love, and for half the money up front."

"I figured you would have your suspicions, and honestly, I never really expected that you'd go along with it. So why?"

"For several reasons. First of all, I was curious why a beautiful young woman would offer to sell her virginity to a total stranger for four million dollars. What kind of trouble are you in, Nia? Why do you want that money so badly?"

"It's none of your damn business. Explaining why I need the money wasn't part of the negotiations."

He uttered a dry laugh. "Neither was you bailing halfway through the deal. Nobody plays me and walks away to brag about it," he stated in a lethal tone. "Nobody!"

Nia thrust her hands on her hips as rage mounted inside her. "What are you going to do, Massimo? What do you rich and powerful people do when peons cross you? You're going to break some of my bones? You're going to threaten my family? Too bad for you, I have none," she hastily added at the quickening in his posture. "What? What are you going to do?" she taunted him.

He stiffened at her questions. "Think what you want about me, Nia. However—"

"You have your revenge." She cut him off, not caring about anything else he had to say.

"Oh, *cara*, revenge is not my desire at all." His voice was oddly resigned and his eyes held a surprisingly gentle softness as he studied her.

"Then what? Humiliation?" She wasn't falling for any more of his charming wiles.

His jaw clenched and his eyes slightly narrowed. "Not that either."

"What is your desire, Massimo? What do you want from me?"

He took a side step, and Nia saw the briefcase and her luggage stacked against the wall behind him. Sheer black fright swept through her. She hoped the cops hadn't gone through her suitcases, and if they had, she prayed to God they hadn't found the passport in Shaina Norwood's name stuffed in the bottom and handed it over to Massimo. If he knew her real identity, there was no place on earth she could hide from him.

She swallowed as he walked around the table and came to stand in front of her. She fought against his bracing masculine scent and the unsteadiness his proximity caused to her system. "You can keep your blood money," she said crossing her arms in an attempt to stop the quivering in her stomach. "Just give me my luggage and let me go. I want to get as far away from you as I possibly can."

His brow pulled into an affronted frown. "What do you think I want from you, Nia?"

She scoffed at the brazen gleam in his blue eyes. "You can't possibly expect me to honor my end of the bargain and sleep with you now. Not after this." Her hands flared in the air.

"I don't care about that." He drew his lips in thoughtfully. "Well, I do care about it, but merely bedding you for a few days, or at most, a few weeks, isn't enough anymore."

"Then what do you want Massimo? What do you want?" she growled.

"*Una moglie.*"

She tilted her head and shot him a suspicious glare. "What the hell is that?"

"A wife. I want a wife." He widened his stance and crossed his arms. "I expressed my desire to you and the world last night. I haven't changed my mind."

"But today at lunch you said you would retract that statement you made to the public."

He shook his head in exasperation. "No, Nia. I did no such thing. You deliberately misinterpreted my words because it suited you."

Tossing her hair across her shoulder in a gesture of defiance, Nia jutted her chin at him. "Well, stop making the same mistake at misinterpreting my words, Massimo. I already told you I wasn't marrying you. I haven't changed my mind, either. Furthermore, you must think I have no shred of self-esteem that I would even consider marrying a man who had me arrested and thrown in jail, just to prove a point."

"I'm sorry about that, but it was unavoidable."

"You're sorry? It was unavoidable?" She smirked with cold sarcasm. "You had me arrested for auto theft and burglary. You accused me of stealing two million dollars and priceless jewelry that has been in your family for generations. I was fingerprinted!" She shook her hands in the air. "They took my picture and gave me a number, Massimo!"

"Don't forget destruction of government property. You

vomited in a police cruiser. Twice. I had to write them a check to clean it."

She glared at the smile playing at the corners of his mouth, the same mouth that had kissed her and taunted her mercilessly a short while ago. Her fingers itched to slap the smug look from his face, but she knew from experience that attempting to slap him would only excite him more. She had no wish to deal with that kind of attention. She balled her fists at her sides. "Thanks to you, I now have a police record. I have a rap sheet. You have ruined my reputation, my life."

"It will all miraculously disappear if you marry me tonight."

"I'd rather rot in jail." The sweetly intoxicating musk of his body finally completely overwhelmed her and she turned and took a few steps to the other side of the small room. She despised herself for allowing him to make her vulnerable and weak. She was not used to anyone asserting authority over her. She was not the helpless damsel-in-distress kind of woman waiting for a white knight to ride up on his steed and rescue her.

She'd been taking care of herself since she was seventeen, and she'd been doing just fine with her life until Eddie found her, forcing her to come looking for Massimo. And now that her plan to pay Eddie back had gone south, she'd have to do the next best thing.

Run and hide again.

This time she was leaving the country, and she wasn't moving next door to Dulcina where both Eddie and Massimo could easily find her again. She was melting away into ultimate obscurity somewhere in Siberia. Aaron would just have to put his plans on hold for a while longer, or change them completely. He could still become an engineer, just not in America.

At least he'd be alive and in good health.

Nia shuddered and blinked back the tears that sprang to her eyes.

"You're sure there's nothing I can do to get you to change your mind, *cara*?" Massimo asked behind her.

"Nothing. I wouldn't marry you if you were the last man on the planet and my life depended on it."

"Perhaps if I kissed you, reminded you of the pleasure you experienced in the limo at my hands, you might eat those words, pussycat." He walked up behind her and wrapped his arms about her. "Think of the magic we can create in bed tonight as husband and wife. Don't you still want to become a woman, Nia? Truth be told, I'm dying to make you one. You drive me crazy with lust. You're under my skin, in my blood, and in my head all the time."

He pulled her hard against him, trekked backwards toward the desk and perched himself on its edge. Nia closed her eyes and stifled the moan that rose to her throat as the heat from his erection burned a hole in her back. She tried to pry his arms from around her. She might as well have been restrained inside a straightjacket.

"You were begging me to take you a couple hours ago, pussycat," he said, bending forward and hauling her up against him, seating her on his groin and tucking her lower body securely between his strong thighs and legs. He swept her hair from the back of her neck and pulled down the turtleneck collar of her dress. "Do you have any idea what seeing you in this ugly schoolteacher's dress does to me?"

The heavy bulge of his erection now pressing into the firm cheeks of her buttocks told Nia just what it did to him, but she wasn't going down without a fight. "Let me go, Massimo. Take your filthy, sleazy hands off of me." She wrestled harder, but her struggles just seemed to excite him more.

"I'm tempted to bend you over this table, hike this dress up to your waist, pull your panties down to your ankles, and take you from behind—hard and deep. You need to be tamed, Nia, brought under control, and I'm the man to do it. I'm applying for that job as your husband." Before Nia could process his threat, he blew his hot breath on the exposed skin at the back of her neck then lowered his mouth and bit into her flesh.

An uninhibited shiver of wanting ran through Nia. The picture of Jabari biting into the neck of the female leopard as they mated in the tall grass appeared in her mind. The more she tried to ignore the image and the yearning it induced inside her, the bolder it became. She was that female leopard in heat and Massimo was Jabari pinning her to the ground. She felt his strength, pressing her down, subduing her, his heat entering her, claiming her…

"No!" She clawed at him, trying to get him off her. She couldn't even budge him a smidgen.

With his teeth sunk into her skin, he pressed the palm of one hand into her belly and used his other hand to fondle the inside of her thighs through the wooly material of her dress. He began to rock against her, titillating her as his hand between her thighs became bolder, more urgent as it crawled higher and closer to the core of her heat.

The erotic act proved too much for Nia. Her knees buckled. She grabbed his steely arms to keep from collapsing on the floor as coils of explosive currents shot through her body.

"Do you still want me to take my filthy, sleazy hands off you, Nia?" He brushed his lips over the tender spot his sharp teeth had made on her neck, the prickling of his new beard intensifying the sensation.

"I hate you." She spat out the words and pulled her neck from his touch. Her flesh stung from his bite and she knew she'd carry his physical mark for days, but his emotional brand she would tote around for years—the rest of her life, perhaps.

He turned her around and cupped her chin in his palm, forcing her to meet his gaze. "We both know that's not true." His gaze traveled over her face. "You are so beautiful when you're mad. I especially love your pouting little mouth. So soft and ripe and juicy."

He stroked the pad of his thumb slowly back and forth across her lips as his eyes held hers prisoner. The gesture was extremely sensual, and her fire quickly returned. She could not resist this man, no matter how angry he made her, and he knew it.

"I can't wait to put your sexy little mouth to good use later tonight," he whispered in a husky voice. "The picture of your juicy lips clasped around my pulsing shaft was another reason I took you up on your brazen offer, little pussycat. I wanted you the moment I saw you, and I can't wait to bury myself to the hilt inside you later tonight."

A new flood of moisture settled in a pulsing pool at the core of Nia's sex. She felt heavy and full and thirsty, all in the same ragged breath. Involuntarily, her tongue came out to wet her dry lips only to make contact with the salty pad of Massimo's thumb.

"*Dolce!*" He circled her body and brought his mouth down on hers.

Nia's lips parted and gave his invading tongue license to enter and plunder at will. He stroked the roof of her mouth and probed the insides of her lips and cheeks with the tip over and over again until finally retreating into his mouth, daring her to follow and reciprocate.

Dazed by desire, Nia's tongue followed his into the wet warm cave of his mouth. He curled his lips around her tongue and sucked on it urgently, creating a throbbing between her legs that matched the tempo of his jaws as he tried to devour her. Nia grabbed the front of his sweater with both hands as he literally sucked the life from her body, turning her into a listless, useless ragdoll.

"*Sì.*" His voice broke with passion.

With their mouths still connected, he bent down, swept his

fingers beneath the hem of her dress and pulled it up to her waist. He then effortlessly picked her up off the floor and placed her feminine heat on the heavy bulge of his erection straining against his slacks. "Wrap your arms and legs around me," he commanded softly as he pushed to his feet.

Rendered powerless by his wicked tactics, Nia wrapped her arms and legs about him.

He groaned, placed his hands on her buttocks, and thrust his rock-hard shaft against her softness, grazing her through the lace of her panties.

Nia's skin was on fire and the flesh beneath it was melting fast, turning into molten lava. She was suffocating, drowning in an ocean of pleasure as wave after wave crashed upon her tender shore. When her heart began to throb as if it would burst from her chest, Nia knew she was about to have her second orgasm for the night, right here, right now in a small interrogation room at Granite Falls Police Station with—God knows who—peeking at them through the door.

Her limbs tightened about Massimo and her body drew as tight as a brand new banjo string. And just as she was about to fly off into oblivion, Massimo lifted her off of him and held her suspended in the air. She crashed back down to earth with an unsatisfied growl.

He released her mouth and gazed deep into her eyes, his dark and stormy with passion and purpose. "You have two options, Nia. One way or the other, you're going to be a prisoner. You can do your time in the women's correctional prison in Concord, or you can serve it out in my bed as my wife, having this." He pulled her back down on his erection and began thrusting against her again. "As often as you desire. It's your choice, but you have to make it now."

"You despicable... Ahhh..." she screamed as he thrust upward, sending a new wave of shocks rippling through her.

"Choose, Nia. It's now or never."

Nia's hands tightened around his thick neck and her fists curled around his silky black hair. She thought about pulling it from the roots and choking him until the life drained from his body, but she didn't want murder or even attempted murder added to her already much too long rap sheet. And she had to think of Aaron. She was no use to him in jail.

If it was just herself she had to worry about, she'd tell Massimo what he could do with his money and his hand in marriage, but it was not just her life that was in jeopardy. Her little brother's life depended on her getting out of this jam. She'd promised their father that she'd take care of him. She just hadn't planned on it coming at the expense of her freedom, the capture of her body and her heart by the insufferable Massimo Andretti.

"Nia, I *will* keep you locked up until you agree to marry me. I can do that."

Family first.

"Okay, okay," she managed between her ragged breaths. "I'll marry you, Massimo. I'll marry you."

"Oh, pussycat, those are the sweetest words I've ever heard."

She thought he would put her down now that he'd gotten what he wanted, but she felt one of his hands slide across her buttocks and make its way to the inside of her thighs, up over the lacy band of her thigh-high stockings. Nia moaned out loud as his fingers eased the crotch of her panties aside and toyed with her soaked flesh.

"How did you know I love landing strips, pussycat?" he whispered, dropping his weight on the desk, and pressing the heel of his palm against her freshly waxed mound.

"Massimo." Nia began to tremble as his fingers parted her flesh. She felt her breath literally being cut off as he eased a finger carefully inside her heat and began to stroke her, slowly and cautiously as she imagined a man would stroke a virgin.

"You like that?"

"Yes." The friction was excruciatingly pleasurable. He pressed a little deeper, but still not deep enough to reach her maidenhead. Nia had never had anyone's fingers but her own inside her, and at those times, she too had stayed close to the entrance of her body so as not to rupture her hymen.

"What about this?" He flicked the pad of his thumb across her swollen clitoris.

The shock of it wrung a loud moan of pleasure out of Nia.

For a split second, she remembered where she was and tried to stifle her screams as Massimo began to strum her with his thumb and finger. She was very much aware that his fingers were thicker and longer than hers, and that the one lodged inside her was massaging previously unexplored regions of her sex. But as her pleasure intensified and fire licked through her veins, Nia held Massimo in a death grip and abandoned herself to the pull of her second orgasm for the night.

As her scream started to erupt, Massimo covered her mouth with his.

Her cry was raw, so raw her throat hurt. Her body remained taut for long shuddering moments, then, breathing like an exhausted cheetah, she finally dropped her head on Massimo's shoulder and let her arms fall limply down his back. She felt Massimo's hand caressing up and down her back, soothing her. Her mouth pulsed from the rawness of his kiss, and the areas around her lips tingled from the grating of his light beard. Nia let herself sink into the thrill of it.

"My God," he said after a long silence, "you're so tight and hot, for a moment there I was afraid you'd either burn or snap my finger off my hand. I can't think of a story to tell our children when they ask what happened to the middle finger of my right hand."

Nia's spontaneous giggles swiftly faded into a groan as her

sensitive flesh tightened around his finger still inside her. "Maybe you shouldn't go sticking it into strange dark holes, then," she said unable to resist. "And you could tell them the cat ate it."

He chuckled heartily. "Ah, Nia, I love the way your mind works. We're going to have so much fun together in bed as husband and wife."

Nia closed her mind to his words and tried to re-erect her wall of defense against him.

"Can I have my finger back now?"

Too weak to speak, she nodded. Nia winched when he slowly pulled his finger out of her then rearranged her panties. If his finger had brought her so much pleasure, she could only imagine what his shaft and his mouth would do for her. She might be a virgin, but Nia was well aware of the carnal cravings of her body and what it took to satisfy them. She'd been taking care of her own needs for years now and each time she made herself come, Massimo Andretti had been right there with her, his blue eyes boring into her, coaxing her on.

He eased her upper body away from his and forced her to look at him. The pale blue rim around his irises darkened with emotion. "I will take care of you, Nia," he said. "As my wife, you will be protected and cared for. No one would dare try to hurt you."

You've hurt me, Massimo, far worse than anyone else will ever hurt me. Can you protect me from you? Nia wished she had the courage to voice her thoughts, but revealing her true identity to Massimo would be a foolish thing to do for several reasons. Just because he'd forced her to marry him didn't mean the conflict between them was over. It had just become more problematical.

"Are you strong enough to stand?' he asked, breaking into her thoughts.

"Yes. I think so." Nia took a deep breath and tried to relax. When he eased her to the floor, she pulled her dress down and straightened the belt, strategically avoiding eye contact with him. Twice tonight he'd brought her sexual release without taking any for himself. He was a generous man. Really generous, she thought as her eyes encountered the huge bulge in his pants.

"Perhaps you should get cleaned up, change into something more flattering," he said curtly before walking around the table. "We have a wedding ceremony to attend." He dropped his weight into the chair he'd been occupying and gave his attention to the papers he'd been studying when she'd arrived. He picked up his cell and proceeded to send someone a text, before he dialed a number and immediately began talking, in Spanish this time.

And just like that, they were back to business, Nia thought, even as her body still tingled from her orgasm and the warm moisture between her legs grew sticky. *It was business.* She'd agreed to marry Massimo to get the charges against her dropped. So even though they'd just shared an incredible intimate moment, there was no need for her to expect any affection from him. Massimo was physically attracted to her, and as his wife, he expected her to make love with him when the need arose.

This was a *quid pro quo* arrangement, and Massimo was getting all the *quid* and all the *quo*.

As that reality sunk in, Nia made her way to the back of the room to her luggage and began digging for fresh underwear, her makeup case, hair stuff, and a suitable outfit to get married in.

As ruthless as Massimo was, she knew in her heart that he would not have sent her to the women's prison in Concord, but he would have prolonged her stay in the jail cell here in Granite Falls for as long as it took for her to bend to his demands. He probably would have provided her with a more comfortable bed and a television and sent her down three gourmet meals from Azi's kitchen each day. He would probably come visit her at nights for conjugal visits right in this very room. He could have waited her out for days, weeks, months, if he had to.

It wasn't a terrible way to kill some time—if one had time to kill. Nia didn't have the luxury of time on her hands.

She had to make Eddie's drop within six weeks. That's all the time she had before she could shed her past like a loose robe and get going with the rest of her life. She couldn't bring Aaron back to the states until her business with Eddie was over.

But how was she to accomplish that task while married to a man she knew would be watching her every move? And not only he, but the rest of the world, as well. If she married Massimo tonight, the news of their nuptials would be everywhere by tomorrow, and Eddie might decide that he wanted more than what he was owed. She'd watched enough movies to know that once crooks knew they could squeeze a pint out of their victims, they would try to squeeze a quart.

With Massimo's billions added to the equation, Eddie would want a few gallons even though he'd promised that she and Aaron would be free and clear of his threats as long as she paid him off within the agreed time. Nia had no doubt that Massimo would crush Eddie like a bug if he attempted to hurt her. But Aaron was still out there unprotected, and who knew if Eddie had already figured out where he was hiding and had someone watching him, waiting for her to mess up. What if he kidnapped Aaron for a higher ransom?

Dear Lord. Nia's mind went into panic mode and her hands froze on the flap of her suitcase. Eddie wasn't the only person she had to worry about discovering she'd married one of the richest men in the world. Aaron was aware of the conflict between the Norwoods and the Andrettis. Like her, he blamed Massimo for their father's death and had more than once expressed his hate for the man.

Nia had allowed him to vent since she'd also hated Massimo

—or at least thought she did. She could never tell Aaron about her indecent proposal to Massimo, nor worse, why she married him. Aaron would lose respect for her. He would see her as a repulsive traitor.

Nia dumped her clothes on top of the suitcase and buried her face in her hands. She'd cleared one hurdle, just to run smack up against another. When would it ever stop? Her throat ached from desperation and defeat.

Nia wished her father were here. He would know what to do, what to say, how to protect her, how to comfort her. She missed him so much. *Daddy!*

Nia moaned as a deep familiar pain settled in her chest.

"Nia, what's wrong?"

Nia stiffened at the sound of Massimo's voice. His tone was laced with tenderness and concern, the kind of tenderness and concern that no one had shown her since she was seventeen. For the past five years she'd been projecting this aura of control and togetherness, primarily for Aaron's sake, but inside she'd always been scared, uncertain, and alone. She'd stayed strong and resolute. As head of the family, it was her duty to do so. She'd had no one to be strong for her. And now that someone had come along, someone who was willing to take on the world on her behalf, she couldn't point out the monsters that were frightening her, threatening her life.

"*Cara?*" His tone had softened, almost to a whisper.

"It's been a long day," she said, fighting back the tears and trying to keep the tremors from her voice. "I'm just tired."

CHAPTER THIRTEEN

Massimo felt a sharp stab in his chest as he watched Nia slump to the floor with her face buried in her hands. She looked frail and beaten down—not the image he wanted her to project while they exchanged their vows.

As her sobs reached him, something told Massimo that her fatigue ran far deeper than the physical. Her emotions and psyche were shattered as well.

He left his chair and, dropping to the floor beside her, he gathered her into his arms and held her tightly as she cried softly. He felt like a jerk for causing her such distress.

Damn it! Not only had he been determined to keep Nia in town and force her to marry him tonight, but he'd also wanted to know why she needed that money and whom she had to pay off. Since Paul had vanished into obscurity, Massimo had been tempted to hire another private investigator to dig further into her background—talk to her friends and neighbors—but unsure of what he was dealing with, he'd refrained from doing so. Tipping off the wrong person about Nia's whereabouts could put her in more danger.

And that was the absolute last thing Massimo wanted to do.

He'd hoped to trick her into revealing that bit of information earlier, but he'd gone about it all wrong and she'd clammed up. It might also have given him a clue as to where he'd seen her before. That image of her eyes staring back at him through the slits of the *khimar* had sparked his hope of recognition. Several times tonight he'd tried to evoke that image again, widen the scope of the lens to include the immediate surroundings, but to no avail.

Massimo sighed as Nia burrowed deeper into his embrace like he'd often watched Jabari's cubs burrow into their mothers' chests. He was tired too, and would love nothing more than to scoop Nia up, take her home, and put her to bed. *It has been a long day*. He'd been up before dawn and needed a good night's sleep himself. He'd never met a woman who worried him half as much as Nia Sylk did. Or perhaps he should say he'd never met a woman he cared enough about to let her worry him.

As he threaded his fingers through her long silky hair, Massimo found himself wishing he'd met Nia six months ago when he'd finally decided to keep his inheritance. He would have loved to take the time to woo her properly, teach her to trust him, to depend on him, to know he was on her side, make her want to marry him instead of forcing her into doing so. She'd stumbled into his life way too late to afford him that luxury.

Massimo tightened his arms about Nia and rested his chin on the top of her head as the sounds of her sobbing ceased. Except for the heavy thudding of her heart—or perhaps it was his—the room was shrouded in silence.

He found the thought that he needed Nia very satisfying for several reasons, but he concentrated on the one most critical. It was imperative that he maintained control of Andretti Industries since Fonandt Energy had secured ninety-five percent of the global wind energy contracts. He and Bryce had been the biggest winners at the meeting tonight, and starting early next week they'd be doing a lot of traveling as they prepared to make the world a better place for future generations. *Theirs included.*

All the good he was set to do would be gone if he lost control of Andretti Industries. As he held her, Massimo once again swore in his heart that he would protect Nia from whatever big bad wolves were after her. He would destroy them, all of them, for threatening her, for pushing her to the point where she thought she had to prostitute herself.

As her husband, he would have every legal right to revenge her honor by any means possible. This might be the twenty-first century, but the customs of the old ways—the old Italian ways—were still entrenched in Massimo's heart. When it came to family, honor and loyalty ruled. Nobody threatened an Andretti and got away with it. *Nobody.*

Even his father had returned to the old customs and sent Judith Carmichael and the bastard child she was carrying packing when he realized how much pain and embarrassment his affairs had inflicted on his wife. Sadly, by then it was way too late. He'd already lost her respect, her trust, and most significantly her love.

Massimo was determined that Nia would not suffer such a fate. Boy, a lot about him had changed in four days, he realized. At what precise moment had he become such a sap?

Massimo tensed at the knock on the door. He turned his head to see the blonde head of his attorney, Steven Lynd, peeking through the narrow pane of glass. He raised his hand to halt his entrance. As Steven drew back out of sight, Massimo eased Nia away from his body so he could see her face.

He felt that sharp stab in his chest again as he gazed into her red teary eyes. "My lawyer and the judge are ready," he said, rather authoritatively. He hated being so rash with her, but he couldn't show one ounce of weakness or she would back out of the agreement. She had to still believe he was a jerk.

"Can't we just go home?" she asked on a sniffle. "I already agreed to marry you. Do we have to do it tonight?"

"I'm leaving the country on business in a few days, Nia."

"Where are you going?"

"To Asia."

Her eyes widened at the news. "For how long?"

He gave a casual shrug of his shoulders. "Two, three days, maybe. I would prefer not to have this hanging over my head." He pushed to his feet then helped her up. "Would you like to go freshen up before the ceremony?"

"No." She wiped her hands down her face. "I don't care how I look. It's not like this marriage is something I want to remember." She slanted her eyes at him. "We're not taking pictures are we?"

"I wasn't planning to, but if you want—"

"I just want one thing. Well, two." She stared challengingly up at him.

He spread his hands.

"I get to keep the money."

"Absolutely. It's yours. You earned it. I had no intentions of taking it back. What else?"

Her lips parted in surprise and she nervously shifted from one foot to another. "I don't want our marriage publicized. Not immediately, anyway."

"Why?"

Her fingers toyed with the woolly strip of fabric around her waist. "I'm not used to that kind of attention, Massimo. You see what happened at the country club when you made that announcement about us getting married. I just need some time to process all this before the circus begins again."

He'd actually thought she would ask that they not consummate their marriage tonight, a promise he would not have been able to keep. "How much time, Nia?" He closed his eyes briefly at the moment of *déjà vu*. "We can't keep our marriage a secret for too long," he added. Particularly when he hoped his child would be firmly planed in her belly as early as tonight.

"Just a few days, maybe a week."

"Your request isn't unreasonable. And we do have up to six days before we have to officially file the marriage license. Is that it?" He knew there was more to it, but he chose not to pressure her for now. All in good time.

She nodded.

"One more thing. Do you happen to have a certified copy of your birth certificate with you? We need it to fill out the marriage license."

She looked flustered for a while, then nodded. "I brought one with me, just in case you wanted more information about me."

Strange. The average person didn't travel with a birth certificate. Then again, there was noting average about Nia Sylk. "Okay, let's get this over then we'll go home." He picked up the white envelope from the table. "I'll go get Judge Thomas while you freshen up. He'll be performing the ceremony," he said, walking briskly to the door.

Massimo stepped into the corridor and closed the door behind him. He motioned for Steven to follow him to the other end of the corridor. "I won't be needing this," he said, handing him the envelope.

"Mass, are you out of your mind?" Steven stared at him.

"Perhaps, but you have no idea what I had to do in order to get her to agree to marry me. Asking her to sign a prenup would be a bad idea," he replied, leaning his shoulder against the wall.

"It'll be a worse idea not to," Steven refuted. "You don't know this woman, yet you're about to grant her access to billions of your dollars."

"I wouldn't have access to any of it without her."

"Not without *her*, Mass. Without a *wife*." Steven eyed him speculatively. "I'm sure Dafne would still go through with the previous plan if you asked her. She was willing to sign a prenup."

"Have you forgotten what she wanted in return?"

"At least you knew what you were getting into. You know nothing about this Nia woman. She's not even the type you normally chase after." Steven set his briefcase on one of the holding benches.

An insightful fact, Massimo thought, pushing his hands into the pockets of his slacks and staring out the window into the dark forest at the back of the police station. Nia was a small fish from a small pond. He never fished in small ponds, not because he thought the catch was unacceptable, but because he didn't want to be accused of corrupting some inexperienced woman or of breaking her heart.

The women he was accustomed to chasing prowled the deep end of the big ponds, hoping to hook giant fish like him. They were used to swimming with sharks. They knew the rules and they played by them. Nia obviously hadn't read the manual when she ventured into the deep end with her little homemade plan— flawed to the max.

Three days in, and she was already drowning. She'd fallen apart tonight just because the rules had changed a little—a fact that deepened his conviction that some nasty little shark had frightened her out of the warm shallows of her familiar habitat into the deep, cold sea. And when he found that shark, Massimo swore he would spear him.

"Mass," Steven said impatiently, pulling Massimo out of his ruminations. "About the next Mrs. Andretti? Should we put Nia on a plane to New York first thing in the morning, and fly Dafne to the States? She could be here by tomorrow evening. The ceremony you had planned for Monday is still good, and," Steven continued, bending down to retrieve a white envelope from his suitcase. "I still have the prenup you had me draw up for Dafne." He waved the envelope under Mass's nose.

"Put that away. Better yet, burn it!"

"I don't get you." Steven tossed the envelope back into his briefcase and slammed the lid. "I've known you for years and I've never seen you act so rashly about any decision you make, especially one so important—perhaps the most important of your life."

"There's nothing rash about my decision, Steven," Massimo stated with a gut-wrenching certainty. "Of all the women I've chased and caught over the years, I've never had the slightest desire to marry one of them until Nia Sylk walked into my life. She is the next Mrs. Andretti. The only thing she'll be signing tonight is our marriage license," he stated with finality.

"I hope you know what you're doing."

"I know exactly what I'm doing." Massimo pushed off the wall and began walking back toward the room where his fugitive bride was waiting for him. "Make sure both prenups are destroyed. I don't ever want Nia to know the real reason we got married tonight. She thinks she has to marry me to stay out of jail and that's the way I want to keep it." He stopped at the door. "Now, I'd really appreciate it if you'll go get Judge Thomas from upstairs. He brought the marriage license that we still need to fill out before the ceremony."

"You're the boss," Steven muttered.

Was he really, now? His father had forced him into a marriage he never wanted, and some peculiar energy was compelling him to marry a woman he knew little about.

He'd never felt so powerless when it came to governing his own life.

❧

Opening her eyes, Nia stretched under the soft down feather comforter like a lazy kitten awakening from a satisfied nap. Flat on her back, she squinted at the colorful stained glass ceiling that was blanketed with a layer of freshly fallen snow, then her eyes darted slowly around the room. The drapes were drawn, and the flickering amber flames from the marble fireplace across the room cast bobbing shadows on the walls, but even from a great distance, she could still feel the warm glow of the fire.

With no natural lighting to guide her, it was difficult for Nia to tell if it was very early in the morning or very late at night. She had no idea how long she'd been sleeping.

Nia cautiously inched her hands across the mattress, expecting to encounter a warm hard body sleeping quietly next to her. She was alone in the huge bed. She lay rigid as bits of memories from the latter part of the night seeped through her grogginess. She'd been arrested and locked up in a cell at Granite Falls Police Station until Massimo had come to rescue her. Some kind of rescue since he was the one who'd put her there. His get-out-of-jail-gift to her was that she marry him, and marriage to a man like Massimo came with unbridled sex—lots of it.

Hesitantly, Nia ran her hands along her body. Her brows furrowed when she realized that she was still fully clothed in the ugly wool dress she'd been wearing last night. Heat rose to the surface of her skin when she remembered Massimo's threat to hike the dress up to her waist, bend her over the table in the interrogation room at the station, and take her from behind. He hadn't carried out his primitive threat then and there, but he'd done some equally naughty things to her in a public place.

Nia tried to throttle the dizzying currents racing through her at the memory of Massimo pushing her panties aside and burrowing his fingers inside her. The fact that any of the four officers at the station could have walked by and peered through the pane of glass in the door had heightened her desire and brought on an orgasm of such magnitude, she'd thought she would die from it. Nobody had ever treated her with such disrespect before, and the current tingling in the core of her sex assured her that she'd enjoyed every moment of the scandalous act.

She squeezed her thighs together and closed her eyes as she recalled the feel of Massimo's fingers thrusting in and out of her. Massimo had said he couldn't wait to make love to her, but Nia knew he hadn't yet fulfilled his promise. If he had, she wouldn't just be tingling from memory, she would have a distinct throbbing between her legs—one like she'd never had before. She would know without a shadow of a doubt that Massimo Andretti had been inside her.

She'd be naked too, since Massimo would never be satisfied with making love to his wife for the first time while she was fully clothed, and then leaving her bed that quickly. Pulling her left hand from under the covers, Nia held it up. The huge diamond of her engagement ring and the studded cuts embedded around the circumference of the white gold wedding band shimmered in the firelight.

Massimo had insisted they get married last night because he would be going away on business in a few days and didn't want it hanging over his head. What he really meant was that he wasn't giving her another chance to run off while he was gone. As her lover, he had no legal rights over her. As her husband, he could use his power and money to track her to hell. He might even be able to have her extradited if he could prove that she'd deceived him. And God, had she deceived him. Nia Sylk wasn't even her real name. It was legally changed, but it wasn't hers.

It's a good thing Massimo had been preoccupied with a business call when she was filling out her portion of the marriage license, or her cover would have been blown. The judge was none the wiser, and hadn't asked any questions.

Nia had tucked her birth certificate away, and then faced Massimo in that small, bare-walled room and promised to love him, cherish him, and take care of him for the rest of her life, and he had promised to do the same for her. But he knew, as well as she, that neither loving nor cherishing each other was part of the contract, and that neither one of them was staying the course of this ruse for life. How could they, when couples who'd married for love couldn't even keep it together?

They didn't have a frog's chance in a snake pit.

Witnesses to their vows of deception were Steven Lynd, Massimo's attorney—whose mouth had been set in disapproval all throughout the ceremony, and the four officers who made up GFPD. The officers had seemed thrilled to be part of such a sacred ritual. One of the richest and most powerful men in the world exchanging vows was probably the most exciting thing to have ever happen at the station.

When the judge pronounced them husband and wife and told Massimo he could kiss his bride, Massimo had done so quite rapaciously as the all-male wedding party—except for Steven— cheered him on from the sidelines.

Nia was certain that Steven thought she was nothing but a gold-digger who would one day cost his client a whole lot of grief, trouble, and money, especially since Massimo hadn't asked her to sign a prenuptial agreement. Nia had no idea how she would have reacted if Massimo had asked her to sign one. She might have feigned insult and refused, at which point he might have ripped it up and gone through with the marriage anyway, or he might have decided to keep her locked up until she signed it. Either way, Massimo would have gotten what he wanted in the end. *Her.* Nia could not have risked being detained indefinitely, and so had gone along with Massimo's plan.

She didn't blame Steven for harboring suspicions about her. She would have been happy to tell him that she already had all the money she wanted from his client since Massimo had told her the two million dollars was hers to keep.

After Steven and the judge left, Officer Jordan, the Chief of Police, had handed her the folder she'd seen on the table in the interrogation room. Her rap sheet, fingerprints, mug shots, and booking report were inside. He told her to put them through the shredder, apologized for any humiliation he'd caused her, and promised it was her first and last arrest in this county, seeing she was apt to throw up in police cruisers.

Massimo had rushed her out of the station as the officers threw rice at them—rice that Massimo had brought from Azi's kitchen for the occasion. He just thought of everything.

Neither one of them had uttered a word on the ride home. He'd just pulled her close. Nia remembered laying her head on his chest and being so tired that it was possible that she'd fallen asleep in his arms. She remembered him picking her up and bringing her inside, and pulling off her shoes and stockings. The last thing Nia remembered about last night was Massimo placing her gently down in the middle of the bed and pulling the covers up over her.

Nia propped herself up on her elbows and peered around the room, half expecting Massimo to emerge from the shadows and demand that she perform her wifely duties now that she was rested. She glanced at the clock on the nightstand. It was a little past six a.m.

So it was morning. Saturday morning. She should be on a plane out of Manchester to New York with her two million dollars sitting on her lap. Instead, she was lying in her marital bed, still fully clothed, still a virgin, and alone.

Where was her husband?

Nia sighed and glanced at the pillows on Massimo's side of the bed. There was no indication that he'd been in the bed. Maybe he'd left early for his trip. Her gaze wandered across the room where her suitcases and the briefcase with the money had been placed on the floor.

She was tempted to carry out her initial plot against Massimo. She was sure he wouldn't leave her alone without commissioning his spies to watch her every move. But Nia doubted any one of them would dare lay a finger on her to try to stop her. They might call Massimo, but what could he do thousands of miles away?

She could still make Eddie's drop today, fly to Florida for her cruise on Tuesday, and be in Dulcina late next week. She would send Aaron back to the States so he could finish up high school and get ready for college. She wouldn't have to worry about Massimo finding him since she'd told him she had no other family. And Aaron would be using his legal name anyway. She was sure the name Norwood wasn't one Massimo would remember and connect to West Gate Mills.

Once Aaron was settled, she would find a remote little town on the other side of the Atlantic to live as Shaina Norwood.

A slow smile parted Nia's lips. Massimo wouldn't want the world to know that his bride had run away from him one day after their marriage. He'd all but admitted that her disappearance would make him look like a fool. He would lose credibility like he had when he began selling off pieces of his father's company and reneging on deals Luciano had made before he died.

The business world had thought he'd gone mad or was simply throwing a spoiled, rich-boy tantrum for a wrong his father had done to him. It was a miracle Andretti Industries had survived that fiasco. A scandal involving a fugitive bride could destroy him for good. How could he control his billion-dollar corporation when he couldn't control his little slip of a wife?

No, Massimo Andretti wouldn't be able to live that one down.

With Massimo and Eddie behind her, Nia would finally be able to live a normal life. If she were lucky, she would fall in love with a man who wanted to marry her because he truly loved her and wanted to spend the rest of his life with her, not trick her into his bed to prove a point.

If Massimo had left the country, she'd be foolish to pass up this opportunity. She was already dressed and packed. Throwing back the covers, Nia hopped out of the bed and checked the bathroom and dressing areas. There was no sign of him. She ran back through the bedroom toward the door that led into the living area. She opened it slowly and stuck her head out. There was no sign of Massimo there either. The dining table was set for two, and the delicious aroma of breakfast heating on the warmer in the kitchenette made her stomach growl.

Promising her stomach that she'd take care of it once she got on the road, Nia pulled her head back in and switched on the lamp on a table near the door. It was then she saw the note propped against the lamp. With her heart fluttering wildly, she picked it up.

Cara, I'm sorry I had to run out on our wedding night. But an emergency came up. Take a bath. Have some breakfast and relax. I will be back as soon as I can! Mass.

Nia had no idea when he'd written that note. It could have been five minutes or five hours ago. His emergency could have taken him out of town, out of state, out of the country, or simply to his office. Only one way to find out. She picked up the house phone and dialed Azi.

"*Yeess, Mizz* Nia." The woman's heavy African accent boomed in her ear.

"Good morning, Azi."

"*Gooood* morning, *Mizz* Nia. I trust you slept well, eh? And I hear congratulations are in *ordaar*. Massimo is a *veeery luucky* man, eh?"

Nia dropped her weight into the chair near the table. Congratulations were not in order, but she liked Azi and had no reason to be rude to her. "Thank you, Azi, and yes I slept well." It was left to be seen how *luucky* Massimo would get. "Do you know where Massimo went?"

There was a short pause before she answered. *"Nooo, Mizz* Nia. Massimo never tells Azi where he's going, only when he's coming back."

Nia was sure Massimo had put Azi on guard and coached her on how to respond to any questions his wife may have. "And when is that? I mean, when is he coming back?"

"He *saaays aroun' nooon.*"

Nia clasped her hand to her mouth to stifle the scream. *Five hours.* She would have a five-hour head start if she left now. Officer Jordan wouldn't dare stop and arrest her for grand theft auto again. She was Mrs. Massimo Andretti and had every right to her Mercedes. He wouldn't want her throwing up in another of his cruisers, anyway.

"Thanks, Azi. And thanks for breakfast," she added before hanging up. She felt guilty that all that delicious food would go to waste.

Nia picked up her stockings from the floor, and pulled them on. She hastily pushed her feet into her pumps, grabbed her purse, luggage, and her briefcase and strolled out of the bedroom without a backward glance.

She walked across the hardwood floor of the living area pulling her suitcases behind her. She could hardly contain her chuckle as she turned the knob on the door leading into the corridor.

Son-of-a…

The door was locked.

She rattled the handle again. *Damn him! Damn him to hell!*

Nia let out a long growl and, dropping her belongings, she sank to the floor in ultimate defeat.

Massimo didn't trust her.

Do you blame him? her annoying inner voice taunted.

Nia dropped her head in her hands. She didn't sigh. She didn't moan. She didn't cry. She just simply accepted the raw truth. There was no escaping Massimo Andretti. He would always be one step ahead of her.

She inhaled deeply as another truth registered in her brain. *She was tired.* She was tired of running, of hiding, of scheming, and deceit. She just wanted to be normal, make friends, form bonds, walk down the street without wondering if someone was following her or if she would collide with death around the next corner. She didn't want to have to worry about Aaron so much. She just wanted to live, take time to breathe and discover who Shaina was.

She'd been living as Nia Sylk her entire adult life and had no idea who Shaina Norwood was. God, she didn't even know if she liked Shaina Norwood. But now that she was Mrs. Massimo Andretti with nothing but time on her hands, she might be able to find herself, figure out who she really was.

Aaron might hate her for marrying the enemy. She had no control over that, but she hoped he would come to realize the sacrifice she'd made to keep him alive and in perfect health, and that Massimo's money had made it possible.

Massimo might be cold and shrewd when it came to business, but in the last four days Nia had discovered a side of him that reminded her of her father. He could be sweet, gentle, and patient and even funny at times. He'd proven that last night when he'd held her in the limo as she slept in his arms, brought her inside and put her to bed. She'd been tired and fresh out of fight, and he could have taken advantage of her vulnerability. But he'd done the gentlemanly thing, and let her sleep. Alone.

Yes, his insensitive actions had gotten her family into the mess with Eddie, but ironically, his crafty plot to have her was digging them out of it—just not quite the way she'd planned. Marriage to Massimo might not be such a terrible thing. She could do worse. Her father would want her to be happy. She wasn't fooling herself into thinking she would be happy just because she was married to Massimo. She'd spoken vows to him, and he to her. So the least she could do was give them both a chance to make or break those promises.

In a few days, when Massimo left for Asia, she would make Eddie's drop, then find a way to tell Aaron about the changes in their lives. Later on, if Massimo proved he could be trusted, she would finally tell him who she really was and give him a chance to explain why he'd reneged on the contract with her father and ultimately caused his death.

Everybody deserved a second chance, but she couldn't risk revealing her true identity yet. Massimo thought she had tried to swindle him because she owed someone money. If he knew it was also because she blamed him for her father's death, he might have second thoughts about sleeping next to her every night or leaving her alone with his food. No man in his right mind would stay married to a woman he knew had come looking for him to avenge her father's death.

He might take back the two million dollars, and she'd probably have to take Eddie up on his offer of trade—that is if Massimo didn't have her thrown into jail for sure this time, which would consequently leave Aaron at the mercy of Eddie and his thugs. If she had to trade her body to keep her brother and herself alive, she would stick with the most desirable trader. That was Massimo Andretti—her husband.

Nia got up from the floor, took her luggage back to the bedroom and unpacked. She ran herself a hot bubbly bath in the Jacuzzi then soaked for a good while, allowing the jet streams to massage her aching muscles and the steam to clear her head. Then she wrapped her wet hair in a towel and her body in a huge bathrobe. She opened the drapes, letting the day into the suite, sat down at the small dining table, and thoroughly enjoyed Azi's breakfast as she watched the local news. The paparazzi had moved on from her and Massimo—for the time being. She cringed at the commotion the news of their marriage would create.

With her stomach full, her hair blow-dried and straight, and her body scented, relaxed, and adorned in a white silky lacy nightgown and matching panties, Nia selected some of her favorite artists on the built-in stereo and curled up on the divan near the fireplace in the sitting area of the bedroom.

From there, she watched giant snowflakes tumble down to the ground while she waited for her husband to come home.

CHAPTER FOURTEEN

Massimo's heart thumped erratically against his chest as he stood at the foot of the divan and studied his sleeping wife. She was the epitome of enchantment as she lay on her back, her arms overlapping above her head on the pillow, one leg fully extended while the other was slightly bent at the knee. Her feet were small and dainty, and he imagined them pressed flat against his chest, her red-tipped toes curling inside his mouth as he thrust deep inside her.

His eyes slid upward to where her white gown had ridden up to the junction of her thighs. From his position, Massimo was awarded a sensational view of the outline of her Venus mound straining against the white lace of her panties. His cock throbbed at the anticipation of a bold introduction to her folds and a tight, wet invitation into her steaming heat. His finger tingled from the memory of her clamped around it last night.

Heat crawled across his belly as his eyes feasted on her belly, her slender torso, and the swell of her voluptuous young breasts, spilling halfway out of the deep V in the front of her gown. For a breathless moment, Massimo focused on the brown mounds of flesh rising and falling to the steady rhythm of her breathing. He shifted restlessly as the subtle bumps of her taut dark nipples pushing against the gown tempted him. His mouth watered at the thought that soon those breasts would be swelling in his hands, then his mouth, those nipples hardening against his tongue.

God, he had so many fantasies about making love with Nia, and had no idea which ones to indulge in first. He sighed deeply. Some of those fantasies should have become reality last night, but he was glad they hadn't consummated their marriage yet. Making love with Nia now would be so much more meaningful, he thought with a bittersweet tug on his heart.

As he studied his wife, it dawned on Massimo that he'd never taken the time to watch a woman sleep before. The desire had never been there. Did they all look this defenseless and innocent, or was it just Nia? And even in her vulnerable state, she was still the perfect picture of sexuality with her long black hair spread out around her head on the pillow, her plump lips slightly parted in slumber, and her dark long lashes brushing her impeccable coffee cheeks. Her face was void of makeup, yet she was the most beautiful, most alluring woman, Massimo had ever seen. In all her waking and sleeping moments, Nia exuded sensuality like Massimo had never encountered in any other woman.

She kept him in a constant state of wanting. He'd be coming home for lunch every day, and his wife would be on the menu every time.

Massimo held his breath as Nia shifted in her sleep, bending her other leg at the knee and widening the space between her thighs. She gave a little half-stretch followed by a soft sigh and brought her left hand to rest on her stomach before settling back down into slumber.

A twinge of guilt shook Massimo as the diamonds on Nia's finger sparkled in the sun streaming through the wall of glass. He closed his eyes briefly at the memory of Nia standing rigidly and despondently in front of him while he'd slipped the rings on her finger and promised to protect her, care for her, and love her for the rest of his life.

Every one of those promises had come from his heart, and Massimo hoped that in time Nia would come to realize his sincerity. Especially now, he thought, as he toyed with the diamond-studded band she'd slipped on his finger while she made similar promises to him.

She was his wife. He was her husband. They belonged to each other.

A tightness gripped Massimo's throat and his heart began to pound with an emotion he dared not try to analyze, but which made him feel very unworthy of such a divine gift. A gift from the most unlikely benefactor.

When Massimo had walked into his bedroom to find Nia fast asleep, he'd been relieved even though he'd had to fight the urge to pick her up from the divan and take her to bed. He'd needed time to think and clear his head of all distractions, and mentally prepare to deal with the events, revelations, and questions that had arisen in the past few hours. He hated that he'd had to resort to locking Nia in like she was a common prisoner. But he'd had no choice.

He couldn't trust her. Not just yet.

Perhaps when he was certain she'd given up all hope of ever escaping him, he'd tell her about the secret passage from her closet into the main house—one she could escape through if dire need ever arose. The one he could have used to sneak into her bed the night she'd locked him out of the bedroom.

Until then, he would dedicate himself to showing her how much he desired her. He wanted to be closer to her than he'd ever been with any other woman. He wanted to show her how special she was to him.

Massimo eased his body down on the edged of the divan

near Nia's feet, being careful not to disturb her. She was a quiet and deep sleeper. He was grateful for that. It had given him the chance to shower and change while he slowly came to terms with the fact that his wife had a perfectly sound reason to hate him. The thought of the life she'd been living for the past five years made his stomach cramp up in pain.

She was Shaina Norwood. The child for whom he'd been looking for five years. The virgin who'd offered to sell herself to him for four million dollars. The woman he'd married last night.

Massimo shook his head slowly and his eyes misted with emotion as he grappled with the truth of his discovery, the way their paths had crossed, their lives interwoven with each other. Those innocent brown eyes he'd been unable to place had stared out at him from a silver picture frame on Ambrose Norwood's office desk at West Gate Mills. He'd been unable to remember his encounter with Nia because it had taken place just weeks after his father's death and shortly before his accident in Kenya.

In the middle of their negotiations, Massimo remembered stopping to ask Mr. Norwood about the eyes behind the *khimar*. He remembered how his heart had stopped beating for a second and how his breath had caught in his throat when he'd first encountered those eyes. Even then, they had mesmerized him. Upon learning they were his daughter's, who'd been dressed in costume for a play, Massimo had voiced his desire to meet her. He was so dumb and narcissistic back then. A real pompous ass to assume that a protective father would appreciate him enquiring about his daughter—who Massimo didn't know was only seventeen at the time. How was he to know from gazing at an image of her eyes? She could have been forty for all he knew.

Massimo had been approached by several mothers and fathers who'd offered to introduce him to their young daughters —some of them barely legal—despite the fact that he had a notorious reputation with women. All they saw were the monetary benefits at the end of his affairs.

Ambrose Norwood was not one of those kinds. His daughter meant more to him than money, than saving his failing paper mill. Their meeting had been recorded, and last night after he'd discovered Nia's true identity, Massimo had headed to Andretti Industries to find the tape. He'd listened to it over and over again until he'd memorized the segment of Mr. Norwood's response to his interest in his daughter. Massimo remembered his brown eyes, bold and imperious, as he'd quite diplomatically put him in his place.

"Excuse my candor, Mr. Andretti, but you're not the kind of man I want pursuing my daughter. You have an unsavory reputation with women. My Shaina is way too young for you—in age and experience. She's still innocent and I want her to stay that way for as long as possible. My daughter is not part of the deal I made with your father, and if you're thinking about adding her as an addendum, we might as well void this contract right now. Shaina is not for sale," he'd finished, attempting to rip the contract into two.

Massimo had developed a fierce respect for Ambrose Norwood that day.

And here he was five years later about to make love to the man's daughter.

But in his defense, she'd come looking for him, and ironically had offered to sell herself to him. She wasn't a young innocent girl anymore. She was a woman, who'd already allowed him to do things to her. Indecent things that she'd enjoyed.

Those facts didn't seem to clear Massimo's memory of the threat in Ambrose Norwood's voice and eyes when he'd told him to stay away from his daughter. The man had been ready to punch his face in, merely for asking. Life couldn't be this cruel, Massimo thought—sending him the one woman in this world whom he wanted more than he'd ever wanted another, but whom his conscience was telling him he couldn't have—shouldn't have—out of respect for her father.

"Mass..."

Massimo went rigid at the soft sound of his name. It was a whisper—barely. A husky murmur. She'd never called him Mass before. He liked the dreamy sound of it. He opened his mouth to respond to her call when he realized that her eyes were still closed, even though she'd shifted again and her hand had moved lower down on her belly. She did have a tendency to talk in her sleep, albeit unintelligible, as he'd discovered the first time they'd slept together.

It was her mumbling in the limo last night that had jarred him into full recollection. She'd been muttering about going to 'the mill' with her daddy on one particular day. Her one-sided conversation indicated that they might have been having an argument.

Why can't I go? Because he'll be there? Why can't I meet him?

Shocked to his core, Massimo had fitted the pieces together as he'd held her securely in his arms. With his gut in knots, he'd dared to ask her who was going to be at the mill. He'd known the answer even before she'd whispered, "Massimo. Massimo Andretti."

Shaina and her father had been arguing on the day he'd given the speech in the cafeteria. It was the second time he'd visited the mill. Ambrose Norwood had been desperate to keep his daughter away from him. Massimo didn't blame him. He would have reacted the same way if some rich arrogant hound had shown interest in his young innocent daughter.

All thoughts, all desire to make love to her had vanished, leaving him with an empty hollow feeling in his chest. Marrying the man whom her father had been trying to protect her from must have triggered her memory of that day and brought on her dream.

After settling Nia into bed, he'd gone to Andretti Industries to find the taped meeting with her father. He'd been paralyzed with the realization that Nia's eyes had been the ones he'd seen while he was drifting in and out of his coma in Kenya. Her eyes had kept him clinging to hope and life—a life that he'd now pledged to share with her.

It had also dawned on Massimo that his marriage to Nia might not be legal since she'd married him under an assumed name. He'd immediately called Steven, and had been somewhat relieved when the attorney said they could work around it. If her name had been changed legally, there was no problem, but if not, it was best he told Nia what he knew and remarried her by next Saturday, the day he turned thirty-four. Steven had also warned him that Nia could be accused of fraud for not producing an ID with her true identity when she signed the marriage license.

Just another problem he had to fix for her.

Before he'd fallen asleep at his desk, Massimo had come to the conclusion that he didn't care about his inheritance that much anymore. He was more concerned with taking care of Nia or Shaina. He didn't want to lose her, and revealing the reason he'd married her would definitely cause her to run again. He wasn't taking that risk.

The moon was still high in the sky when Massimo opened his eyes again and immediately began wondering how to approach Nia with his discovery. Had she disobeyed her father and snuck into the mill, anyway? Massimo smiled as his eyes caressed her. Knowing how persistent she could be when she set her mind on something, he would bet his prized orange Lamborghini that she'd been in the cafeteria the day he'd promised her father and his employees that the contract was solid and that the mill would remain open.

As far as Nia was concerned, he'd lied to her father, to his employees, and to her and her brother. In her eyes, he was a lying bastard. Aching with the knowledge, Massimo stared out the glass as snowflakes swirled around the tops of the evergreen trees. Fire and ice flowed through his veins.

On his way back to the mansion, Massimo had called Azi and asked her to prepare Nia a breakfast and take it to the master suite. Nia was still asleep when he got there. He'd written her a note and left to find more answers.

He hadn't been able to save Ambrose Norwood. After losing everything, the poor man had had to resort to cleaning snow off roofs in the winter to feed his children, and had slid to his death from one of them. Massimo had managed to save his business once Maurice's treachery had been exposed. He was now determined to save his children and restore their family legacy. He would try to make up for all the pain they'd suffered, no matter how long it took. Whether they liked it or not, the Andrettis and the Norwoods were bound to each other for the rest of their lives. He would turn them into one big happy family, or die trying. Massimo felt honored at the thought of Ambrose Norwood's blood flowing through the veins of Andretti heirs.

"Yes… yes... Mass… Massimo…"

Massimo stilled as Nia spoke his name again. This time there was no misinterpreting it. Nia was dreaming—about him. He held his breath as he turned to see her left hand sliding slowly to the V of her thighs, and her right over the mounds of her breasts. Blood pounded against his temples when she began to caress the curves of her hips and the soft flesh of her inner thighs while she undulated the lower half of her body on the divan. His mouth opened in silent awe when her fingers spread over her sex and she began to stroke herself through her panties. Soon a damp spot appeared in the crotch.

Massimo's erection stood at attention making a huge tent under his silk robe. He was hotter and harder than he'd ever been in his entire life. Unable to help himself, he placed his left hand on his shaft and began to stroke it beneath the thin fabric of his robe as he watched Nia caress herself.

This was quintessential eroticism.

Her soft sighs sent his gaze riveting to her face. Her little pink tongue darted erratically in and out of her mouth, moistening her lips, making them shimmer in the afternoon light. She moaned softly as her head thrashed back and forth on the pillow, her right hand earnestly kneading her swollen breasts, her palm opening occasionally to glide across her taut nipples before closing to knead again.

So that was how she liked to be caressed.

The increased thrusting of her hips brought his attention back south where her hand had found its way inside her panties. From the movement beneath the lace, Massimo knew that his wife had inserted one of her fingers inside herself. Perhaps two. He couldn't tell.

He toyed with the idea of pulling her panties down to her knees and licking her clit as she strummed herself, but decided that he liked watching her more—for now.

"Mass..."

Unable to resist the stimulating effects the live erotic scene was having on him, not to mention Barry White's deep baritone chanting *I Get Off On You* through the surround sound system, Massimo opened his robe and clasped his hand around his shaft. It was hot, hard, and hurting with need. With fire spiraling through him, he leaned back against the foot of the divan and stretching out his legs on each side of Nia, he began to stroke himself, trying to match his rhythm to that of his wife stroking herself.

Pleasure hummed through Massimo. He'd jerked off many times in his lifetime, and a lot more recently in the last couple months, and even more in the last four days, but no pleasure compared to the waves of ecstasy that now rolled through him, that threatened to drown him in bliss. Being inside Nia would be his ultimate undoing. His heart might stop beating, but what a way to die, tangled up in bliss.

Massimo sucked air into his lungs when he felt the heel of Nia's foot brush against his belly. She'd shifted again in the throes of passion and her fingers were still working magic between her thighs. Her breath was coming in hard gasps and the tightening of her body warned Massimo that she was on the verge of an orgasm.

The thought of her bringing herself to a climax in front of him ripped a groan from his throat.

The sound must have startled her, because her hands stilled. Her lashes fluttered up and her eyes widened in both surprise and a bit of confusion. Their gazes locked for a few tense moments and Massimo felt a fierce sensuous flame pass between them. It was a flame of acceptance, submission, promise, and expectation.

His body shuddered as her gaze skidded down his bare chest, past his stomach to where his hand was wrapped around his pulsing shaft. He felt no shame. He heard her quick intake of air as her eyes widened even more. He'd gotten that kind of reaction from women in the past who'd been amazed by his length and girth.

"Impressive set of family jewels," she murmured, appreciation evident in her sexy eyes. "What big stones you have."

There was no trace of the contempt he's seen when she'd said her vows to him last night. Perhaps she'd accepted him, willing to give them a chance. "I'm glad you like," he responded, loving her uninhibited remark.

"Do you know how to handle such a powerful tool?" She licked her lips.

His gut contracted painfully. "Question is, will you be able to handle such a powerful tool?" He was guessing that he was the first naked man she'd seen up close and personal. He wasn't kidding himself into believing that she'd never peeked at pictures or even watched sex tapes. He knew a lot of women who did, although some would never admit it.

But the fact that his nakedness was the first his wife had ever seen brought him a sense of joy and gratification he never knew possible. His eyes shifted to the junction of her thighs where her hand, though now motionless, was still shoved inside her panties, her finger still buried inside her woman's heat, he supposed.

"Only one way to find out," she said, attempting to pull her hand from inside her panties.

"Leave it there," he commanded, his eyes holding hers captive as his hand tightened around his shaft. "I want to savor the vision of you pleasuring yourself."

A sensual smile curved her lips. She worked her finger inside her slowly raising her hips to meet her downward plunges, her sweet chocolate eyes ablaze with passion and wickedness as she held his gaze, watched the play of desire roll over him. Oh yes, his wife was a pro at self-stimulation. He was proud of her.

"So you *do* like to watch," she said in a silky voice, still laden with sleep.

"Yes, I like to watch," he responded, remembering bits and pieces of their first conversation the day they met. "Do you like to watch?" His voice was gravely with emotion.

She spread her thighs a little wider to give her more room to play, or perhaps it was for his viewing pleasure. "I don't know. I've never watched before."

"Then watch then tell me." Only for her, he began to stroke himself again. Slowly and steadily he pumped his fist along his shaft from the base to the tip, squeezing and rotating as he watched the curiosity in her eyes turn to awareness, then desire, and enchantment.

"I like to watch," she finally confessed, her passion-filled eyes coming back to his face. "But you should stop before you come. I want you to come inside me."

Dear Lord, he wanted that, too. Massimo released his shaft that was now so hard, it slapped against his belly and pointed straight up toward the ceiling. He wanted to come inside her, make a baby with her—not to keep his inheritance, but to bind her to him forever. She would never knowingly run with his child in her belly. He'd only known her a few days, and they'd only been married a few hours, but Massimo already knew that he didn't want to move into the future without her. He couldn't imagine his life without Shaina Norwood in it.

She pulled her hand from inside her panties, and to his amazement, she brought it to her mouth and without breaking their gaze, she began to lick her juices off her fingers like a cat cleans its paws after a kill. His wife was full of surprises. Shrugging out of his robe and tossing it on the floor, Massimo crawled up the divan to perch on the side. He was careful not to touch her, but the heat from her body was scorching the hairs on his skin.

Her eyes widened in surprise and her luscious lips froze in an *O* around her middle finger when he reached across her, grabbed her other hand and pinned it to the divan above her head.

"You don't think I'm gonna let you clean all that up by yourself, do you? This is a marriage, a partnership. We share everything—the good, the bad, the dirty." He dropped his head and curled his lips about hers. He felt her quiver at the contact, then she giggled, then moaned as he began licking her fingers and her mouth, tasting her, as the musky smell of her sex sent his heart leaping inside his chest.

"Sweet. So sweet," he murmured as their tongues worked

together to clean all traces of her wantonness from her fingers and her rings. When she was panting under him and he was satisfied that she was clean, he raised his head and smiled down at her. Never had he performed such sensual acts with a woman before. He'd never even conjured them up. But he liked them.

"There's more where that came from, you know," she said on a tantalizing smile.

"Are you asking me to eat your——"

"Yes, but only if you want to. Don't want to be accused of making you do anything you don't want to do," she said, her lips pouting in mock disappointment.

Massimo chuckled as he caught her other hand and pinned it above her head near the other. "You're definitely a virgin," he said, watching her intently. "Your hymen is still intact, but you're no innocent, Nia Sylk."

"I never told you I was innocent. You misinterpreted my words." She wriggled in pleasure.

"We seem to do a lot of that, don't we?" He held her fast, his eyes raking down her vulnerable body as a slow fire began to build in him again.

"Yes we do."

He gazed deeply into her sweet brown eyes, wanting so badly to tell her what he'd discovered, but afraid of how she'd react. Would she stay with him if she knew he knew her secret, or would she try to run again out of embarrassment or fear of what she thought he might do to her? He wasn't willing to take that risk—again, not because of his inheritance.

Massimo surrendered to the stark naked truth. For the first time in his life, he was afraid of something. He was afraid of losing Nia.

Her eyed narrowed and a frown settled on her face as she gazed at the scar in his side. "Mass, what's that? It's too big to be a bullet hole. It looks more like a——"

"I was in an accident a long time ago," he said cutting her off.

"What happened?"

Massimo's heart raced at the concern in her eyes. "One day I'll tell you all about it." Now was not the time to discuss his face-to-face encounter with death. If he told her the truth, she'd know he could not have possibly given the order to close her father's mill, and that would lead them into a different discourse. No, he'd rather stay in this one. When she opened her mouth to ask more questions, he bent down and kissed her long and hard until she sighed her surrender into his mouth.

Assured that her questions about his scar were forgotten for now, Massimo released her mouth. "There's one thing we can't misinterpret," he said, releasing her hands and pushing to his feet.

"What's that?" Her eyes zeroed in on his erection.

"Take off your clothes and I'll show you." He wanted to test her desire for him, her commitment to their marriage. He wanted her to want to make love with him, not because she thought he expected it, but because she truly desired to give herself willingly and completely to him.

"Slowly," he advised, walking back to the bottom of the divan to reclaim his previous position. He felt a tingling along his spine as she pushed to her knees, gathered the hem of her gown in her hands and slowly pulled it up along her slender body. She raised her hands above her head, taking much, much longer than necessary to pull it completely off. Massimo groaned as his eyes grazed down her perfect brown body, her beautiful perky breasts, high on her chest, her round brown nipples a little taut with the promise of growing darker and harder with his love, the flat dip of her belly tapering off into her still hidden Venus mound—the place where he would ultimately unleash his passion for her. Dark and lovely suddenly had meaning for him.

Her gown fluttered to the floor next to his robe and she swung her head, tossing her long black hair over her shoulders— so sexy. Massimo held his breath as her thumbs hooked into the waist of her panties and she proceeded to push them slowly off her hips, over the curve of her thighs. She dropped back to her buttocks and pulled them completely off, baring her sex, swollen and glistening from her self-stimulation.

Massimo was standing beside her, their bodies so close he could feel the heat rising up inside her. "You're beautiful," he said, running his fingertips along her arms, feeling her shiver from his touch. "The most beautiful woman I've ever seen."

She trembled at his words, and gathering her into his arms, he picked her up and took her over to his bed. He set her gently down on her back in the middle of it like he'd done last night as his fully clothed virgin bride. Only this time she was completely naked and she would no longer be a virgin when she left.

Massimo came down over her, supporting his weight on his elbows and arms on either side of her. He glanced down between their bodies, loving the contrast in the tones of their skin. It was erotically stimulating.

He cradled her face in his hands and gazed deep into her eyes, his heart trembling at the emotions she aroused in him. "I'm sorry for locking you in this morning," he said, needing to clear the air. "But I couldn't take the chance of you running again."

She touched her finger to his lips. "It's okay. You don't trust me, and you were right not to because I did try to run."

He swallowed at her honesty. There was no reason for her to tell him the truth, but he was happy she did. "I want to trust you, Nia. Can you promise me that you'll stop running?"

She nodded. "Yes," she said on a choked whisper. "It's pointless. There's no place on this earth I can hide from you. And I wouldn't want to miss this, anyway," she added, thrusting her hips upward to graze her silken belly against the firmness of his, trapping his erection between them.

Heat generated in his belly. He dipped his head and pressed his lips against her forehead, and as her arms circled his shoulders, he began to drop a series of kisses along her face, working his way down to her mouth as passion rolled through him. "How long have you been dreaming about me?" He imagined it had been six years since she first saw him at her father's mill.

"Forever. I've been dreaming about you forever, Massimo, and I'm ready to make that dream come true."

Massimo swallowed at the spark of desire he saw in her eyes. There would be no fighting him, no pretending that she didn't want him. She was giving herself willingly, erotically, and exquisitely to him. She was trusting him to quench the fire burning inside her, to release the passion she'd been bottling up for twenty-three years—to make her a woman, bring her pleasure she didn't know possible.

Nia came easily—much more easily than any woman he knew, and he was dying to sink his aching need inside her while she came, but he had to proceed with caution because she was a virgin. He'd heard rumors of some newly deflowered virgins not wanting to be touched for days, sometimes longer. Massimo didn't want to have to stay away from Nia. They were going to come together multiple times today.

"Do you want me, Nia? Truly want me?" he asked needing to hear her say the words.

"Yes, Massimo. I want you. I want to mate with you."

"Then let's mate, pussycat," he whispered against her mouth.

CHAPTER FIFTEEN

As Massimo's mouth closed over hers, Nia wrapped her arms about his shoulders, and gave herself over to the passion of his kiss. It wasn't demanding, or ravishing like his kisses in the past, but slow, lazy, and drugging with a dreamy intimacy that made her quiver at the sweet tenderness of it. He moved his mouth over hers, savoring its softness, sucking and nibbling on her lips as if he were enjoying a delicious piece of chocolate candy. This was a new side to his lovemaking and she loved it.

Massimo was no longer the rat-bastard she despised and was eager to swindle and humiliate. *He was her husband.* She was no longer a scared young girl forced to offer her body to her nemesis in exchange for money to pay back a loan shark. *She was his wife.*

Suddenly the conditions of their union didn't matter to Nia anymore. Maybe she was naïve. Maybe she was crazy. Even stupid to be feeling the way she felt about him, but her life had changed the minute she walked up to him in that cabin on Bristol Mountain four days ago. Or perhaps it was six years ago when she'd hidden in the back of the factory cafeteria and listened to him lie to her father and his employees. In spite of his deception, she'd still pledged her heart, mind, body and soul to him.

For better, or worse? She didn't know. The one thing she was certain of was that she was done denying herself the pleasure of Massimo Andretti. She wanted her husband. True, she'd just forgiven him for locking her in the master suite today, and she'd promised him that she would not run again, but their marriage was grounded on so many lies and deceit.

There was no trust or love between them. Just pure unadulterated lust and passion. A whole lot of lust and passion, she thought, as the bracing scent of his freshly showered body made her tingle all over.

When Massimo's tongue finally sought entrance into her mouth, Nia opened wide to receive him. She sighed as he traced the soft fullness of her inner lips and cheeks and stroked the roof of her mouth with the tip, and when he delved deeper seeking hers, she offered it up with a deep moan.

He echoed her moan as he began to suckle her, pulling little sighs of pleasure from her. As their tongues twirled around each other, fire began to build in Nia again. She felt restless, and her hands ran erratically up and down his powerful shoulders, molding his smooth hard flesh, loving the way his muscles contracted beneath her palm. As his dark silky chest hairs lightly brushed them, her breasts began to tingle and swell and her nipples tightened and hardened with excitement. She felt a throbbing in the core of her womanhood and seeking connection, she wrapped her legs about Massimo's waist and arched upward.

Understanding her need, he lay flat on her, crushing her swelling breasts beneath his chest and fitting the ridge of his hard sex against her moistness. Skin to skin, they were one. A searing heat sang through Nia's core and a harsh groan ripped from her throat as Massimo began to gyrate against her with slow excruciating sweetness, dipping and rolling, and each time the ridge of his sex made contact with her clitoris, he thrust his tongue deep inside her mouth. He kept up his tantalizing assault on her mouth and her sex until the ache inside became too much to contain.

She screamed his name, but his mouth on hers kept it locked in her throat. Trapped, the echo of his name spiraled down inside her like a roaring ball of fire and settled into the deepest part of her body. Nia dug her nails into his back and tangled her legs around his as he pushed her deeper into the center of the twisting firestorm. As her body tightened about him, he pressed her into the mattress with his whole body, holding her down while the raging ball of fire that was his name exploded inside her.

Gasping for air and robbed of all her strength, Nia lay listless under him.

Her body was still trembling when he released her mouth and raised his head to smile down at her. "*Vuoi piu*? You want more?" he asked, the light of desire illuminating his mellow blue eyes.

"*Si*," she responded in the only Italian she knew.

"Say, *voglio di più*, Massimo. I want more."

"*Voglio di più*, Massimo." Nia shivered as the aching walls of her sex contracted. She couldn't tell if it was from slaked passion or renewed desire. It didn't matter. The ache suggested she wanted more of her husband. She'd always want more of him. She could never get too much.

"*Poi ti darò più*, pussycat. I'll give you more." He lifted his body off hers and kneeling between her thighs," he smiled up at her. "Didn't I say you'd bring me to my knees one way or the other?"

Nia's giggle died in her throat when Massimo's lips fluttered over the delicate hollow of her neck. His soft feathery kisses, light nibbles, and gentle suckling of her skin sent dizzying sensations rushing through her. The sensations mounted as Massimo's mouth began a blazing trail of desire across her chest, kissing, nibbling and licking his way to her aching breast. She buried her hands in his hair, tangled her fingers around his silky strands and moaned deeply as his large warm hands moved over her breasts. Cupping them in his palms, he began to knead them, then massage her taut nipples with his open palm, the way she'd done countless times over the years as she'd dreamed her fantasies of him.

He'd been paying attention as she'd lain on the divan acting out her fantasies about him in her dream. And now he was playing her like a pro. He'd learned her tune, studied her rhythm. He wasn't just a playboy. He was *her* playboy. Strumming her, stroking her, leading her like a conductor leads an orchestra.

"*Che è buono?* Is that good?" he asked, his breath hot and moist against her chest as he brought his lower body back down on hers and once again settled the ridge of his sex along her moist heat.

She shook her head on a moan, too delirious to speak.

While he continued to massage her right nipple with his open palm, his left hand closed around the underside of her left breast pushing it upward, and squeezing with just about the right amount of pressure. He dropped his head and began to lick and nibble on her nipple as his hips began another slow dance against hers.

Nia's heart pounded out an erratic rhythm and her body heaved on the mattress as the conflicting vibrations rippled through her. She didn't know which triggered the need in her most—his palming, his licking, nibbling, or the provocative movements in his lower body. She didn't care, and just when she thought she could stand it no longer, his mouth closed over her entire breast and he began to suck her in earnest, switching up his tactics, bringing even more confusion to her convulsing body as he rotated his hips urgently against her.

She pulled on his hair frantically. He groaned without missing a beat, sending more passion pounding through her heart, chest and head until she cried out in wanton pleasure. While she was still screaming his name, he trailed his mouth over to her right breast, his hand to her left and repeated the assault.

Nia's third orgasm of the day exploded inside her. She lay trembling and soaked beneath him, clinging to him until her body relaxed and her limbs dropped lifelessly on to the mattress.

"You're going to kill me," she said on a breathless whisper when he lifted his head to feast on the passion spilling from her eyes.

"Then let it be a sweet death, *cara mia.*"

The hungry look in his cobalt eyes told Nia that he intended to come back to her table of delights for seconds, thirds, fourths, and fifths today. He intended to feast until there was nothing left of her.

And to prove her right, Massimo's hands circled her waist as he dropped his head to the valley between her breasts. Spreading her hands above her head, Nia closed her eyes and gave herself over to the exquisite sensations of her husband kissing his way down her body, dipping his tongue into the sensitive hollow of her belly button turning each pore of her skin into a fire-spewing volcano. Her belly quivered and her skin burned beneath his hands and mouth, and when she felt his hot breath against the waxed mound of her flesh, her body coiled at the unfamiliar, yet awesomely delicious sensations. She needed to see this.

Breathing in deep soul-drenching drafts of air, Nia pushed herself up on her elbows. He stilled and looked up at her, a sapphire fire burning brightly in his eyes. Knowing exactly what she wanted, he spread her thighs, and hooking his arms around them, he settled himself between them. Their eyes locked as his tongue darted from his mouth and made contact with the outside of her lips, very, very softly. Her body convulsed at the initial contact, and her legs began to shake.

"Delicious," he murmured, his hot breath burning her sensitive spot. He held her fast and licked at her again, smiling when her mouth opened on a sigh. His next assault was bolder, hotter, sending electrical shocks scorching through her entire system.

Nia moaned deep and long when his lips closed over her and his tongue probed the inside of her moistness. She watched his mouth open and close over her as he sucked on her like she was a ripe fruit, parting her with his tongue, kissing her with his mouth. Passion rose in Nia like the hottest fire and too weak to support her weight any longer, she tumbled back against the mattress.

That was his cue to have his way with her. She felt his fingers parting her, then his tongue probing at her entrance, flickering, tickling, teasing, edging deep inside, sending her careening into a another firestorm of delight. Nia grabbed handfuls of the sheet as Massimo's mouth moved up to her sensitized clit while one of his fingers slid inside her. She arched into his face as he stroked her and sucked her until she shot a deluge of love juices into his mouth.

There was no recovering from this one she realized as he moved up over her, supporting his weight on his elbows. His face was contorted with passion, hunger, and lust, but deep in the recesses she saw a tenderness she never expected. He gazed at her as if he knew her, had figured out her secrets, but still loved the bareness, the rawness of her.

Some unexpected recognition unlocked inside Nia, but before she could analyze it, he brought his mouth down on hers, and reaching between them, he positioned his shaft at the entrance of her body. They both groaned at the initial contact of their naked flesh—heat, power, rigor, succulence, and tension, fusing into one.

"*Guardami.* Look at me," he said as Nia closed her eyes to absorb the pleasure zapping through her.

She opened them to encounter the hot desire in his.

"*Sarò gentile.* I'll be gentle. I will love you until you scream, "*Abbastanza!*" Remember that word. It means "*Enough*". Can you remember that?"

Nia nodded and swallowed as she repeated the word in her head.

He gave her a passion-filled smile then began to thrust against her gently, the wide tip of his sex stretching her, seeking access inside her at every tentative lunge.

The tantalizing attempts caused a deep ache in the center of Nia's womanhood, and on its own volition, her body began to respond to the call of mating. She spread her thighs wider and higher inviting Massimo to come inside, finally yielding to the searing need that had been building up for years.

He thrust against her with a little more force than before and as the wide head of his sex gained entrance, Nia dug her nails into the flesh of his chest and tightened her legs about his waist.

He pulled out to the opening and thrust in again.

"Big," she moaned. "You're so big."

Sei così stretta e umida. You're so tight and wet. *Calda,*" he hissed, his body rigid and solid above her like a glittering chunk of Italian marble.

Nia moaned aloud with an erotic pleasure as she felt him moving deeper than either of their fingers had ever been. He massaged untouched and unexplored regions of her sex, causing friction that bordered on pain and pleasure. She quivered and groaned on a powerful thrust that caused a stabbing burning sensation deep in her body. She became very much aware of Massimo's size and vigor. He was a large man and he was filling her up to overflowing, stretching her, forcing her to accept him, embrace him. She groaned and quivered again.

He stilled for a moment, and Nia could feel him trembling over her and inside her as he fought to control his own passion, his need to thrust into her. "*Sei mia adesso. Tutto mia. Per sempre,*" he rasped as he clasped her hands in his and brought them to lie on the mattress above her head, intertwining their fingers together.

"It hurts," Nia whispered, not feeling so brave at the moment.

"I know, and I'm sorry." He kissed her lips. "Relax," he said in a gravelly voice, staring into her eyes with his electric blues. "Breathe deeply and slowly, listen to the rhythm of my voice. Think of the multiple times you've come today, think of the fire rushing through your veins, of the passion building in your flesh, of the throbbing of your heart threatening to burst from inside you. Think of me, Massimo, your husband, loving you, cherishing you, enjoying you, creating and feeding your pleasure, taking you to passionate heights like you've never known before. Nia… Sweet Nia… *Ti voglio cosi tanto. Ho bisogno di te cosi tanto.* I want you so much. I need you so much… Nia… my love, my sweet hot love…"

As his hot, hard shaft grazed the pulsating walls of her sex and his broad tip batted cautiously against her hymen, seeking complete entrance into her body, Massimo serenaded Nia in Italian, then in French, then in a number of other foreign tongues. The warm husky sound of his voice reached deep inside her, caressing her, enveloping her in velvet desire, his raw sensuousness carrying her to levels of ecstasy she didn't know existed. Nia felt herself tumbling, spiraling into a universe that seemed to strip her of all knowledge of Nia, the girl she used to be, transforming her into an undulating ball of hot aching flesh where she was wrapped up, tied up, enveloped in Massimo, floating on a cloud with him, dipping and dancing with him, breathing him…

"Oh God… Oh God… Oh God…"

Nia gasped in sweet agony as she felt Massimo thrusting deep, deep inside her, grunting out his pleasure above her as his huge hard body slapped against her smaller softer frame. She had no idea when he'd pierced her hymen, but the pulsing fullness of his engorged sex moving in and out of her with deep steady thrusts alerted Nia to the fact that she was no longer a virgin.

The knowledge brought a womanly smile to her lips and a liberating flush to her body. She opened her eyes to stare into the face of her husband's contorted with raw passion, his eyes gleaming like slivers of tinted crystal. She didn't know how long they'd been making love, but the sheen of sweat covering their bodies, the love welts on his arms and chest, and the warm stickiness where their sexes joined told her it had been for a while.

With the turbulence of Massimo's passion swirling around her, Nia wrapped her legs higher around his waist and gave herself over to the delightful fire pulsing through her. Their bodies fused and danced as one as they aroused a new torrent of hunger in each other, as they rode out the hot storm of desire that raged through both of them.

As she sank beneath the waves of another orgasm, Nia called out his name as her body tightened and quivered around him, creating such a friction between them she thought she would explode from the inside out. And as her climax wrapped about her, Massimo moved up over her like a powerful merciless sex god.

"*Guardaci*! Look at us!" he commanded on a hoarse whisper. "Look at us mate."

Nia followed his gaze to the spot where their bodies were joined so intimately, so erotically. It was the most beautiful thing she'd ever seen. She could feel Massimo's eyes burning into hers as she watched him sink deeply into her—to the hilt, with a loud, tormented groan of ecstasy. He pulled out slowly and thrust back in again. The sight of his strong golden body mounted over her, the convulsing muscles of his well-defined chest and washboard stomach, and the feel of his turgid sex sheathing itself inside her brown slender form over and over again sent deep, earthshaking tremors gushing through Nia, and she came again, clutching the sheets to keep from soaring off into the ceiling. As she continued to spasm like molten lava, Massimo clasped his hands beneath her thighs, pushed her knees into her chest, changing the angle of her body to give him deeper access to titillate nascent regions of her rippling sex, regions that had never been touched before.

The intimate picture and sensations of her husband loving her were so thrilling, so gloriously, excruciatingly galvanizing, Nia thought she would literally die from it. Her need had surpassed the physical. It was no longer lust that spiraled through her, because even after her lust was satisfied, her heart remained flooded with yearning for him.

She loved Massimo. Had loved him for six long years. She could forgive him for forcing her to marry him, for locking her in the master suite today, because deep down inside, Nia humbly admitted that she didn't want to leave him. Never wanted to leave him.

She was doomed. So doomed. She began to cry.

"Nia, sweet Nia. Baby." With a harsh groan, he came down on her, captured her mouth with his, swallowing her sobs as he pumped inside her again and again, swinging his hips with hysterical speed and depth as she fell to pieces under him. When his pleasure overtook him, he raised above her again, his mouth opening and closing, his eyes rolling back in their sockets as his desire peaked to unrestrained proportions. He was beautiful to her. Placing her palms flat against his chest, Nia grabbed the rippling muscles beneath his damp skin as her insides gripped him, sucking him deep, making him growl out his delight as he pumped even harder and faster inside her.

"Massimo…" She clawed at him, thrusting her hips into him, matching the tempo of his passion as their hearts thudding against each other became one beat, their bodies becoming one rhythm, communicating in the language of love. Nia opened for him as he entered, and held him tight as he tried to leave, creating such unbearable friction and heat around their throbbing sexes that she thought they would literally meld into one. Yet, she wanted more.

"Deeper. Harder," she spurred him on as she felt the onslaught of another orgasm coming on, the spinning wave of pleasure pulling her down into a fiery furnace, melting her flesh from her bones.

When she literally saw stars shooting across her universe, Nia knew she'd reached her limit. She had nothing more to give. "*Abbastanza. Abbastanza,* Massimo!"

"*Si, picolla. Chéri.*" He dropped his head beside hers on the mattress, his body convulsing like a wave caught in a tempest as he tried to suck air into his lungs.

Nia answered his call by raking her nails across his back and shoulders and sinking her teeth into his chest, punishing him, wanting to inflict the same degree of pleasure he'd inflicted on her. He groaned deep as he pulled all the way out of her then slammed back in. She could feel every inch of his shaft trembling, quivering out of control as he gyrated trying to hold on to his passion. He pulled out one last time and slammed into her, locking their hips together, stamping his claim as he whispered her name.

This time, he stayed and as Nia felt his hot seed spurt into her womb, her teeth sank deeper into his chest. Her back arched, her body tightened, and she held him close as tremors rocked her, as electricity raced through her, then fizzled out into an arousing blast of release.

He collapsed on top of her, pushing her into the mattress, his stomach jerking, his body shaking as he pumped the last drops of his seed into her.

The harsh sound of their breathing as they struggled for air echoed around them.

Nia couldn't move. Her husband had loved her to death. And it was sweet.

Massimo was used to awaking to the softness and warmth of a woman in his arms. So when he opened his eyes to the dawn of a new day, he was not overly enthusiastic until he remembered that the delicate form snuggled up against his chest was his wife. A wife with whom he'd made love multiple times yesterday and into the night—each time more intense, more rapturous than the last.

His heart raced with blissful memories and he took a deep breath as his mind flooded with visions of Nia twitching about on the mattress as he kissed his way down her body, at her moans of pleasure as he thrust deeply into her over and over again. Kissing her was like eating fire. Touching her like holding electricity. Sheathed inside her like being trapped inside a continuously erupting volcano with thick boiling lava spewing down its sides.

She was so hot, so sensual, much more so than any woman he'd ever known—and just when he thought he was utterly satiated with her sweetness, the delectable taste of her, his body hungered to meld with hers, his soul yearned to connect and soar with hers on inexplicable plateaus of ecstasy, his spirit desired to dance with hers on the pleasurable thresholds of Nirvana. She aroused feelings in him that Massimo never knew he was capable of. Feelings he'd heard Bryce and Erik talk about when referring to their wives, feelings he'd jokingly told them were sentimental loads of crap—perhaps out of jealousy at their happiness and contentment at sharing their lives with that one special woman.

Feelings Massimo had sworn never to harbor for any woman for fear of letting them down. After all, he was an Andretti. Andretti men were masters of letting women down and blaming it on the curse. He'd been breaking the curse by keeping his relationships short, making himself different from his forefathers. But as he'd made love to Nia throughout the night, Massimo had come face to face with the feelings he'd been running from, or perhaps seeking in the multitude of women he'd been with over the years.

His was a different kind of curse.

He was in love with a woman who didn't, couldn't love him, who blamed him for her father's death, and perhaps hated him for it. A most profound and cruel irony, yet not strong enough to dissuade his feelings for her.

Massimo's entire body trembled. He tightened his arms around Nia and a possessiveness and protectiveness he'd never experienced before riveted through him. She was his wife, his life, the future mother of his heirs, the candle that brightened the dark corners of his heart, the sweet essence of his being where existence and nonexistence merged into one, where the flames of their passion consumed the earth, wind, and sky.

Of all the women he'd had over the years, Massimo had never experienced the kind of optimum passion he'd had with Nia. His virgin wife had just proven that climbing peaks of absolute sexual gratification and then plunging mindlessly into the twirling abyss of ecstasy had nothing to do with the experience of the woman, but simply the woman herself.

Nia was *his* one special woman and Massimo hoped that one day soon she would come to see him as *her* one special man.

A man, who would die for her and kill for her without batting an eyelash.

CHAPTER SIXTEEN

"So, Nia, Bryce told me how you and Massimo met on Bristol Mountain. Very romantic. The first time I met Bryce I wanted to choke him, or slap him, or do something awfully painful to him, but I was too short to reach his face."

Nia glanced over at Kaya who was sitting in a rocking chair in her first-floor nursery nursing her infant son, Eli—under the privacy of a nursing blanket—while Elyse, his twin sister slept in a nearby basinet.

"The first time I met Erik, I thought he was a stiff-shirted snob, but that didn't stop me from wanting to rip his clothes off. He was hot. Still is, even after two years of marriage," Michelle murmured as she fell back against the sofa with a soft sigh.

Nia smiled at the two women who were close to her age, and who were married to men as rich and powerful as her husband. She'd only met them a few hours ago, but already she liked them.

Michelle was tall and slim and wore her straight black hair in a short chic cut. She seemed to be the wilder of the two. She had a take-charge attitude with a twist of dry humor and Nia would bet that with a flash of her black eyes, she could convince Erik to do just about anything she wanted him to do.

They'd just been discussing Michelle's vision for her *Children of the Future Foundation*. Nia was quite impressed with her dedication to disadvantaged children and her determination to save as many of them as possible. Nia had also learned that Michelle had written two books based on the lives of some of the children who frequented the youth center she'd pioneered in her hometown of Manchester—a city three hours south of Granite Falls. She was working on the third and final book in the series. The woman was an amazing philanthropist with a heart as big and warm as the Indian Ocean.

Kaya was quieter, and petite with brown eyes, and dark-brown curls reaching past her waist. She looked like a delicate flower—like the orchids Nia had seen in abundance around the house. It was hard to believe that she was married to a formidable giant like Bryce, whom Nia was quickly learning was nothing but a big teddy bear who thought the sun rose and set on his lovely wife. He gave her an orchid every single day, even if he had to have them flown in from abroad, Kaya had told her. Kaya, who grew up in foster care, was also involved with Michelle's charity. She was the lead interior designer for the building that would serve as the headquarters of the organization. They were set to break ground late next spring.

The LaCrosses and the Fontaines were two couples who were very much in love with each other, and with their adorable children as well, Nia thought. Michelle had three children—a twenty-month-old son, Little Erik, a five-month-old daughter, Tiffany, and a nine-year-old stepdaughter, Precious, whom she treated as if she'd given birth to. In addition to her twins, Eli and Elyse, Kaya was also raising her ten-year-old nephew, Jason, and her nieces, five-year-old Alyssa and one-year-old Anastasia.

Nia had been touched with Kaya's selflessness in giving up her life and a thriving interior decorating career in Florida to take care of her nephew and two nieces after their parents were killed in a car accident last year. The children called her and Bryce Mommy and Daddy, and anyone observing that family would never know that Bryce and Kaya hadn't given birth to those three children. Their love and commitment to them was undeniable.

All of the children were presently in the home theatre watching a movie with their doting grandparents—Felicia and Philippe, Erik's parents, and Lillian and Henry, Bryce's parents who reminded Nia of her own.

The love, trust, and respect that these people shared for each other was phenomenal—nothing like Nia had ever witnessed from people who were so diverse in so many ways. They were more like one big happy family than friends—especially the four men, who'd disappeared into Bryce's man cave to watch a game. Not a bad circle to be part of Nia thought on a ragged breath as she thought of Aaron. How would he fit in? *Would he fit in?*

"So what was your first impression of Massimo when you met him?" Kaya asked, pulling Nia out of her reverie.

Nia took a deep breath and decided to be perfectly honest. "I thought he was hot. The hottest man I'd ever seen and I swore he would be mine one day, and *voila!*" She held up her left hand and waved it in the air. "Come on, girls, do you really think my fall in front of one of the hottest, richest, most eligible bachelors in the world was an accident?"

They all burst into laughter.

"You go, girl." Michelle slapped her arm. "You lassoed yourself a real Italian Stallion. I hope you rode him hard and fast and put him away dripping wet."

"Michelle!" Kaya sent her friend a look of feigned shock.

But shivers ran up and down Nia's spine and her whole being throbbed as she remembered doing exactly that—riding her Italian Stallion all day yesterday and all night last night. They'd taken short breaks to refuel with food and sleep before reaching for each other again and again.

"What?" Michelle cut her eyes at Kaya. "Like you and Bryce don't get freaky and dirty in the bedroom?"

"Who said we keep it in the bedroom?" Kaya's mouth twisted mischievously. "As a matter of fact, Bryce gave me my very first orgasm right there on that sofa."

"Eww!" Both Michelle and Nia jumped up from the sofa as Kaya doubled over laughing, interrupting her son's feeding, which caused him to whine in protest.

"You're nasty," Michelle said, traces of humor still ringing in her voice as she sat back down.

"Sex is a freaky, messy business, girl," Kaya said, her eyes brimming with obvious steamy memories with Bryce.

"Hmm. *Gooood* sex," Michelle acquiesced, her eyes glazing with apparent equally steamy memories of Erik.

Nia sat down again, flushing at the women's openness about sex. "So was Bryce your first?" she asked Kaya, then immediately realized her forwardness. "I'm sorry. That was too personal. Forget I asked." What the hell was wrong with her asking this woman such a private question just hours after meeting her? But it felt as though she'd know her and Michelle for years. She'd never felt this instant connection with women before, not even Amber, one of her two best friends. It had taken her a long time before she could warm up to Amber, who used to run a flower shop beneath the Manhattan apartment of a child Nia used to tutor, and then to Amber's friend Josie who frequently visited the shop. She was happy she'd formed the friendships though, because it had given her a place to hide Aaron from Eddie.

"No, it's okay," Kaya responded with a tender smile. "Bryce *was* my first, but not because I had some hang-up about sex before marriage. It was just circumstances, but I'm glad I waited for him. Can't imagine sex being better with anyone else. The way he loves me… Ohhh." She shivered. "I know I'm not missing anything."

"Erik was my second," Michelle offered without prompt, "but I wish I'd waited for him because I really hadn't made love until I made it with him. And amazingly it gets better between us as time goes by." She glanced at Nia.

"Massimo was…is my first," Nia responded to the question in her eyes. She felt a hungry tug between her thighs and she could feel moisture gathering in her panties at the memories. "I had sex for the very first time yesterday and I absolutely love it, but Massimo is so experienced, I'm afraid he might think I'm… naïve, maybe even boring." That's why she'd been so uninhibited with him. He was an Andretti and although he'd promised never to cheat on her, the possibility worried her.

"I felt the same way about Bryce's reputation with women," Kaya said. "It's one of the reasons I kept him out of my bed for a month after we got married."

"A month is a long time to wait to consummate a marriage." Nia said.

Kaya chuckled. "Yeah, he called me his reluctant bride. It was a waste of time. When we finally got together, it was just simply amazing. I have no doubt that I bring him far more pleasure than any of the experienced women he'd had in the past. As a matter of fact, he has told me so."

"I wouldn't worry about Massimo thinking you're boring," Michelle piped in. "I've seen him with a lot of women in the past two years, but from the way he's been watching you all day, I could tell that you are special to him."

Nia doubted that, but she couldn't voice her thoughts without going into details about her relationship with Massimo—why she'd come looking for him, and how he'd tricked her into marrying him. She liked these women, and believed they would eventually become her newest best friends and confidants, but not yet when she suspected that they told their husbands everything. If Bryce and Erik knew the truth about her, they would deem it their honorable duty to tell Massimo. She didn't want him hearing it from anyone but her. So until then…

"I never thought Massimo would ever settle down," Kaya said, switching her son to her other breast. "Marriage wasn't something he ever wanted. I was surprised when he became engaged to Gabrielle Berkley, but not surprised when it fell apart. But he surprised me again when he dropped that bombshell on the reporters at the country club. That was the talk of the night during Michelle's fundraiser. But now…" She shrugged. "You must be a very special woman to make him change his mind, Nia."

"And so suddenly, too," Michelle added. "I couldn't believe it this morning when Erik told me you and Massimo got married Friday night. You did the right thing in not waiting. Erik and I would have saved ourselves a whole lot of heartbreak if he'd just been honest and upfront about how he felt about me the first time we got married."

"You were married twice?"

"Yep. Unlike Massimo and Bryce—no offense." She held up her hand in apology. "Erik had only been with one other woman before me—his deceased wife, Cassie. He had a hang-up about sex before marriage. He married me just so he could have guiltless sex with me. Nobody but the judge who performed the ceremony knew we'd been hitched. I was his secret bride."

"Secret bride. Reluctant bride," Nia said, pulling her legs up under her. "I guess I'm the fugitive bride."

"Huh?" The women's brows rose in question.

"Massimo had me thrown in jail." It was best she put it out there. She was sure it was bound to become public knowledge soon.

"For what?" Michelle stared at her.

"I was mad at him and tried to run away in the Mercedes he'd bought for me. He had me charged with grand theft auto, and burglary because I was wearing his mother's jewelry." *And other things I can't tell you.* Nia took a deep breath. "He had me arrested and swore he would keep me locked up until I agreed to marry him that very night. My wedding ceremony took place in an interrogation room at Granite Falls Police Station."

Their responses puzzled Nia. Instead of being appalled and calling Massimo a heartless jerk, and offering her sympathy, they doubled over laughing.

"A woman running away from Massimo Andretti? Now that's a first." Michelle slapped her palm against the arm of the sofa as her laughter took hold of her.

As Nia watched them, she began to smile, then grin. It hadn't been funny on Friday night when she'd thought her and Aaron's safety had been jeopardized. But now that she could still pay Eddie on time and lead a somewhat normal life as Massimo's wife, she allowed herself to see how comical it all was—all the planning and scheming Massimo had to do in order to pull it off.

How had he explained to Officer Jordan and to his lawyer the fact that a perfectly healthy and beautiful young woman was running away from him in the middle of a cold winter night with two million dollars in tow? Why would any woman run away from him when he treated them so well? It must have taken a little starch out of his ego, knocked him a few rungs down his playboy pedestal. Nia began to giggle at the sticky situation Massimo had found himself in, and then she was laughing until tears sprang to her eyes.

"Leave it to Massimo to go to such extremes to get what he wants," Kaya said, finally wiping a tear from her eye and taking a sleeping Eli from her breast. She fixed her clothes and prepared to rise from her rocking chair.

"And you are worried that Massimo doesn't want you, doesn't

think you're special." Michelle, who was closest to Kaya jumped up to help her. "Girl, he had you marked from the moment he set eyes on you, but he isn't going to reveal his feelings until he's good and ready. He's just like Erik and Bryce. Most people fall in love and get married. These men marry then fall in love."

"You and Bryce weren't in love when you got married?" Nia asked Kaya, after she'd settled Eli in the basinet next to his twin sister. She wondered how these babies slept through all this noise then she remembered how many children lived in the house. They were probably used to it, had adapted to it, like she would have to adapt to a lot of changes in her life.

"No," Kaya said, coming to sit on the sofa, sandwiching Nia between her and Michelle. "Bryce and I got married to give my nephew and nieces a stable home after they lost their parents last year. But we grew to love each other. I can't imagine my life without him."

"Did either Erik or Bryce ask you to sign a prenup?" she asked, looking from one woman to the next.

Michelle and Kaya exchanged wary looks before shaking their heads.

"Why, did Massimo ask you to sign one?" Kaya asked.

"No," Nia said, still not knowing what she would have done if he'd asked her to, but grateful he hadn't. She had a lot in common with these women it seemed.

Kaya shrugged. "See, Massimo would not have married you if he didn't think you were the woman of his dreams. These men believe in family and forever. They don't believe in divorce, especially when there are children involved. They would walk barefoot across Antarctica to keep their wives happy because they know that if we aren't happy, they won't be happy. They get enough stress at the office, and they come home looking to us to relieve that stress. They respect us and support our ambitions even if they're different from theirs."

"Kaya is right." Michelle laid a hand on Nia's shoulder. "And I'll tell you the same thing I told her last year when she was worried about the reason Bryce married her. Massimo could have married any woman in the world. Any!" she reiterated with emphasis. "But he chose you, Nia. You, and no one else. Look at what he did to make you marry him. He practically made a fool of himself," she said on a chuckle. "That alone should tell you how he feels about you. You're his one special woman. And I for one am ecstatic he chose you 'cause we definitely need some more color up in this town," she said, flipping her wrists.

They laughed.

"Seriously," Kaya agreed on a chuckle. "Just give him time for his heart to catch up with his libido."

Nia felt a warm flush in her body at the mention of Massimo's libido and memories of their first day as husband and wife. Early this morning Massimo had awakened her with a kiss that turned into another long session of slow lovemaking. They just couldn't get enough of each other. Neither one of them had wanted to leave the warmth and coziness of their honeymoon bed, but Massimo couldn't miss the christening since he'd promised to be godfather to Bryce and Kaya's twins.

Nia had been amazed at the feeling of peace and contentment she'd felt at Granite Falls Community Church as she sung spiritual songs, read passages from the Bible, and listened to Pastor Reuben Kelly deliver his sermon about God's grace and favor to mankind. Her eyes had misted at one point because she'd been taken back in time to when she and Aaron used to attend church with their parents. She'd thought of Aaron —about how much she missed him, and had wondered how she would go about explaining her sudden and seemingly treacherous marriage to Massimo.

She'd sent up a silent prayer, asking God to help Aaron to forgive her and to eventually accept what she'd done.

Amazingly, Massimo had sensed her internal turmoil, and had reached over and taken her left hand in his, intertwining their fingers so that their wedding bands nested against each other on his thigh. He'd placed his other arm around her and pressed her head against his chest, holding her securely against him. The gesture was so possessively tender, Nia had to fight the need to break down and cry in his arms.

After the service, she, Massimo, Adam, the LaCrosses, Steven Lynd and his pregnant wife, Libby, and the Kellys had been invited to Bryce and Kaya's lovely lake house for an elaborate lunch. In addition to being drop-dead gorgeous, Kaya was also an exceptional cook. Nia had thoroughly enjoyed the lunch she'd prepared. It was late afternoon now, and the Kellys and Lynds had left a while ago.

Before he left, Steven had pulled Nia aside and apologized for his lack of enthusiasm over her marriage to Massimo. He was just looking out for his client, but after observing Massimo today, seeing how happy he was, he realized that his suspicions of her were misplaced. He wanted them to be friends. Nia had no idea if Massimo had put Steven up to it, but she'd accepted his apology and had even given him a hug.

Since she was new in the town, and to this very exclusive circle, it would be wise for her to garner friends and not enemies. The one enemy she had in this town was now her husband—a husband whom she loved, but whom she was afraid might despise her when he found out she wasn't the woman he thought he married.

Erik and Bryce had grown to love Michelle and Kaya after they exchanged vows and rings because they were the women they married. But such was not her case. Massimo had married Nia Sylk, an alias she'd adopted, and not Shaina Norwood, the woman she really was.

Would Massimo forgive her deception when he found out

she'd neglected to tell him the truth before they exchanged vows and rings?

Only time would tell.

&

"Did you have a good time with the girls?" Massimo asked Nia as they drove down Fontaine Harbor Road, away from Bryce and Kaya's home as the beginning of dusk hung suspended in the air.

"Yes. I like them. They are really fun to be around." It had been a long while since she'd laughed that much, felt lightheaded and giddy. *Those are the kind of friends Shaina Norwood would have if she existed.* She had to find a way to bring Shaina back to life—both her and Cameron—her brother's real name.

"I'm glad. It's important for you to have close friends. Women friends," he added as he turned on to Crystal Lake Road that ran along the lake.

"Why, are you threatened by the idea that I may develop a close relationship with a man?"

"*Sì.* I will take down any man who is presumptuous enough to think he can be my wife's best friend."

"Okay, I'll put out a bulletin warding off any potential offenders. Don't want to be responsible for another man's demise," she said cheekily.

His eyes burned up the cramped space between them. "I want to be the only important man in your life. The only man who needs you. The only man you need."

But you're not. I have a little brother who needs me as much as I need him. "I didn't know you were the jealous kind, Massimo," she said, sending him a smile even as her heart thumped against her chest. Maybe what Michelle and Kaya had told her was true. Maybe she was Massimo's one special woman, and she'd just have to give him time to come to terms with that fact before he could share it with her. After all, he'd only just met her five days ago. She was certain he was too pragmatic to believe in love at first sight and even more so to admit it so quickly, especially to a woman he didn't quite know.

He reached over and took her hand. Raising it to his lips, he kissed her rings before replacing it on her lap. "I didn't know that either, pussycat, until I met you, married you, and made love with you." His eyes were blazing with passion—past and impending.

"Especially when you make love with me. We do burn up the sheets."

He chuckled. "I think we set the mattress on fire. I swear I saw some scorches on it this morning."

Nia laughed. Sex was the one thing they could be honest about. "Maybe we can add a few more when we get home."

"Oh, we will. You have no idea how hard it was for me to sit beside you in church and follow Pastor Kelly's sermon. All I could think about is what we did with each other yesterday, last night, and this morning, especially this morning."

The walls of Nia's insides throbbed at the memory of making love with Massimo this morning. It was excruciatingly slow and beautiful, almost sacred. Massimo had brought her close to an orgasm about half a dozen times and backed off before she reached the point of no return. He guided her with breathing exercise, and each buildup was more intense, more powerful than the last until neither he nor she could control the force of nature. Her body had exploded as he came inside her. The memory made Nia hunger for more of him, made her grateful to be married to him. "How hard was it?" she asked with a wicked grin as she reached across the middle console of his orange Lamborghini to fondle his thigh.

He had a knee-jerk reaction to her touch, and had to grab the steering wheel with both hands to keep the car on the road.

"What are you trying to do? Kill us both?" he asked, when the car was stable again.

"Why wait until we get home?' she asked capturing her lower lip between her teeth as she squeezed her thighs together to combat the urgent throbbing between them. All that sex talk with the girls had made her horny. She was soaking wet and burning up inside, burning up with a fire that had spread to her belly—a fire only Massimo could put out. She wanted to get freaky with her husband.

She brought one hand up to fondle her breasts as the other ventured toward his inner thigh to find that his shaft had hardened. She massaged him gently as she listened to him suck air into his lungs and watched his stomach convulse as he teetered on the edge of lust and logic.

"I want you now, Mass. I want to feel you inside me. Deep, deep, deep inside me, filling me up. I'm aching for you." She squeezed the lovely column of flesh through his slacks.

"Nia." He groaned, and the car swerved as he took a sharp turn off Crystal Lake Road on to an unpaved road. He drove like a madman for a few yards and Nia took the opportunity to unbuckle his belt, unzip his fly, and pull his dress shirt from inside his slacks. He made another turn that took them into a narrower clearing that offered some privacy by the evergreen trees surrounding them as well as a lovely view of Lake Crystal and the abundance of trees on the other side of it.

As Massimo put the car in park, Nia unbuckled her seatbelt, hiked her dress up to her waist, and pulled off her panties. He unbuckled his seatbelt and hit some buttons to push back the driver's seat and lower the back down as far as it would go.

There was no need for words between them. The harsh sounds of their breathing, the erratic thudding of their hearts in each other's ears, and the hysterical haste with which they shed their clothes was all the communication they needed.

As his upper body reclined with the seat, he worked at pulling his slacks and silk briefs halfway down his thigh while Nia straddled him. She gasped as she felt his sex spring up and slap against the inside of her thighs, reminding her of his strength and power. With her whole body quivering in anticipation, she reached down between them to hold him. He was hard and hot and so huge, she couldn't wrap her fingers all the way around him.

But knowing it was the only thing to ease the throbbing ache in the deepest region of her being, Nia raised her hips and planted the tip of his pulsing sex at the slick entrance of her body. She leaned forward, and locking her arms around his neck, she stared deeply into his beautiful eyes, aglow with passion and love. It had to be love, she told herself as Massimo wrapped his hands around her waist and pulled her down as he thrust up inside her. Hard and deep.

They both cried out at the primeval onslaught, of the fierce invasion of male into female.

As Massimo forced his way deeper into her, Nia's body began to shake as a series of powerful electrical shocks ripped through her. There was nothing tender in their quest for sexual gratification today. There was no giving, only taking from each other this time.

Massimo crisscrossed his strong arms across her back, clasped his big hands on her shoulders and pulling her chest to his, he held her down and began to pump up into her with boundless speed and force. His grip on her upper body was so tight, the only part of her body Nia could move was her hips and she worked them, slamming them into his, angling her thrust so that her clitoris hit his pubic bone every time they connected. She felt every ripple of his pumping flesh scraping the inner walls of her sex, sending fire and desire roaring through her. Her breasts had become so swollen, her nipples so rigid trapped between their chests, it caused a sweet pain in the core of her heart.

As they ravished each other, Massimo's tormented groans intensified Nia's ache, amplified her itch, deepened her lust, fed the flames licking through her body until she felt the sway of her orgasm pulling her into the tidal wave of ecstasy. When it completely submerged her, she curled her body into Massimo's and cried out in the cramped space of the small car as she felt a flood of juices gush from her body and trickle down between their thighs.

Massimo didn't ease his hold or even miss a thrust as her walls convulsed around him. It were as if his shaft had been transformed into a monstrous lust machine with a ferocious life of its own, and her sex had become a hot wet velvet vacuum, clinging to him like a bloodthirsty leech, clutching him in an eternal contraction of delightfulness as he rammed in and out of her.

Nia was still quivering on the aftershocks of her orgasm when she felt Massimo's palm collide with her bare bottom. She bucked as a sensational mixture of pleasure and pain rushed through her entire body.

"*Prendimi! Scopami!*" he yelled, slapping her again.

Nia bucked and, sinking her teeth into his shoulders, she began to ride him again. Her limbs were rubber, her whole body a moving mass of fire as she rocked back and forth on her husband. Her heart was flooded to such capacity, Nia found it hard to breathe and just when she thought she would detonate, Massimo began to roar like a lion as his body jerked in a crazy frenzy under her.

"*Vengo! Vengo!*" he shouted on an upward thrust more powerful and vicious than any Nia had ever received.

It felt as if he'd pierced through every resistance inside of her. She felt him stiffen, then she felt his hot seed flooding her womb, quenching the fire that he'd created inside her She sank her teeth further into him and let herself drown in her own release. They quivered above and beneath each other and stayed locked together until their harsh cries of pleasure dwindled to low moans, and their hearts and breaths returned to their normal pace.

Nia opened her eyes to find that they were shrouded in the darkness of night. Massimo was asleep beneath her, the steady rhythm of his heartbeat echoing in her ears, and the cry of loons reaching her from their nests on the lakeside.

Massimo's sex, though far less rigorous now, was still nestled inside her. She would have loved to stay that way a little while longer, but it was cold inside the car. When she attempted to move, she found she couldn't. Her foot was lodged between the car seat and the door. She ached all over. Inside and out. It was going to be a while before she could walk without pain.

Nia smiled at the thought that she'd ridden her husband exceptionally hard and put him away dripping wet. Lowering her mouth to his, she awakened him with a tender kiss of love.

CHAPTER SEVENTEEN

With a large bulky envelope clutched under his arm, Massimo stepped inside a Spanish restaurant in Upper Manhattan, and walked up to the front desk where two hostesses stood. "Excuse me," he said to the unoccupied one. "I'm meeting a Mr. Wallace."

The young girl checked a seating chart, then glanced up at him, as if expecting him to remove his sunglasses. When he didn't, she smiled and said, "Yes, Mr. Wallace has been waiting for quite a while, Mr. Andretti."

Yes, I know. An hour to be exact.

"If you'll follow me this way, please."

Massimo shadowed her as she wound her way through crowded tables filled with noisy lunch patrons. He'd picked this restaurant because they served the best *Cochinillo Asado* he could find outside of Castile. Whenever he was on an extended business trip in New York, he tried to stop in for lunch. Today wasn't one of those days. Although he'd already put in an order, lunch was the furthest thing from his mind, but he hoped Mr. Wallace would appreciate his recommendation.

The hostess turned a corner that led into a smaller dining

area at the back of the restaurant. He'd paid handsomely for absolute privacy, so he knew right away that the man sitting at the table under a window overlooking the Hudson was none other than Mr. Wallace.

He seemed to be in his early to mid-forties, was taller than the average man, and wore a mustache and a goatee. The expensive black suit he wore fitted his solid frame perfectly. His hands were wrapped around a liquor glass and the multitude of diamonds on his fingers flashed against the sun streaming through the window. Even from a distance Massimo detected the beads of sweat on his clean-shaven head and forehead. A smile curved Massimo's lips. He'd asked the restaurant manager to turn up the heat in the room and to seat Wallace at the window so the midday sun could beat down on him. He wanted to make him as uncomfortable as possible. The fact that Wallace seemed fit and able to defend himself gave Massimo a modicum of relief. If he had to deck the man, he didn't want to be accused of not picking on someone his own size. It would be a fair fight.

Wallace looked up as they approached the table and when he saw Massimo, he nodded and raised his glass in acknowledgement.

"Here you are," the hostess said, stopping at the table.

Wallace held on to his silk tie and attempted to rise.

"Don't bother." Massimo stared down at him, a mixture of emotions swirling around in his belly. He wanted to punch Wallace just because he'd had to take time out of his life to meet with him. He would have much preferred to remain in the warm cozy comfort of his bed with his wife for a few more hours before he boarded his jet to Asia. But then again, if it weren't for Wallace, his and Nia's paths might never have crossed.

Tugging at the knot of his tie, Wallace stared at the waitress. "Hey, doll. It's a little hot in here. Do you think you can turn down the heat? Maybe turn on the AC?"

"I'm comfortable," Massimo said without taking his eyes off Wallace. "Perhaps it's just you."

Wallace uttered a shaky laugh. "Yeah, yeah, I guess it's just me." He mopped at his scalp and forehead with his napkin. "I guess I'm a bit overdressed," he said, taking a swift look at Massimo's attire: designer jeans and a gray sports shirt.

Massimo turned to the hostess. "Would you be so kind as to have the order delivered in about fifteen minutes?" That was all the time he needed with this piece of garbage.

"Yes, Mr. Andretti."

As the hostess took her leave, Massimo removed his sunglasses and placed them in the case that was clipped to the side of his belt.

Wallace's forehead crinkled and his eyes eyes narrowed, then widened. "Andretti? *The* Massimo Andretti?"

Wallace stared up at him with the dazed look of a child discovering Santa Claus—the real one—standing under his Christmas tree. The expression was totally idiotic on a grown man.

"The woman who called to set up this appointment said I was meeting with an Italian businessman who wants me to negotiate business on this side of the pond," Wallace said. "Be a middleman in a sticky situation, so to speak. I thought I was meeting someone who lives in Italy, who needed an American contact. Your reputation with the ladies precedes you, Mr. Andretti. Perhaps you can give me a few pointers, if you know what I mean." He bared his teeth in a smile Massimo assumed was meant to impress him.

"I am an Italian businessman. Andretti just happens to be my name, and I will be commissioning your services as a middleman. So I suppose everything my assistant said is correct."

"All right then," Wallace said, beaming. "It's an honor to meet you at last." He held out his hand.

Blatantly ignoring it, Massimo pulled out the chair on the other side of the table and sat down. He dropped the envelope he was carrying on the table, and moved his folded napkin and the pitcher of ice water to the other side of the table.

Wallace's eyes zeroed in on the envelope and his expression assured Massimo that he knew it was stuffed with cash. He'd no doubt been handed numerous bulky envelopes in the dark confines of many of New York's back alleys.

"Would you care for a drink while we talk business?" he asked Massimo.

"I only drink with friends."

Wallace's lips cracked into a smile. "I understand. We just met, but I hope by the time the meeting is over we'll be friends, at which time I'll insist you call me Eddie. All my friends call me Eddie," he added picking up his glass.

Massimo clenched his teeth. "And what do your victims call you?"

Eddie's hand froze halfway to his lips. "Wha—what kind of question is that?"

Reaching into his shirt pocket, Massimo pulled out a photo and carefully placed it in the center of the table. "Tell me, what does this young woman call you?"

Wallace stared at the photo, then at Massimo, then back to the photo again.

Massimo choked back a mixture of emotions as he stared at the photo of his wife he'd taken yesterday in the foyer of Granite Falls Community Church. They'd been posing for photographs with Bryce and Kaya and their children after the service, and he'd secretly snapped a few candid ones of Nia with his smartphone. She'd looked so lovely in a black pencil skirt, and a gold silk blouse, her hair tumbling down her shoulders, the wavy strands brushing her swelling breasts. He swallowed and pulled his thoughts back to the present. "Do you recognize her?" he asked Wallace.

Wallace raised his head to meet Massimo's stare. "Yeah, I recognize her. I wouldn't really call her a friend. Not yet, anyway, if you know what I mean." He grinned.

Massimo's hand curled into a tight fist under the table. The thought of this disgusting piece of garbage ogling his wife, much less laying a finger on her generated a murderous rage inside him that Massimo had never experienced before. He forced composure into his system. "If she's not your friend, what is she to you? An acquaintance? A commodity? Asset? Victim?"

Wallace straightened up and immediately went on the offense. "Look, I don't know what game you're playing, Andretti, but you asked me to meet you so we can talk business—under false pretenses, I might add. What does she have to do with anything? Is that what you want? You want her? I don't know where she is right now, but in six weeks I will, and if—"

"Our meeting has everything to do with her, Mr. Wallace," Massimo stated, leaning back in his chair and draping his arm around the back of the one next to him. "Here's the thing. You threatened to hurt her brother, and then her if she failed to pay you back the money her father borrowed from you six years ago. You even threatened, or should I say, offered to pimp her out to work off the debt."

"Where'd you get that information?"

"I spoke with some of your thugs."

Wallace flinched. "I don't have thugs."

"Oh, sorry. Your employees," he drawled. "And, she came looking for me, seeking my help in paying you back."

A slow creepy smile spread across Wallace's face. "No wonder she turned down my offer to work off the debt. She has higher ambitions than I realized. Sweet young thing, isn't she? How much did you pay her for—"

The next thing Massimo knew, he was standing over Wallace, who was sprawled on his back on the hardwood floor surrounded by overturned chairs—one with a broken leg—shreds of glass, ice cubes, and the remains of his drink. His left hand was covering his left eye, and he was peeping up at Massimo with his remaining good one. His lips were swollen and there was a trickle of blood on the side of his mouth. Massimo held his cold stare, daring him to attack so he could take out his other eye, pound him to pulp into the floor. When Wallace dropped his gaze, Massimo regretfully accepted that the fight was over. *Yellow bastard.*

His fist hurt. Damn, it hurt. Without breaking a sweat, he'd delivered about five swift jabs to the face before Wallace even realized what was happening to him, but Massimo smiled inwardly with the knowledge that Wallace was hurting a hell of a lot more. Picking up his napkin, Massimo dipped it into the pitcher of cold water and wiped Wallace's blood from his knuckles, grateful to realize that his skin hadn't been broken.

He sat down, patiently waiting for Wallace to collect himself and return to his seat. He had to fight to contain his humor at watching the man try to raise himself up off the floor with one hand since his other still cradled his injured eye. He slipped and slid a few times in the remains of his drink until he found a dry spot to give him some leverage. Once on his feet, he bent down and picked up the chairs as if he thought Massimo expected him to clean up his mess. He leaned the broken one up against the wall, and sat down, still holding his eye and trying awkwardly to lick the blood from the side of his mouth.

"Now," Massimo stated, as if the flow of their conversation hadn't been interrupted, "this young woman doesn't know that I'm aware of her true identity, and I would like to keep it that way. Therefore, your confidentiality is most appreciated. Can I count on you to keep my secret, Mr. Wallace?" He stared into the man's good rapidly blinking eye that had started to mist and twitch from the strain of assuming the workload of two.

Wallace shook his head, probably still too stunned and in too much pain to get words past his swollen lips.

"I'm a businessman, as you are. And I expect people to pay me back when they borrow from me. In the cases where they're unable to meet their obligations, I weigh the situation and act accordingly. But I don't go after their children. I don't threaten their health, their lives, or offer to pimp them out. I don't kidnap, enslave, or force them to work off their parents' debts, especially when that parent is deceased. It's neither right, nor fair. Don't you agree?"

Wallace nodded again.

Massimo pushed the envelope toward him. "I'm aware of the amount of money Mr. Norwood borrowed from you. And since I'm a businessman, like you, who expect a return on my investments, I went ahead and calculated interest for the past six years. You forfeited all late fees and penalties when you threatened his children. I realize it's not nearly as much as you expected, but I consider it fair—comparable in today's economy."

Now that they were talking money, Wallace found his voice. "Look here, Andretti, if you think you can just—"

"I'm not finished," Massimo stated, raising his hand to stop him, and like the coward he was, Wallace shut his busted trap and settled back into his seat. "I have enough on you and your shady business practices to put you away for a long, long time, but since your business is not my affair, except where this young lady and her brother are concerned, I'm willing to look the other way. I want you to forget these people exist. If you fail to adhere to my warning, I will have some of my Italian and Russian friends who live in the city pay you a visit. Believe me, they won't be as congenial as I am. They shoot first, and never ask questions. And just in case you still don't get my point, here's a little more incentive." He reached into his other pocket and dropped another photo on the table.

Wallace dropped his hand and picked up the photo. His damaged lips dropped, his good eye bulged, and his swollen eye wept as he stared at the image of his wife and four young children. His good eye looked crossways at Massimo while the other one squinted out of a red socket. "You can't threaten my family. You have no right."

"I have every right. You threatened mine. Not a pleasant feeling, is it?"

"What are you talking about? How can I threaten your family when you don't have one?"

"Oh, I have one now." Massimo held up his left hand and tapped his wedding band, then the photo of Nia. "There are three of us, and soon there will be more."

"You married her?" Wallace sucked in his lower lip, but apparently too swollen and numb to be controlled, it popped right back out with a loud smack.

Now that he knew Wallace posed no further threat to Nia and Aaron, Massimo almost felt sorry for the man. Where had he gone wrong? His background check on Edward Wallace had produced some unexpected facts. He'd come from a decent middle-class family and had graduated with honors from Harvard School of Business. He was obviously intelligent, but instead of putting his brain to good use, he'd chosen to victimize the weak and innocent.

Just went to show that *what* you become isn't always directly linked to *where* or *from whom* you come. It's your heart, your mind, and your spirit that carves the soul inside you—the soul that makes you who you are.

Massimo picked up the picture of Nia and returned it to his pocket. "Besides the return on your investment, this envelope contains some instructions for you to follow, before, during, and after my wife makes the drop to you. I suspect that she will be coming to the city tomorrow, so I suggest you begin preparing today. You'd better convince her of your sincerity, Wallace, or NYPD Blues will be fishing you out of the Hudson." He paused, and when he was certain Eddie understood him, he continued. "I've also included a—"

Wallace tried to frown. "If you're settling her account, why's she still making the drop?"

Massimo shook his head slowly and sighed aloud in frustration. "Forgetting already, Wallace? My wife is not to know we spoke. She will deliver the million dollars you requested from her." His chest rose and fell on another deep sigh. "Now, as I was saying, I've included a list of children's charities right here in New York City, and I've written down the amounts I want you to donate to each one in Ambrose Norwood's name. And let me suggest you start supporting your community instead of trying to destroy it. Your children are growing up here, for God's sake. Believe me, it will give you a sense of pride and accomplishment. Remember, stay away from my family, and I'll stay away from yours."

Massimo pushed to his feet just as the waiter entered the room. *Perfect timing.* "Hmm, lunch has arrived. I hope you like *Cochinillo Asado,*" he said on his way to the door.

"Never had it. What is it?"

"Roast Suckling Pig. Enjoy your lunch, Eddie."

Massimo exited the restaurant and climbed into the limo waiting on the side of the street. He sat down in the seat next to his cousin, but opposite his two dearest friends. He'd told them about Nia's background and about Eddie while they'd been hanging out in Bryce's den yesterday. He hadn't told them about Nia's proposal, just that Eddie had threatened her and her brother, and that she'd come looking for him because she blamed him for her father's death. They'd finally accepted his obsession with her, his marriage to her, and had pledged to protect her as he'd pledged to protect their wives in their absence.

"That was quick," Adam said, as Massimo buckled in.

"You pounded that bastard, didn't you?" Bryce asked, as the limo pulled away from the curb and began its journey to JFK where the Fontaine jet waited to take them to Bangkok, the first stop on their Asian trip as CEOs of Fonandt Wind Energy.

"He most certainly did." Erik said, watching him intently.

"Not as soundly as I wanted to." Massimo tried to make a fist and grimaced.

"Let me see that hand."

Massimo grimaced again as the doctor probed and prodded the back of his hand, his knuckles, and fingers, even his arm. "Nothing broken," he said, releasing him. "But you should put it on ice. That should bring down the swelling by the time we land. If you need a painkiller, I have some in my bags on the jet."

"Gee, thanks, Doc." Grinning at Erik, Massimo stuck his fist into the ice bucket nearest him. Erik was a member of Global Doctors, an organization that serviced war-torn countries and those that suffered from natural disasters. He was among a group of doctors traveling to Thailand to try to convince the Thai authorities to allow them to service non-documented refugees who were being held in detention camps in that country. But instead of traveling with his colleagues, he'd opted to fly with his friends. He would meet up with the other doctors in Bangkok.

"Nothing like having your own personal physician at your service," Adam said.

Massimo smiled. Adam was just along for the ride, although he'd mentioned his interest in the possibility of a Hotel Andreas in the region. It was nice to have the whole gang together. Their expanding businesses and equally growing family obligations had been cutting into their group time, so they cherished the moments they could spend together and talk about manly stuff without their wives being present.

"Do you feel better now that you whipped his ass?" Adam elbowed him in the side.

"A lot better. I wanted to wrap my hands around his neck and watch the life drain out of him."

"I know the feeling. I almost killed Kaya's ex when I found out he was using her. The things we would do for the love of a good woman."

Massimo frowned over at him. "I never told you I love her."

"Didn't have to. The fact that your hand is shoved into a bucket of ice says it all."

"Have you told her yet?" Erik asked.

Massimo's heart leaped around in his chest. "No." He pulled his hand from the bucket of ice and wiped it on the napkin Adam held out to him.

"Do it as quickly as possible," Erik admonished. "Let her know exactly how you feel. How deep your love is for her. I'd already lost Michelle before I told her how I felt. I'm just lucky that she has one of the most forgiving hearts in the universe."

"I agree," Bryce said. "I almost lost Kaya because I was afraid to open up to her. Michelle was the one who encouraged her to forgive me, and just love me. Don't make our mistakes, Mass, especially with a wife who has a propensity to run when she feels cornered. She might make it over the town line next time. Maybe even out of the country."

They all laughed, even Massimo who saw the humor in his scheme to keep Nia in town.

"Speaking of propensity, do either of you notice anything about your wives after they've all been together? How overly amorous they are?" Erik glanced from Bryce to Massimo.

"Like yesterday?" Massimo asked with a silly grin on his face. "I think they talk about us, share notes."

"Yeah," both Erik and Bryce said with equally silly grins on their faces.

"What happened yesterday?" Adam asked.

The husbands stared blankly at him.

"Once you get yourself a wife and she joins the brides' club, you'll know," Massimo told him. "Until then, you'll just have to wonder, little cousin."

"Seriously? From a three-day-old husband?" Adam said satirically.

Yep, the wives definitely shared notes, even his three-day-old one, Massimo thought, closing his eyes briefly as his mind wandered back to the erotic scene in his Lamborghini. He still felt cramped, the welts on his back and shoulders were unbearable, and his pectorals hurt where his wildcat had bitten into him. He was going to have to start wearing protective gear to bed. Perhaps he'd take one of Erik's painkillers when he got to the jet. When he'd pointed out his injuries to Nia, she'd smiled and told him it was his fault for being such an amazing lover, and that that's how pussycats behave when they're aroused. He guessed even optimum pleasure had its price.

Massimo turned to Adam, and couldn't even believe the words coming out of his mouth as he spoke them. "Marriage isn't such a bad thing Adam, as long as you're with the right woman."

"That's something coming from you, Mass. You married Nia to keep your inheritance. Lucky for you, she just turned out to be the right woman for you." He paused and glanced out the window, a sadness settling into his features. "I gave up on marriage after Claire. I loved her, and she hurt me. I'm not doing that again. I guess I'll never experience the kind of happiness you all have." He shrugged and brought his attention back inside the car. "I'll always be a bachelor I guess. The lone billionaire bachelor," he added with a wary chuckle.

Massimo felt for his cousin, but he said nothing because he had no idea what to say to someone who'd been hurt by a woman, by love.

"Don't close your heart to love and happiness, Adam," Erik —the expert on being hurt by a woman said. "You thought Claire was right for you. Obviously, she wasn't. Your heart and your ego were crushed, but she did you a favor by leaving you at the altar. The right woman for you will find you. And your heart will know it when you see her. But you have to keep it open."

It became suddenly quiet in the car as if each man was savoring his individual happiness.

Then Bryce spoke. "Now that your inheritance is somewhat secured, I think you should reach out to your brother, Mass," he said, fixing his black eyes on Massimo.

"Never gonna happen," he answered through clenched teeth. "I can't prove it, but I know his mother caused my mother's and my baby sister's deaths."

"Galen had nothing to do with their deaths, Mass. Your father and Judith Carmichael are the guilty parties. Children don't decide their DNA composition or the circumstances under which or into which they are born. Children are innocent and should not be held responsible for their parents' mistakes. I've always believed that, but even more so since I have my own."

When he didn't respond, Bryce leaned forward and planted his elbows on his knees. "Look, I can never say that I understand your pain and anger, my friend, but I know that Kaya still regrets not reaching out to Lauren and getting to know her when she had a chance. You still have a chance to know Galen. He's your brother, Mass. You share the same Andretti DNA. Don't make the same mistake Kaya made."

Massimo glanced out the window as they sped along the Brooklyn-Queens Expressway toward JFK. He agreed with Bryce's opinions about not holding children responsible for their parents' mistakes, especially since he'd learned about Eddie. And he understood Kaya's regrets about not forming a relationship with Lauren when she had the chance.

But his situation was different. Galen didn't know the identity of his father and the vast empire he'd left behind. He didn't know he had a half brother, who was worth billions of dollars. There was no evidence that the waters had been stirred where Galen was concerned, and he'd be an idiot to go looking for trouble now when he needed all his focus to remain centered on his new bride.

There were still a lot of issues he had to work out with Nia, secrets to reveal, and misconceptions to set straight before they could settle down and learn to trust and love each other freely and unconditionally. The most significant of all was forming a relationship with Cameron Norwood. That held more importance to Massimo than forming one with Galen Carmichael.

Nia loved her brother, and he could only imagine how hard it must have been for her to send him away while she figured out how to protect him. He loved her bravery, her sense of loyalty and commitment to her family. She would make a fantastic mother, willing to do anything and everything to protect her children—his heirs—just as he would do any and everything to protect them and their mother.

Massimo also knew that he would never have all of Nia's heart, her trust, her love, until she and her brother were reunited —a reunion he was certain would be taking place by tomorrow night. He hoped that by the time he returned home on Friday, Nia would be ready to open her heart to him.

CHAPTER EIGHTEEN

From the living area of her penthouse suite, Nia looked down on the moving mass of twirling skaters of all ages—some graceful and some not so—as they glided across the ice in Wollman Rink. In a couple hours, New York would light up and the sky would be teeming with millions of twinkling stars transforming Central Park into a magical, enchanted oasis of excitement, adventure, and romance.

She'd lived in this city—the most exciting in the world—for the past four years, but she'd never been able to fully enjoy it. How could she, when she'd been living as someone else and always on the alert that her past would catch up to her? She'd been afraid of so many things. That Maine's child welfare services would find her, take Aaron away, and put her in jail for kidnapping him. That the hospital would catch up to her and start garnishing her wages to pay off her father's medical bills. Little did she know that those two problems were the least of her worries, that there was a greater, more evil force lurking in the shadows. A force by the name of Edward Wallace.

Nia shivered and tightened her arms around her midsection.

It wasn't from fear, just stark realization that if it wasn't for Eddie, she might not have sought out Massimo Andretti. In fact, she knew she would never have done it. There would have been no reason to. Any hope of ever seeing Massimo again had died when he'd voided the contract between their fathers. But Eddie's threats had rekindled that hope. Eddie had inadvertently given her back her life, a chance to resurrect Shaina Norwood.

Nia took a sip of her herbal tea as her mind swam in a haze of conflicting emotions. Yesterday morning, as she'd basked in the rapturous aftermath of Massimo's lovemaking, her fear of Eddie had transitioned into a debt of gratitude toward him. She'd even thought that he deserved his one million dollars for sending her into Massimo's path, his arms, his bed, his life, and hopefully, one day, his heart.

So far removed were her anxieties that before Massimo left for his trip to Asia, she'd told him she was coming to New York to take care of some business. He'd looked at her expectantly, but when she'd offered no further explanations, he'd simply told her that his pilot was at her beck and call to fly her anywhere she wanted to go. He'd also told her that since he would be away for a few days, she should extend her stay, go shopping, catch up with her friends, and such.

Nia had needed no convincing. She did have to spend a couple days in the city since she had to settle Aaron back into school and make some kind of living arrangements for him until June when he graduated. She couldn't share the details of her trip with her husband, not just yet, but she did tell him she would stay a couple nights, at which point he'd promised to book her his favorite penthouse suite at one of New York's finest five-star hotels.

It was comforting to know that he trusted her to come back home to him. And as if to remind her of what she would be missing should she harbor any thoughts of running again, he'd made slow, drugging love to her before reluctantly pulling himself out of their bed. Nia had followed him into the shower and made love to him under the warm sprays—just to remind him of what would be waiting at home for him, should he be tempted to stray.

She wasn't forgetting that Massimo was an Andretti and that Andretti men had wandering eyes.

After Massimo left for the airport, Nia had spent the day preparing for her trip to New York. She'd called to tell Aaron to pack his bags for home. She hadn't told him that he would be flying first-class from Puerto Rico to JFK. He would have asked too many questions that she preferred to answer in person. Her intentions were to give him a taste of the new life he was returning to. Maybe if he saw how the other half lived, he wouldn't be so hard on her.

The first thing Nia had done when she arrived in New York this morning was make Eddie's drop. After handing over the money, she'd been asked to wait while they counted it in a back room of his check-cashing establishment. A short while later, a woman had come to the front and handed her an envelope. With shaking fingers Nia had opened it to find a hand-written notarized letter from Mr. Edward Wallace, stating that her father's debt had been paid in full and that she and her brother were safe from all further threats from him and his associates. He'd even apologized for his insults to her. He'd written that his change of heart had come about when his wife discovered the sort of business he was mixed up in. His wife was appalled that a man who had children would treat another man's so despicably, especially his daughter. He was trying to change his ways, and wished her all the best in life. He hoped she could forgive him. At the end of the letter, he'd listed the names and contact information of some local charities where he was planning to donate portions of the money in her father's name.

It had taken Nia over an hour to get over the shock of the contents of that letter. She must have read it half a dozen times just to make sure she hadn't imagined it, and once the reality had sunk in, she'd broken down and cried in relief. She could bring her brother home and not worry about leaving him alone in the city.

She'd spent the rest of the day looking at apartments—happy that she could now afford an upscale one. She would love to take him back to Granite Falls with her, but it would be foolish for him to change schools when he was so close to graduation.

She'd found a one-bedroom apartment within walking distance of his school. It was in a secured building, fully furnished, and equipped with a washer and dryer, and surrounded by good restaurants and a supermarket, so she wouldn't have to worry about him wandering the streets too much. The three-month lease cost more than a year's rent on their old apartment, but she had the other million dollars from Massimo and had deposited half of it into her old bank account. Tomorrow, she would take Aaron to the bank to add his name to the account and get him a debit card with spending limits of course. She didn't want the access to so much money going to his head.

She'd spoken to her old landlord who'd told her that her boxes were still at the apartment because he hadn't had time to transport them to a storage facility. Nia was elated he hadn't moved them and had made arrangements to truck them to Granite Falls. That is after Aaron took what he needed to get him through the rest of the school year.

As her heart fluttered away in anxiety, Nia left the window and sat down on the sofa near a roaring fire. She checked the time on her Smartphone as her anxiety began to grow. Aaron would be arriving at the hotel very soon, and she still had no idea how she was going to tell him about her marriage to Massimo. Even though he'd said nothing when he'd called to let her know he'd landed and was in the car she'd sent to pick him up, Nia was certain that he'd already figured out that a lot had changed in the short time he'd been away.

She would have to explain that change tonight. They'd suffered through many over the past six years—each one as challenging as the last, and they'd survived because they loved and trusted each other. She was banking on that love and trust to get them through this final, but most difficult change of all—the change back to themselves, to the people they used to be. The most challenging of all would be their change of attitude toward Massimo Andretti.

If Eddie could change, so could they—all of them—she, Aaron, and Massimo. They could learn to live as a family.

She hoped.

Massimo glanced at his ringing cellphone, and when he saw the identity of the caller, he let it ring a little longer before setting aside his copy of the report he and Bryce had been discussing— over breakfast—before their first meeting for the today. It was Wednesday morning in Bangkok and Tuesday evening in New York City. He picked up the phone and pressed it to his ear. "Andretti."

"Good morning, Mr. Andretti. It's Eddie. Mr. Wallace," the wooly voice on the other end said.

"Good evening to you, Mr. Wallace. What can I do for you?" Massimo sneered when Bryce rolled his eyes at him. He knew full well why Eddie was calling, but he had to keep him in his place.

Not for a minute did he want Eddie to get the idea that they were equals.

"You told me to call when your wife made the drop. She did this morning at which time she received the letter."

Nothing he didn't already know.

"Also," Eddie continued without prompt, "her brother just got to the hotel."

He knew that, too. Massimo walked to the window of his hotel suite and looked out at the spectacular network of Bangkok's streets and *sois,* bristling with skyscrapers and mega malls, and further in the distance the Chao Phraya River lined with ancient temples clashing against a modern skyline. It was truly a unique city and he wanted to bring Nia here sometime in the near future. More urgently, he longed to take her to Bellagio and Kenya, show her the world he'd originated from. "Anything else to report?" he asked Eddie.

Eddie cleared his throat. "She rented an apartment for her brother. It's close to his school and in a really nice neighborhood. He'll be safe there."

"Of course he will be safe, Eddie. Do you know how I know?"

"I'm gonna make sure of it."

"Good, Eddie. Remember if anything happens to him, anything at all, your wife will become a widow and your children will be fatherless."

"Nothing will happen to him, Mr. Andretti. You have my word on that."

Bryce was shaking his head and grinning when Massimo hung up and turned around. "You've definitely made a puppy dog out of that man," he told Massimo.

"Yep," Massimo said, walking back to the dining area of the elaborate suite he was sharing with Bryce. "Edward Wallace is now my bitch."

"And a fine bitch he is." Bryce burst into laughter. "That's what I should have done with Kaya's ex. Turned him into my own personal bitch." He took a sip on his coffee.

Massimo sat down and looked at his friend. "You were going through a tough time last year Bryce, and you had to deal with it alone. Now, if Erik, Adam, and I were home, we would have happily turned him into your bitch for you. It's what we do. We take care of each other's problems."

Bryce shook his head. "You're right. The only thing on my mind this time last year was the welfare of my godchildren, helping them cope with losing their parents. Plus, after my experience with Victoria and Pilar, the last thing I would have wanted was Kaya's ex hanging around her."

"My point exactly. Our situations are different, but I still don't want Eddie Wallace anywhere near my wife. I don't even want her to know what he looks like. I don't want his image in her thoughts. Her business with him is done, and she'll never have to see him or think about him ever again. Her brother is a different story, though. He will be safe—ironically—*from* and *with* Eddie as his own personal invisible watchdog."

"When are you going to tell Nia that you know who she is?" Bryce asked.

"When I get home. I thought it would be best if she told her brother about me first."

"That's good. You don't want to prolong it." He paused. "We have three meetings set for today, but I can handle the one tomorrow by myself if you want to go home a day early, you know. You're a newlywed and must be missing your bride like crazy."

Massimo sighed. "I do miss her. I've never missed a woman in my life before, Bryce."

Bryce smiled. "You've got it bad, brother. Welcome to Love." Bryce stood up. "I'm gonna go video chat with my wife, check on my family before we leave for our meetings, and they go to bed." He picked up his laptop from the table. "Maybe you should call Nia."

"I can't. She's with her brother now."

"Oh yeah. I forgot. Later, man." He walked across the floor toward his bedroom.

Massimo leaned back in his chair and locked his hands behind his head as he thought of the reunion Nia and Aaron were having at the moment. He knew it would be difficult for her to explain why she'd married him, and Massimo wished he could be there to share her burden. But he had every confidence in her.

She'd caused him, a man she'd hated for six years, to fall in love with her. He was certain she could convince Aaron, a boy she'd loved all her life, to forgive her.

Massimo prayed they would both forgive him, not for causing their father's death, because he had no hand in it, but for not being there to prevent the sale of the mill, which ultimately led to his death. He should have been there to prevent so many things, but he'd let another of his father's mottos keep him in hiding.

If your enemies know your weakness, they'll attack it. Never let them know when you're down. And if you're ever down, call your most trusted friend and have him fight on your behalf.

And he'd been weak—physically, emotionally, and psychologically. If Maurice Spencer had known he was incapacitated, Massimo would have lost Andretti Industries for sure. So he'd called Bryce, his most trusted friend and asked him to fight for him until he was well enough to fight for himself again.

Looking back now, Massimo realized that he should never have gone on that lone safari in such a fragile state of mind. But after learning about Galen, and what he had to do to gain control of his inheritance, he'd wanted to bury his father in the deepest part of the jungle he could find, in a place where his ashes would never cross paths with his mother's. She'd had no peace in life. He was determined to give her some in death.

He'd been so engrossed in his internal turmoil that he'd been paying little attention to his external surroundings, and by the time he'd noticed the injured rhino charging at him, it was too late. A month later, he'd awoken on a cot in a Masai village fighting for his life, only to learn that during his drifts in and out of his coma, Maurice had made a move to dismantle Andretti Industries by selling off a number of companies, claiming the orders had come from an absent Massimo. And to make matters worse, Massimo had discovered that huge chunks of his most recent memories had been lost.

The first thing Massimo had done on his return was fire Maurice, ninety percent of the employees, and the entire board of directors. He'd replaced them with people he could trust. He'd been called ruthless and heartless for closing his companies and putting so many people out of work, but rather than waste time defending himself, he'd taken the blame and exerted his energies to rebuilding Andretti Industries, and carving out his own niche—Bianchi Incorporated—and regaining his reputation in the business world.

Leaning forward, Massimo picked up his phone and opened his camera app. His heart thundered in his ears, and a tightness settled in his belly as he slowly clicked through the images of Nia he'd taken on Sunday.

Nia had called him from her hotel. She said she missed him. She didn't say what she would be doing in the city, and he never asked because he didn't want her to lie. There were enough lies and distrust between them already, and for that reason, he'd halted all surveillance on her once he knew she'd made Eddie's drop and Aaron was back in New York.

Massimo sighed. He couldn't wait to get back home, hold her in his arms, gaze into her beautiful brown eyes, hear her sweet voice calling his name, tell her that he loved her, and then tell her everything else. He hoped they would finally be able to begin a life—free of lies, secrets, deceptions, and misconceptions.

❧

Nia took a deep breath and told herself to remain calm and dignified. She was a married woman now—a very rich and powerful one—and she had to maintain a certain decorum when in the presence of others, like the bellman who was accompanying Aaron up to the suite.

But when Nia opened the door and saw the muscular, six-foot, one-inch frame of her seventeen-year-old baby brother standing on the other side, her reserves went flying down the hall. She shrieked like a hyena, threw herself into his arms, and burst into tears. Happy tears.

"Hey, big little sister." Laughing, Aaron wrapped his arms about her and, picking her up off the floor, he spun her around and around.

Nia felt like she was a little girl again when she and Aaron used to lurk near the door and pounce on their father when he came home from work. He would pick them up and dance them into the kitchen, or the living room, or wherever their mother was busy doing whatever mothers did. *Such sweet memories.*

"Ahem."

At the sound of a throat being cleared, Nia opened her eyes to stare at the bellman. He still had Aaron's two duffle bags draped around each of his shoulders. "Put me down," she told Aaron.

He immediately placed her on her feet. She swooned a little from the excitement and from being spun around, and grabbed on to his arm for a few more seconds. "I'm sorry. I'm just so excited to see him," she said to the bellman.

"I understand. I have a little sister," he replied with a smile and a nod. "Where would you like the bags, Mrs. A—"

"Just right here." She hastily cut him off. Now was not the time to drop the Andretti name, especially with a *Mrs.* attached to it while addressing her. "You can leave them here."

"Yes, Ma'am." He placed the bags on the floor.

"Allow me," Aaron said, stopping her when she reached into the pocket of her jeans to retrieve the tip she'd stashed there earlier. He reached for his wallet, counted off some bills, and pressed them into the man's hands. "Thank you," he said, giving him a big smile.

"Thank you, Mr. Sylk, and please let us know if we can be of further assistance to you. Enjoy your stay." He bowed and left, closing the door behind him.

"Where'd you get all those bills in your wallet?" Nia asked, linking her arms about his waist and leading him over to the sofa. She loved his new scent—sunshine, ocean, sand, and tropical nectar.

"I was working on Dulcina."

"What kind of work were you doing to make that kind of money?" She pushed him down on sofa and dropped down beside him.

"I used to go fishing with one of Josie's uncles. Uncle Luther."

"You, fishing? In the ocean?"

"Mm hmm. I went out with Uncle Luther on his boat four days a week. He even gave me my own traps and nets. He said that whatever I caught, I could sell and keep the money. I made around five thousand dollars. U.S."

"Wow, that's a lot in such a short time. I never even made that in a month."

"I was doing it for you, for us, Nia." His soft gray eyes that he'd inherited from their mother shone with pride. "Since Dad died, you've worked so hard to take care of me. You've sacrificed so much to raise me. I know I can never pay you back, but I wanted to try. I wanted to make things easier for you, especially after you called me last week and told me you were moving to Dulcina—which isn't a bad place to live," he added. "But then yesterday when you called to tell me I was coming home, the first-class ticket, private limousine, and now this…" His voice trailed off as he glanced around at the grandeur. "What's going on, Nia? Did you win the lottery or something?"

Something. Nia swallowed as she gazed at her baby brother. He'd grown up so much in a few weeks. He'd left New York a boy, and returned a man, a man who'd earned five thousand dollars working with his hands. She would respect him and treat him like a man. There was no need to protect him, keep things from him anymore. Soon he'd be going off to college and finding his place in the world. She took his hands in hers, hands that were calloused, dry, and sunburnt, hands she didn't recognize.

"I have something to tell you Aaron, something that might upset you." She looked away for a second. "It will upset you, but you have to trust me. You have to believe me when I say it was the only way to keep us safe and alive."

He was taken aback. "Keep us safe from what? From who? I'm too old for Maine's child welfare services to put me back into foster care."

Nia wished that that had been her only fear all these years. She released Aaron's hands and reached toward the coffee table. She picked up a magazine to reveal her wedding and engagement rings sitting underneath it.

Aaron's eyes bulged. "Holy crap! Those stones are huge. Are they real?" He leaned forward, blinking as the diamonds shot blinding sparks into the air.

Nia picked them up and placed them on the appropriate finger of her left hand. "As real as the man I married."

"You're married?" He slapped his hand against his forehead. "The bellman started to call you Mrs. Something, but I thought he had you mixed up with another guest. When I left New York, I didn't even know you were involved with anyone. I've never seen you with a guy. Ever. I don't think you ever went out on a date. Did you?"

"I didn't have time for guys." *Thankfully*. She was created for Massimo. Born to love him.

"I feel bad about that," Aaron said. "You were so busy taking care of me that you didn't have time to take care of you. Is this guy rich?" He cast his eyes around again.

Nia nodded. "He's a billionaire."

Aaron's mouth dropped open for a few seconds, then he squinted at her. "Is it a marriage of convenience? You could not have met, fallen in love, and married a stranger in three weeks time, Nia. What do you know about this man? He could be a dangerous criminal."

He is dangerous. "He isn't a stranger, Aaron. Not in the real sense. I'd met—I'd seen him once before—before Daddy died. Our paths crossed again last Wednesday and we got married on Friday."

"That was lightning fast. Do I know him?"

Nia held her breath and his gaze. "You don't *know* him. You've never met him, but you know *of* him. You've heard his name and seen his picture in magazines and on TV many times over the years."

"Is he some kind of Hollywood celebrity, professional athlete? They're the only billionaires whose names I might know."

"No, Aaron. He's not a Hollywood celebrity or a professional athlete. He's in business. Textiles. He owns Andre—"

Aaron jumped to his feet and glared down at her. "Don't you dare say that name, Nia! Don't you dare tell me that you married that—" He balled his fists and growled.

"Massimo Andretti. I married Massimo Andretti, Aaron. He's my husband. I'm his wife."

Nia watched the life, the excitement, and the pride she'd seen when he walked through the door drain from her brother's face. The youthful façade of a teenage boy had instantly hardened into the vicious image of a man. His body had become a hard mass of anger. Murderous anger. She didn't like the picture she was seeing. Her stomach was in knots. She wrapped her hands around her middle.

"How could you?" Aaron found his voice and it was laced with disgust. "How could you marry the man who's responsible for our father's death, Shaina? How could you betray his memory like that?" His eyes were filled with disdain. "Have you slept with him? Please tell me you haven't."

Nia dropped her gaze against the humiliation she was suddenly feeling. For the first time, she felt dirty for making love with Massimo. A medley of erotic images of them together flashed across her mind and she had to fight hard to hold back the bile that threatened to rise to her throat.

"Oh God!" Aaron exclaimed. He took a step back from her as if he'd suddenly discovered she was carrying some kind of infectious disease. "How could you sleep with that jerk? How could you let him touch you? Don't you have any pride?"

Those were questions she'd asked herself, mental obstacles she'd had to overcome.

Aaron growled. "You think because you're his wife, you're better than all the other women he's had? You're just a trophy wife, Nia. Nothing more, and when he's done with you, he'll toss you aside like the others. I thought you were smarter than that."

Nia's chest rose and fell on some harsh gasps as she tried to cope with Aaron's reaction to the news of her marriage to Massimo. She understood his disappointment, even his disgust, but she'd be damned if she was going to sit here and let him talk to her like that. Who the hell did he think he was? Her father? He was just a kid. A kid she'd sacrificed her entire life for. A kid she'd raised and protected and watched grow into a man she loved, and was currently proud of. Of course she had the same fears about Massimo, but no way in hell was she going to sit quietly and let her little brother insult her like that, make her feel shamed about the choices she'd made. As if she had any choice at all.

It was time little Aaron knew exactly what she had to do to protect him. She was telling him everything, each dirty little detail. "Sit down, Aaron," she said to him.

He turned and headed toward the door. "Dad must be turning over in his grave. I want no part of this. I'm not staying here—"

"I said, sit down, Aaron!" Nia didn't even bother to get up. She was still the boss of him for a few more months and she was exercising her authority. "Cameron Norwood, get your oversized, seventeen-year-old ass over here and sit down, or I swear to God, I'll—"

"What? What you gonna do, big little *Sista*?"

Nia clenched her teeth. "You're gonna hear me out. It's time you know exactly what I had to do to keep your bigheaded, stubborn butt safe and alive. Why you'll never become fish food in the Hudson."

He stopped and turned to look at her, shock, confusion, and fear replacing the anger and disgust in his eyes.

"If you still want to leave after you hear it all, I won't stop you. You can take your five thousand dollars and go live your life however you want to live it. But you're hearing me out. You owe me that much."

He dropped his head and slouched his shoulders as he walked slowly back towards her. He sat down on the other end of the sofa, far away from her. He didn't look at her, but kept his gaze straight ahead out the window as dusk began to descend upon them.

Nia pulled her feet up under her and leaned back against the arm of the sofa. She took a deep breath and kept her eyes on her brother's rigid frame as she began to talk. She started at the beginning, the first time she'd seen Massimo when she was the same age Aaron was now, and how she'd felt about him. She told him about the promise she'd made their father to take care of him and to leave Maine. She told him about the detective who'd been asking questions about them in Philadelphia—the reason she'd fled to New York and changed their names.

He flinched when she spoke about the first letter she'd received from Eddie. He turned and looked at her while she spoke about the second letter with the threats. He was shaking when she told him about her proposal to Massimo, and by the time she got to the part where Massimo had her thrown in jail and forced her to marry him, tears were streaming down his face.

"Shaina." He was kneeling on the floor in front of her, holding her as they cried together. "I'm so sorry. I'm so sorry. Why did you keep all this from me? Why didn't you tell me about this Eddie guy? Where is he? I'm gonna beat the crap out of him."

Nia smiled. "That's why I didn't tell you, Aaron. I knew you would think it your duty to go after him to protect me. The best way I knew to protect you was to send you away. And the only way to save us both was to proposition Massimo. As sick as it may sound, I'd happy he took me up on my offer."

He stared at her. "Did—um—your husband pay him off?"

She shook her head, understanding that he wasn't ready to speak Massimo's name. "No. Massimo doesn't know anything about Eddie. But since he let me keep the two million dollars, I gave Eddie his one million this morning." She'd also discovered that Massimo had paid off all her credit card balances and her school loans. She had no debt, except the one owed to her husband.

"How can you be sure Eddie will leave us alone now?" Aaron asked. "You came up with a million dollars in less than a week. He might see you as an easy ride to more."

Nia pulled away from him and went over to a desk. She brought back the letter she'd received from Eddie that morning and handed it to Aaron who sat on the floor with his back propped against the sofa while he read it.

"Is he for real?" Aaron asked, looking up at her.

"I don't know. He seems sincere. Let's just hope he means it."

Aaron was quiet for a moment then he shot to his feet. He held Nia's hands. "I'm sorry for the things I said earlier. Forgive me?"

"Already did."

"Do you love him? I mean your husband?"

"Yes." She wasn't going to lie to him.

"I don't understand how you can, knowing what he did to our father, our family."

"I understand how you feel, Aaron, but I've just spent a week with the man, and I have to confess that I have doubts."

"About Dad's claims?"

"No. Not about that. I feel like Massimo isn't the same person he was six years ago. He was young and inexperienced back then. Maybe he thought he was doing the best thing for his company." She shrugged. "I don't know. Maybe he's changed."

"He couldn't have changed that much. He was a hound back then, and he's still a hound, Nia. He changes women faster than I change my socks. Didn't he cheat on his fiancée not too long ago?"

Nia tugged her hands from his and tucked her hair behind her ears. "Massimo wouldn't cheat on me."

"How can you be sure? You yourself said that cheating was in his blood."

"Because he promised," she said with an emphatic shake of her head.

Aaron chuckled sarcastically. "He also made promises to our father, and look where he is."

Nia swallowed the feeling of inadequacy this conversation was causing in her. "You think I haven't considered that?" she asked, staring at her brother, meeting the concern in his eyes. "Massimo promised me he wouldn't cheat and I believe him. Ever since I walked up to him in that cabin, he's been nothing but caring, sweet, funny even," she said.

"You've been in love with him for years. You'll think that about him. Love is blind."

"Maybe it is. But Eddie changed, and he's a notorious gangster. I've changed, and before he died, Dad did say to forgive Massimo." She waved her hands at him. "And you, you've changed. I can't believe you've morphed into this man. This man with eloquent speech, and a sense of direction and purpose. A man who earns thousands of dollars in a few honest weeks' work. What happened to you?" She poked him in the chest.

He chuckled. "Her name is Monica."

"Josie's little sister?"

"Well, she isn't *that* little. She's my age. I like her. She's really smart, and she's interested in engineering, too. She's applying to colleges here in the Northeast. We're dating."

"Wow." Nia walked to the refrigerator and pulled out two bottles of water. She turned around and stepped on Aaron's toes. They both laughed. Aaron had been shadowing her ever since he could crawl. Every time she turned around, she was stepping on his toes. It was just that his toes were really big now—much bigger than hers. She handed him a bottle of water. "I have to ask you this—"

"You want to know if we're doing it," he said.

"Are you?"

"No. I'm not ready for that, and neither is Monica, but we're serious about each other."

She let out the breath she didn't even know she was holding. "You're kind of young to be serious about any girl." She unscrewed her bottle and took a long sip.

"No younger than you were when you fell for that hound you're married to." He raised his bottle to his lips.

Nia socked him in the gut, and then laughed as water spilled down his chin and splashed on to his colorful Caribbean print shirt.

He chuckled as he dabbed at the water. "I guess I deserved that."

"You did."

"Does he make you happy?"

She nodded. "Very."

"So why haven't you told him who you really are?"

"Everything happened so quickly and unexpectedly, and once we were married and I realized that I loved him, I wanted to talk to you first."

"Is he here in New York with you?"

"No. He's in Asia on a business trip. But as soon as he gets home, I'm telling him everything." She pulled out a chair from under the dining table and sat down. "I don't even think my marriage is legal."

"Right." Aaron pulled out the chair next to her and sat down. "Nia Sylk isn't your real name, and Aaron Sylk isn't mine. "Boy, we're sure in a lot of mess."

Nia sighed. "Since the change was legal, I don't think it's too much of a mess. I talked to a lawyer yesterday, and he's on it already. The biggest problem for you is having yours changed for your school records, and for MIT."

"Is it going to be an issue?" His voice was ripe with worry about his future.

"Not too much. It's being handled. I got you, little brother." She bumped his arm with her shoulder. "Massimo is due back on Friday, and I plan to tell him everything then. It wouldn't be pleasant because he has to explain why he voided the contract between our fathers. He has to take responsibility for Dad's death. He has to atone for that. If we can get past that problem, and if he still wants me, I'll ask him to marry me again." She wanted to wake up in his bed as Shaina Norwood-Andretti on Saturday morning, on his thirty-fourth birthday. "I can't wait for him to come home, so we can start fresh."

"I guess home for you isn't New York anymore. It's Granite Falls now." Aaron looked sad.

"New York was never our home. We were just hiding out here. But Granite Falls is your home, too, Aaron. And I would love it if you'd come visit this coming weekend to meet Massimo and all the other friends I've already made."

"Pff. Thanks, but no thanks." He placed his arm around her shoulders and pulled her close. "I'm really happy for you, Nia. I'm happy that you're married to the man of your dreams. But the man of your dreams is the man of my nightmares. I'm not ready to meet him. I don't know if I'll ever be."

"I know. I understand."

"But if he ever hurts you, if he ever makes you cry…" He made fists with both hands. "His Italian-American face will meet my African-American fists."

Nia chuckled and snuggled against his chest. Massimo had promised to fight her giants for her as well. It felt so good to have two men who were willing and ready to fight for her and over her. It felt so good to lay down the burdens of responsibility she'd been carrying for five long years. *So good.*

"Come on," she said, snatching her purse from the table.

"Let's go explore New York in style. Cruise around in a sleek limousine, check out some ritzy restaurants, order some raw oysters, ceviche, and caviar, even try some escargot—see what the rave is all about."

"Hey, as long as Massimo Andretti is paying, I'm all in."

Nia smiled. Aaron had said Massimo's name. It was a good sign.

CHAPTER NINETEEN

As the limousine cruised along 42nd Street toward Times Square, armies of butterflies fluttered around in Massimo's belly and his heart was pounding so ferociously, he could hardly breathe. He'd never experience butterflies in his belly or pounding of the heart, except when he was caught up in the throes of passion—a basic physical reaction to lust and sexual release.

These strange sensations happening inside him were brand new. His body had never been this eager for meaningful, heartwarming feminine contact, his emotions never so positive, his spirits never so uplifted at the prospect of floating away into a cosmos of love energy with Nia. His love for her had superseded a level, much higher and deeper than he'd ever imagined.

Nia possessed everything he'd ever wanted, would ever want in a woman. She was the one who satisfied his deepest human need—the need to be loved.

His breath caught in his throat. What if Nia didn't feel the same way about him? What if she didn't love him? He'd forced her to marry him because after spending three days with her, he'd realized that he couldn't live without her. He loved her, even if he hadn't known, hadn't admitted it to himself at the time they'd exchanged vows. She, on the other hand, had married him because she felt she had no other choice.

It was that realization that had driven him to take Bryce up on his offer to return home early. Well, that and the provocative video Nia had sent him during his second business meeting yesterday. His phone had buzzed in his pocket, and when he'd seen the text from Nia, he'd turned it on.

Never before had Massimo taken a call from a woman while he was occupied with business. But he'd taken this one and had almost exploded in his pants. He'd immediately excused himself and hurried to the men's room. He'd locked himself inside a stall and watched the mouthwatering video of his wife slowly peeling off a baby blue camisole and panties, touching herself seductively and intimately while her body swayed to Barry White's *Baby Blues*. He'd been as hard as a rock by the time she edged her baby blue panties down her tempting body.

Completely naked, she gracefully crawled up on the bed and positioned herself on all fours—animal style—as Barry sang *Can't Get Enough of Your Love, Babe*. She pushed her delectable buttocks into the air, smiled seductively into the camera and began simulating the act of lovemaking, rocking, bucking, thrusting, and writhing while she caressed her breasts, her belly, and down between her thighs where he was certain her fingers had found their way inside her dripping heat. When her pleasure peaked, she dropped her shoulders on the mattress and closed her eyes, her mouth opened in wondrous ecstasy to Barry's *You're The First, The Last, My Everything*.

Massimo hadn't even realized that he'd freed himself from the constrictions of his trousers and that he'd been stroking himself, that his sighs and moans of pleasure had blended with Nia's as her body spoke to him in the sensual language of love, until the warm evidence of his release poured into his hand.

There was no way Massimo could go back into the conference room after that. He'd called Nia to thank her for the video, but he hadn't told her that he was coming home early. He wanted to surprise her, and what a surprise it would be, he thought as his entire body seemed to quiver with the anticipation of seeing her again.

It was around two o'clock in the morning when he entered the hotel, but he was rested since he'd slept and showered during his eighteen-hour flight from Bangkok. As he rode the elevator up to the penthouse suite, Massimo hoped Cameron—who Nia said was staying with her until tomorrow—was asleep on the other side of the suite. As much as Massimo wanted to meet the young man, his wife's was the only face he wanted to see, her voice the only voice he wanted to hear for the next few hours. But he had to admit that his quiver of excitement was tainted with a rush of trepidation.

He had to tell Nia what he knew about her, even before he told her that he loved her—had loved her for the past six years. He couldn't keep that secret any longer. He didn't even think he'd be able to make love to her again until he got it off his chest. The next time they rode the waves of desire together, he wanted to whisper, scream her name—*Shaina*!

He wanted her to know that he was making love to her, the girl who'd enchanted him with her eyes six years ago. He wanted to tell her that it was her beautiful brown eyes that had guided him back to life after his collision with death. He hoped, he prayed that she felt the same way about him.

Massimo slid his key card through the slot and pushed the door open. He stepped inside and glanced about the semi-darkened living area. It was empty and quiet. *Excellent.* As he made his way toward the master bedroom, he noticed the multitude of shopping bags littered around. He recognized the names of some of the most exclusive boutiques and department stores in New York. He smiled at the thought that his wife felt at liberty to spend his money. For the first time in his life, Massimo felt useful, needed.

His heart was thumping even louder as he opened the door and stepped inside the spacious room. The drapes were drawn against the twinkling lights of New York City, but a glowing fire in the fireplace gave him just enough light to make out Nia's sleeping form in the gigantic bed. He dropped his bags near the door, toed off his shoes, and began stripping his clothes as he walked across the carpet. By the time Massimo stopped beside the bed and gazed down at his wife's angelic face, he was naked and aching. They'd been apart for three days, yet it felt like three weeks or even months.

He pulled back the cover and tossed it to the foot of the bed. She was naked. His eyes swept down her beautiful, golden body, glowing in the firelight as images of her dancing in the video heightened his arousal. He slid in beside her and spooned her against him. A fierce hunger ripped through Massimo as her soft buttocks collided with his groin. His cock responded by pulsing and growing in length and girth, as it nestled itself between the warm, moist comfort of her buttocks. Massimo buried his face in her hair, in the sleepy hollow of her neck. She was soft, and warm, and she smelled exquisite—fresh, yet musky from her own juices—a heady combination of subtle clean and earthy arousal. He had to get her some toys.

He pulled her closer with one hand and brushed his nose and lips along her neck and back, tenderly, sensually—intoxicating himself with her essence while his other hand moved slowly up along her silky body. He applied extra pressure to the taut flatness of her little belly, wondering if his first child was already planted inside her, bonding them together forever.

She moaned in her sleep, and pushed back into him, wriggling her buttocks against his cock so erotically, his stomach cramped from the thrill of it. The heat from her body merged with his, sending a fiery ache deep inside of Massimo. When his hands cupped her breasts, she began to undulate against him, cradling and caressing his shaft between her cheeks. Massimo thrust lightly, creating an intimate exchange that was beyond delicious. He kneaded her breasts and kissed and licked her earlobes, her neck, her shoulders and back until she began to groan and shiver.

Her breathing now shallow and rapid, sent electrical shocks pounding through Massimo, and needing a more intimate contact, he reached between them and fitted himself between her thighs. He thrust back and forth, rubbing his length against the hot, moist swell of her sex. He groaned when she squeezed her thighs on a sigh and shuddered, trapping him in her velvet prison.

"Massimo," she finally whispered his name.

"Hi, baby."

Her body tensed as her awakening mind tried to catch up with the heat and sensations in her body. Once she realized he was real, she tried to turn around in his arms.

He held her fast and kissed the soft flesh between her shoulder blades.

"I thought I was dreaming, but you're here. You came back early."

"Mhm. Thanks to that provocative video you sent me. You're a naughty little girl."

She chuckled, causing her wet sex to glide along his shaft. "You want to spank me?"

Massimo gritted his teeth against the intensity of his passion. He would love to spank her and then possess her, but they needed to talk first. "I would love to spank you, *cara*." He was careful not to say her name. Shaina was the name her parents had given her and it suited her perfectly. She was 'Beautiful' like the Yiddish meaning of her name. Although, he had to admit, since the Swahili meaning of Nia was 'Purpose', he could say she was a Beautiful Purpose—for so many things. "But we need to talk first," he said on a sigh.

"Not now." She kissed his arm that was wrapped around her upper body, then reaching down between her thighs, she dipped her fingertips into her own juices, and began to lather it on to the tip of his shaft with light little tentative caresses. "I've missed you."

Massimo sucked in air as his excitement weakened him. Her caresses became bolder, and as his groans increased in volume and depth, she reached behind her and clasped him in her small hand.

"We…must…um…Mmmm. We…. talk…" Her seduction of him and his desire for her overrode everything else, robbing him of his ability to speak coherently. "Mmmm. We need—talk…"

She turned her upper body slightly and, curling her arm about his neck, she pulled him in and seized his mouth in a deep, hot kiss, silencing him. She was a smoking hot she-devil, and he felt buffeted by the winds of a savage harmony when she began to suck on his tongue, matching the tempo of her hand sliding up and down his shaft, around and around, squeezing, pumping— lightly, tightly, urgently, she varied her speed and grip sending blood pounding through his heart, his chest, and his head.

"You still want to talk?" she panted against his mouth.

"Yes…No…Yes…Oh God…Mmmm…" He tingled all over.

"Okay, let's talk, but with our bodies. I want you to take me from behind." She curved her back, pushed her buttocks toward him, and positioned the tip of his cock at the entrance of her hot body. "Take me like Jabari takes his mate," she whispered, rocking back and forth, rubbing her wet sex all over his tip, teasing him, drawing him just centimeters inside of her, clinching and squeezing the head of his shaft in a tight velvet ring of pleasure, then releasing him, only to come back for more. "No more words," she said, moaning and groaning out her desire like a shameless hussy.

His hussy whom he loved.

Massimo's heart and his breath lodged inside his throat as spurts of hungry desire spiraled through his veins. He fought the need to thrust, and simply flexed his buttocks, holding himself still and stiff as his wife danced around. His mind was reeling, spinning wildly as he glanced down at the inflamed head of his cock grazing the entrance of her body.

He breathed through the pleasurable pain as he continued to massage her breasts, her belly, her thighs, and the little knob of pleasure between her folds. He kissed her neck, her shoulders, the side of one breast, and he waited—he waited until her movements became erratic and she slid back further onto him, taking a little bit more of him inside her. Still he fought the need to thrust until her body began to quiver with the power of her orgasm. Soon she shattered, screaming his name, and when he felt her hot juices coating him, Massimo pushed forward with one powerful lunge. He felt every inch forcing its way into her. She was burning hot and soaking wet, and she squeezed her muscles around him, causing a friction so severe, his eyes rolled back into their sockets. He drove deeper and deeper, pushing through her tightness until there was no further depth to conquer, until he was sheathed to the hilt inside her, until there was nothing separating them, not even air. Her body melted against his and his world was filled with her.

Securely lodged, Massimo grabbed a pillow and aligning it with her hips, he rolled her over on to her stomach. He straddled her, and held her in place between his thighs while his hands on her hips kept her immobile. In total control, he began to pump her, pulling out to the tip and ramming home, over and over again, loving the slushing sound of their damp bodies colliding in the night. He threw his head back and groaned at the insatiable pleasure that washed over him, the prickly sensations racing up and down his spine, giving him the strength to thrust into her, while at the same time robbing him of the desire to leave the silky vortex of her love.

In and out, side to side, he pumped into her while she whimpered and moaned beneath him like a jungle cat in heat. His heart rumbled at the sight of her round buttocks jumping and jiggling against his groin each time he rammed into her. He watched her hands curl around the sheet as her body began to quiver uncontrollably. Her passion fueled his own and he thrust harder and faster, gritting his teeth against the fiery sensations of her muscles gripping every inch of his cock as he plunged higher and deeper. She looked so erotic, so sensual trapped beneath him with firelight flickering across her damp brown body, edging him on, testing his strength, his endurance, his control.

Changing things up a bit, Massimo worked his thighs between hers, allowing her a little room and freedom to strut her stuff, show her appreciation, give back a little of what she was receiving. And she did, digging her heels into his buttocks and pushing herself into his groin, meeting him on his downward thrust and releasing him on his upward. Their bodies, their souls and spirits were so in synch, Massimo saw stars and moons and entire universes flickering across his mind.

He wanted to shout her name. God, how he wanted to shout out her name.

She turned her head and smiled at him, her eyes dreamy and lovely and bewitching in the firelight. It was too much for Massimo. Her body tightened and she came on him, moaning and twisting as her muscles quaked and convulsed around him. He held himself tense and closed his eyes against the need to come with her.

When he felt her relax, he leaned over her and dropped

feathery kisses along her damp back and up toward her shoulders while his hands passed beneath her to clasp her voluptuous breasts. Her nipples were hard against his palm. She reached a hand up and pushed her long hair out of the way, baring her glittering neck, for him. Knowing exactly what she wanted, Massimo licked the tender flesh, loving the salty taste of her sweat on his tongue. He brushed her soft skin with his lips, salved her with his tongue, and grazed her with his teeth, over and over until she began to moan with renewed pleasure.

He squeezed her breasts as he pulled out of her, all the way to the tip, and as he drove slowly back in, he sank his teeth into the skin at the back of her neck. He bit her fiercely, lovingly, and tenderly. His love for her was so deep, so strong, it brought tears to his eyes. He wished he could swallow her whole.

She purred, growled like a pussycat, and curved her body into his, grinding against him as she rocked in orgasmic euphoria. Their bodies locked and fused. His stomach churned fire and his cock seemed to melt from his body dissolving into the tight, moist heat of her. He eased the pressure of his teeth as the power of her climax waned.

Realizing that this was the final act before the curtain dropped, Massimo began to ride her again, slowly and sweetly at first and then more urgently and fiercely as he felt the passion build, and crest inside him. She was hotter, wetter, and tighter than before, and soon a breath-stealing explosion of ecstasy engulfed him. As he felt his seed twirling inside his groin and rushing along the length of his shaft, Massimo surrendered everything to the intensity of his climax and sank his teeth further into his wife's flesh.

He shot his hot seed deep inside her womb. He groaned out his satisfaction and pleasure, roaring like a lion that had been caught in a trap. His release was endless and wonderful, yet was over too soon.

"Shaina," he whispered, collapsing against her back as a series of earthquakes racked his body. "I love you, Shaina."

"Ahhhh." Her body stiffened in pleasure and shock, and dear Lord, she had another orgasm as her lush walls milked the last drops of semen from him.

She was quivering and crying and moaning and whimpering and he held her tightly as they lay joined together in the most basic, intimate, yet animalistic way a man and a woman could be joined. He stayed with her long after their hearts had quieted down and she lay beneath him silently, but not completely relaxed. How could she be relaxed after the bombshell he'd dropped on her? Well, two bombshells, simultaneously. It wasn't the way he'd planned for it to happen, but it was out in the open and they would have to deal with it now.

Finally, she spoke. "How long have you known?"

Massimo didn't want to leave her, but he knew this was a conversation he needed to have while looking into her eyes. With his hands wrapped about her to keep them connected, he glided on to his side and arranged her next to him with her back on the mattress and her lower body angled to cradle him—the way they were when she first began to seduce him.

He reached up and turned on the wall lamp over the headboard, then turned to gaze into her eyes that were wide and muted and filled with lingering passion, and questions. His heart ached at the bit of fear he noticed in their depth. Did she think he would retaliate for her lying to him? He pulled a pillowcase from the nearest unoccupied pillow and dabbed at the sheen of sweat on her face and neck.

She whimpered when the silk fabric brushed the spot where he'd bitten her. He turned her so he could see the evidence of his passion. "I'm so sorry sweetheart," he said, bending down to brush his lips against the darkened, raised flesh.

"It's okay." She actually smiled. "I enjoyed it. I'll get you next time."

Massimo laughed—delighted that she'd enjoyed it and for the promise of a next time. He proceeded to dry the rest of her body, then he patted himself dry before tossing the damp pillowcase on the floor. "Now," he said settling down and brushing strands of hair from her face, "how long have I known what? That I know who you are, or that I love you?"

Her lashes fluttered down briefly. "Both."

He trailed his fingertips up and down her arm. "I think I knew I loved you the day we were at the country club and my cousin began asking about my intentions toward you. I didn't like the idea of another man even thinking about you as a potential girlfriend. Especially not my cousin."

"You were jealous?"

"Yes, and that's why when I was backed into a corner by the local press, I announced to the world that we were getting married. I wanted to put the Andretti stamp on you."

She swallowed. "Why didn't you just tell me then and there instead of going through the motions, having me arrested and forcing me to marry you like that?"

He chuckled then groaned as her silky muscles gripped him, reminding him where he was. "I had to go through the motions because at the time I still didn't know who you were. I didn't know anything about the woman I was falling in love with, especially since I knew you were hiding something from me." He shrugged. "I'm sure by now you've suspected that I had you investigated. The night we met, I had a friend who's an FBI Special Agent do a background check on you."

She stiffened and looked away. "Is that when you found out who I really was?"

"No. Paul—my friend—simply verified what you'd told me about yourself. But before he could give me any more information, he fell off the map. Probably went undercover. He does that a lot. But while I was waiting to hear more from him, I realized that I didn't want to lose you. I was willing to do anything to keep you in my life. By then, it didn't matter to me what Paul found out about you."

"Obviously." She looked away again. "So when did you realize I was Shaina Norwood?"

"The night we got married."

"Before or after?"

"After."

She recaptured his gaze and her mouth tightened just a fraction. "How did it make you feel to know you'd married the daughter of the man you lied to, the man whose death you caused?"

"Is that why you came looking for me? Were you seeking revenge, restitution, retribution?"

She tried to pull away, but he tightened his grip and thrust his hips to remind her where she was, and what they'd just shared. There was no need for her to feel ashamed or frightened of him. He wasn't going to hurt her.

Her chest rose and fell on a deep sigh. "You lied to my father and caused his death. I hated you for years. I wanted to punish you," she said, her voice cracking, and her eyes tearing up with pain. "But on his deathbed, my father told me to forget you and to go on with my life. I was trying to, but then..."

He realized she'd stopped because she hadn't yet told him about Eddie. "But then Eddie happened?"

Her eyes became wide and luminous. "You know about Eddie?"

"I know about a lot of things, Ni—Shaina."

She recoiled slightly. "No one has called me that for a long time. I missed it."

"It's beautiful, like you." He kissed her forehead. "And with your permission, I would love to begin calling you Shaina. Shaina Andretti."

A tentative smile parted her lips. "Well, it's my name."

"Yes, it is." He watched the sparkle return to her eyes. At least she wasn't opposed to Andretti as her last name. There was hope, he supposed.

"Okay. I'm Shaina from this moment forward. No more Nia."

"Shaina. Shaina," he whispered then bent to kiss her lips.

"You said you discovered my true identity the night we got married. How?"

He waited a moment before responding. "Do you know you talk in your sleep?"

"I do not." She slapped his chest.

He chuckled. "You do. You fell asleep in the limo on the way home and began mumbling about going to the mill yard with your father. I think you might have had a fight or something. When you said my name, I knew instantly who you were."

Her eyes narrowed as her mind wandered back down memory lane. "Oh yeah." She smiled. "It was the day you were visiting the mill for the second time. Daddy didn't want me there. He was adamant about it."

Massimo smiled. He would tell her why later.

"But I got one of my friends to give me a ride, and I snuck in anyway and hid at the back of the cafeteria and listened while you...lied." Her voice dropped an octave.

"Give me your hand."

She hesitated before obeying. He kissed her wrist before placing her fingers on the scar on his right side.

She stared at him.

"Feel that?"

She rubbed the scar, sending a burning sensation into

Massimo's skin. "I asked you about it a couple days ago. How did you get it?"

Massimo took a deep breath. Now was the moment of truth. He held her gaze. "After my father died, I discovered something about him. A secret from his past." Talking about his father and Galen took all the excitement out of him and his flaccid sex slipped out of her.

She moaned at the loss and turned fully around in his arms so they were lying belly to belly. She kept her hand on his scar, though. "What? What did you discover?"

He took a moment to ponder, wondering how much he should divulge. It bothered him that she hadn't responded to his declaration of love. He'd told her that he loved her, and she'd said nothing. He'd never spoken those words to any woman but his mother. And he'd envisioned that when and if he spoke them, the woman would jump into his arms and tell him that she loved him, too. That woman was lying in his arms, unaffected by his love.

Massimo swallowed the panic that rose in his throat. It would be so damned painfully ironic if she rejected his love. There was no doubt that she enjoyed his body. But did she want his heart? Was it good enough for her? "I discovered that I had a half brother, ten years younger than me," he said to relieve his mind of the apprehension he felt.

"What? That must have been a shock."

He shook his head regretfully while he told her about the day he'd found his father and his secretary together at Andretti Industries. "She's the mother of his bastard child," he finished, as the disgusting images swirled in his mind. He never wanted to speak of them again.

"You were so young. Too young to witness something like that."

"That's when my relationship with my father took a nose

dive. I lost all respect for him. I despised him for cheating on my mother."

"Well, all Andretti men cheat. That's a fact." Her ironic tone concealed the true emotions he imagined she was feeling.

He broke their gaze and looked across the room as he recalled her pointing out that fact to him before. It was the most significant reason she'd given for not wanting to marry him, but he'd forced her to. She could never know the real reason he'd demanded they get married that night. "It's the curse," he said with a sour twist to his lips.

"What curse?"

He pulled her more securely into him and flung a leg across her hips. "A few generations back, one of my ancestors fell in love with a young girl from a Masai village in Kenya. She was the daughter of the Chief. The Masai are very proud people and entrenched in their traditions. They didn't allow intermarrying with other races, especially the white race. So, Amadore, my ancestor, stole Itifaki and ferried her back to Italy. Unfortunately, Itifaki was already promised to the son of the *Laiboni*, or medicine man of the village. Mbari was his name, and he cast a curse on Amadore and the entire Andretti bloodline."

"What was the curse?" she asked in a breathless whisper.

"No Andretti male would ever find happiness with any one woman, and further more they will never father a daughter." He chuckled. "Of course I don't believe in such nonsense."

"Why not? It seems to have worked. You've all cheated, and as far as I know, there have only been male offspring in your family tree. Even your half sibling is a male." She paused on a shaky breath. "I will never have a daughter." Her voice was dull, void of the heated passion they'd just shared. She pulled her hand from his scar and fisted it. "You will cheat on me, Massimo. Andretti men cheat. It's in their blood. Your blood."

"No! Never! I will never cheat on you, Shaina. I would cut

my heart out of my chest before I hurt you. What I believe is that my ancestors used the so-called curse as an excuse to cheat. I'm not like them." When she tried to turn away, he held her chin and forced her to look into his eyes. "I love you, Shaina Norwood-Andretti. I will never be unfaithful to you. And we will have daughters. Lots of sons and daughters. You have to believe that, believe me." His heart pounded against his chest with fear —the fear of losing her, not just physically, but emotionally as well. The way his father had lost his mother long before she died.

Shaina closed her eyes against the piercing blueness of Massimo's. She was cursed. He was cursed—not by some medicine man, but by the force of habit he'd adopted from his ancestors. They were doomed. She would never be happy, and neither would he. Maybe the moments they'd just shared were the happiest she would ever have. She would have to cherish them. Grief seized her. She didn't know if she should leave Massimo now before she invested more of herself into their relationship, their marriage, or wait for him to be unfaithful.

He shook her shoulder. "Shaina, say something."

Shaina felt ice spreading through her stomach. "What do you want me to say? Just because you said you loved me and that you'll never hurt me doesn't make it true. I don't believe in the curse either, but I'm sure your ancestors made the same promises to their wives, and they all broke them. Those aren't the only promises you broke," she added, pulling away from him. She was surprised he let her go. "You lied to my father. He died because of you. I need to know why, Massimo."

"Okay." His voice was tainted with frustration and impatience. He pushed himself to a sitting position and reached for the sheet, pulling it up along the bed with an aggravated deftness. He leaned his back against the cushioned headboard and reaching for her, he settled her next to him and spread the sheet over them. He returned her hand on his scar. "This scar proves that I had nothing to do with the demise of your father's company, or his death."

"How?"

"When I learned about my—Galen." He stopped to catch his breath. "I was livid. I was hurt. I can't prove it, but I know my father's affair with his secretary had something to do with my mother's death. At least her will to live."

"How do you know that?" Shaina asked, still not understanding where his story was leading and what it had to do with her family's tragedy.

"The day my mother died, she and my father had just emerged from *Il Nido d'Amore.* It's a private intimate room on the third floor of the mansion where they used to sequester themselves for hours, sometimes days at a time. It was their own little love nest where no one, not even I was allowed. It wasn't until I was much older that I understood the significance of that room."

"I guess that's why you never showed it to me on my tour," Shaina said. How much was he still keeping from her? "I know *amore* means love. What does *nido* mean?"

"It means nest. *Il Nido d'Amore* means The Love Nest," he said dropping a kiss on the top of her head. "After my father left to return to his office, my mom took me into the music room with her. She sat down at the piano and began to play Beethoven's *Fur Elise.* She played that tune whenever she was happy, and her smile that day was radiant. I so loved to watch her play, her fingers sliding across the keys and her body swaying to the music. I remember she was wearing this floral print cotton dress. She looked so beautiful, like an angel."

He smiled and looked across the room as if he could still see his mother sitting at the piano, playing for him. But soon his smile slithered away to be replaced with a look of sheer sadness.

"The phone rang and she got up to answer it. I watched her

smile die and the color leave her cheeks. She went white as a ghost before she slid to the floor. Somebody must have told her about my father's other child. It's the only thing that would have sent her into shock, and then early labor."

"I'm sorry." She laced her hands around his waist and nuzzled her face in his shoulder. He smelled musky, all male, and… She drew back. She couldn't allow herself to be hypnotized by him, not until she heard the rest of the story. "Go on."

His chest heaved on a sigh. "After I met with your father, I left for Kenya to spend some quiet time in one of my favorite villages and to scatter my father's ashes in the Mara Lands."

"Weren't your mother's ashes scattered there too?"

"Yes. They met at the Masai Mara National Reserve, and every year, they went back to celebrate that day. They wanted to spent eternity together there."

"That's so romantic."

"It could have been," he said blandly. "But after learning about his other child, I took my father's remains deep into the jungle where his ashes would never cross paths with my mother's." His muscles tensed. "Once that was done, I started off on a lone safari to clear my head. I was distracted, of course, and didn't notice the injured rhino charging toward me until it was too late. Weeks later, I woke up on a cot in a Masai hut in excruciating pain and fighting for my life. I went in and out of a coma for several more weeks while the villagers tried tirelessly to keep me alive. It was months before I was strong enough to return home, and to make matters worse, I had lost some of my most recent memories."

He paused to catch his breath before turning to look at her. "By the time I made it back to the States, the then executor of my father's estate had sold off a number of our companies and reneged on several contracts my father had signed before his death. The bank had already foreclosed on West Gate, and unfortunately your father had died and you and your brother had disappeared. I am not responsible for your father's death, Shaina. I liked your father, very much. I respected him, and I regret not being here to prevent what happened to his company, to him, and to you and your brother."

CHAPTER TWENTY

Shaina closed her eyes as her heart began to palpitate in her chest. *He almost died.* The love of her life almost died. While he was fighting for his life, she was cursing him, damning him, wishing him dead.

Shaina pressed her palm against his scar and the pain he'd suffered all those years seemed to seep into her hand, up along her arm and into heart. Her limbs felt numb and sweat beaded her forehead. She pressed her hand against her chest, as her breath seemed to solidify there. She clung to Massimo in desperation. "I can't breathe. I... I can't breathe," she panted between gasps, as her convulsing stomach seemed to careen toward her chest, bringing a gallon of bile with it. The room spun around her.

"Shaina. Shaina. Breathe. Breathe, *cara.* In through your nose, out through your mouth. Two counts in, three counts out. Yes, baby. Yes, like that. Breathe..."

Massimo was holding her, his strong hands stroking her back, his voice calling her name and telling her to breathe. "There. There," he said as her anxiety calmed, as the pressure in her chest eased, and her stomach stopped convulsing and returned to its rightful place.

"Water," she said, needing to wash the bitter bile from her mouth.

Massimo scooted off the bed and hastily returned, holding a glass of water to her lips. "Slowly, slowly," he crooned. His other hand massaged her temples as she tried not to gobble down the cool liquid.

She pushed the glass away. "Okay, I'm good. Thanks."

He placed it on the nightstand and his arms were about her again. He laid her head on his chest and stroked his fingers through her hair. "What happened?" His voice was a tormented whisper.

"The thought of you dying was too much for me to handle." Tears ran down her cheeks. "You were fighting for your life while I was cursing you, wishing you dead for what I thought you'd done to my family. I'm sorry. I'm so sorry, Massimo."

"It's okay." He kissed the top of her head.

"Did one of the villagers find you?"

"Actually, it was Jabari who dragged me back to the village. I didn't even know he'd been following me. Animals do have a sixth sense, and he must have sensed the danger even before I started out. Somehow he knew a rhino was injured and on a collision path with me."

"Oh, my God. That's amazing. You two do share an uncommon bond." She snuggled closer to him, happy that he was here with her, and grateful to Jabari.

"Yes. I owe my life to Jabari, and to you," he added in a choked voice. "You kept me alive. Your eyes kept me clinging to life while I drifted in the darkness of my coma."

"My eyes? How?"

"When I met with your father the first time, I saw a picture of you on his desk. Well, your eyes, only. You were dressed in a *khimar.* Do you remember that picture?"

Shaina nodded. "Yes. It was for a play."

"I was mesmerized by your eyes even then, and I asked your father about you."

"You did?" Her lips parted on a smile. He'd been infatuated with her as she'd been with him. So much time had passed and they'd still ended up together. They were truly made for each other, destined to be together. "What did my dad say when you asked about me?"

"That you were too young and too good for me."

"He did not."

"That's why he didn't want you at the mill the day I visited for the second time. He was trying to protect you from me. Hey, if you were my daughter, I would have done the same thing. I was a hound dog, Shaina."

"Yes, you were." Shania's smile widened as she recalled the argument with her father. She also realized that it wasn't because of Eddie that her father had told her to leave Maine. It was because of Massimo. He was trying to protect her from him, yet here she was in his bed.

"When you approached me in the cabin, I knew I'd seen you before, but I couldn't remember when or where."

"Because you'd lost your memory."

"I tried to find you and Cameron. I wanted to make that wrong right. My detective tracked you to Philadelphia, but by the time I got there, you were gone."

Shaina shot up in the bed and stared at him. "That was you? I thought it was Maine Child Welfare looking for me because I'd stolen Cameron from his foster home."

"Is that when you fled to New York and changed your names?"

She nodded.

"Did you do it legally or—"

"It was legal. But I was so scared and alone. I missed my dad so much. I didn't know what else to do." Tears stung her eyes.

He pulled her back into his arms. "I'm sorry. I'm so sorry for all the pain you suffered."

She held him tightly. "We could have been together all that time." The tears rolled down her cheeks as she thought of the wasted years on the run, hiding, scrimping, and almost starving.

He pushed her away so he could see her face. His blue eyes were glittering with gentleness and kindness and love. "I can't even begin to imagine what you and Cameron went through, but as horrible as this may sound, I'm glad I didn't find you back then. My mind and heart were in the worst place possible. I would have used you, and you would have ended up in my pile of broken dreams like all my other conquests. My heart wasn't ready for love. It wasn't ready for you. Your father was right. You are too good for me."

Shaina stared at him as the meaning of his words sank into her brain. He'd said he loved her so many times tonight and she'd ignored him, refused to believe him because she still blamed him, harbored resentment toward him, was confused and suspicious about him, didn't fully trust him, doubted he could ever be faithful to her. But now…

She threw herself into his arms. She straddled his lap, and began to drop eager kisses on his face. "I love you too, Massimo. I love you. I love you. I love you. I've loved you since the moment I saw you from the back of the mill cafeteria."

He uttered a happy, triumphant laugh and wrapped her in his arms. They laughed. They cried. They kissed. They cuddled. And soon, without either of them realizing it, they were both in a state of arousal.

"Now I know exactly where you got this impressive

sledgehammer from," Shaina said, running her fingers up and down his rigid shaft, pressing the veins that were full and pulsing with blood, watching him jerk and moan from her caresses. "You've got black in you. You've got jungle fever."

"Yeah, I'm burning up with jungle fever. And you're my cure, my black pussycat."

Shaina's giggles turned into a gasp of delight when Massimo lifted her up and fitted the head of his erection at the wet entrance of her body. All humor left them. This was serious business, now. She placed her hands against his chest and held his gaze and her breath. She tightened her muscles as she sank ever so slowly down on him.

His hands cupped her tender breasts and he kneaded them, pressing her aching nipples into his palms as she began to move slowly up and down on him, simmering and rolling on him, being filled by him as he stimulated and caressed her every crevice and curve. The friction was sharp and intense. The fire, fierce and engulfing. The intimacy, sweet and soothing. The love, deep and overwhelming.

Their eyes spoke to each other in streaming rivers of delight, as adoration, appreciation, and ecstasy swirled around and inside them. And when the pinnacle of their passion was reached, when their fever spiked, and the great dams of their desires broke, they whispered each other's names, clung to each other, and rode the waves over the falls together.

As soon as Massimo opened the bedroom door and stepped into the living area of the hotel suite, he realized he should have taken the time to dress. It was after ten in the morning and Shaina had assured him that her brother had already left for school.

She was evidently mistaken, because standing directly in front of him was seventeen-year-old Cameron Norwood—all six feet plus and a half-mile wide of him. He was obviously on his way to his sister's bedroom. Half an hour earlier, and he would have caught them in the act. Massimo hoped he'd planned to knock.

He looked him over. A true quarterback, and handsome to boot, he was the spitting image of his father—and like the older, deceased Norwood male, Massimo could tell that Cameron didn't think too kindly of him. Boy, he'd clearly picked the wrong family to marry into.

Talk about first impressions, Massimo thought as the fact that he was buck-naked registered in his brain. It was one thing to walk around naked in front of his friends in the men's locker room at the country club, but an entirely different story to parade his junk around in front of a teenager. Worse, his younger brother-in-law.

Thank goodness the young man had the decency to keep his eyes riveted on his face. Never once did he look south. His stare was paralyzing. What should he do? Retreat to the bedroom and return fully clothed? Offer him a handshake with a "Hello Cameron. I'm Massimo, your brother-in-law. How are you? Nice to finally meet you."

No, it was best he went back into the bedroom and put on some clothes, Massimo thought at the unmistaken loathing he saw in the young boy's intense gray eyes. Too late, he realized, as he felt Cameron's right fist smash into his jaw, sending him staggering back against the closed half of the double door.

"That's for my father," he said with lethal calmness.

Damn, the boy was strong, Massimo thought as the shock of the unprovoked attack wore off and the sharp pain set in. He moved his jaw around to see if anything was broken. He was clearly in no condition to fight. He wasn't expecting a fight. He'd just come out here to get the damn paper.

In addition to the fact that he was naked, he'd been making

love all night, and thirty minutes ago, he'd spent the last atoms of his energy inside his wife. He was weak, and he was certain Cameron knew it. The hickeys on his neck and fresh welts on his chest were evidence of his most recent activities. Seemed the whole Norwood family had it in for him for one reason or the other.

While Massimo was still reeling from the first blow, Cameron delivered an upper cut into his other jaw, sending him crashing against the door again. "That's for my sister. For having her arrested. And this is for me." He punched him in the gut this time, sending him to the floor doubled over in pain.

Massimo grunted. Who the hell was this kid? Mike Tyson's apprentice? Thank God, he'd missed his precious family jewels—he hoped intentionally, and not in error.

"What is going on out here?" Shaina appeared in the doorway, tying the belt of her big white fluffy hotel robe around her waist. "Oh my God." She dropped on the floor next to Massimo, shielding his nudity from her brother's eyes. She held his face between her hands and caressed his jaws. "Mass. Massimo," she called in a broken whisper, her brown eyes soft and misty, and full of love and concern.

"I... I'm all right. I think," he managed through the pain, then thought it best if he didn't try to speak for the moment, or move for that matter.

"There's no blood," she said, her eyes inspecting his face. "Is anything broken?" When he winced under her testing fingers, she glared up at her brother. "Cameron, what have you done?"

"He had it coming for what he did to our father. He destroyed our family."

"He didn't do anything to our father or our family."

"Oh, so now you're defending him? You're defending the man who killed our father?"

"I don't need to defend him. He didn't kill our father. He was in Kenya fighting for his life when all that crap was coming down. He didn't know what was happening until it was too late."

"You'll believe whatever he tells you. You're in love with him, but I'm not. I hate the bastard. I told you I wasn't ready to meet him. That's what you get for forcing him on me."

"I thought I raised you better than this. Violence doesn't solve anything. It makes things worse. You don't go around hitting people, especially naked people in their own home."

"This isn't his home. It's a hotel."

"Which he's paying for. Same difference."

Cameron growled. "It always comes down to money, doesn't it? Whoever has the most money has the most power, and all the say."

"Cameron, you know that's not true."

"Isn't it? You're taking his side against me. Your own brother. Your flesh and blood."

Massimo raised his hand. "Um… may I say—"

"Stay out of it," they shouted in unison, glaring at him before turning their attention back to each other.

Okay. So this was what it was like to have siblings. He knew they loved each other more than life itself and would fight for each other, die and kill for each other, but they weren't afraid to fight each other either. Because at the end of the day, one fact remained—blood was thicker than water. And right now, he was the water in this steaming brew. God, he could sure use some water.

Massimo sought support against the door as the heated exchange of words and angry stares between his wife and her brother continued. They'd clearly forgotten he was naked and lying on the floor helpless—the injured party. He could sure use some ice for his jaw, too, but since he couldn't move without embarrassing himself, he sat patiently and listened while Shaina relayed the story about his accident in Kenya six years ago.

Finally, she got through to Cameron who shot him an awkward look of apology. "Sorry man. I didn't know. All I had to go on was what went down six years ago. I guess I should have trusted my sister. I should have known you were okay from the simple fact that she loves you. Forgive me?" He took a step forward with his hand outstretched.

"Don't you come any closer," Shaina yelled, extending her arms like a mother hen spreading her wings to protect her young. "Turn your back."

"Yes, big little *sista*." Cameron turned around. "I'll go back to my room."

"Why aren't you in school?" Shaina demanded.

"I don't have any classes until noon."

"Get your butt back out here in half an hour when you can apologize to Massimo properly before leaving for school. You'd better make it good since you won't be seeing him again for a while."

"Yes, big little *sista*." He marched across the room and closed his door behind him.

Shaina turned to Massimo and cradled his face in her small hands again. "Oh, Massimo. I'm so sorry about what Cameron did. There's no excuse for him hitting you, but he's been angry for so long. He's been carrying that around for years."

Massimo tried to laugh then grimaced. "I understand. I would have done the same thing. I'm glad you have a brother like that, a man who'll fight for your family honor, your honor."

She giggled. "*Two* men who'll fight for my honor and that of my family. You went to see Eddie. That's the only thing that could explain his letter of apology and so-called transformation to the good side of the law."

"You got me." He hung his head sheepishly. "But I couldn't let him get away with threatening you. What he made you do was inexcusable, but I forgive him since if it weren't for him, we might not have met. You are the best thing that has ever happened to me."

"I love you," she said softly, coming in to kiss his lips. "Will you marry me later today when we get back to Granite Falls?"

"We're already, married, *cara*."

"I know, but I want to pledge my life and my love to you as Shaina Norwood. Tomorrow is your thirty-fourth birthday and I want to wake up in your bed as your real wife, Shaina Norwood-Andretti. That's my special birthday gift to you."

Massimo couldn't believe his ears. Marrying Shaina would definitely take care of any doubts about his rights to his inheritance. There was no need to bring up the real ugly reason he'd forced her to marry him. He could bury that with all the other skeletons in his closet. Let her continue to believe that he'd married her because he loved her, because that was the honest to God truth. He'd had choices—he could have married Dafne to secure his inheritance—and he'd chosen Shaina.

"Mass, did you hear me? I asked you to marry me. Again."

Tears welled in his eyes. He cradled her face in his hands. "Yes. Yes. I will marry you again, Shaina Norwood. You are my best birthday gift, ever." He hugged her to him and kissed her passionately, ignoring the pain that seared through his jaws and his belly.

"Okay, then, it's a date," she said when he finally released her. "Let's get you cleaned up and presentable before Cameron comes back out." She helped him up and he grimaced from the pain in his gut. "Just lean on me," she said, lacing her arm around his waist. "I got you."

"Yes, Ma'am." Massimo surrendered to her motherly concerns. It was nice to have a woman care about him. Really care. Azi was the only woman who ever fussed over him since his mother died.

Half an hour later, after Massimo's jaws had been iced, they were all seated at the dining table enjoying a scrumptious breakfast. Cameron had apologized over and over again for hitting him and for unjustly accusing him for a wrong he hadn't committed. They'd hugged and expressed their eagerness to get to know each other.

Massimo liked him. He really liked him, and it made his heart flutter in his chest to observe the young, intelligent, sophisticated, and well-rounded man Shaina had raised. Their children would be so lucky, so blessed to have a mother like her. His sons would be strong and fearlessly loyal and protective of their sisters. She was indisputably the cream of the crop.

"So, Cameron, Shaina tells me you're interested in engineering. And that you received a full scholarship to MIT."

Cameron flashed him a big grin from across the table. "Yeah, like father like son, I guess. You must be relieved you don't have to pay for it."

"I had no intentions of offering to pay for your education." He watched his reaction over the rim of his coffee mug.

"Oh, come on. What's the point of having a rich brother-in-law? I already apologized for hitting you. Give a brother some slack."

Massimo held back his chuckle, knowing it would cause him pain. "Well, maybe I would have paid for it, but you would have had to work it off during breaks and summer vacations."

"I have no problem with that. It would be an honor to do internships at Andretti Industries. I'll still do it if you'll have me. I could learn a lot from you."

"Yeah that would be great, Mass." Shaina, who was sitting beside him, turned and gave him a big hopeful smile. "That way I'll get to see him more often."

"What about internships at West Gate Mills?" Massimo said, giving his attention back to Cameron.

"West Gate? The new owners probably wouldn't allow it.

They might think I'm trying to steal it back," Cameron said, popping a slice of bacon into his mouth.

"You can't steal something that's already yours. Yours and Shaina's."

Massimo smiled as Cameron's mouth dropped, and Shaina gasped.

"Ours? West Gate is ours?" his wife asked, wide-eyed.

Massimo cupped her chin and gave her a quick peck on the lips. "I bought it back and rehired most of the former employees. When I met with your father, he told me the amazing history about West Gate Mills, about your ancestor, Thomas—a run-a-way-slave—who started it. It has been in your family for generations and it shouldn't have been taken away. So, I've been waiting for this day."

"What day?" Cameron asked with bated breath.

Massimo reached into his shirt pocket and pulled out an envelope. "The day I give you the deed. It's just a faxed copy, but the mill is in your name. West Gate Mills is now back in the hands of the Norwood family." He passed the envelope to Cameron. "You better make damned sure it stays in the family this time."

Cameron sat there with tears running down his cheeks as he read the deed. Shaina hugged him, sobbing with joy and excitement. Massimo was so happy he could do this for them, help them keep their father's name, his legacy alive.

"I don't know what to say, man." Cameron stared at him. "Thank you. Thank you so much, Massimo. I won't let you down. I'll work my butt off to make sure West Gate continues to thrive. I'll make you and my father proud." He was out of his seat and bending over Massimo, hugging him, even kissing him on the cheeks.

Massimo hugged them both, loving the nascent feel of family in his arms.

For some inexplicable reason, his thoughts wandered to Galen.

CHAPTER TWENTY-ONE

I t was two weeks to the day that Shaina and Mass had renewed their vows. Just for the sake of nostalgia, they'd renewed them in the interrogation room at Granite Falls Police Station, and she'd worn the ugly gray dress she'd worn before. Officer Jordan had called them a pair of crazy lovebirds when she and Mass had asked if he and the rest of the force would be their witnesses again.

After the ceremony, while the entire police force was upstairs gorging themselves on the food he'd had catered in from Andreas, Massimo had covered the piece of glass in the door, locked them inside the room, bent her over the table, hiked up her dress, eased her panties aside, and taken her from behind.

A tremor rushed through Shaina's entire body and she curled her toes as the wicked memory assaulted her. While she was still raining Massimo, they'd gone upstairs where he'd given a press release and allowed the local paparazzi to take pictures of them. Since there was nothing more to fear, Shaina had smiled proudly for the camera, while her body quivered and glowed from within.

Back at the mansion, they'd spent the rest of the day proving their love for each other. And on Saturday, Shaina had awakened

Massimo with the best birthday gift ever. The tingling and throbbing in her body deepened at the memories of his sleepy blue eyes fluttering open to the sight of her mouth clasped around his…

"Mizz Shaina."

Shaina jumped at the sound of Azi's voice. She shook her head and tucked the memory back inside her heart. "Hi Azi," she said, looking up from the interior decorating magazine she'd been leafing through before her thoughts began wandering. Mass had left on a three-day trip to Europe this morning, and she was planning on asking him about renovating the interior of the mansion when he returned. Kaya had already given her some ideas, and she was anxious to get started. She wanted her home to look and feel as modern and sophisticated as Kaya's and Michelle's. Both the exterior and interior designs were magnificent and she wouldn't dare think of changing a thing, but the atmosphere, the colors were cold and unwelcoming.

In addition to modern living and dining rooms, she also longed for a cozy family room with a huge sectional, a humongous wall TV, big comfy chairs, and oversized pillows strewn around the floor. She and Massimo had that kind of place in the living room of the master suite, but she needed a place to hang out, kick back with family and friends in front of a fire on a cold winter's night.

Azi had informed her that the house hadn't been renovated since Massimo's grandmother was alive, so she didn't think Mass would put up too much of a protest. Even Azi was excited about having a state-of-the-art kitchen with all the modern smart appliances like Mrs. Hayes, the LaCrosses' housekeeper had.

"The mail has arrived," Azi said, placing a pile of envelopes and magazines on the kitchen table. "One of the guards just dropped it off."

"Thank you, Azi." Shaina glanced at the pile of mail, then smiled at the housekeeper, of whom she'd grown extremely fond.

"Are you feeling okay, my dear?" Azi asked, placing a hand against Shaina's forehead. "You look a bit flushed."

"I'm fine, Azi." Shaina felt a bit of embarrassment as her nipples tingled and moisture gathered between her legs. She couldn't tell Azi that she was blushing because she'd been fantasizing and reminiscing about intimate moments with her husband, but she was sure Azi knew. Nothing was lost on that woman. She was not just a housekeeper to the Andrettis but a distant relative from the tribe Massimo's ancestor had been stolen from. When Azi was still a teenager, Luciano had taken her to Europe and sent her to several of the best culinary schools in the world. She'd been with the family for years. She'd also discovered that Azi slid into her native accent, only when it pleased her. She also spoke Italian and French as fluently as Massimo. She was a complex woman, keen and observant, too.

"Would you like Azi to make you some lunch, Mizz Shaina?"

"That would be wonderful, Azi. Thank you." It was a little past noon and she was getting a little hungry, which surprised her since she'd had a snack—more like a brunch—just a couple hours ago. She was eating like a pig, much more than usual, but who could blame her? The chefs at Ristorante Andreas had nothing on Azi. If she didn't cut back on eating, Shaina knew she'd be big as a whale soon. She had to start making use of the fully equipped home gym.

"Azi will make for you a chicken sandwich from last night's leftovers, and warm you up some soup, eh?"

Shaina smiled as Azi made herself busy. Azi was like the grandmother she never had, and it had been such a long time since Shaina had had a female role model that she soaked up all the attention Azi had been lathering on her. When Massimo was at the office, Shaina spent her days with Azi, learning a lot about the Masai way of life, and about Massimo—like how for months after his mother's death, he used to wake in the middle of the night screaming for her. The only comfort he'd found was in Azi's arms. No wonder he and Azi had such a close relationship. She'd felt that special bond between them the moment she'd stepped into his house.

Shaina had also learned that Mass supported a number of Masai children in Kenya and since many of the tribes had been forced to relinquish their nomadic customs, he'd built schools for them to attend, and sent others to universities worldwide. He'd installed irrigation systems in villages to aid in farming and to provide running water in each compound so the women wouldn't have to walk for miles for that most precious commodity. And just recently, Fonandt Energy had begun erecting wind farms to bring electricity to some of the most remote areas.

The more Shaina heard about Massimo, the deeper her love for him grew. She'd married a remarkable man. She still could not believe that he'd bought West Gate, and handed it over to her and Cameron, and that he'd eliminated Eddie as a threat to them. Her father was so wrong about him not being good enough for her. He was just good for her, and she for him.

"Here you are, Mizz Shaina." Azi placed a plate with a huge sandwich, a bowl of vegetable soup, and a tall glass of milk in front of her. "Eat up now. You don't want the little one to starve."

Caught momentarily off guard, she stuttered. "Little one? What—what lit—little one?"

"Azi knows these things, Mizz Shaina. You will make Massimo *veeery* happy. *Veeery* happy, eh?" She grinned, flashing her big white teeth.

Of its own volition, Shaina's hand went to her stomach and a warm glow passed through her. Dear Lord, was she really pregnant? Her mind wandered back to the day she and Massimo first made love a month ago. It was possible. She'd been ovulating the night they got married. Nia grabbed up her phone from the kitchen table and opened her calendar. She should have had her period two weeks ago. She'd been so preoccupied with learning how to please her new husband, she wasn't paying attention to anything else. The shock of the realization hit her full force, and she took a few quick breaths.

She stared at Azi. "But I don't have any symptoms."

Azi brushed her hand down Shaina's hair, much like her mother used to do to comfort her when she was a little girl. "It's still early. You will have your symptoms, Mizz Shaina. Now eat up while Azi takes care of the laundry," she said on her way out of the kitchen.

Shaina ate up. All of it. Massimo's child—the next generation of Andrettis and Norwoods was on its way. Joy bubbled up inside her. She couldn't wait to tell Massimo that he was about to become a father. But first, she needed to confirm it with a home pregnancy test and an appointment with Kaya's doctor—Dr. Jillian Walsh—Erik's colleague.

Michelle and Kaya had brought her up to date about the billionaires, and the brides clubs. One of the rules was that even though Erik was the best OB-GYN in the area, he wasn't allowed to attend any of the wives. He would assist if complications arose. Made sense. What man wanted his best friend poking around in the most intimate part of his wife's anatomy? There were some things that needed to remain secret and sacred between them.

Her lunch finished, Shaina put her dishes into the dishwasher and collected the pile of mail on her way from the kitchen. Out of habit, she shuffled through the bundle not expecting anything for her... She came to a halt as she stared at a white envelope addressed to Mrs. Massimo Andretti. The return address was that of a local law firm. Shaina frowned. Why would any lawyer

—other than Steven—be sending her mail? Propelled by curiosity, she ripped open the envelope.

She could feel the blood siphoning from her veins and her body growing cold as ice.

Massimo had lied to her. He'd lied. The letter slid from Shaina's trembling fingers and slithered to the floor as fat tears of hurt, disappointment, and outrage slid down her face.

❧

"After all the things he's done right, you're going to punish him for this one little infraction?"

"It's not little."

"Seriously, Nia—I mean, Shaina, it is little in comparison to everything else you told us about him."

"Whose side are you on, anyway?" Shaina frowned at her friends, Josie and Amber, as they faced her across a table on the veranda of Josie's magnificent beach house. After reading the letter, the only place she could think about running to was Dulcina where her old friends could offer her some comfort and support. The embarrassment of Michelle and Kaya knowing the real reason Massimo had married her was too much to bear. But Josie and Amber weren't being very supportive. They were being pragmatic instead.

She supposed it was because they were happily married to two wonderful men—Colby and Mark who were both pilots. They were stable in their marriages and family lives, and wanted the same for her. Josie and Colby had a one-year old daughter, Justine. Amber had seven-year-old twin girls, Paige and Payton, from her previous marriage, and she and Mark shared a six-month-old son, Mark Jr., or MJ as everyone called him. They owned a majestic beach house, a few palm trees down from Colby and Josie. To give the women time alone, Mark and Colby had taken the kids to church and then to visit with Josie's parents on the other side of the island.

"We're not on anyone's side," Josie said. "We just think you have a good thing going with this Massimo guy. I mean he sounds like the perfect man."

No one was perfect, Shaina thought, even as she grudgingly agreed with her friends' opinions of Massimo. He'd done a lot of good, but she just wished he'd been honest with her, at least when she'd asked him to marry her the second time. She could understand how he would have kept it from her the first time, but not after all they'd shared and definitely not after he'd told her he loved her. *Was that a lie?*

She'd been crying since she read that letter. And even though she'd hardly slept last night, she'd been too agitated to stay in bed this morning. Her body just refused to relax. Her eyes wandered off behind her friends' heads to the green manicured lawn, the line of palm trees swaying in the cool morning breeze, and the open stretch of sandy white beach beyond. The calm blue water of the Caribbean Sea was inviting as it sparkled under a clear blue sky. The magic and beauty of the island had been beckoning to her since her arrival yesterday evening, but she'd been too hurt, too distraught to enjoy this wonderful paradise.

She felt betrayed and used in the worst way possible. She was sure Massimo didn't expect her to ever find out. He obviously thought he could just bury his little secret in a snow bank somewhere. He forgot one thing about snow banks: they eventually melted, leaving your little secret lying exposed on the ground for all to see.

Amber got up and came over to sit next to her. She placed a hand around her shoulder. "Look Shaina, you were there for me during my nasty divorce from Josh, and I have no intentions of encouraging you to go down that painful path. Josie and I aren't trying to make you feel any worse than you already do. What we're saying is that you should talk to your husband, give him a chance to explain. I believe that he loves you, and that he didn't tell you because he was scared."

Shania scoffed. "Massimo scared? I can't imagine him being scared of anything."

"When it comes to matters of the heart, all men are scared. Yes, they fluff their feathers and beat their chests in public, but once behind closed doors, the one thing that scares them to death is losing that one special woman in their lives, messing up the best thing that ever happened to them."

Shaina wrapped her arms about her belly. "Then he should have just told me the second time around. I would have understood why he had me thrown into jail and forced me to marry him the first time."

"He knew you'd react by running, and you did. He didn't want to risk it."

Shaina shuddered on a deep sigh and her arms tightened around her. "He didn't want to risk it until I was pregnant. He thought that a child would be the only thing that would keep me from running, keep me bonded to him. The one last thing that would secure his inheritance."

As the nasty truth hit her hard, Shaina pushed her chair back and raced into the house. She reached the bathroom just in time. She dropped to the floor and held her face in the toilet bowl as her stomach heaved, forcing up the salt fish and johnnycakes she'd had for breakfast.

She felt Amber's hand brushing her hair from her face.

"You know," her friend said, handing her a glass of water, "not too long, I was in this very same spot heaving my insides out while Mark held my hair. I think that was the instant I fell in love with him." She took the empty glass from Shaina and helped her to her feet.

"Well at least he didn't lie to you." Tears welled in her eyes.

"No he didn't, but I was lying to myself, just as you are doing now. You love Massimo and you will forgive him." She patted Shaina on the shoulder. "It's gonna work itself out in time. Love always conquers."

Finally alone, Shaina locked the guest bedroom door and crawled into the bed. How would it work itself out? A marriage could not survive on love alone. It needed trust, and right now, there was none between her and Massimo. He didn't have enough trust in their love, in her, to tell her the truth.

Shaina was never the kind of woman to fall apart and weep when trouble set in. She'd always had to be strong for Cameron, but now as helplessness and uncertainty about her future assailed her, Shaina opened up her soul and wept her heart out. Empty and numb, she finally curled up into a ball and fell asleep. When she opened her eyes again and stared out the patio doors, the sun was hovering above the horizon and the blue sky above it had been transformed into a giant picturesque canvas of orange, yellow, and blue hues with the swaying palm trees in the forefront. It was a lovely sunset, but Shania was robbed of the strength and liberty to enjoy it.

The sounds of adults talking propelled her from her bed. She took a quick shower and pulled on a white cotton dress. She didn't bother with makeup, not even gloss. The smell of dinner cooking made her stomach growl. She was starving, and she was starving the tiny life inside her. "I'm sorry, baby," she said, rubbing her stomach. "Mommy promises to start taking good care of you from this moment on."

With that, she left the bedroom and walked down the hall toward the great open room that served as a kitchen, dining, and living areas, and that looked out onto the patio and beach on one side, and the majestic three-thousand-foot mountain known as Dulcina Peak on the other side.

Mark and Colby were on the veranda, drinking beer and

talking, their deep voices floating on the evening breeze. Josie and Amber were busy in the kitchen, chattering as steel drum music spiked the interior air. It was a lazy, comforting, welcoming atmosphere.

"Hi there," Josie said as she walked up to the breakfast nook. "Feeling better?"

Shaina nodded. "Thanks for letting me sleep."

"You needed it, especially in your condition."

"Do you guys need help?" she asked, watching them ladle dishes from pots into serving bowls.

"No," Amber replied. "Just sit there and relax. You're our guest. When we visit you in your mansion in Granite Falls, you can wait on us then. You must be hungry. Here, munch on these." She pushed a platter in front of her. "Dinner will be ready soon."

Smiling, Shaina climbed up on a bar stool at the nook and dug into the assortment of fruits, cheeses, and crackers on the platter. "Where're the kids?' she asked, glancing around.

"Monica took them for a walk on the beach. By the way," Josie said, stopping in her task of slicing tomatoes for a salad. "Your husband called."

Shaina almost choked on the piece of juicy papaya in her mouth. "What? How does he know I'm here?"

"My nosy sister."

"Monica?" Shaina had met the spirited young lady last night when she'd accompanied Josie to the airport to pick her up. She'd liked her then. Now, she wanted to throttle her. She braced her hands against the cool marble countertop, trying to control her ire.

"She called your brother and he called Massimo. She was worried when you emerged from the plane all puffy-faced and red-eyed. She doesn't know what's going on. She just thought he should know that his sister was upset and crying," Josie said, in defense of Monica.

Shaina took a deep steadying breath. "What did Massimo say?"

"Not much, but he sounded pretty mad."

"Good!"

"We're to keep you here until he arrives," she added, with a skeptical look in her eyes.

"Yep," Amber said, grinning. "We've been instructed to hog-tie you to a tree, any tree, if that is what it takes to keep you on the island."

"Don't make us do it," Colby warned from the veranda, holding up a spool of rope.

"But just in case, we already picked out the tree." Mark pointed to a tamarind tree near a gazebo a few yards across the lawn. "At least you'll have some shelter from the sun and the rain. And we'll even let the kids out to play with you, keep you company."

Everyone thought the idea of her tied out to pasture was hilarious, and they doubled over laughing while she glared at them.

"Oh come on, Shaina, you gotta admit that it's funny." Amber slapped her on the wrist.

"Yeah, yeah, yeah." She snarled. "When is he due to arrive?" She didn't know whether to feel relieved or anxious over seeing Massimo again.

"Some time early tomorrow."

Colby and Mark strolled inside, their imposing physiques sucking up the air and their charming sun-kissed faces grinning like servants of the evil one. They were eagerly following Massimo's orders and they hadn't even met the man. But that was Massimo. He had that kind of effect on people. He could make them do whatever he wanted them to do. Herself included.

Shaina watched each man walk automatically up to his wife, laced his arms about her, and kiss her on the lips. These two old friends of hers shared something special with their husbands, just like her two new friends back in Granite Falls. She wanted what they had, what her parents had. Living Cinderella's story was every little girl's dream.

She and Mass were supposed to be leaving on a three-week honeymoon next month. They were going to spend one week in Kenya with Jabari, one week in Bellagio, and the last on a private island in the Mediterranean. Two days ago, her future seemed so certain. Now she had no idea where she was headed.

CHAPTER TWENTY-TWO

Crickets chirped and birds cooed in the flamboyant tree outside her window, and on the other side of the room, the ocean roared and waves flapped as they broke upon the sandy shore. The symphony of nature in the early dawn coupled with the cool breeze fragranced with hyacinth and jasmine coaxed Shaina out of a deep sleep.

She took a moment to revel in her tropical surroundings and then tried to stretch.

"What…" Her eyes flew open and her forehead crinkled as she came fully awake. She tried to move her body only to realize that her arms were stretched above her head and her wrists were tethered to the bedpost with scarves. Something that felt like the trunk of an aged cedar tree was lying across her lower body. "Massimo."

A huge dark figure rose from the mattress beside her and loomed over her, but not touching her. "Good morning, pussycat." His devilishly handsome face was an olive effigy of frustration and rage, and his blue eyes glittered like glacial rocks in the morning sunrise streaming through the glass. The sexy masculine smell of him made her dizzy.

Shaina yanked on the silk scarves that held her captive. The knots weren't tight on her wrists, and her arms weren't stretched enough to cause her discomfort, but she was restrained, nonetheless. "Massimo, untie me. Right now!" she ordered as his lips tightened and a muscle twitched at the side of his mouth.

He tossed her a smile that did not indicate compliance. "I don't think you're in any position to be making demands, my little flight bird." His eyes caressed the length of her body, which was scantily clad in a pair of pink panties and a matching camisole that only came down to her midsection. His lazy gaze returned to her face and he held her eyes steady as his fingers crawled along her leg, up, up toward the inside of her thighs, leaving a fiery wake on her skin and sending tingling sensations shooting through her.

Shaina swallowed as her breathing increased and her body began to respond to him in the familiar trembling fit. She stared up at the slowly spinning blades of the ceiling fan—anything to distract her mind from the betraying sensations in her body. "Mass…" She twitched as the warm heel of his palm pressed into her groin.

"What?" he asked, in a throaty whisper as the soft pads of his long fingers splayed across her belly, stirring a dull aching need in the core of her womanhood.

For one thrilling moment, Shaina caved to the arousing desires as her body flushed and moisture rushed to the junction between her thighs, the place where he was massaging her ever so erotically. She could feel her breasts swelling and her nipples hardening beneath her camisole. She wanted…she wanted… to…touch him…

"Stop!" she shouted, when the restraints on her wrists reminded her that they were at odds, that she was mad, hurt. For the first time since she learned she was pregnant, Shaina wished she suffered from morning sickness just so she could throw up all over him. "Massimo, untie me, or I'll scream." She glared at him.

"Go ahead. I already warned your friends that you have the habit of screaming when you're in the throes of passion. They won't be barging in to rescue you."

"I hate you!"

"Of course you do. I wouldn't respect you if you didn't." He pulled his hands from her belly and pulled back his hair at his forehead. "See this?" He pointed to a spot at the full line of silky black hair.

Shaina squinted. "See what?"

"It's a gray hair, Shaina. I've been turning gray with worrying about you ever since you walked into my life."

"Well, you just got a year older," she retorted. "Maybe it's just age."

He sat up and shook his fists in the air, then waved his hands around like a bona fide Italian. "*Dio! Mi fai impazzire*, Shaina! *Pazzo! Pazzo! Pazzo!*"

"English! English, Massimo." She felt like she was in an episode of *I Love Lucy*.

He frowned with cold fury. "You make me crazy!" He shook his head on a groan then swinging his feet over the side of the bed, he stood to his six-foot, three-inch frame and glared down at her.

It was then that Shaina realized he was fully dressed in khaki slacks and a white linen short-sleeve shirt. He was even wearing socks.

"Yes," he responded to the question in her mind, his tone changing drastically to warm sensuality. "I tied you up, and I slept fully clothed to protect myself from your wicked, seductive wiles. I'm not ashamed to admit that I'm whipped. I can't keep my hands off you. I can't resist you, even when you make me madder and crazier than anyone else in this world ever has.

You're in my head all the time. I can't concentrate on business when visions of our bodies tangled up in love dominate my brain. You've got that kind of whip appeal on me, baby."

A vision of them making love to Baby Face's *Whip Appeal* flashed across Shaina's mind, and those words he'd just spoken to her... "Believe me, I wouldn't have tried to seduce you. In fact, I have no intentions of ever seducing you again." Now that her legs were free of his weight, she crossed them to combat the lingering effects of his caresses still zinging between her thighs.

"Promises. Promises." His chest rose and fell on a deep sigh, and he rushed his fingers through his hair. "I can't do this, Shaina," he said, dropping his weight into the chair near the head of the bed.

Something melted in Shaina's heart at the sight of him slumped over in the chair with his elbows on his knees and his hands clasped. She became aware of the black circles under his eyes. He looked defeated, haggard, tired, like he hadn't slept in weeks. Maybe she was making him old. Maybe... "Mass, I have to go to the bathroom."

"Oh no, you're not tricking me into releasing you."

"Seriously, Massimo. I do have to go. Please." Shaina was quickly realizing that pregnant women needed to frequent the bathroom a lot more than usual, but she would eat sand before she told Massimo she was pregnant with his child. She would not give him the satisfaction of reaping the benefits of his lies and deceit. No wonder he took her to bed every waking minute he could afford. *Yeah, like you don't enjoy it, too,* her annoying inner voice said.

"Okay." He knelt beside the bed, untied her wrists, and helped her up. "You have two minutes. Don't make me come in there to get you. And just in case you're thinking of jumping through the window, I have two of my men stationed outside."

Fuming with anger, Shaina hurried to the bathroom and

answered the call of nature. Of course she was tempted and glanced out the window. Massimo hadn't lied. Two of his guards were sitting on the gazebo under the tamarind tree where Colby and Mark had threatened to tie her out to pasture. There was only one way to beat the devil she realized: face him head-on.

Shaina almost collided with Massimo when she opened the bathroom door. He towered over her, glaring down at her. She thought of asking him not to restrain her again, but his tight strained expression told her that it would be useless. Since a physically struggle with him might hurt her baby, when he took her hand and let her back to the bed, she lay down like a martyr and allowed him to tie her wrists again.

He frowned at her. "What, no protests, no pleas?"

"Would it matter?"

His eyes narrowed. "No. Now, where were we?" he asked, sitting in the chair again.

"You were saying you can't do something," she said in a terse, dry tone.

"Oh yes. I can't be worried each time I leave home that you won't be there when I get back. You promised me you'd stop running, yet here we are." He spread his hands in frustration. "I had to cancel a meeting that was set in stone two months ago in order to fly halfway around the globe to find my wife."

"I wasn't lost. I didn't ask you to come looking for me."

"I lost fifty million dollars for failing to close that deal," he continued, as if she hadn't spoken.

Crap, that was a lot of money, even for a billionaire. But then again, fifty million was a drop in the bucket compared to the billions he would lose if... "You have no one to blame but yourself," she said, refusing to accept any blame for his financial dilemma.

"How do you figure that?" His expression was one of pained tolerance.

"You lied to me."

"About what?"

She glanced away briefly, still feeling embarrassed about the revelation. "The real reason you married me."

He straightened up in the chair as if she'd struck him. He gave her a level look. "I married you because I love you, Shaina. You are the love of my life. The one woman I never knew I'd been searching for all these years. You are my soul's counterpart."

Knowing that he would say anything to get what he wanted, Shaina yanked on the scarves. "Untie me, Massimo."

He shook his head. "No."

She glared at him. "You married me to gain your inheritance. To secure it, you have to stay faithfully married for three years, and produce an heir within a year. You promised you'd never cheat on me, but you failed to add that it was only for three years. And all the talk about sons and daughters, all you need is one."

Her mind wound back to the day she met his friends at the country club, the day he announced to the world that they were getting married. A thought froze in her brain as she recalled the coded conversation between the men. His need to marry before his birthday was the unmentioned topic of conversation, and his break-up with Gabrielle... "Oh, God," she said with disgust. "That's why Gabrielle Berkeley dumped you, isn't it? She found out the real reason you wanted to marry her." She pounded her feet on the mattress. "This marriage is a farce. I want a divorce, Massimo! I want out."

Massimo slumped against the back of the chair as if he'd been caught up inside a whirling tornado, stretched wide and thin, and then dumped on a cold hard patch of concrete. How the hell did she know all that? He knew none of his friends would betray him. Their wives didn't even know about the conditions in his father's will. The only other people who knew were his attorney and Dafne.

Steven wouldn't dare say anything to her for fear of breaching their attorney-client privilege. He'd told him to burn his copy of the will and the prenup he'd drawn up. Steven had assured him that he'd followed his orders. The only remaining copy of the will was in his home vault. Shaina had no access to it since the key for that compartment was inside the Granite Falls branch of *La Banca di Bianchi*. So, that left Dafne. Could she be that vindictive, that jealous to try to destroy his one chance of happiness? When he'd told her about his love for Shaina, she'd seemed excited for him. Could she have been masking her true feelings? No, he refused to believe that. He'd known Dafne all his life. She would never do this to him. He glanced at his wife. "Where did you get that information?"

"Does it matter?"

"Yes, it matters a lot." It was crucial that he knew who his enemies were, because anyone who wanted to hurt him would use Shaina to get to him. He needed to know whom he had to eliminate from his circle of trust. He sprung from the chair and perched on the side of the bed. "Who told you?" he asked, staring down into her face. Even when shrouded with anger, she was still so damned hypnotizing. He would put all that fiery passion to good use later.

"Your father." She flung out the words brutally, as if to tell him that all Andrettis stank.

"My father?" Taken aback, Massimo tried to keep the rancor from his voice.

"He wrote me a letter welcoming me into the family. Well, not me exactly. The letter was addressed to Mrs. Massimo Andretti. She just happens to be me," she said, her brown eyes flashing with hurt and loathing.

It was the kind of loathing he'd detected in her when they'd first met, when she thought him responsible for her father's death. Massimo never dreamed he'd see that cold look in her eyes again. "My father is dead. How could he have written you a letter?"

She rolled her eyes as if she were dealing with a daft child. "Apparently, he left it with another attorney with instructions to deliver it to your wife. It's over there in my purse on the dresser. You can read it yourself."

"Stay right there," he said, rising and going over to the dresser to rummage through her purse. He found the letter and, walking to the sliders, he silently read it in the early morning light. Would he ever be free of his father's dominance and control over his life?

Massimo ripped the letter to shreds and stuffed the pieces back into the envelope. He folded the envelope into his pocket and strolled back over to the bed. He sat down on the side again and held his wife's gaze. "I want you to listen, and I want you to listen well because we're never, ever going to have this conversation again."

"The only conversation we're going to have is through our lawyers. I can't trust anything you say."

Teetering at his breaking point, Massimo whipped off his silk socks and balled them in his fist. "Do I need to stuff these into your saucy little mouth, or are you going to listen to me? Next time you open it, in they go."

Her chest heaved on a sharp breath, then she pressed her sexy lips together and settled down into the mattress.

Satisfied that he had her full attention, Massimo placed the socks on his lap and held her beautiful gaze. "There is no denying my father's terms for gaining my inheritance, which I initially had no intentions of fulfilling. He died six years ago, and since then, I started Bianchi Incorporated and made my own money. However, the closer I got to the deadline, the more I realized that the only thing I never wanted to lose was the home where I spent the best part of my life with my mother. I didn't give a damn about Andretti Industries, but I detested the thought of my half-brother owning the place where my mother's spirit and memories still linger."

She nodded with understanding.

"Yes, I asked Gabrielle to marry me to meet the terms in the will. She didn't dump me. I broke off the engagement when I discovered that she was addicted to prescription drugs. If I didn't have to produce an heir, I probably would have still married her, but I couldn't make a baby with a drug-addicted mother. I encouraged her to check herself into rehab and told her she could tell whatever story she wanted about the breakup. She chose to tell the world that I was unfaithful." He paused. "You are never to repeat this," he said, wagging a finger at her. "Do you understand?"

She shook her head in agreement.

"I was set to marry someone else a few days before my birthday. She's an old childhood friend who lives in Milan, Italy. She offered to marry me, but," he added, needing to be completely honest, "she would produce my heir by artificial means only. You see, we had a brief sexual relationship when we were quite young. We were each other's first, actually, but we later decided that our friendship meant more to us than an occasional sexual encounter. We didn't want to mess up what we had, still have."

Her eyes grew wide with questions but she kept silent. He would answer all her questions later. He just needed to get this out.

"I had a prenuptial agreement drawn up, and Dafne was to fly over to the States the day after I met you to sign it and settle in before we exchanged vows. But the moment I gazed into your eyes, I knew that I could not marry Dafne, and I began plotting a way to keep you in Granite Falls and force you to marry me. I also had a prenuptial agreement drawn up for you, but at the last minute, I decided that what I felt for you was more important than anything else in this world. I didn't want to lose you, and that's why I never told you about my father's will, because quite honestly, it has nothing to do with the reason I married you, Shaina. None whatsoever."

Massimo noticed the changes occurring in her body. She was a lot more relaxed and her sweet brown eyes were no longer spewing hate and anger, but had softened to a deep chocolate richness that made his heart pound and tears to well in his eyes.

He swallowed the lump in his throat. "I had choices, Shaina. I could have married Dafne and secured my inheritance, but I chose to marry you. I married you both times because I love you. I didn't tell you the second time because I didn't want you to doubt my love, question my feelings for you. And yes, I didn't want you to run, because the thought of not having you in my life brings me much pain. I don't ever want to be without you, live without you, Shaina. And if you ask me to, I would relinquish my rights to Andretti Industries. I would even give up the mansion for you. And we don't have to make a baby anytime soon. In fact, let's wait a year. That'll give us more time to devote undivided love and attention to each other."

Massimo didn't even realize he was crying until his tears splashed on her face, mingling with hers. He dabbed her cheeks with the back of his hand as her mouth opened and closed in an attempt to talk. "You can speak," he said, his heart racing inside his chest, his breath solidifying in his throat. God, he loved her so much. The thought of losing her…

"You can't give up the mansion. I already have renovation plans for it—that is, if it's okay with you."

Chuckles erupted from deep inside Massimo's throat. After all he'd just told her, all she could say was "You can't give up the mansion." He dipped his head and covered her mouth with his, then scooped his arms beneath her and held her close. She was sweet, and soft, and warm. Forgiveness came in many forms he realized as he inhaled deeply, drinking up her fragrance as their tongues twirled around each other like dancing ballerinas.

"Mass," she said, struggling against him.

He released her and gazed down at her, happiness and joy bubbling inside him like the hottest fire. "Yes, pussycat."

"About waiting a year to make a baby—"

"Yes," he bent his head again and began to drop a series of kisses on her face, paying particular attention to the corners of her voluptuous mouth. "We can use whatever method of birth control you want. Just no condoms. I've used them all my life. I'm not using them with you."

"It's too late for birth control."

He froze and raised his head. The smile in her eyes, the joy on her face said it all. His gaze wandered down to her stomach. "Really?" His stomach crunched up in knots.

She nodded. "Really."

"How far?"

"Dr. Jillian said a month. I think I got pregnant the first time we made love."

Massimo's entire body trembled as the news sank in. He was going to be a father. He traced his hand down her body to her soft flat stomach and caressed her, closing his eyes and willing his soul to connect to his child growing inside her. Finally, he opened his eyes, and drowned himself in the passion and the love he saw spilling from inside the brown depth of hers. "I promise you, Shaina. I will love our child. I will respect him and value his opinions and wishes. I will not try to control him like my father tried to control me. I will make his mother the happiest woman in the world—as happy as she has made me."

"She already is," she responded on a choked whisper. "And it might be a girl. You're not cursed, Massimo. You're blessed."

He offered her an arresting smile. "Because of you. I'm not

only blessed, but I'm changed. I'm trying to be a better man, a husband you can be proud of, a father our children will admire and want to emulate. I want to be perfect for you. And so I called my brother."

"You did? That is nice, Massimo. He's your family and you should get to know him."

"I was planning to pay him a visit on this trip, tell him who he was, but then I got the call from your brother, and here I am." He spread his hands.

"I'm sorry." She pouted her sexy mouth. "Untie me so I can show you how blessed you are and how sorry I really am," she said, giving him such a sensual smile, his cock went from semi to rock solid hard in a split second.

"Oh, I know I'm blessed, but you're not getting away that easily, *cara*."

"I'm not trying to get away with anything. I want to make up for the worry I caused you."

"I'm glad to hear that. You once offered me the joy of having you for four million dollars. I'd say your price just went up."

Her brows furrowed in question.

He smiled as he pulled his shirt over his head and tossed it across the room. "You owe me fifty million dollars, Shaina, and I intend to claim every cent of it in trade from your sexy little body."

"So untie me so I can start paying you back."

"Uh-uh." He shot to his feet and began unbuttoning his slacks. "I plan to keep you tied up until you promise—really, really promise never to run away again. And if you weren't carrying my child, I'd spank your delectable little rear end for causing me so much trouble."

"Mass…" She pulled against her restraints, even as her pupils grew large and dark with a mixture of uncertainty and desire.

Massimo felt fire racing along his spine and settling into his groin as he slid his slacks and his briefs off his hips and down his thighs and legs. He stepped out of them and stood tall, strong, and ready for her, his erection so painfully hard, it pointed straight up to the ceiling. This was a new experience for both of them and he intended to enjoy it to the max.

"Mass," she pleaded again, struggling with hesitation and primitive wantonness as her eyes caressed his engorged shaft with its multitude of full pulsing veins running the length of it, and a sheen of pre-pleasure love juice coating its head.

"I would bound your silky legs as well, but for now I prefer them wrapped around my waist or slung over my shoulders. Maybe next time," he said, stepping closer to the bed. At least he was coming out of this one without battle scars.

Shaina gazed at her husband, love flowing freely and copiously inside her. She loved him more now than she'd loved him yesterday, more than a few minutes ago, and she knew that love would only grow more fiercely as time went by. She just hoped her heart had enough room to contain it.

How could she not love him when he'd been looking out for her and Cameron even before they met? She hadn't even known until recently that he'd paid off her father's hospital bills. He'd taken care of her legal issues and restored her family legacy.

He said he was changing his ways because he wanted to be perfect for her. He was already perfect for her. Neither one of them was perfect, but they were perfect for each other, in every possible way. Especially sexually, she thought as he sat down on the side of the bed.

"Are you ready to be loved beyond your wildest dreams, *cara*," he asked, his deep voice and sexy blue eyes brimming with passionate promises for years to come.

Realizing her absolute vulnerability, Shaina struggled against the silken tethers even as a whirlwind of erotic fear and delight swept through her. She knew her body and the overwhelming intensity of her orgasms. She'd always been able to stay grounded by biting or digging her nails into Massimo's flesh, or grabbing the sheets, or something—anything when they made love. With her hands bound above her head, and her body under his total control, she wouldn't be able to do anything but surrender to the masterful lovemaking tactics of her husband.

She could lose her mind and remain forever locked in a state of orgasmic hysteria, walking around with an idiotic grin on her face. The stares. The stares. "Mass… Massimo…"

"Mhm. Mhm… Call my name. Call out my name, pussycat," he said, reaching for her.

THE END

TRANSLATION PAGE

Italian	**English**
Abbastanza	Enough
Andiamo	Let's go
Andiamo a letto, poi	Then let's go to bed
Aprire la sua boca.	Open your mouth.
Avvolgere le braccia intorno al nio collo	Wrap your arms around my neck
Bambina, mia. Piccola, mia.	My baby
Bellisima	Beautiful
Buonasera, Signore Andretti	Good evening
Cara. Cara mia	Dear. My dear
Che è buono?	Is that good?
Como sei graziosa bella e molto dolce	Very beautiful and sweet
Cresci in esso, quello piccolo	You'll grow into it, little one
Guardaci	Look at us
Guardami	Look at me
Ho bisogno di te cosi tanto	I need you so much
Il Nido d'Amore	The Love Nest
La Banca di Bianchi	Bank of Bianchi
Mama, che bel tettone	Mama, what beautiful big tits
Nono	Grandfather
Poi ti darò più	I'll give you more then
Prendini	Take me
Sarò gentile	I'll be gentle
Scopami	Fuck me
Sei così stretto e umido. Calda	You're so tight and wet. Hot
Si picolla.	Yes baby
Ti voglio cosi tanto	I want you so much
Una moglie	A wife
Vengo.	I'm coming
Voglio di più	I want more
Vuoi più	Want more?

Swahili	**English**
Jambo	Hello
Punda milia	Donkey's ass

French	**English**
Chéri	Baby

THE TYCOON'S TEMPORARY BRIDE

CHAPTER ONE

Tashi Holland took a deep breath of the summer air as she exited one of her favorite shops at Stone Crest Shopping Mall Outlets. Bags in hand, she strolled along the walkway, wheeling her way through the throng of residents and tourists who frequented this delightful small town nestled in the foothills of the White Mountain National Forest of New Hampshire.

She headed for one of the many gazebos in the plaza and, setting her bags on a stone bench, she pulled her camera from her backpack and began clicking away at the breathtaking views of the shimmering waters of Crystal Lake and the green majestic mountains in the background.

Granite Falls was a long way from New York City, the place she'd gone to study photography, and even farther from Ohio—the place where she was born and raised, but never felt any real connection to. Granite Falls wasn't a bad town for settling down and starting over, but it was remote and lonely. Lonelier, because she hadn't made any friends and had spent the last few months trying to make sense of the events that had changed her life a year and a half ago.

Sometimes it felt like yesterday, and other times it felt like a lifetime. And then there were times when it felt as if it never even happened. She'd listened to the news and searched the Internet day and night for weeks, then months, trying to find evidence that her nightmares weren't just some figment of her imagination.

But there was nothing. Never anything—except for one fact.

Tashi sighed and, putting her camera away, she sat on the bench and folded her arms across the stone tabletop and indulged in her favorite pastime. Watching people mulling about and speculating about their lives had helped to keep her mind off her own lifeless existence.

Who was she, anyway? She was a girl with a name, and only a name. One she couldn't use. She couldn't open a bank account or use her credit cards. Her driver's license was useless since she couldn't rent or purchase a car, or even book a hotel room for a night.

She had the cell phone the FBI agent who'd rescued her had given her—her only communication to the world beyond Granite Falls' border—but she had no one to call, except the closest pizza parlor and Mountainview Café for occasional deliveries during the past cold winter nights. She kept her phone charged and protected like it was an infant, hoping and praying each day would be the one she would receive *that* one call she lived for— the call that would give her back her life.

Maybe she would never get her life back. Maybe they thought she'd died during the shootout in that house in New York City, fifteen months ago.

But then again, who were *they*?

She had no family. She'd never met her father. Her mother died when she was four, and then her uncle who'd raised her suddenly and unexpectedly lost his life to pancreatic cancer almost two years ago. She'd been alone and scared in the craziest city in the world until Scottie showed up. He'd seemed real and charming and had treated her like a princess until…

Tashi covered her face with her hands as visions of that night stormed into the forefront of her mind. Those visions never surfaced gently. They always came at her like a silent freight train speeding around a bend. She only knew it was there after it hit her.

What if Scottie was real, but the man who'd claimed he'd come to rescue her along with the others who were posing as guards and parents were just actors his real parents had hired to get rid of her? After all, she was a nobody, and Scottie was the heir to some multi-million-dollar corporation. Maybe they thought she wasn't good enough for their son. Tashi had watched enough movies to know that rich people could get away with almost anything. What if they were all fakes? Except…

She wrapped her arms around her middle as the pain seared through her. The one thing about that night that wasn't fake was the fact that she'd killed a man. She'd climbed undetected into the back seat, pointed a gun at the back of his head and pulled the trigger. *Twice.* Then she'd watched, numb from head to toe, as he slumped against the steering wheel. It was the blare of the horn that had propelled her into action. She'd pushed the dead man out of the car, and driven off.

His death was the only event that had made the news. It was described as a drug deal gone wrong. He'd left behind a wife and three young children. There were no suspects and last she'd read, the case had been closed.

What if killing the driver was the only real event about that night? What if Scottie's parents were using that incriminating fact as a means to keep her away from him? If the man who'd claimed to be an FBI agent had made it out alive, where was he?

He'd promised to find her and explain everything to her. What was 'everything'? What did he need to explain?

Tashi didn't know what to believe anymore. And here she was in a strange town where the agent had sent her in search of a man who was supposed to protect her. A man without a face and a name. Tashi scanned the crowds as she'd done countless times in the past months, hoping beyond hope that her *savior* would see her, recognize her, and help her.

He could be anybody, even that giant of a man with his arm around the petite woman as they pushed a set of twins in a double stroller. He reminded her of the FBI agent—large, dark, and handsome. The couple nodded and smiled at her as they walked past.

Tashi smiled back. She felt as if she's seen them somewhere before, but then she quickly averted her eyes as the woman said something to the man, and he turned and gave her another smile.

"She said you're very beautiful, and I agreed," the man said over his shoulder.

"Thank you. And so is she." Tashi's smile deepened, as the couple disappeared into the crowd.

One thing she could say about this town was that the majority of people were nice and friendly. They probably didn't think the same of her since she never made any attempts to engage in conversation, nor did she respond to personal questions about herself—legitimate questions people ask when they were interested in someone.

Not knowing whom she could trust, she trusted no one, not even Mindy, her garrulous neighbor, whose kids she'd babysat on a few occasions.

Tashi gathered her bags and left the gazebo. It was laundry day, and she didn't have a washer and dryer in her one-bedroom apartment—an apartment in the not-so-nice side of town. But it was the only place where the landlord would allow her to pay cash—no questions asked.

The FBI agent had given her a bag of cash and she'd carved out a hole in the back wall of her bedroom closet and hidden the bag inside it. It wasn't like she could take the money down to the local bank and make a deposit. Her closet was the safest place she could think of to hide it. She'd bought a piece of plywood, painted it white and leaned it up against the wall to hide the hole. Every time she left her apartment, Tashi worried about someone breaking in. But so far so good.

The car she'd driven to Granite Falls, and the gun with which she'd killed the man had become real estate for fish in the deepest parts of the Hudson and Aiken Rivers, respectively. She had enough money to last her a decade, if she spent it wisely. Hopefully, before it ran out, she'd have some answers to her past and be able to live a normal life.

Her stomach rumbled, reminding her that she'd had a light breakfast. Tashi smiled at the idea of enjoying a juicy, smoked ham sandwich from Mountainview Café, just two blocks over from the outlets. She would grocery shop tomorrow after her kickboxing class. On that thought, Tashi headed for the café.

Having no job, and no people to visit, she'd learned to spread out her outdoor excursions over several days, just to have a reason to leave her apartment, and keep herself from going crazy. It had been hard during the cold long winter months. Sometimes she didn't know which was worse—sitting in her apartment reading, or watching TV and snow fall through her window, or braving the freezing temperatures and trekking through snow banks to do her laundry and groceries. On milder days, she'd walk six blocks to the public library, curl up in front of a warm fire, and read. A few times, she'd even fallen asleep in one of the oversized comfortable chairs, only to wake up to face the long walk back and the destitution and isolation of her apartment.

Tashi prayed that something would change before winter came around again. She didn't think she could survive another six months of cold in this lonely town. She'd thought of leaving, but that promise from the FBI agent to find her and explain everything had kept her grounded. She didn't want to miss him when and if he ever came looking for her.

An hour later, Tashi placed some money next to her empty plate and grabbed her bags from the floor. As she stood up and spun around, she collided, head-on with a solid wall of hard muscle. She immediately felt strong arms close around her.

"Whoa…"

Was that thunder? Was this an earthquake?

Tashi stiffened as a flicker of fear rushed through her. Her face was pressed tightly against a hard expanse of human flesh that smelled so good. A man was holding her. A strange man.

You're a witness. They'll be looking for you. Don't trust anyone.

She panicked, her heart thundering as she fought against him. "No! No! Let me go!"

"Hey, take it easy. I was only trying to catch you before you fell flat on your pretty little face."

The man abruptly released her. Then he bent down and retrieved her bags that had fallen to the floor. He straightened up and handed them to her.

So it wasn't thunder. Tashi tilted her head back to gaze into a pair of the bluest, most intimate eyes she had ever seen.

Her heart did a double take and something hot sizzled through her stomach. More adrenaline rushed through her as she took a good look at him—from his waist-length wavy black hair to the tips of his black leather shoes. He wore designer jeans and a gray shirt. Or maybe they wore his tall, hard, sexy frame.

The food stains on the front of his shirt caused Tashi to look behind him where he'd parked a baby stroller. A little girl, who looked about two years old, was fast asleep inside it. Tashi took a long, deep breath as her panic subdued. He couldn't be one of the mob's men. He didn't look the type. They wouldn't be running around after her with a baby in tow. And how would they have found her, anyway?

"I'm—I'm sorry," she stuttered. "I really should look where I'm going."

"Don't apologize," he said in a deep, rumbling voice. "I'm the one who sneaked up on you. I hope I didn't hurt you." He gave her body a bold raking gaze, then his soft blue eyes came back to her face, and that something hot sizzled through the core of Tashi's body again. It was nothing like she'd experienced before.

Their eyes locked for tense moments as if they were both waiting for the other to make the next move.

"No. I'm fine." Tashi licked her lips that had suddenly become parched. She tugged her eyes from his, only to stare at his wide and generous mouth with lips that reminded her of blooming rosebuds. They were so pink and succulent.

She studied his face. It was passionate, beautiful, and irresistible, down to the narrow, hollow grove etched into the taut skin under his straight nose. His features were sculptured so perfectly, so symmetrically, that he was almost too beautiful for a man. *Italian? Greek?* Tashi took another look at the adorable baby-girl sleeping in the carriage.

He's married! Not that it really mattered. She wasn't looking for a husband. Heck, she wasn't even looking for a man. Well, she was, but she didn't know who that man was. She didn't know if he was supposed to be black or white, old or young, rich or poor… All she knew was that he should be single and his name began with an *A*. She didn't even know if the *A* stood for a first or last name.

"I—I have to go," she said in an awkward, tremulous voice.

He opened his mouth as if he were about to say something, but instead, he gave her a sensuous stare that made her heart turn over in response. Close Encounter of the Magnetic Kind, Tashi thought on a raspy breath as she hurried away. What a man! God, she didn't realize they made them like that. His appeal was extremely unsettling. She'd never been this affected by a man before. It was scary and exciting at the same time.

When she reached the sidewalk, Tashi looked back at the café to find him standing at the wall of glass in the front, looking at her. He smiled, and waved. She smiled, and waved back. His smile turned to a charming grin and it was then that Tashi felt as if she'd seen him before. It was the second time today that she'd run into slightly familiar faces.

For some reason, she didn't feel threatened by the man who was now watching her, especially when Miss Felicia, one of the owners of the café, came up and hugged him before bending over to pay attention to the child sleeping in the stroller. She was probably his mother-in-law, Tashi thought, since Miss Felicia was black, the man was white, and the baby had olive-toned skin, an indication that she was biracial or multiracial.

No, Tashi thought walking away, this man wasn't after her. Nevertheless, she decided not to head home, just in case he was tempted to follow her. She crossed the street and entered the supermarket. She'd do her laundry tomorrow. She didn't have her list, so it took longer than expected to get her shopping done.

With two bags filled with groceries, and two filled with additions to her new wardrobe, she exited the automatic sliding doors of the supermarket and froze. The tall handsome man was standing near the entrance, talking on his cell, his back to her. He must have heard her gasp, because he turned around and immediately ended his conversation. His dark shades obscured his eyes, hiding his expression from her. For all she knew, he could have been talking to the men who were after her, letting his boss know that he'd found her.

Real fear gripped Tashi this time. Scottie had been charming and sweet, just like this man, but according to the FBI agent, he'd been hired to befriend her and trap her.

Her bags slid from her hands. She heard glass crunching, and then red liquid leaked around her sandals. *Blood. Blood splattered on the windshield, on the dashboard, and ran down the back of his fat neck, staining the collar of his white shirt.*

Tashi's heart thundered and her stomach clenched tightly. *Dear God. No.* She started to run, but didn't get far. Her eyes closed in defeat as he caught her and spun her around. "How did you find me?"

"Who are you running from? Why are you so paranoid?"

She opened her eyes and stared at him. He'd removed his shades and his blue eyes pierced through her as if he were trying to read her soul. "Why are you following me?"

"I'm not following you. I swear I'm not following you. I wouldn't do that. Stalking is illegal in this town." He smiled, and the afternoon sun illuminated his soft blue eyes. "I came to the market to get some pull-ups for Tiffany. Her mother didn't pack enough this morning."

Tashi's breath came out hard and rapid. Of course. He wasn't one of them. He was married. He had a little girl.

She felt so weak. She was so tired. Tired of hiding. Tired of the unknown. She just wanted a life. She wanted to feel safe and secure, just for one moment. Tashi gave in to the overwhelming emotions that had been building up for fifteen months. She was only human, after all. She fell weakly against the strong, hard chest. The hot tears ran in torrents down her cheeks, dampening his shirt. She felt his arms close around her. His fingers tangled in her hair as he pressed her face into his chest.

"Hey, it's okay," he whispered gently in a deep voice as he

held her, his hands soothing and comforting as he caressed her back and shoulders. "It's gonna be okay..."

They stood holding onto each other in the parking lot with curious people watching and the warm July sun beating down on them.

After a while, he put his hand under her chin and lifted her face to his. "It's gonna be okay," he reiterated, gazing into her eyes. He backtracked a few steps with her, bent down, picked up her backpack and shopping bags, and handed them to her. "Your groceries are ruined." He bent down and began to scoop up as much as he could of the mess of food from the ground.

Tashi slid one strap of her backpack over her arm and bent down to help him. As they carried the soggy paper bags with ruined groceries over to the trashcan and deposited them inside, Tashi felt an unexpected warmth from his tenderness. His genuine concern for her—a stranger—was touching.

"If you come inside with me, I'll replace your groceries," he said.

"You don't have to do that." She could have salvaged most of the items and washed off the spaghetti sauce once she got home, but she was too tired to bother. "It's my fault for being paranoid."

"Why do you take on so much blame?" he asked. "In the café, you blamed yourself and now... I snuck up on you there, and I scared you just now. It's not all your fault, you know."

A heaviness settled in Tashi's stomach. But it was. *If I hadn't been so naïve that nice FBI agent would be alive today, and that driver too— even though he was a bad man.* It was her fault.

"At least let me reimburse you." He pulled his wallet from his back pocket.

"No. It wasn't that much. I'm fine." She hoped her camera was fine. It was expensive and she didn't want to have to replace it. At least her phone was tucked safely inside the pocket of her dress. She would die if it was ever lost, damaged, or stolen.

The man's eyes continued to bore into hers as he replaced his wallet. "Are you in some kind of trouble?" His voice was deep and rich, and it made her feel safe.

Tashi needed that voice at night as she lay in bed trembling and frightened, whispering that everything would be all right. She needed that voice to bring her out of the nightmares that continually plagued her sleep. She swallowed and shook her head, then pressed her hands against her temples. "No. I'm just tired. It's been a long day."

"It's only noon," he pointed out in a patient tone.

She tried to smile, but the corners of her mouth just trembled. "Where's your little girl—Tif—Tiffany, right?" she asked, noticing what she supposed was green dried baby food in the tresses of his long black hair. She envied the woman who had this gentle, loving man to comfort and protect her. She wished she had someone like him to lean on. To trust.

"She's with her grandmother," he answered, offering her a smile that made her knees weak, not from fear or heartache this time, but attraction. "Come back to the café with me. Have a smoothie and some apple pie. It'll calm your nerves, make you feel better. I promise."

Tashi shook her head. "The apple pie is delicious. I usually have it for desert." *Usually*, she thought in wonder. She hadn't ordered it today, and if she had, she would still have been sitting at her table when this stranger walked in. She would not have stood up and bumped into him. "I just ate and I'm really full."

"Maybe another time then?" he asked, on a warm smile.

"I'm sorry for crying all over you," Tashi said, willing herself not to fall victim to his charm. The lingering smell of green beans and applesauce on his shirt made him even more irresistible. He was somebody's dad—the one thing she never had growing up.

"Why did you cry all over me?"

She hesitated before responding. "It's just that, when I saw you standing there talking on the phone, and then when you turned around, I panicked. I thought you were—" She stopped, and dropped her gaze.

"You thought I was someone else. The person you are running away from?"

"I'm not running from anyone." Tashi's defenses instantly returned. She didn't know this man. He was nice, but he had his own family to take care of. If she were his wife, she wouldn't appreciate him paying so much attention to another woman— especially one who in spite of the mental brakes she was trying to apply found herself highly attracted to him. She stepped back and glanced up at him. "I have to go." She hooked the other strap of her backpack over her shoulder.

"Where? Where do you have to go?" he asked, the beginning of a new smile tipping the corners of his sexy mouth.

"Bye." She turned and walked away, clutching her two garment bags in her hand.

"I'm Adam. Do you live around here?" he called after her.

Tashi stopped in her tracks. *Adam. His name was Adam. His name began with an A...*

Her mind rewound fifteen months to the night in New York and the split second just before the first round of shots blasted around her: "*When you get to Granite Falls, look for A—*" and just before that, "*I'll send word to my friend. He is to give you the protection of his name and family by making you his temporary bride.*"

Tashi did not dare turn around. It was too good to be true. He couldn't be *that friend*. The agent hadn't said anything about him having a child, and she was certain that if Adam was already married, the agent would not have asked that he marry her. What if he'd gotten married in the fifteen months she'd been wasting away in this town? Well, if he was *that man*, he could still give her protection, just not as his wife. "Yes," she said in a voice squeaky with hope. "I live around here."

"What's your name?"

"Tashi. Tashi—" She hesitated, then decided to go for it. "Tashi Holland."

She waited for some indication of recognition. A "My goodness, I've been looking for you for months," or something along those lines. When none came, Tashi continued on her way.

Tashi.

"Tashi Holland." Adam whispered her name as he watched her walk through the parking lot, her long jean dress flapping loosely around her ankles. When she exited the lot, Adam realized that she didn't own a car. The thought that she couldn't afford a car upset him. How many other basic necessities of life —things people like him took for granted—did she live without?

He was tempted to follow her, even though he'd told her he hadn't been following her. That was then. This was now—now that he knew she was afraid of something or someone, the urge to run after her and hold her again mounted by the second. Twice in one day, within the hour, he'd held her against him, pressed her cheek close to his heart—his heart that was now beating madly out of control.

Adam pressed his palm into his chest where her cheek had lain. His shirt was damp from her tears. His skin tingled from her heat. He fisted his hand as if he could capture her sadness and make it his own.

"What frightens you, Tashi? Who scares you? An obsessive boyfriend? An abusive husband?" he asked out loud as he watched her cross the street and walk west on Beacon Avenue, pass Mountainview Café, toward Union Street.

Soon she would be out of sight, but positively not out of mind, he thought as he recalled her eyes—wide sapphire pools of mystery and magic, bright open windows to her timid soul. His pulse quickened as he remembered the rich golden glow and enthusing aroma of ginger scenting her soft auburn curls, and the sensuous bouquet of jasmine and vanilla emanating from her smooth silky skin.

Exotic. Sweet. Enticing. *Lei era la spezia e il sapore al suo stufato* —yes, the spice and the flavor to his stew, indeed. The kind of woman a man wished he could bump into again and again—all pun intended.

Adam's excitement waned when she made a right turn onto Union Street—the low-income part of town, littered with rundown multi-family houses where people existed from paycheck to paycheck. His heart squeezed mercilessly. A woman like Tashi didn't belong in that kind of neighborhood. She belonged in a palace surrounded by servants eager to grant her simplest request.

As her diminishing figure disappeared from his view, Adam walked into the supermarket. His concern for the girl sprouted wings and his protective instincts toward any damsel in distress bulldozed through the barrier he'd erected several years ago. It ripped through him like a fist smashing through the surge of a waterfall.

Tashi was in trouble. Not the kind that went away with a threatening phone call or a letter from an attorney. She was in deep. The girl was a bundle of nerves, and seemingly as defenseless as an alley cat trapped with its back against the wall.

Much like Claire, sans the entourage of negative vibes.

As he pulled the box of disposable diapers from the shelf and headed to the checkout, Adam tried to put all thoughts of Tashi Holland out of his mind. He told himself that she was not his concern. He berated himself for asking her name and if she lived in the vicinity. Why couldn't he have left well enough alone?

It wasn't that he was opposed to helping damsels in distress. It was just that damsels in distress were his weakness.

He'd discovered his Achilles' heel at age twenty-one when he'd rescued Claire, a damsel in distress from an abusive relationship. A practicing yogi and meditation guru since the age of twelve, he should have known that a woman with that kind of baggage and high levels of toxins circling her orbit would tip his Libra scales way out of equilibrium.

Perhaps the challenge of teaching her to trust again, to show her that not all men were cruel, and most emphatically the fact that she was the first woman he'd made love with had clouded his mind, made him think he was in love with her, and pushed him to propose. It could also have been his father's frequent referral to the fact that since Adam was his only heir, it was his duty to carry on the Andreas bloodline.

Or perhaps it was that longing in his heart to share his life with someone special, to create his own home with a wife and children that was filled with joy, happiness, laughter, and respect —much like the one he'd grown up in. Whatever it was that had pushed him to ask, Claire had accepted his proposal, and had seemed excited about marrying him in the months they'd spent planning the elaborate wedding of the decade.

Then she'd broken his heart.

Eventually, his heart had healed and had forgotten the ache of rejection. A true believer in love and Happy Ever After, he'd opened up to another damsel in distress. He never got as far as the altar with Denise, and he couldn't say that his heart had been broken the second time around—just a little hurt and somewhat disappointed at failing again.

That kind of consecutive rejection could wreak havoc on a man's confidence, not to mention his ego—even if that man practiced yoga and meditation on a daily basis. While yoga and meditation were efficient in helping him regain and maintain balance in his inner universe, they, however, were ineffective when it came to matters of the heart and soul.

The heart and soul, he'd discovered, were restless teammates —forever on perpetual journeys to find their one true love—the ultimate mate to complete them. Twice burned, Adam had learned that the best way to deal with his heart and soul was not to engage them, to keep them away from things that affected them most.

For him, that *thing* was a woman in distress, since the moment he thought he had to rescue a woman was the moment he began falling for her.

After his emotional disasters with Claire and Denise, he'd made a conscious effort to only pursue independent women who didn't need to be rescued, women who wanted a career more than they wanted love and a family, those who bowed out as graciously as they bowed into their affairs with him. To be fair, he was always mindful to let them know right up front that there was no permanency in a relationship with him. Consequently, he was known as "Temporary Adam" to some, and "The Temporary Tycoon" to others.

Adam had been initially surprised that there were actual women out there who didn't see marriage and children as the prime reason for their existence, that it wasn't a goal they needed to attain to feel complete and valued by the opposite sex, or by society. What many women *really* wanted had changed in recent decades. Some of them just wanted to have fun.

Adam appreciated their contemporary philosophies, and while the opposite was true for him, *temporary* was working out just fine. The heart couldn't always get what it wanted, and since he'd conditioned his not to fall in love, it seemed to have ceased its endless quest.

The safest way to keep *temporary* permanent was to stay away from damsels in distress. That meant no opening of Pandora's box—well, in this case, Tashi's box—for a quick and curious peek inside.

By the time he walked back to Mountainview Café and handed the box of diapers to Felicia, Adam had succeeded in putting all thoughts of Tashi Holland out of his mind.

At least that's what he thought.

NOTE FROM THE AUTHOR

Dear Reader,

I hope you enjoyed following Massimo and Nia, aka Shaina, on their journey to love and *Happily Ever After, and* your introduction to Adam and Tashi from The Tycoon's Temporary Bride.

May you catch and tame your very own Massimo.

Ana

ABOUT THE AUTHOR

Inspired by the strong heroines and flawed alpha heroes in the stories she read as a young girl, *New York Times* and *USA Today* Bestselling Author, Ana E Ross writes steamy and sophisticated, multicultural contemporary romance novels. Her drama-filled stories feature charming, powerful, larger-than-life billionaires and strong, independent women who fight and love with equal passion.

Born and raised in Nevis, Ana now lives in the Northeast, U.S., and loves traveling, tennis, yoga, meditation, everything Italian, and spending time with her daughter.

www.anaeross.com
ana@anaeross.com